D0291244

To Stew
With Love
Anne Lynn Cruz

LaBajada Lawyer:

A LEGAL THRILLER OF NEW MEXICO

by JONATHAN MILLER

Stephen
Good Luck
On your
book

[signature]

P.S.
Can't wait
to
see
Boulevard
On
the
big
screen

T I T L E S

Published by
Cool Titles
439 N. Canon Dr., Suite 200
Beverly Hills, CA 90210
www.cooltitles.com

The Library of Congress Cataloging-in-Publication Data Applied For

Jonathan Miller—
Labajada Lawrer: A Legal Thriller of New Mexico

p.   cm
ISBN-10: 09673920-8X, ISBN-13: 978-09673920-80
1. Mystery   2. American Southwest   3. Legal Thriller   I. Title
2008

Copyright 2008 by Jonathan Miller
All Rights Reserved
including the right of reproduction in whole or in part in any form.

Printed in the United States of America

1 3 5 7 9 10 8 6 4 2

Book editing and design by Lisa Wysocky, White Horse Enterprises, Inc.

For interviews or information regarding special discounts for bulk purchases,
please contact us at njohnson@jjllplaw.com

DEDICATION

To my mother, who is a far better mother than
all the characters in this book put together.

ABOUT THE AUTHOR

Jonathan Miller is an author and an attorney practicing criminal law in Albuquerque. He is a graduate of the Albuqerque Academy, Cornell University, the University of Colorado Law School, and the American Film Institute; and has taken writing courses at the University of New Mexico and UCLA-Extension. He hopes to use the proceeds of this book to pay off his student loans before he dies.

Also by Jonathan Miller:

Rattlesnake Lawyer
Amarillo in August
Crater County
Volcano Verdict

Jonathan Miller dedicates this book to his family.

Prologue: The Checkerboard Mile

"OPEN CELL FORTY-TWO," the guard yelled from out in the pod.

The cell door clicked open. I nearly fainted as I rose off my hard cot and stumbled into the main area of Segregation/Intake Pod Number Nine of the Albuquerque Metropolitan Detention Center. A sliver of sunlight came down from the small skylight. I shut my eyes in pain. Had I forgotten sunlight already?

"Shepard, some chick's bonding you out," the bored guard at the desk shouted. Another guard, the heavyweight champion of the penal boxing league, cuffed me for the walkout. As a high-risk inmate in a maximum security unit, I never walked anywhere alone, especially since they knew I was a defense lawyer. At least I hoped I still was.

"Tell your lover to bond me out!" Pocahontas, a tall Native American inmate who resembled the animated princess, pounded on the bars of his cell. "I can't wait to meet him!"

"Meet her!" I shouted. "She's a her!"

They had run out of orange MDC jumpsuits, so I still wore my gray Ralph Lauren pinstriped suit with the purple Jerry Garcia tie. I'd have NASA sterilize this suit before wearing it again. It hung loosely over my body. I had thrown up nearly every meal during my stay. I won't mention how I used the tie. I was amazed it was still purple.

We clicked out of Pod Number One, but stalled in the sally

port. The sally port was a small room with one door that opened to the pod and one that opened to the hall. The sally port was the size of a gas-station bathroom. It smelled even worse, as someone had been stuck here too long and couldn't hold it. My claustrophobia kicked in. I shut my eyes, and tried to pretend I was on a beach somewhere, but the sky itself closed in on me.

After an eternity and a half, the metal sally-port door on the other side clicked open. The air still felt thick; I wasn't out of jail yet.

We then walked down the hallway. Well, Heavyweight dragged me. The narrow walls, electronic doors, and bulletproof glass reminded me of a Nazi submarine. After we passed the Sex Offender Pod, the Double Detox Pod, God's Pod, and finally the female pod known only as the Maximum Bitch Unit, we arrived at the main hallway of the Metropolitan Detention Center.

I called the mile the Checkerboard Mile because of the pattern. It could also be a chessboard, and that would make me a pawn. But was the queen I was serving the black one or the white?

Still sore from being in a cramped room, I begged Heavyweight to let me catch my breath near the kitchen. Bad choice. Breathing the remains of the afternoon's green-chile stew made my lungs feel even worse. I didn't know green chile could ferment.

An inmate passed by me. I recognized him as one I called "Isotope."

"I know you!" he said, laughing.

"Let's get going," I said to Heavyweight.

He took his time. There were drugs smuggled in here, but speed certainly wasn't one of them. Still, every step I took away from the Segregation/Intake Unit, the air grew a little fresher, a little lighter. Each step took me closer to the surface.

We stopped suddenly and made a hard right turn. We had to wait again, then click out to the main exit corridor. A final guard waited by a metal detector, like St. Peter guarding heaven. The only thing the guards hated more than inmates were lawyers.

I was both.

Heavyweight took off my cuffs. It had only been a minute, yet my hands felt like lead.

St. Peter nodded and let us walk past. I waited for the last door to click. Nothing.

"Let me the hell out of here!" I yelled.

St. Peter laughed at me. "Just push it. It's open."

I pushed.

Nothing.

Had my muscles atrophied in jail that quickly? I pushed really hard with all my might, and it finally inched open, just enough for me to squeeze through. Heavyweight followed from behind.

I blinked a few times to let my eyes adjust to the sunlight on the other side of the window. I was still inside, in the lobby, but someone had opened the door to the parking lot outside. Fresh New Mexico desert air blew toward me. It was the sweetest air I had ever breathed. It was surprisingly warm for January.

Then I saw her.

"Oh my God, it's you!" I said.

Why the hell did it have to be her?

"I bailed you out," she said.

I couldn't read her emotions.

I turned to Heavyweight. "Could you please take me back?"

Act I
Ophelia

Eldorado: Two Months Earlier

"THE POLLS ARE OFFICIALLY closed. We'll have the results momentarily," the young reporter said. "We're live from the Governor's campaign headquarters at the Eldorado Hotel in Santa Fe. Back to you, Jill."

"And we're clear," the cameraman said.

He nearly tripped over me as he walked out the door. I didn't care, I was too happy. Yes, Dan Shepard—former public defender, failed writer, still unmarried after all these years—had finally made it to the next level in life. At thirty-nine, my hair had a few touches of premature gray around the sides. I still looked like Clark Kent with my glasses, especially now in my blue glen plaid suit and red Armani tie that resembled a rattlesnake's skin. I finally felt like the Man of Steel.

I scanned the Anasazi Room of the Eldorado. It was warm and cozy on this snowy November night. The room had a feminine quality to it, soft adobe earth tones, blue pastel accents, and a whispering fireplace of mesquite. This was epitome of "Santa Fe style," the self-proclaimed "City Different."

The Anasazi, or ancient pueblo people, were the original tribe in the Southwest, the most native of the Native Americans. This room kept much of the majesty of their ancient sandstone *kivas*, round sandstone buildings often used for mysterious ceremonial purposes. The primitive etchings on the wall of this room might be looted from one of their sacred sites. I noticed an unearthly glow emanating from the wall; perhaps the Anasazi were slightly pissed about tonight's election.

I waited in the line at the bar behind an anorexic woman dressed in black who treated the governor's election bash as just another Hollywood premiere.

"Dude, do you mind if I cut in?" an energy lobbyist asked. He didn't wait for an answer. His gun metal gray suit made him look like a high class hit man. I nodded. A few state officials in brown polyester politely got behind me. Santa Fe definitely had its pecking order.

I took a deep breath and scanned the room again, this time with my X-ray eyes. Loneliness was my Kryptonite. A few Native Americans in dark suits could have passed for Wall Street bankers except for their ponytails and turquoise bolos. They talked casino profits over by the fire. In the corner, a few local Sikhs, many with Long Island accents still intact, watched the proceedings with a look of bored bemusement. No one met my gaze; perhaps I hadn't made it after all. I had almost decided to leave when an arm grabbed my neck from behind.

"Dan, I'm here! Stone drove me from Albuquerque, and he was running late."

"Lia!" I said with a smile. "I thought you'd never make it."

Ophelia Paz, a.k.a. Lia Spaz, hugged me tightly from behind.

"You can let go now," I said. I wasn't used to public displays of affection with Lia, even though she was my officially my girlfriend . . . I guess.

"I am so glad to see you," she said. "So very glad."

If I were Clark Kent, she was a Latina Lois Lane. Well, Lois with learning disabilities. Lia had dark-hair with blond streaks. I hated the streaks, as they took away the natural beauty of her hair. Lia was petite, the former cheerleader from hardscrabble Albuquerque High, turned thirty. She wore a pink outfit that could only be described as "hip peasant," as if an East Coast designer had gone into a Mexico City barrio and given Lia a million-dollar make-over.

There was still some making-over left, as Lia was a work in progress. Her Navajo turquoise fetish necklace dangled a bit too much, and the trademark flower in her hair was too big for her delicate ear.

I had met her a few weeks ago when she was handing out the Governor's campaign literature at the law library. I made a joke about repealing the laws of gravity, and she had laughed, a nice warm laugh. I asked about her flower and she said it was a scarlet begonia.

"She wore scarlet begonias tucked into her curls," I had sung to her from an old song. *"I knew right away that she was not like other girls."*

Lia wore an identical begonia tonight.

"Tonight might be the night," she hinted.

Tonight? We hadn't slept together yet, but we had napped together a few times. She had closed her eyes while lying with me on my couch. Everyone once in a while, she would jerk as if having an unpleasant dream. I'd hold her tight, then I'd drive her home for the night. For all I knew, Lia was a virgin. She seemed so innocent, so childlike, that I didn't want to force the issue, and remained content with her amazing back-rubs.

I politely changed the subject.

"You're just in time," I said with a nod toward the door. "He's making his entrance."

On cue, Governor Gary Mendoza entered with a Mariachi fanfare of "Hail to the Chief." Everyone in the room knew of his unstated goal of national office. He was a big man who came across like a big friendly bear. His tie had the New Mexico state symbol, a red Zia cross settled uneasily on a red, white, and blue background.

After a few minutes of shaking hands, actually crushing hands in his big paws, he arrived in our corner.

"You're Dan Shepard, right?" He held his vice-like grip. "Athena Shepard's son."

"Call me Dan." My mother's reputation often preceded me. "This is my friend, Lia Paz."

"We've met," Governor Mendoza said. "Once. At a campaign event. What was your name again?"

"Ophelia Paz," she said in her childlike voice. "I worked on your campaign down in Albuquerque, Mr. Governor, sir, your honor."

"I've heard about you, Lia," the governor said. "All good."

All good? What had he heard? I glanced at Lia. I didn't look at her clothes, the streaks in her hair or the turquoise jewelry. I looked at her mouth. When Lia got nervous, she often said something out of left field, sometimes out of the whole damn ballpark.

Governor Mendoza embraced her, a literal bear hug. This bear had supposedly hibernated with half the female gallery owners in town. His record in New Mexico was mixed: he was more popular outside the state than within it. The press joked that his ratings now hovered at the mythical "Mendoza line," a reference to a baseball hitter who hit below .200. Hopefully he was above the political Mendoza line of fifty percent tonight.

The bear hug lingered. Shit. He came to Albuquerque quite often. Had they really only met once at an event? Had he slept with her?

"Governor, make sure you don't let them repeal Article Seven of the Children's Code," Lia said when the Governor let go. She was very passionate about issues, especially those involving children. A "Rain Man of Politics," she knew every arcane fact about every district, but when she talked, it came out sounding like gibberish.

"Don't worry about Article Seven on my watch," he said.

"Dan here is so brilliant," she said. "He's so talented. Hopefully you can find a place for him in your administration. Either here, or when you go to Washington."

"Don't believe everything Lia says," I said.

The governor smiled back. "Dan, Ophelia, thank you so much for coming to my party," he said, glancing back at the TV. "And thank you for all your help. Hopefully, C de Baca is history after tonight. Oh wait, speak of the devil."

Tom C de Baca, the Governor's opponent, suddenly appeared on the giant plasma TV screen. He, too, was bigger than life, on camera or off. The old Spanish name "C de Baca," came from *Cabeza de Baca,* head of a cow, and his face resembled the Chicago Bull's fierce icon.

Behind the candidate, his older brother, Xavier, stood guard. I knew the "X-man" from his social worker days.

"He's not just my brother, he's also a client," Xavier once joked.

The image was a still-photo with the caption, BREAKING NEWS: NEW MEXICO GUBERNATORIAL CONTENDER TO MAKE ANNOUNCEMENT. The announcement came from a national feed. Something was about to break.

C de Baca then vanished off the screen; I almost expected a cloud of smoke to signal his disappearance. The party munchkins sprang to life the moment he flickered off, happy that the great and powerful wizard had gone away.

"Kormanyzo!" a woman shouted.

The governor smiled. "I never thought I'd have to learn Hungarian as part of my job," he said. "That means 'Governor' by the way."

He hurried over to his trusted secretary, Eva Jonas.

I had met Eva at another event and nicknamed her Eva Braun after Hitler's secretary, since I figured she'd stick with the governor all the way to the end. There had been rumors of an affair between the two many years ago, but now he supposedly had a taste for younger women. Eva was in her fifties, and was the descendant of Hungarian royalty. Now she was royalty here in New Mexico—well, the secretary to royalty.

"Ja napot, Danika," she said to me from across the room. I was amazed that she remembered me after only one prior meeting. I hoped her words meant "Hello, Danny."

She would have come closer, but she was intercepted by Judge Kurtz, Chief Judge of Albuquerque, who was there in a wheelchair. Eva didn't acknowledge Lia. As a peon on the campaign, the two had probably never met. Eva was too big for mere politics; she decided who had access to the real players. The governor hurried over to her.

I breathed another sigh of relief there in the middle of the Anasazi Room. It was all downhill from here. I felt like El Dorado himself, the golden man of the Conquistadores legend.

"Dan, don't forget the deposition tomorrow!" It was my boss, Joel Lipschitz, Esquire. He appeared suddenly, as if he had jumped out of one of the Anasazi etchings. He looked "oh-so-Santa-Fe chic" in a vaguely western black outfit with no tie. I thought of a Jewish Johnny Cash. Joel was younger than I, but far more successful. He had never taken detours in life, as I had.

I had just started at the Joel Lipschitz Law Firm a few weeks before, and I wasn't sure whether we were friends yet. He introduced me to one of our clients, Santa Fe Gallery Owner/Real Estate Whiz, Rhiannon Goldstein Manygoats. She wore a million-dollar outfit that combined the worst of the east coast and the southwest.

"This is Dan Shepard, my new associate," he said, his voice neutral. "His mother is Athena Shepard. *The* Athena Shepard."

"And where is Athena tonight?" Rhiannon asked, as if mentioning the Greek Goddess herself. "This would be her kind of party. We did International Women's Forum together."

Rhiannon wanted to go on forever about my mom; Mom had achieved international success as a lawyer and a humanitarian. My parents had recently semi-retired and moved to Santa Fe.

"My parents are taking a world tour right now." I said. "I think they're in Indonesia by now. Or Malaysia."

"Indonesia is the largest Muslim country in the world," Lia said. "I'm Lia Paz. I'm Dan's *girlfriend*."

"Nice to meet you," Rhiannon said to Lia. Then she gave me an evil smile and winked, as if to ask 'What are you doing with this girl?'

"I do love your hair. And your flower. Is it alive?" Rhiannon asked Lia. Then to me she asked, "Has your mother met your new little *girlfriend* yet?"

"Not yet."

"I'd love to be a fly on the wall for that meeting."

What the hell did she mean by that?

"Don't forget the deposition tomorrow," said Joel. "Bright and early."

"I'll be early," I said. "I don't know how bright I'll be."

He didn't laugh. He never did. I think in his deal with the devil he had traded a sense of humor for material success. Well, and his soul of course. Joel left to mingle.

"Joel said you're looking for a house up here," Rhiannon said, trying to mask her Chicago north shore accent with a drawl, or was it a lilt?

"Hopefully," I said. "Once I get my Christmas bonus."

"He's so brilliant," Lia said. "He can do anything he wants."

I smiled. "I want to buy a place near that gallery. You know, the one that's really overpriced, sells weird stuff that's kind of Native, but really made in California by hippies, and the staff has nose studs?"

"I know which one you're talking about," she replied.

"I'm talking about *all* of them," I said with a smile.

Rhiannon walked away in a huff. I had insulted Santa Fe. Oh well. I finally felt confident enough to joke about the city where I almost lived.

"You definitely should move up here," Lia said. "And buy a luxury estate. Maybe two. You can have one in the foothills and a condo within walking distance of the plaza. Didn't Oprah have a place up here? In Tesuque or Pojoaque, one of those towns that end with a 'que.'"

"I already live in Albuquer-*que*. I'm not in the Santa Fe big leagues yet." I hesitated to explain to Lia that the only affordable housing for locals in Santa Fe was the prison.

"You will be," she said. "I believe in you. I believe in you with all my heart."

I wanted to believe her. Out the big bay window, the snow accumulated on the adobe roofs of Santa Fe. Smoke came up from the fireplaces. Bright and early might be a problem. I wanted to spend the night here in Santa Fe, rather than driving back home to Albuquerque. I was still a "La Bajada Lawyer." La Bajada was the steep hill marking where Albuquerque's exurbs ended, and Santa Fe's began. I drove that hill several times a day.

Lia kissed me on the cheek. "Tonight's the night."

"It's going to be all right," I sang, forgetting my anxiety of minutes earlier.

I almost wanted to cry. Life was finally perfect. I just knew something had to go wrong.

Itches are Deadly

THE BIG SCREEN DISPLAYED an EMT rappelling into a ditch trying to rescue a drowning woman from the raging waters of a concrete arroyo in Albuquerque. Arroyos in their natural form were big ditches that were usually dry, but became raging rivers during rainstorms. In urban areas like Albuquerque, arroyos were often paved. In good weather, they were a haven for skateboarders and cyclists, but during rainstorms water in paved arroyos ran much faster than their natural cousins and presented very hazardous conditions.

"Would you do that for me?" Lia asked. "You remember that ad campaign about the dangers of flash flooding: ditches are deadly?"

The burly EMT lifted the limp body out of the water, the woman dead weight in his massive arms.

"Details after the election!" the announcer intoned excitedly, then shifted back to "New Mexico's Night," the local broadcast.

"They're showing the first *valasztas*, election results from the rural counties. Everybody quiet!" Eva said, playing den mother.

The room quickly grew silent.

"We're up in Mosquero County," the governor said. "We got

60 percent of the voters, and 100 percent of the cattle."

"Mosquero went the other way last election," Lia said. "It's primarily ranching. I don't know which way the cattle voted."

I couldn't tell whether she was joking, or not.

Joel stood next to the governor and Eva. A million-dollar contribution bought that kind of access. I had hitched my star to their wagon. If Governor Mendoza could just hold on, stay in office two more years, maybe I could even return to D.C. as the conquering hero when he got tapped as vice president.

But this election was hard fought. C de Baca had run a ruthless campaign. A gang-leader from Albuquerque's tough Barrio Wells Park, he'd found God at thirty, became a teacher, then went into politics as a "values candidate." He still approached politics like a drive-by shooting, and some of his bullets had hit the governor, hard.

One scandal had drawn blood. Governor Mendoza stood to make a million dollars from a land deal, nicknamed "Agua-gate" after the *Agua Caliente* creek that ran through a piñon forest. There were rumors that the governor would hit back hard with a November surprise. That hadn't happened yet.

The governor frowned as he listened to his phone, swore under his breath, then hung up. He hurried into the other room with Eva and a few trusted aides.

Lia and I wandered around the meeting rooms of the Eldorado, each named for a local tribe. The art on the walls was appropriate for each room. Next was the Taos room, named after the Taos tribe, who were renown for their silver work. There were several silver sculptures in cases near the wall.

"Make new friends, but keep the old," I said.

Lia smiled. "One is silver and the other gold. That's from the Brownies."

Lia then told an obese state senator about pork subsidy amendments as he ate a tamale. He shrugged, swallowed the tamale whole and chased it with a *Tecate*, a light beer flavored with salt and lime. I pulled Lia away before she could tell him about changes in the breath alcohol retrograde extrapolation, the rate that alcohol leaves the body after drinking. It's something every criminal defense lawyer doing DWI defense has thoroughly memorized.

As for my own breath alcohol, I knew I had to drive back to Albuquerque so I stuck with coffee.

"I like my coffee the way I like my women," I said to her with a smile. "Short, dark and sweet. And a little nutty."

"Then I like my coffee the way I like my men: tall, dark and strong."

"I'll try to be strong," I said. How hard could that be?

Someone swore. Apparently C de Baca had conquered Aguilar County, where I'd been a public defender.

"Aguilar's pretty conservative," Lia said. "So we expected to lose by twenty percent. I sure hope the snow doesn't dampen the turn out in Rio Arriba County. *Sixty Minutes* once did a show about heroin addiction up there. We're polling sixty percent positive on heroin addicts, so hopefully they'll make it out to the polls for us."

Lia went on about how heroin addicts voted more conservatively *after* completing rehab, since many church groups had their own rehab programs. Her observations were right on. The governor won that county by a plurality, just below the Mendoza line.

"I hate that asshole C de Baca," Rhiannon said from across the room when she heard the bad news that Mendoza had less votes than expected. "I'd kill him and his bitch wife if I could."

We next entered the Santa Clara Room. Here there was a party for Attorney General Diana Crater, who ran for re-election unopposed. This room focused on the shiny black Santa Clara pottery, and some pots were in glass display boxes.

Lia excused herself to freshen up. "I held it all the way up," she said proudly, like a child.

Lia gone, my attention turned to two women standing in a corner by a black Santa Clara pot under glass. One was Latina, the other Asian. The Latina was in her mid-thirties and had a touch of gray in her hair, just like I did. Her outfit was shiny black and fit tightly against her lean, tan body, as if a Santa Clara potter had spun it specifically to compliment her flawless skin.

She smiled at me, as if she recognized me from somewhere. I walked over.

"Dan Shepard," I said.

"Luna Cruz."

"Not *the* Luna Cruz?"

"Not *the* Dan Shepard?" She smiled. "Wasn't your nickname the Rattlesnake Lawyer when you were out in the boonies?"

Before I could reply, Lia burst through the room like a guided missile. I wondered if she had even made it to the bathroom.

"My name is Lia Paz," she said to Luna, somewhat out of breath. "Dan is my *boyfriend*."

"Lia?" Luna said. "That's funny. We almost have the same name. My name is Luna. Luna Cruz. Is that Leah with an 'e'?"

"No, with an 'I'. It's short for Ophelia," said Lia.

There was a weird vibe between the two women. Luna was the upgraded version of Lia. Lia was gas station coffee, Luna was cappuccino; Lia silver to Luna's gold. I then thought of the obvious: Luna was Santa Fe to Lia's Albuquerque.

Lia went into her rote speech about growing up and how her nickname started as "O" then "Ophie" then "Fee" until they ran out of syllables and ended at "Lia."

"Ophelia was the crazy woman in *Hamlet*," Lia had to add. "She died at the end, you know. Drowned herself."

"*Hey nonny, nonny*," I sang badly. "That's a line from the play."

Luna rolled her eyes. "I've read *Hamlet*," she said.

"You're a famous lawyer, right?" she asked Luna.

Luna smiled. "More infamous. This is Jen Song." Luna paused as she thought how to best describe the women next to her. "My best friend and legal assistant. She's in law school at UNM."

"Do you like law school?" Lia asked Jen. "I might go some-day."

"I'd rather practice law than having someone practice it on me," said Jen. "Before I decided to be a lawyer I was all set to run this huge business that kind of fell into my lap, but then I realized that it took a lot of math. I hate math.

Lia looked at Luna for a second. "Didn't you defend a crazy woman who killed a lawyer? The case was on TV. You know, that weird slutty girl."

Luna smiled. "That weird slutty girl was Jen here."

"I was like totally innocent," Jen said. She then smiled a guilty smile. "Well, mostly."

Lia touched Luna on the arm, as if capturing her. Luna recoiled, ever so slightly.

"I might need you to do a case for me." Lia said.

"What kind of case?" Luna brushed the arm off gently.

"It's about political signs in my yard."

"Is it a violation under the Albuquerque city code?"

"I don't know yet." Lia said. "It could get complicated."

Before, Luna could answer, more bad news came from the big screen. Harding County's handful of votes went for C de Baca as well. Channel 8 kept hyping a major development from C de Baca.

Luna looked at me. "I just bought a building in Albuquerque. I need someone to rent it and it would be perfect for you, if you want to stay down there."

I took another look around at the beautiful room. "Hopefully I'm moving here quite soon. It suits me."

Just then, Lia grabbed my arm.

"There's something going on the Anasazi Room," she said.

On the big screen, C de Baca had finally made it to the podium of Albuquerque's Pyramid Hotel. His brother held C de Baca's left arm for support.

C de Baca cleared his throat. Lia leaned closer to me as C de Baca's stare penetrated though the screen. I stepped back to avoid his gaze. The screen showed a close-up of the three cross tattoos on his right hand. Either they were emblems of his new religious life, or indicative that he had killed three people in his earlier life.

Perhaps both.

C de Baca clinched his teeth. "It is with great pain that I announce the death of my wife, Portia Smith C de Baca, who was murdered tonight. Yes, murdered. That was my wife they pulled out of the arroyo."

The Anasazi Room went silent.

"I loved Portia," he said, then waited a moment for the emotion to pass. "I've called the governor and he knows how to reach me, but I will stay in seclusion for the rest of the night, regardless of the results."

C de Baca took another deep breath. "I have also heard that the alleged murderer might have ties to the Governor Mendoza's campaign. This was a dirty campaign, but I had no idea . . . ."

The Anasazi Room gasped. Was Portia's killer in the room with us?

Suddenly the TV blacked out. Governor Mendoza had switched it off by remote. "Win or lose, we're going to sue that bastard for even suggesting that horseshit."

Some of his closest advisors huddled closer, afraid that the governor would utter another obscenity that might get picked up. A very short man, Vladimir Stone—very hairy, very New York—had the governor's ear. Stone's nickname was "The Werewolf." He was the man who had driven Lia up for the night.

"The party is over. Everyone needs to leave now! You got a ride back?" he asked Lia.

"Dan is taking me." She turned to me. "You will take me, right?

"I will," I said.

"I know you will." Lia gave me a hug. "Tonight's the night."

Giant Slalom

WE HURRIED OUT TO find my old Saturn coupe, parked way out on a side street. Someday soon, I'd park inside the Eldorado with the big boys. Once I put a down payment on a nice Prius hybrid with my signing bonus, parking places would magically open up for me, even in Santa Fe. I could smell the leather of my next car already.

I knew that the next bonus, the Christmas bonus from Joel, would be even better. That money would be for the down payment on the house here in Santa Fe. I could smell the piñon wood crackling in the fireplace.

I thought of the old joke, "It's better to have a car than a house. You can always sleep in your car, but you can't cruise in your house on a Saturday night."

We took a few wrong turns before I found my Saturn in the maze of adobe buildings downtown. Nothing was straight here, not the tan stucco walls or the streets. I had parked all the way down on Burro Alley, a windy street a few blocks away.

Once I found the car, we made fresh tracks in the rapidly accumulating powder as we left downtown Santa Fe on Guadalupe Street, and then on St. Francis Drive. The streets were empty, except for a white car that followed us all the way from downtown.

A Crown Victoria? No real Santa Fean would be seen dead in a car that big, ugly, and environmentally incorrect. The white car had "cop" written all over it.

A figure with a crew-cut sat rigidly in the driver's seat. The figure had "cop" written all over him as well. He was definitely tailing me. Maybe he thought I was a drunk driver, or perhaps he just wanted to bust a Mendoza supporter coming from the party. I drove slowly just to be safe. I didn't even run the yellow light on Zia Road like I always did.

Lia turned on the radio. The conservative station was heard all over the state, while the liberal station barely made it out of the UNM student ghetto. The announcer was ecstatic. Every mile we pulled away from the Eldorado, another county went to C de Baca.

Oh well, the northern counties would go our way, heroin addicts or not, and they always counted their results *manana,* right?

"Don't worry, there's going to be a happy ending no matter what." Lia leaned closer to me and touched my shoulder. Her smile glistened in the moonlight. She kissed my cheek.

Tonight was the night, indeed.

A happy ending awaited me in just forty-seven miles. As we ascended the hill outside of Santa Fe, we first passed a giant radio tower, then over a brief flat before heading down La Bajada hill. I sometimes called it La BJ.

La Bajada means "the descent" in Spanish. The highway here was like a sharp circumcision in the earth, and was the real boundary between Albuquerque and Santa Fe. The road was slick, as if paved with turquoise, a real turquoise trail. La Bajada had been tough on trains that crossed the pass for over a hundred years, and it wasn't kind to cars either. More people died on this stretch of highway than anywhere else in New Mexico, espe-cially in winter. One couple even vanished in the fog up here, never to be seen again. It was a Bermuda triangle with snow.

I could not make it up La Bajada in my Saturn without downshifting a gear or two. Gravity pulled stronger here. Suddenly the headlights of the car behind me pulled off to my left, trying to pull alongside us. Was he trying to bump us?

My Saturn hit a patch of ice, black ice. My car careened from side to side. Lia screamed a horror-movie shriek. I wasn't much of an ice driver, having lived in the desert for so long. The other car slid behind us.

"Dan!" she cried, then she lapsed into something unintelligible, like the war-cry of a distant ancestor.

I grabbed the wheel tighter and tried to remember how to drive in snow. The other car went into a ditch along the side of the road. Was the driver alive? I couldn't tell, I had to keep my eyes on the descent or I'd be off the road as well.

I swerved off the Interstate and hit a hard metal guardrail. Sparks flew. On the other side was a drop-off, a hundred feet of nothing but New Mexico night. Luckily, I bounced back and spun toward the median and oncoming traffic. It was foggy now, and the snow came down faster. I tried to turn into the spin, but still had no traction. Had someone cut my brakes?

Lia kept screaming; her voice was so high I was surprised it didn't shatter the windshield. My life flashed before me. It was not much of a life, a few good cases, no kids, no property, nothing. Everything I owned was in this car. Not that I owned Lia.

We kept spiraling, and did two three-sixties down La Bajada. An Escalade managed to swerve out of our way before starting its own skid. Lia prayed in Spanish.

I suddenly felt lightheaded. I hadn't eaten much. I barely had the strength to turn into the skid, or was I supposed to turn away from it?

Lia looked at me, pleading. Somehow I managed to keep the Saturn on the road. I tensed for a moment, awaiting a slam from the back.

Thankfully the roads were mostly empty tonight. La

Bajada's descent ended abruptly at the Rio Galisteo riverbank. My car slowed as we rose on the other side. I pulled over to the shoulder and uttered a small prayer of thanksgiving.

"You saved my life!" Lia yelled. "You saved my life!"

"What do you mean?"

"That car. I think it was following us. It tried to pull up. I think he had a gun or something."

I looked back. I saw lights about a mile uphill. They weren't moving.

I breathed a sigh of relief. There was a God. Maybe it was a sign, but a sign of what? I didn't want to push my luck. One miracle was enough for the night.

"We'd better keep going," I said.

"Wait," she said. She gave me a kiss on the lips. "I love you so much. So much."

I felt Lia's lips against mine, felt her heart beat with a mixture of lust and adrenaline. I almost wanted to do it right there at the bottom of La Bajada Hill, stalker or no stalker. And yes, the emotion rang though my body, through my heart.

"I love you too," I said.

Did I just say that out loud?

The City Similar

THE SNOW LINE WAS now safely behind us. In addition to dividing the areas around Albuquerque and Santa Fe, La Bajada was the sharp divide between the mountains of the north and the deserts of the south. In skidding down the hill, we had dropped nearly a thousand feet in elevation. The desert was nice and empty here; it hadn't changed much since Coronado's day. The moon looked so big and close, as if it could roll right down La Bajada to the Rio Galisteo riverbank. I kissed Lia again, but kept one eye on the moon just in case.

The headlights on the top of the hill went out. Perhaps Mr. Crown Victoria wanted to chase us on foot.

We released our embrace. I drove back onto the dry Interstate, and quickly gunned it up to eighty-five. I could afford to pay a ticket or two these days, or do a day in driving school. I was cool as long as I didn't get a reckless driving charge, which was a mandatory four days in jail.

We passed San Roberto Pueblo's casino. The casino had really packed them in tonight. The number of cars in the parking lot showed that most people in New Mexico preferred penny slots to politics.

Lia grabbed my crotch and rubbed slightly. There was something incredibly romantic in the flashing casino lights below.

"I want you right here," she said.

But she tensed when she saw a C de Baca billboard off to the right. His face exhorted us to Return to Values, New Mexico!

Lia closed her eyes and I wondered again why he had such a strange effect on her. "We'd better keep moving," she said.

Slightly disappointed, I said nothing and kept driving. After Algodones, Lia called her mom on her cell, not bothering to use the Bluetooth.

"Mama, I'm staying with Dan tonight. I know. I know. I didn't say anything. I won't say anything."

Say anything about what?

Lia talked to her mother for a few more minutes. I could hear no sound from the other end. None at all, and there never was. I had never met her mom; I sometimes wondered if her mom really existed. Guess I'd meet her at the wedding, right?

Wedding? The word didn't sound so bad right now. I looked at Lia. Should I ask her? No, I wasn't ready yet. I didn't know her that well, but perhaps in a few months. Maybe I would know her well enough then.

Have Faith, New Mexico! C de Baca's next billboard said.

"Show a little faith, there's magic in the night," I sang with Bruce Springsteen. "You ain't a beauty, but you're all right."

The big moon must have rolled right up behind us from Santa Fe. I thought about waking up in my beautiful Santa Fe home, next to my beautiful wife. "Letting the days go by . . . Same as it ever was."

A mile further, another C de Baca billboard appeared. Return to Justice, New Mexico!

Once we hit the suburb of Bernalillo the desert sprouted fast food restaurants amidst the cacti. Moments later, we reached the outskirts of Albuquerque. If Santa Fe was the City Different, Albuquerque was the "City Similar." We could be in Los Angeles, or we could be in Louisville, as we headed down I-25.

On polluted winter nights the city of Albuquerque often prohibited its citizens from using their fireplaces. One convict did twenty years for burning on a "no burn" night. Of course, he was trying to dispose of a large stash of marijuana before his parole office made it to his living room. Tonight was a "no-burn night," but people burned anyway. Eight lanes of interstate now jutted though the smoky air.

After the Paseo del Norte exit, we passed the twelve stories of the Pyramid Inn, a concrete approximation of an Aztec step pyramid. C de Baca was probably still in seclusion there. I picked up the pace.

Up ahead loomed the largest building in Albuquerque, twenty-two stories of glass and granite. It had a pyramid top, and looked like the Washington Monument with a weight problem, or a massive rocket about to launch into space. The building was named after a bank, but the bank kept changing names so I called it the Rocket Building. The Albuquerque skyline with its rectangles and bold lines was masculine, relative to a Santa Fe skyline that was distinctly feminine.

I exited at Lomas Boulevard, did a few quick turns through the adobe bungalows of the Martineztown barrio, then pulled into my sprawling apartment complex nestled under the shadow of the massive Big-I, the interchange between I-40 and I-25.

The complex could pass for something of a lesser Orange County suburb, as it featured Spanish style red roofs over crumbling white stucco. I called it Neverland, since most residents were college kids at nearby UNM, with a few getting their grades at the local community college. Every semester new kids moved in to replace the graduates. No one ever got old in Neverland—except for me. The guard at the gate eyed me warily, then mumbled something into a walkie-talkie.

I looked at Lia one more time. All my doubts had died when we had gone off the road. God had a plan for me, and that plan was Lia. We pulled into the lot. I opened my car door and immediately heard sirens. Loud sirens.

"Don't move!" I heard a female voice call through a loudspeaker.

Then a SWAT team, guns drawn, surrounded the Saturn like a ring.

"Put your hands on your head," the female voice said in an Asian accent. The voice was calm, not much different than a Tokyo Rose propaganda broadcast during World War II.

I panicked. I put my hands on my head, which I had never done before. Lia got out of the car.

"Now lie down."

I tried to think what I had done. I had cheated on the SATs, taken an extra minute to fill in questions on Section A when I was supposed to be working on Section B. I had put twenty dollars into a stripper's g-string rather than a trust account. Well, actually, two hundred dollars, but who's counting? Jesus, what else had I done in my checkered past? That's when I realized that they didn't care about me. No one bothered to come over to me. They had surrounded Lia.

"Ophelia Paz," the voice continued in that distinctive accent.

The accent made me wonder if this was an international incident.

"You're under arrest for the murder of Portia Smith C de Baca."

Coronado's Waitress

I DIDN'T KNOW WHAT I was supposed to do. Lia would have a lawyer already. Some kid from the public defender, my former employer, would handle the Metro Court arraignment Wednesday morning. A monkey could handle a Metro Court arraignment, waive a formal reading and utter the magic words—not guilty. Lia had no record, so hopefully they'd let her out on her own recognizance. Lia didn't need me for that.

I was still in too much shock to deal with anything. This was all a case of mistaken identity or something, right? It would be over by noon.

I couldn't visit her in the Albuquerque jail because I had to head back to Santa Fe for the deposition in a big medical malpractice case. I was somebody's lawyer all right, Joel's.

Still, I wanted to be there for Lia for moral support. I called Joel's cell at seven a.m. and tried to weasel out of an overly early return to Santa Fe. Joel picked up, a little hung-over both from alcohol and the election results. A printer hummed in the background; he was already hard at work at the office.

"I'm sorry," he said. "But trial's next week and if we don't do this before then, we're dead. You have the file in the car. Be here by nine, or don't be here at all!"

I took a quick, cold shower and headed out the door. I

always ran late, so I never wiped all the ice off the windshield before heading out. Every morning I dreaded going east on Indian School Road before turning north onto I-25, because my defroster didn't work that well. The sun always shone directly into my un-defrosted windshield turning it into a cracked kaleidoscope.

Albuquerque High, aka "Burque High," Lia's alma mater, stood across the street. The school was always crowded with pedestrians. A short, squat man who looked like a human bulldog yelled at a student loitering in the crosswalk. I almost hit the Bulldog while making my left turn into the sunlight. The sunlight formed a psychedelic rainbow of shifting patterns on the cracks in the glass.

"This is a school zone, asshole," he yelled.

"No blood, no foul," I whimpered.

"Watch yourself," he yelled.

Luckily I made it to the Interstate without any more near misses. I glanced at the massive Sandia Crest to my right. God must have stepped on a mountain range and flattened it to form this gigantic block of granite ten miles long.

As I headed north, my body ached. I had developed a chronic tightness in my right calf from putting my foot on the accelerator. Every morning I swore I wouldn't put my wallet in my back right pocket because it caused more pain. Every morning I forgot. I was a relatively young man with an old man's right calf.

I had once divided the sixty-mile trip into thirds. Albuquerque to Algodones was the first third, Algodones to Cochiti was the second. The home stretch was Cochiti up to Santa Fe.

I made up some time on the first third. By seven forty-five, halfway there, I stopped for gas, food, and bathroom at San Roberto Pueblo's Casino and Travel Center. I had seventeen minutes for all three activities.

San Roberto Casino was in a natural formation too big to be called an arroyo, but too small for a valley. The casino jutted out of the desert floor like a series of stalagmites with neon trim. The casino had been there forever, perhaps Coronado and his Conquistadores had played a few hands of no limit blackjack, then hit the peso slots.

Inside, the Pueblo's restaurant had some tribal decorations. The San Roberto were famous for their bead work. All the waitresses were pony-tailed Native women. One looked particularly ancient. Maybe she was the one who had served Coronado his scrambled eggs with chorizo, a spicy form of barbecued pork.

The woman had a great smile and wore layers of beautiful beads. Coronado had probably tipped her well. She brought me a cup of coffee without my asking, and I was about to go into my usual "I like my coffee the way I like my women" routine, but I was at a loss for words. I drank my coffee pitch black, just like my life.

I glanced at the Albuquerque paper. C de Baca was on the cover. Triumph and Tragedy was the predictable title. The Journal had called the election his way already. I had backed the wrong horse. Not the first time in my life.

According to the paper, Portia Smith C de Baca had been out canvassing by herself in the late afternoon during the rainstorms. Her nickname had been the "Canvass Goddess." The Canvas Goddess made house calls to any and all potential worshipers through rain, sleet and snow. Yesterday she had gone to a neighborhood, Lia's neighborhood. For some reason, Portia followed a resident into the home. No one saw Portia come out. She was not seen alive again.

A short time later, the EMT plucked Portia out of the drainage ditch a few miles downstream. She must have been carried down by the floodwaters during the raging rainstorm. If it hadn't been for the belated rescue, her body would be in the Gulf of Mexico by now.

I closed my eyes. Lia's house indeed abutted the concrete arroyo that flew all the way from one of the canyons up in the Sandias to the Rio. I had never actually entered Lia's house. Lia kept saying the time wasn't right. I realized how little I truly knew her.

I had seen Portia Smith C de Baca on TV with C de Baca. He was a giant. She was not. She couldn't weigh more than one hundred pounds max on her tiny five-foot frame. The former Portia Smith was almost a Nordic double of Lia. They next showed a picture of Portia with smiling Chinese children while she worked as a missionary. Many of the children were as tall as she was.

I tried to calculate Lia's strength and Portia's weight. Lia was no athlete, but her grip had been tight around my neck. With a little heave and a little ho, Lia could indeed have dragged Portia from her house. The sides of the arroyo were wet from the rain, so Lia would only have to slide Portia down into the rushing waters below.

Concrete walls surrounded all the yards. It was dark by five in the evening, and no one was out in the rain anyway. Lia certainly wouldn't be the first person to throw some litter into an arroyo.

Why couldn't that litter include a body or two?

Why not, indeed?

Why did I even think this way? Lia wouldn't even throw a wrapper out the window. Once, she had made me get out of the car to pick up a wad of gum that I had spit out while stopped at a traffic light. I had nearly killed myself picking it up before the light changed.

"It serves you right," she had said. "Littering is the worst thing in the world. Did you know that the average New Mexican tosses out over one hundred pounds of trash every year?"

The state was now charging Lia for one hundred pounds of littering.

My seventeen minutes were nearly up. I asked for the check from Coronado's waitress, and she ran my card through the world's slowest machine. Yesterday, murder day, I had not seen Lia before she arrived at the election party. I had been in Santa

Fe all day playing lawyer. Lia said that that The Werewolf had driven her up. Technically, she would have had time to kill Portia and then clean up, but Lia took forever to get ready, so it was highly unlikely.

But not impossible.

I got back on the freeway and headed north and tried to read Joel's file while I drove. I couldn't make sense of any of it. What the hell did Joel expect me to do when I got there?

Adobe Bubble

BY THE NEXT EXIT snow dusted the hills, making the small, isolated juniper trees look like sleeping white Dalmatians. After a few more Dalmatian canyons, I passed the Cochiti Pueblo exit. Now for La Bajada, and the final third.

The evil white car that had pursued us had vanished. Had the chase just been my imagination? Over La Bajada's summit, I had to stop at the rest stop. Perhaps it was stress, but the caffeine wanted to exit my body.

I expected a sign to read Watch for Rattlesnakes, like some of the other rest stops on the freeway. It didn't. Apparently in Santa Fe, the rattlesnakes knew how to hide.

I quickly got back in the car and began my own bajada, my own descent. Off to the left, I saw a rise that I called "Nipple Hill," after a petite Asian porn star with the world's smallest fake breasts. The northern mountains—the Sangre de Cristos—were rounder, much more feminine compared to the hard rectangular granite of Albuquerque's Sandias.

Traffic slowed to a halt between Nipple Hill and the high walls of the Penitentiary of New Mexico. There must be an accident, or perhaps a prison break. Why did inmates always make a run for it during rush hour?

Joel's office was in a little adobe development on the edge

of downtown. This was the last gasp of "Santa Fe style." I had heard that few blocks over, on Cerillos road, Santa Fe had Wal-Marts and Wendy's like everywhere else. Way out on the east side, on Airport Road, the town apparently even had a full-fledged barrio. I wouldn't know. An imaginary turquoise curtain separated the two Santa Fes.

I have never passed through the turquoise curtain. I always went down St. Francis, never down Cerillos. My Santa Fe was in an adobe bubble. Joel owned the "A" complex, which looked like the illegitimate offspring of the Taos Pueblo. The Taos Pueblo was made famous in a Georgia O'Keeffe painting and was a gigantic multi-storied complex of red adobe structures more than a thousand years old.

Thankfully, Joel's complex had better plumbing, but he was cheap on heating, so the original pueblo was probably warmer. Nearly every office in the building had been rented by a "healer" of some sort, Acupuncture in A-2, Natural Therapeutics in A-4. Mystical Readings were done in A-5. Even Fidel's, the "free trade" coffee over in A-6 offered aura readings with the decaf. We were in A-7, and the court reporters were in the building next door.

I hurried inside Joel's office. I didn't have my own little office decorated, didn't even have furniture yet. Joel had mentioned something about hiring a designer for me once I settled in. I'd have my pick of the litter. Santa Fe had nearly as many decorators in town as lawyers. Many locals did both law and decorating, along with real estate of course.

Joel had already gone over to the court reporters' office. Inside, they went with a South American variation on Santa Fe style, slightly more primitive but with some bolder teak accents. I would have to find out which decorator they used.

I checked my watch. I was late again. Joel said nothing. He pointed at the thousands of dollars of legal talent waiting for my entrance. Like cab drivers, their meters kept ticking even if nobody was moving.

"So this is the famous Rattlesnake Lawyer?" a civil lawyer commented under his breath.

Civil lawyers were such assholes. Civil law isn't civil, the old saying went. I know that if it weren't for the criminals, I'd be back in criminal law in a heartbeat.

I had worn a suit and tie, forgetting that Santa Fe lawyers were different from Albuquerque lawyers. They didn't wear ties or jackets. Still, their sweaters were often more formal than a suit.

To Joel, a deposition actually was a gallery opening party. Every question was an unveiling. To me a deposition was just a deposition.

Today's case involved medical malpractice, the least civil practice of all. We represented the hospital. My head still hurt. I had to question the alleged victim. I couldn't even remember the basis for her suit. She sat in a wheelchair and stared at me as if she thought I wanted to roll her off a cliff.

I was off my game. I didn't like wearing the black hat, especially with an orange tie. Everything I asked drew an objection. Unlike a trial, no judges refereed it, so the deposition resembled pro wrestling rather than boxing. I couldn't remember the rules of evidence either, and confused Rule 404(a) with 405(b) like I always did. What's the difference between pattern and habit, and which one are you allowed to ask about?

During a break an hour later, Joel pulled me aside.

"What's going on with you?" he asked. "You're not fully engaged."

For a brilliant lawyer, he sure favored clichés in his non-legal conversation.

"Personal stuff," I said. "Really bad personal stuff."

"Personal stuff is not a valid excuse. We're professionals here."

"I'll just go home."

Joel smiled. Under his contract with the client, he could bill me for the entire deposition as long as I showed up for part of it. It didn't matter if I stayed or went.

"Don't forget to bill your time," he said as I headed out.

I'd do that tomorrow. I made it to the freeway quickly, as Lia waited on the other side of La Bajada. She should be out by now. No answer on her phone. I called the jail to check on her, and found that she was still an inmate. The bond was a one hundred thousand surety bond, which meant that someone would have to post ten thousand with a bondsman. Gee, who did Lia know with ten thousand dollars burning a hole in his pocket?

Shit!

Bedknobs and Broomsticks

I WORRIED ABOUT LIA spending even an extra five minutes in jail. My right leg jammed against the accelerator until I hit one hundred miles per hour downhill on the La Bajada stretch. According to the New Mexico statutes that kind of speed was "per se" reckless driving, mandatory four days in jail. If I had hit someone, the charge would be vehicular homicide or perhaps even depraved mind murder. I slowed to a slightly less deadly eighty-five. If tragedy struck now, it would be misdemeanor manslaughter. Three-hundred-sixty-four days tops, a day less than a year. County jail. I could probably serve it on house arrest.

Even house arrest scared me. I slowed to under seventy-five.

Once I made it to Albuquerque on I-25, I then headed west on I-40 over the Rio Grande, then up the treeless incline of Nine Mile Hill to the Metropolitan Detention Center, otherwise known as MDC. This was the high desert, no tress, no grass, just brush. A few miles north, Albuquerque's dormant volcanic cones looked as if they were ready to blow.

As I entered the cinder-block building, a very petite female police officer escorted several men in suits into the inmate entrance.

Sucks to be them, I thought. I wanted to play "guess the

crime." Insider trading perhaps? Or soliciting? Or worse, giving insider stock tips to prostitutes?

From a distance, the petite officer stared at me, and waved. I waved back. I knew her from somewhere.

I entered MDC's bland lobby, which looked more like a dentist's office than a jail. I scribbled my name in a battered old log book. A correctional officer (or CO) of indeterminate gender didn't bother to check for ID. I beeped when I went through the metal detectors of course. The CO waved me through anyway, not looking up from a copy of that legal thriller that everyone in the jail seemed to love. It was a paperback of course. Hardbacks were banned in jail because the inmates might use them as weapons.

He stared at my orange tie. "Your tie matches their outfits."

Lia was held in a minimum security unit, D-9, which inmates considered the Kappa Kappa Gamma of jail sororities. The bad one, the Maximum Bitch Unit, was just as bad as the male units, and even worse during certain times of the month.

D-9 held the multiple drunk drivers, the meth whores, and a few serious first time felons like Lia. Before I could enter D-9, I had to wait in a tiny sally port. In the claustrophobic space I started to breathe heavier, and that made the air quality even worse, like breathing into a paper bag with a sandwich still in it.

My claustrophobic panic attacks began a few years ago. I could barely handle visiting the jail for extended periods of time any more, so even two minutes in a sally port was brutal.

Bulletproof glass separated the sally port from the unit. The physical layout of D-9 could pass for an army barracks in Iraq, but the female residents weren't soldiers, they were overweight, tattooed, and middle-aged. Their hair was straight, or shaved off, because the pod was stingy with shampoo, stingy with style. The sixty women of D-9 didn't have cells. Instead, their bunk beds lay randomly around the pod. Many of the women left their bunks to gather around the sally port, anticipating my entrance as if I were the last man on earth.

I placed a notebook over my crotch. Thank God my fly was zipped up.

Lia saw me from her bunk. She wore the red of a high-risk inmate, like Little Red Riding Hood in a forest of orange wolves. Without her make-up and a few pounds lighter, Lia looked sixteen rather than thirty. And she just didn't look right without the flower in her hair. Lia immediately ran to the glass.

"No running in jail," the guard said in a matronly voice. Lia stopped right by the door.

I felt so helpless trapped in the sally port.

"Can someone let me the hell inside?" I shouted to the intercom. Profanity never worked, but I couldn't help it.

Just as I breathed the last of the fresh air in the sally port, the door clicked open. I hurried into the relative openness of D-9. Lia hugged me right there.

"No hugging in jail," the CO shouted. "Ain't no love in D-9."

"Why is she in red?" I asked the guard. "She doesn't have a record."

"She's on suicide watch."

With her tattoos, the female CO looked like one of the inmates, rather than an authority figure.

She smiled. "Remember when you represented me for beating up my girlfriend?"

"I won your case, right?"

"I wouldn't be a CO if you had lost," she said.

She then made me go over to the control desk and sign a form. As a male in a female unit, they took extra precautions. I had left my pen in Santa Fe of course.

"Anybody here have a pen?" I asked.

The inmates laughed. Sharp objects were forbidden in the unit.

As the CO searched for a working pen on the control desk, I recognized a famed female boxer, Knock Out Noriega, strutting her considerable bulk. Knock Out once had some serious facial piercing, but since metal wasn't allowed, she filled the hole in her chin with the end of a plastic fork. She put the end of a comb through her ears. I would have laughed, but Knock Out could easily take me out with one punch.

Knock Out had some words with the small Vietnamese woman mopping the floor. The woman scurried over to me and introduced herself as Thuc Doan Le. She must have learned English on the inside, but the language still came hard to her.

"Will you represent me? I gotta get outta here."

"What are you in for?"

"Prostitution, and I violated my probation through mental health court."

Thuc Doan Le was about sixty and had no teeth. She was definitely not a pretty woman, nor a sane one. I had often joked that the only attractive prostitutes in Albuquerque were cops.

A posse of similar women surrounded me.

"How's that pen coming?" I shouted to the guard.

"Still looking," she said. "I gotta get a key to a meeting room, too."

Lia hid behind me. She was small, and most of the women were very big. Lia looked even smaller than she had the day before; she probably couldn't hold anything down due to stress. When female inmates de-toxed meth and coke, they often gained significant weight on the fatty jail food.

One woman exposed her stomach, checking the new rolls of fat. "I gotta get me back on the Jenny Crank," she said, apparently referring to the amazing dietary advantages of doing meth on the outside.

I politely told them that I wasn't taking new criminal cases any more.

"He doesn't have time for you," Lia said. "He's my lawyer now."

The tattooed CO finally found a pen, and I officially signed into the unit.

"Could you please hurry and get us inside the meeting room?" I asked.

The CO finally found the right key and ushered Lia and me into a small blank room with a single bulletproof window between it and the pod, then locked the door behind us. I had five minutes in here max, before the claustrophobia got to me. There was one chair. Lia sat while I paced around the room.

She had tears in her eyes.

"I'm so glad to see you," she said. "I missed you so much, so much, so much."

"I missed you too," I said. "I nearly got busted for reckless driving on the way down."

"Will you be my lawyer?"

"I don't know," I said.

"Please be my lawyer," she said.

"I don't know."

"You're so brilliant," she said. "You're a brilliant lawyer."

She probably said "brilliant" twenty times. Damn, the girl didn't get it. Finally I relented. "Okay, I'll do it. For now."

She got up and would have hugged me if I hadn't put a straight arm up like a running back trying to avoid a tackle.

She backed off. "Thank you so much, so much, so much." She wanted to keep going with the "so muches," but I wouldn't let her. Something wasn't right.

"Are you on meds right now?"

"No, I'm doing something called Siberian trancing. Someone developed it while in a Siberian labor camp so that you pretend that you're really on a tropical island. Once—"

"I don't care about Siberia right now. Just tell me what really happened," I said.

Why did I just ask that? You never ask your client what really happened. Had I forgotten how to be a defense lawyer in the few weeks I had worked for Joel?

"I had all my campaign signs out in front of my house," she said. "The homemade signs. It was afternoon, around five. I was getting ready for the party, to be with you. Portia Smith C de Baca was outside. It was pouring."

"Did you hit her?"

"Not even. I was totally calm. I told her to come inside and we'd talk about her husband's campaign She came into the house and we had a little argument about her husband. I said he was pure evil. I didn't touch her at all. That was it. The whole thing took five minutes."

No one saw Portia Smith C de Baca leave during the torrential downpour. Any people who could have been possible witnesses stayed inside. I wondered how anyone even knew Portia had gone inside with Lia. I supposed I would find out when I looked over the documents provided by the State.

"When I left she was still alive. Stone picked me up. The guy you call The Werewolf. He just honked; he didn't come in. I ran out to his car, and then I saw you in Santa Fe. I was as surprised as you were to learn she had died."

"Was anyone with you in the house?" I asked.

At that moment, Knock Out took a swing at another inmate, the one who wanted to be on Jenny Crank. Jenny Crank could take a blow surprisingly well, due to her bulk. She had a good left jab that broke Knock Out's plastic chin piercing, drawing blood.

"It is so on!" Jenny shouted.

The inmates starting yelling; they had ringside seats to a championship cat fight, right there in the pod. Another inmate pushed someone right up against our glass, leaving a blood stain.

I had visited inmates for years, but this was the first real live female inmate fight I had seen. I could barely hear Lia over the yelling. Lia said something about her mother.

"It is so on, you fat bitch," Knock Out said back to Jenny Crank.

The tattooed CO hurried over. Knock Out got a good right to the CO. The CO then took out her wooden baton.

I stood by the door. It was locked right? Could I protect Lia if the door gave way? I hoped so.

I kept my eyes on the door; Lia kept talking through the

entire fight. I think I heard her say the word "illegal" over the riot outside. If Lia's mother were illegal, this opened a mess of worms. I wanted to pursue the issue of Lia's illegal mother further, but the fight spread to other inmates. One knocked on the window in a threatening manner. I would have to stay vigilant.

The tattooed CO hurried back to the control desk. More inmates came closer to our room, now that the CO stood on the other side of the pod. I braced myself for them to break through. The tattooed CO pressed the panic button at control desk.

Silence.

The inmates began laughing. They owned the pod now.

Lia kept talking.

When the alarm finally went off it was the loudest alarm I had ever heard. Within moments, back up poured into the pod, male and female guards with clubs. Lia still kept talking. I couldn't hear anything at all, even if I wanted to.

After a few swings of the clubs, the guards quickly gained control.

The alarm went silent.

Finally, my ears still ringing, the guards herded the inmates back to their bunks, hands over their heads. Once there was relative quiet, the tattooed CO knocked on our door.

"I've got to get you out of here," she said.

"That might be best," I agreed.

The tattooed CO double-checked all the bunks before she let me out. All the inmates were in their bunks on the perimeter, and I was relatively alone in the corner with Lia. Now that they had relative anonymity, the inmates shouted louder and louder. Some shouts were aimed at me, but most were aimed at Lia.

"Broomstick," one said. I knew what they meant. I sure didn't want to explain it to Lia.

"One more thing," Lia said.

"Yes?"

"I don't have any money. And my mom can't help right now. Could you bond me out? It's a hundred thousand dollars bond.

That's ten thousand to a bondsman. Wouldn't your signing bonus cover it?"

I took a final look at Little Red Riding Hood, then at the wolves back in their bunks.

"Broomstick!" one shouted again. "Give her the broomstick."

Lia now realized what they were saying. Her skin was ghost white.

"Broomstick," the entire pod yelled at once.

"Don't worry," I said. "Who needs a new Prius anyway?"

The CO clicked me out of the pod as I watched the guard put Lia back on her bunk. Once again, I stalled in the sally port of D-9. I clicked the outgoing button repeatedly. Nothing.

The inmates now chanted: "Fuck you, lawyer."

Sweat poured thought my suit by the time I finally emerged into the main hallway. On the way out, somewhere in the middle of the Checkerboard Mile, I ran into Luna Cruz, the lawyer I'd met at the election party. She looked fairly ridiculous in an oversized leather jacket and baggy sweat pants. She looked like she'd just had a drunken one-night-stand in the D-7 pod and grabbed the first available clothes from the intake room on the way out.

"Luna Cruz, right?" I said. "What's up with you?"

"Sam?"

"It's Dan."

"Sorry." Luna was more educated than Lia, but she certainly lacked Lia's photographic memory. She looked sheepish to be seen in such a state.

"I had forgotten that you can't show too much skin in jail," she said. "I can't even wear heels. Apparently they're afraid I'm going to drive the inmates wild with the flash of my ankle. Luckily I had an old boyfriend's clothes in the car."

"I'm sure you have a nice ankle," I said. "You here visiting a client?"

She looked uncomfortable. "No, it's personal."

Her face betrayed nothing. I couldn't help but wonder what she was wearing under the sweats and the jacket. Lia wore her emotions on her sleeve, while Luna hid hers under a cast iron corset. Why couldn't Lia be more like Luna?

"How about you?" she asked. "Are you visiting a client here?"

"That's personal, too."

Phantom Menace on Line One

BONDING LIA OUT OF MDC was not easy. I used James Barcelona of the Barcelona family of bondsmen.

"Just call me Bond. James Bond," he said over the phone. "I have a license to bail."

I was too nervous to laugh. Lia finally emerged late in the afternoon. I wanted to wait outside in the fresh air, but tumbleweeds roamed the mesa like a wolf pack, so I reluctantly waited in the lobby with the families. The lobby smelled like an airport after a maintenance workers' strike. I sat in one of the hard plastic chairs, the same kind of chair that was inside the pods. Many of the family members knowingly gossiped about life inside. Apparently the deputy warden in charge of the Maximum Bitch Unit had had an affair with Knockout Noriega herself.

Lia's nice pink outfit from the party looked only slightly worse for wear, but her turquoise necklace was a stone or two lighter. Behind us, an eighteen-year-old in an Albuquerque Isotopes jacket let out a wolf whistle. He had some scary gang tats on his neck, just like Dad.

I called him Isotope, both for the jacket and the fact that his face looked mottled from stray radiation and acne. Had a nuclear bomb gone off in Albuquerque while I was in Santa Fe?

"Hey Donna, you wanna?" Isotope said to Lia.

We ignored him.

Lia hugged me so tight it hurt, but in a good way. She had just a whiff of the jail smell too, which, combined with Lia's body chemistry, created a new perfume. One of my old girl-friends had called it *Incarceration*, for the woman who can't be caged. Incarceration had never smelled this good. Neither of us let go.

"Get a room, *ese,*" Isotope yelled.

"Ese" was supposedly a term of familiarity. I certainly didn't want to be too familiar with Isotope, so I ignored him and let the hug linger. Nothing else mattered at that moment; Lia was free. From now on I would protect her from the Isotopes and Knock Out Noriegas of the world.

"Tonight can be the night," Lia whispered as we hurried out the door.

"Where to?" I asked, after we fastened our seatbelts in my messy car.

"Let's pick up stuff from my house. I reek." She sniffed her-self. "Then let me stay with you."

"I kinda like the smell," I said with a smile. "You know I've never been to your house before. Will your mother be there? I want to meet her."

"Weren't you paying attention when I was talking?" Lia asked.

Before I could answer, Lia's entire body started vibrating. For one moment, I thought she had ants crawling around her body. Finally she found her phone and put on her Bluetooth.

She listened intently. I heard nothing.

She then replied. "But he's my lawyer."

It was unnerving, watching her talk into thin air. She listened for another minute and then responded. "Okay, I understand. I promise I won't say anything to him. I don't think he was lis-tening anyway."

She then put her head set down. "I can't talk any more. My phone is dying."

I had no way of knowing whether she had actually talked to any one or not.

"I can't say anything more to you about what happened that night," she said. "I promised."

"Who was that?" I asked.

"I told you, I promised."

"But—"

"I *promised*," she repeated.

I didn't want to press her. I called this the "Don't ask, don't tell" rule. As a defense attorney, ignorance wasn't just bliss, it was often an ethical obligation under the canons of ethics. If I didn't ask and she didn't tell, I had a lot more options at trial.

Although Lord knows, I prayed it wouldn't come to that.

We drove east on the interstate as it passed by the giant sand dunes known as Hell's Hills, descended to the Rio Grande, then climbed toward the Sandia Mountains. A few uphill miles later, we exited to an aging subdivision in the northeast heights. Lia's house was a boring brick, in a boring brick subdivision. It could be anywhere in America, except for the yellow crime-scene tape around the front yard and the squad car waiting patiently in front.

Lia's handmade political signs lay face first in the mud. The cop who got out of his car looked like a miniature Arnold Schwarzenegger. He approached us warily, his hand near his gun.

"Can I help you?" Arnold asked.

"She needs to get her things," I said. "She lives here."

"Who are you?" he asked.

"I'm her lawyer," I said, flashing my crumbling bar card.

"You should get that validated," Arnold said.

"You mean laminated."

"Whatever. I'll have to go inside with you," he said. "It's officially a crime scene."

Inside, the tiny house was immaculate. Her mother must be an amazing housekeeper. Apparently, since her dad died a few years ago, Lia and her mother had lived off his life insurance from the city. He had been a city maintenance worker and was big into the city worker's union. One picture showed him with a very young Lia posing with the mayor at that time. Perhaps that's what got Lia interested in politics. Elsewhere in the house religious icons shared the walls with some very old family pictures. Mama was an immigrant from Chichen Itza, Mexico. Dad came from a family in the southern part of this state, Deming, a one-McDonald's town near the Mexican border.

In the pictures Mom was as dark and obese as a Mayan fertility idol. She looked far sturdier than Lia. In one picture, she posed next to a pyramid with pride, as if she had built it herself. She easily had the meat to beat up Portia and drag her out the door, another human sacrifice to a Mayan deity.

Several Spanish language religious tracts lay on the table. The pamphlets had dust caked on top of them. I didn't see a single recent photo in the entire house. Not one.

In the quaint living room, there was a broken vase with dead flowers on the table. A drop of blood stained the tan carpet next to a turquoise stone. The stone had a chalk mark around it. As I bent down to look at it, Arnold grabbed my hand.

"Don't touch that!" he yelled.

I sheepishly walked away, and headed instead out the glass door to a dirt back yard. The messy yard had some plastic trash. Drag marks led to a door at the edge of a wall at the back of the yard. If memory served, a bike trail along the arroyo lay on the other side. I had ridden that trail during my brief flirtation with triathlons. Someone could easily exit unseen via the bike trail and then re-emerge almost anywhere in Albuquerque.

Lia had made it to her bedroom. I followed.

"My computer is gone," Lia said to Arnold. "Did you guys take it?"

Arnold frowned. "There wasn't a computer here when we got here," he said.

That sounded suspicious. Maybe the plastic I saw in the backyard was a broken part of the computer. Whoever killed Portia might have disposed of the computer as well. Lia owned a five-pound laptop, so that would make it one hundred and five pounds of littering.

Lia looked at her closet absent-mindedly. She was in another world right now, about to change clothes right there in front of the cop.

Officer Arnold grabbed her wrist. "Don't touch anything. Just get your clothes from the closet and get the hell out of here before I arrest you for tampering."

He looked at me. "That goes for you, too."

He stayed to make sure she didn't contaminate anything. I wandered to her mom's room as if walking on eggshells. It was immaculate, but dusty. No one had been here for weeks, or perhaps even years. The bed looked like it hadn't been slept in, ever. I coughed from the dust.

I did see a picture of Lia's mother, possibly in her forties, standing with Lia in front of the Sandia Crest. Lia wore a junior varsity cheerleader uniform for Albuquerque High. Lia was thirty now, so that was twelve, thirteen years ago. Like the living room, I saw no recent family photos.

I couldn't help but realize that I never heard Lia's mother call Lia. Lia had always called her. Until tonight. If that really was her mother.

Lia had put her phone down in the living room to charge it. I hurried over to see the caller ID. Unfortunately, nothing came up. Either the call came from an unknown number, or it never came at all.

As I turned, I saw a wig on the top shelf of the closet.

A wig?

Was her mother still alive? If Lia's mother had called her from the afterlife, at least she waited until after seven o'clock, when the rates went down.

A very scary thought hit me as I picked up the wig. Suppose Lia was playing the Norman Bates game from *Psycho?* Suppose Lia had two personalities: normal sweet Lia and evil Lia who dressed up like her dead mom and killed the wives of rival political candidates. Or maybe Mom just had ugly hair and wore a wig. Or she was an illegal alien who spent considerable time on the road and she wanted to blend in.

As I moved to pick up the wig I heard water running. Was Lia taking a shower? Or changing into her dead mother?

I glanced into the bathroom where Lia washed her hands under Arnold's watchful eyes.

"Dan," Lia said. "He said we've got to get out of here. Right now."

Eggshells or not, I could not have run faster out the door.

Neverland Nookie

PART OF ME WANTED to drop Lia off at a motel near the freeway. Just end it there, a clean break. Hell, I'd take the motel room; she could have the apartment, along with her mother, alive or dead.

"You're my white knight," she said.

"Your white knight is tired," I said.

I didn't know what to feel about her anymore. White knights usually saved the maiden and then went on their way to find the grail. I couldn't abandon her.

Lia had found a slightly wilted red rose to put in her hair. The rose seemed to bloom a little bit more with every passing moment, as if gaining sustenance from her aura.

We made it back to Neverland. I almost expected another SWAT team to wait for us in ambush, but the parking lot was completely empty. Sometimes I thought the other residents knew about a secret party and never told me.

We went inside my studio apartment. I never understood the term "studio." If I were an artist, I definitely would not have enough room to fit a full-size model in it. I could barely fit in an easel. Since I had begun working in Santa Fe, I hadn't bothered to clean the place. Hopefully this sty was temporary, just until I moved into that big place up north in Tesuque or Pojoaque, whichever was the cooler "que."

Any "que" but Albuquerque.

The tan carpet tried vainly to resist an occupying force of dirty laundry and fast food wrappers. Lia began undressing, and left the flower by the bed. The jail smell wafted into the tight confines. I snuck a glance at her, and felt guilty.

If I was truly her lawyer, could I see her naked?

"No peeking," she said.

I covered my eyes.

She went into the bathroom and steam quickly filled the apartment, as if we were at a naturist resort in the midst of the Amazon rain forest. She must have turned up the heat to over a hundred. It was so hot I had to wipe my glasses.

Minutes later, the place was a nice, sultry hell. Lia had changed into some of my gym clothes, and put the rose back in her hair. I tried to be a gentleman. I wanted to tell Lia to sleep on my bed, that I would take the couch. But she pulled me to the bed before I could protest

"You look tense. I'll give you a back-rub."

I hesitated. Technically, I hadn't entered my appearance yet on her case. I hadn't stood in as her lawyer for any hearing. Just visiting her at the jail didn't count. I visited a lot of people at jail. She could still give me a back-rub, right? There was no canon of professional responsibility that said a client couldn't touch her attorney's rhomboids, right?

I thought again about the wig. Could Lia be an insane killer? Did I have a death wish? Did I secretly want Lia to kill me right now because I felt some failure in my life?

No, I didn't just have a death wish, I had a hard on. She pulled my shirt off my back. Lia once told me that she had wanted to learn acupuncture. She knew all the right trigger points. She touched a spot on my shoulder and the warmth shot down into my toe.

She then took off my pants, so I was in my underwear.

"Quit wiggling," she said with a giggle.

"It's hard," I said, not necessarily referring to the difficulty of staying still. She went a little deeper into the flesh by my lower spine, as if trying to enter me through one of my *chakras*. Somehow that made me even more excited. She even used the thorn of the rose, ran it down my back, over my butt and down my legs.

"Say you're firing me as your lawyer," I said. "Other than the statement to the cop, I technically haven't entered yet."

I regretted using the term "enter."

"You're fired," she said. "For now."

"Say it three times," I said. "That's what it takes in some jurisdictions."

"You're fired. You're fired. You're fired."

I had never been so happy to be fired in my life. It was cool, right? At least that's what I kept telling myself. Perhaps I could get Luna Cruz to take over the case.

"Are you sure you want to do this?" I asked, rolling onto my back. This would be our first time.

"Tonight's the night!"

Lia jumped on top of me. I felt crushed. With the wind out of my lungs, I had less energy to resist. She kissed me, then she told me over and over how brilliant I was, how wonderful I was, how sexy I was.

For a moment, I actually believed her.

When I finally went to sleep, exhausted, I wondered if she would kill me in my sleep. I didn't care. I would die happy.

God, I hoped she wouldn't re-hire me.

Not So Grand Jury

WE MUTUALLY DECIDED IT would be best if Lia stayed at her house for the duration. When I took Lia back the next evening, APD had removed the crime tape. Still, I didn't want to go inside, and dropped her off in her driveway.

I did remember one thing about the attorney-client relationship from my days as a public defender. I could never put on testimony I knew to be false. Not if I wanted to remain a lawyer. If I ever wanted to put Lia on the stand, I'd better not ask Lia too much about her mother. Murder could be a team sport. Conspiracy was a felony as well. Mom's phone calls could make Lia part of that conspiracy.

In the eyes of the law, silence was golden.

Over the next week Lia resumed her usual good spirits with every new hour of freedom. She kept up with the Siberian trancing chants instead of popping anti-depressants. The trancing worked almost too well.

"I mean, why worry?" she said to me one night on the phone. "They haven't taken it to Grand Jury yet. A Grand Jury will throw it out once they hear the truth, that I left while she was still alive."

A therapist would call it denial of course. Grand Juries in Albuquerque had never failed to indict. Even the innocent. In some ways it was good that Mama was gone to either Mexico or the afterlife. I certainly couldn't tell Lia about my "Plan B" of blaming Mama for everything. Lia wouldn't like Plan B.

Lia's name did make the papers later that week, complete with her mug shot. Lia's eyes were open way too wide, so she looked like a deer getting booked.

I kept waiting for Joel to say something to me. He ignored everything as he worked on the malpractice trial and relegated me to the firm's land use work. When he called me into his office that Friday, I grew nervous. Was the jig up?

"They settled the malpractice case." he said.

He gave me a four hundred dollar bonus check from the client.

"But I didn't do anything," I said.

"You will."

Sunday night I called Joel and told him I couldn't make it to work on Monday. It was Lia's Grand Jury. I certainly couldn't tell Joel that, so I made up an excuse about my tires getting slashed by ravaging teen-age hoodlums from nearby *"Burque* High." Santa Fe people had this vision of Albuquerque as an Hispanic Baghdad, so he bought it immediately.

Santa Feans made a deliberate point not to follow Albuquerque murders, much like Yankee fans don't follow the Mets. Supposedly Santa Fe was a violent city as well, but that occurred on the other side of the turquoise curtain.

I hoped I would be a partner in the firm before Lia's case actually made it to trial. I knew I'd have to take off a few days here and there. Joel would be cool with that, I hoped.

The next morning, Lia's case made it to Grand Jury at the Second Judicial District Court in Albuquerque. The Second Judicial District Courthouse had been designed by three different committees, and looked like the past, present and future in seven stories. The bottom was one story of adobe bricks, something out of territorial days; the middle was six modern stories of gleaming concrete and glass, something you'd see off the interstate in Silicon Valley; the blue roof on top could pass for a flying saucer.

The Grand Jury room was in a far corner of the third floor. I couldn't actually enter the room, since after considerable begging, I had convinced Lia not to testify.

"Remember, I'm not your lawyer yet," I told her over the phone. "I'm just doing recon on your behalf."

A line of witnesses waited to check in. Two Albuquerque Police Department (APD) cops stood looking out the window. The male cop, Onate, was the standard APD bodybuilder. On his arm was a barbed-wire tattoo. Onate didn't even glance at me as he walked toward the Grand Jury room to testify.

I recognized the female Asian cop—Bebe Tran. "Like you *tran't nguyen* them all," she would joke when people screwed up her name. Her four foot eleven frame was all muscle. She had a tattoo of a handcuff on her left wrist, with the word EMPATHY written underneath.

Empathy for whom?

Bebe had been the petite officer escorting the men in suits into the jail. Up close, her ninety pounds could easily have taken them all.

"You're not supposed to be here," she said, all edge.

That's where I knew the voice. She had been the arresting officer with the bullhorn.

I had said that Lia was Albuquerque, and Luna was Santa Fe. So who was Bebe? At first I thought Las Cruces, because she was underrated and underappreciated, but then the answer was obvious. She was Roswell. No one really knew what the hell had happened there, but there were a lot of rumors. Some of them had to be true.

A recent APD recruiting television ad showed Bebe pretending to be a lowly secretary who transformed moments later into a Laser Geisha superhero in Blue, gun drawn, taking down an evildoer.

In reality, Bebe was hardly a poster child. She didn't play well with most of the barbed-wire bodybuilders. They often made her work Vice, forced her to pretend she was right off the streets of Saigon, as opposed to having a Master's Degree in Criminology.

Bebe could be nice. She would play "bad cop" with some of my clients and tell them if they didn't take the nice deal Mr. Shepard had negotiated, she would be forced to come down hard with the full force of the law.

"Just passing through," I replied. "Are you still in Vice?"

"Burque Vice." She hummed the theme song from the old *Miami Vice* show. "Except I don't get to be Crockett or Tubbs. I'm the girl in the skimpy outfit that only got one line a show. At least I'm now half time in a special unit. Crisis Intervention."

"That sounds impressive."

"The salary sure isn't," she said. "Are you representing the lovely Ms. Paz?"

"I don't know yet," I said. "You the one who busted her?"

"You know she's mentally ill," Bebe said. "Our unit has been watching her for years."

"Mentally ill?" I looked at Bebe for a moment. "Have you ever seen her mother?"

"Until the date of the alleged murder, none of the neighbors ever reported anyone other than Lia actually going in the front door. And Portia went in, but didn't come out."

I shook my head. "There is a back door out to the arroyo trail."

Bebe smiled. "If the mother was going in and out the back door for ten years, that definitely is a bad thing."

I stared at Bebe. "I'm sure you have the pictures of her mom tagged into evidence. Maybe you could run something through NCIC or whatever it is you do."

"I'll try," Bebe said. "One more thing. You were there when we busted her. They did see someone matching your description drop Lia off a few times. Please tell me you're not sleeping with her. Craziness is contagious."

I said nothing.

"Are you going to stay in the courthouse?" she asked. "I'll find you."

"There's a woman who knows everything up on the seventh floor," I said. "I'll be up there."

More Than Kin, But Less Than Kind

AFTER MY CHAT WITH Bebe, I went up to the seventh floor to wait out the Grand Jury. Usually I would hang out with Chief Judge Kurtz's secretary, Beverly, who looked like Jennifer López. Unfortunately, there was a new face at the desk.

Out of context, it took me a moment to recognize Eva Jonas, a.k.a. Eva Braun, Governor Mendoza's former secretary. Apparently after the defeat, the governor had pushed her out of the bunker. Someone like Eva would only work for the best, and needless to say, with Mendoza on his way out she needed a new job.

Secretary for Judge Kurtz, chief judge of the biggest district court, was the best job in the state right now, even if she was on the wrong side of La Bajada.

On her desk was a rare volume of Shakespeare's collected works. She was reading *Hamlet*. I guess that made her Gertrude, she had gone from one king to another.

"Hello, *Danika*." Eva spoke trippingly on the tongue. She must have a photographic memory for everyone who was at the party.

"I guess," I said. I pointed at her book. "To be or not to be." She laughed. "You're no Hamlet."

"Eva, right?" I almost said Eva Braun, but wisely refrained.

I didn't attempt to pronounce her Hungarian last name. Continuing with my New Mexico cities analogy, Eva would be Taos, the more intense, more ancient version of Santa Fe. She was the governor's age, but people said she had been more like a mother to him. I sure needed some matronly advice these days.

Eva had let her hair go gray in the last week, as if she didn't have to try so hard now that she was in Albuquerque.

"Are you okay, *Danika?*" she asked. "You look stressed. I was a nurse in Budapest. You can tell me everything."

She put her hand on my forehead, taking my temperature, then made some tea for me. I told her about Lia over sips of tea. I didn't tell her the sex part, of course.

"*Hagyd beken.* You should stay away from that Ophelia Paz. She's *orult,* crazy. You don't know the half of it."

When she said the word "half" in her BBC/foreign hybrid accent, I could tell that she knew a lot more than she let on. "Half" really meant infinitesimal here, as in "You don't the know the barest fraction of what is really going on."

"Did you work on the campaign?"

"No, I'm a state employee," she said. "It's forbidden to work on a political campaign. That was left to the *Kormanyzo,* the governor's political team—Vladimir Stone and his ilk."

It took me a moment to remember that "ilk" was an English word.

"I was alone a lot. He would practically leave me in charge of the state when they went off to campaign headquarters. But I knew your Ophelia. Everybody does."

The memory of the election loss stung her; she obviously wanted to change the subject. Eva picked up the local bar directory.

"You know who would be perfect for you? Your *igaz szerelem,* your true love?"

"Who?"

She flipped to a picture of a brunette. "Luna Cruz, the pretty lawyer you were talking to at the party."

"I think she's out of my league," I said. "She may be the perfect women, but women like that are looking for the perfect man."

"Don't sell yourself short," she said. "Come out to the balcony, I need to smoke a cigarette."

"I thought you were nurse," I said. I was a vehement non-smoker. "Don't you know that stuff will kill you?"

"I *was* a nurse, *Danika.* I don't always follow my own advice."

The balcony faced west, toward Albuquerque's dormant volcanoes. There was a cloud over the biggest one. Maybe it was ready to blow. Eva lit a cigarette that smelled more of sulfur than nicotine. I scanned the modest Albuquerque skyline, the twenty-two story "rocket building" towered over the motley collection of ten story boxes.

I turned down Eva's offer of a sulfur cigarette.

"You remind me of my own *fiam,* my son," she said.

"I do?"

"He was like you, *Danika,* very smart, but a little lost."

"That's me to a 'T.' Is he here in town?"

She frowned, drew a cigarette. "My son and my husband had a *balesat,* a car accident, back in Hungary. I had nothing, so I came here to America, New Mexico. Long story."

Time to change the subject.

"Do you think Lia's charges are politically motivated?" I asked. A strong breeze blew past us and the balcony shook.

"What do you think?"

"I don't know. It just seems there isn't enough evidence to charge her."

"They had to charge somebody," Eva said. Her cigarette went out in the wind, so she lit another. This one smelled of brimstone, whatever that was. "And Ophelia was that somebody. What was that line from *Casablanca?"*

"*Round up the usual suspects,*" I said. "But Lia is pretty unusual."

"You don't know—"

"The half of it," I said. "I know. I think her mother did it. Assuming she's still alive."

"Her *anya?* Her mother?" Eva thought for a second.

"I bet it was an accident," I said. "Lia leaves her mom alone with Portia. Portia has a heart attack or something. The mother freaks, dumps her, then goes to Mexico and hides out for the duration."

Eva thought about it. "That's an interesting theory."

I decided to impress her with my other theory.

"But then again, perhaps Lia's mother is dead, and Lia dressed up like her mother and killed Portia doing the Norman Bates thing . . . . No, I still think it was the mother. I bet she's in Mexico."

"You do have an imagination," she said.

I liked the way she pronounced the word. Hungarian was the sexiest accent. If she was just twenty years younger. Or if I was twenty years older. After spending time with Eva, I was positive she once had a "thing" with the governor.

"Speaking of mothers, how's yours, *Danika?* The world famous Athena, goddess of wisdom? She must be proud of you, an *ugyved,* a lawyer and all."

I looked down at Fifth Street, seven stories below. It was an effort, but I made a point to look up and watch the volcanoes instead. The clouds grew bigger, darker. I purposely didn't answer the question. My parents hadn't been proud of me in a long time.

"I haven't heard from them in couple of days: they're still in on a slow boat to Shanghai or wherever."

Eva sensed my loneliness and put her hand on my shoulder.

"*Dani. Danika*. You should just be yourself, not try to prove anything to them."

I began to feel dizzy from the view.

"Could we go back inside?"

Eva finished her cigarette and flung it into the Albuquerque air. I wanted to tell her that she shouldn't litter, but what would they do—arrest her? She was secretary to the chief judge.

When we went back inside she showed me the card of a lawyer/publisher in Los Angeles.

"This guy's interested in my book project. He's always looking for good material," she said.

Eva smiled an evil smile, put the card into a desk drawer, then locked it. Was she writing about the governor?

As I waited with Eva for the Grand Jury to finish with Lia's case, Joel called a few times and asked me about a various cases I had worked on. I was a little nervous and confused the medical malpractice case with the one involving municipal bonds. I told him I'd be up for the afternoon.

Eva called the clerk downstairs twice to find out whether the Grand Jury had come back.

I closed my eyes and said a prayer. "Please God, don't let the Grand Jury indict her."

"True bill or not true bill," I asked. "That is the question."

My phone rang. It was Bebe Tran. "Good news!"

"They didn't indict?" I asked.

"They didn't indict?" Eva asked me.

"No, they did." Bebe said. "After only thirty seconds. By 'good news,' I meant it was good news for me. It was my case after all."

I clenched my fist and swung it down in rage. I accidentally hit the cup of hot tea I left on Eva's desk. The tea burned my hand.

"Shit!"

Judge Kurtz wheeled himself out of his inner office. He looked as if he wanted to roll right over me

"Excuse me, Eva, are you working for him or for me?"

The last thing I wanted was to get a judge mad at me, on top of everything else. On the way out I thought of Hamlet's last words: "The rest is silence." Something told me that with this judge, I had better keep silent.

Fried Fugu

I HAD TO RETURN to Santa Fe that afternoon. I tried to call Lia three times to tell her the bad news, but I couldn't get through. Perhaps she was in the midst of a Siberian trance and didn't want to pick up. Once I hit Algodones, I stopped trying and forced myself to think of Santa Fe. I knew I'd better do some actual legal billing for Joel or it would be my actual legal ass.

At the office, Joel seemed happy with my work for a change. In one brief, opposing counsel had said we had "perverted the spirit of the collateral estoppel case law." Collateral estoppel had to do with re-litigating issues that were already decided in a lower court. I wasn't sure what this particular opposing counsel meant, but I put in a zippy reply anyway.

Joel smiled a rare smile. "If you learn the rules here, every once in awhile, I'll let you break them."

"Thank you," I said.

Lia called right at that moment, of course. I snuck out to the front to talk to her, and tried to sound cheerful.

"It will all work out," I said.

"They dropped the charges, didn't they?"

She was serious. The Siberian trancing had tranced out her fears a little too well. She should be panicking. Instead, the situation hadn't sunk in yet.

On the job front, I apparently hadn't made a clean getaway. Joel opened the door, and shouted, "Is something wrong?"

I hung up the phone. Lia didn't need to hear me get chewed out by my boss.

"No, nothing." I whimpered.

I went back to my office and pretended to work on the computer for a few minutes, then hurried to the bathroom. I didn't want Joel to interrupt me as I told Lia the bad news. I locked the door as if I were doing a drug deal. I called Lia, but she didn't pick up. Come back from Siberia, damn it!

I left a message on her machine, but what could I say? "You've been indicted on murder charges, call me tomorrow night?"

Instead, I just said "Meet me at Fugu, that place you're always talking about, around six thirty."

I hung up. Fugu sounded great.

"Fugu is the rare poisonous puffer fish from Japan," she had said. "It's a delicacy that must be prepared by an expert chef. Bad fugu could kill you."

"Can you buy real fugu in New Mexico?" I asked.

"There's going to be a fugu importation bill in the next session," she said. "I think it will pass, but C de Baca will veto it."

One more reason to hate C de Baca. He was anti-fugu. I hoped that we'd dine tonight in some dark romantic corner. I would ply her with *sake* before I told her the bad news.

I heard footsteps outside the bathroom. Why couldn't briefs just write themselves? I unlocked the door and quickly got back to the computer. Somehow I managed to finish my project for the day. I printed it out and looked for Joel.

"Out here," he said.

Joel was outside on his private patio, sipping the famed Sheep Springs Mineral Water with that addictive after-taste that could be anything from sugar beet to sheep shit. He threw me a bottle.

"Relax for a second."

The air was cold out here, but the sun was bright and the rays made the adobe somehow look like they'd had a fresh coat of stucco.

I had a Santa Fe moment. I breathed in the high altitude air, tasting the mesquite fireplaces, the organic coffee from Fidel's, even the lightly scented erotic massage oils from all five massage places in the building. The sun had begun its descent, and the snow on the top of the Sangre de Christos now looked pink. One mountain looked so close in that clear, clear air that I was tempted to lick the snow like a snow cone.

Joel didn't say anything. Perhaps the sheer beauty of the moment got to him as well.

"Some day this could all be yours," he said.

I nodded as I sipped the cool water.

"I'd like that."

I had mixed emotions as I drove home. Still in Santa Fe, my cell rang just as I hit St. Francis Drive's exit to I-25. I wanted to pick it up, but a motorcycle cop rode next to me and he must have heard it. Driving while using a cell-phone was illegal in Santa Fe. I had never bothered to get a Bluetooth. They killed my ears.

The phone kept ringing. Shit, Santa Fe cops could lock you up for less. Talking on the phone certainly wouldn't give me "street cred" on the inside. The cop stared at me. The ringing eventually died a slow and lingering death.

Once I was on the open road, the sunset was magnificent. Georgia O'Keeffe would have loved a sunset like this. The clouds looked like pink flowers, or whatever it was she was *really* drawing. New Mexico was the Land of Enchantment after all. On an evening like this, I wished that UNM's teams were called the Enchanters instead of the Lobos. Well, maybe something slightly more macho along the lines of Notre Dame—The UNM Fighting Enchanters.

There was some light snow on La Bajada, and yet another accident. I was gun-shy after the miracle survival the other night, so I descended the hill like a snow-plow, rather than a downhill racer. After La Bajada, it was bone dry back to Albuquerque.

Fugu was packed when I arrived at six forty-five.

"Dan," I heard Lia's voice inside the restaurant. "I've got us a table. They put on a show here!"

A show?

I sat next to Lia, who had a yellow rose in her hair. The restaurant had steel teppen grills in the middle of the tables so the chef could prepare the meal right in front of the customers. We had a corner table with some tourists from Amarillo, who were as excited as Lia and complimented her on her rose. I grimaced as the chef came to our table and turned on the heat in the middle. He had a long ponytail and a kamikaze headband, but when he began to speak, something didn't sound right.

"*Konishiwa*," I said, a gift of gab from an old Japanese girlfriend.

"*Ya ta hey*," he replied with a smile.

That didn't sound Japanese.

"Where are you from?" I asked.

"Sheep Springs, out on the Navajo rez."

"I love your bottled water," I said.

He told us he was a Navajo who had wanted to be a *ninja,* but cooking was the logical next step after failing *ninja* school. He played with an egg, juggling it before letting it break on the table. He then put in some rice and did somersaults with rice and egg, then peas and carrots. He even used his knives to play ping-pong with the peas. He was quick. He could have been an amazing ninja, no matter where he lived.

"What are you making?" a tourist asked.

"Fried rice," he said. "Just like mom made back in Sheep Springs to go with the fry bread."

He acted as if that was funny, so we all pretended to laugh. He then dished out portions to the six of us, spinning his knives all the while.

"There's a place like this in Amarillo," one tourist said.

"Been there," he said. "All over Texas. I trained under the great *sensei* in Muleshoe."

I didn't know if he was kidding, or not.

The Navajo Ninja now emptied the meats onto the table, starting with the pork. It sizzled like bacon.

"So what happened with my case?" Lia asked, talking over the sizzle. "The Grand Jury let me go?"

She devoured the fried rice. At the other side of the table, the Navajo Ninja did some pre-op surgery on the beef, then sliced and diced some sirloin into cubes.

"You were indicted," I said. "True bill."

"What does that mean?" She knew politics, but she didn't know law.

The Navajo Ninja now threw both knives in the air, like a juggler. He was good.

"The case was *not* dismissed." I tried to whisper, but Lia couldn't hear me above the clatter and the sizzle.

"Speak up," she said. "So what am I being charged with?"

There was no easy way to say it. "Second-degree murder."

The chef looked right at me. "My cousin got indicted on murder once—the big Yazzie case out in Crater County."

"What happened to him?" a tourist asked.

The chef now shifted to the vegetables, he cracked an egg and then fried a mysterious substance with a fishy smell. Was that the fugu? The grease on the table sizzled like a volcano. "He was executed," the Navajo Ninja shouted over the sizzle. "They strapped him to a slab and fed him bad fugu."

He smiled. The fish smell got worse.

His levity didn't work. The enormity of all suddenly hit Lia. Her façade crumbled at that moment, and not even seven days of Siberian trancing could stop a new onslaught of stress. All of a sudden she turned ghostly white. The fried rice burst out of her and landed right on the table. The peas and carrots apparently didn't get along too well either, as they came down directly on the hottest part of the grill. The peas caught on fire.

The Amarillo contingent all ran to the bathroom, and I felt like I was about to purge myself as well. All the deep dark crap that churned inside, stuff that I had kept down for years, all of that wanted to burst out of me and onto the burning table with the burning pork. My lost loves, my failed jobs, my C+ in Criminal Procedure mixed with my current trauma: fears about Lia, anxiety about keeping Joel happy and my parents proud. The smell of the burning peas cranked it up a notch.

For one brief moment, my body felt like a volcano about to erupt. The chef looked at me with horror. If my whole life spilled onto the burning table, he knew he wouldn't get a tip from the folks from Amarillo.

"Hold it together!" I said to myself.

I didn't know whether what I was did Siberian trancing, but I did something. My stomach finally settled. I then did what I always did at moments like this. I made a joke.

"I hope you're not going to charge her for the peas. She sent them back."

The Navajo Ninja held up a knife for a moment. He could easily carve up my face and turn it into teriyaki. But the manager gave him a look, then came over to him. "This is not our way," he said.

Ninja then put the knife down and began to clean the table with a scraper.

Lia wiped her mouth, then cried until she ran out of tears. I held her hand all the while. She stared blankly at the small fires on the table.

"I'll protect you," I said.

"Thank you," she said. "I know you will."

At the end of the night the owner comped our meal, but asked us never to return.

I now opposed the importation of Fugu.

Pitcher in the Rye

LIA FOLLOWED ME TO my place that night. There was no enchantment here, only interstates crossing in both directions. It was another "no burn" night, yet the night was filled with smoke. Unlike Santa Fe where they burned mesquite, the Albuquerque sky smelled like burning tires.

My place was still a sty. The insurgent underwear had now completed a takeover of the entire apartment. I tried to make Lia wait outside while I threw all the underwear and socks in the closet, but she ignored me, headed into the bathroom and flushed the toilet.

We sat in my one room on the couch and sipped wine out of my only clean glass. There really wasn't enough room for both of us, along with my big stereo and the TV on the other side of the room. I turned off the lights so Lia couldn't view the mess.

"Have you heard from your mother?" I asked.

"Don't ask me about my mother," Lia said, insistent. "If you're my lawyer, you can't ask me about certain things. I read that in an article today."

"Was your mom the one who called you the night I got you out?"

"Dan! You should know better!"

She rushed into the bathroom and slammed the door.

Lia was right. I should know better. If she told me that she had any knowledge of the conspiracy whatsoever, she wouldn't be able to deny it later. She came back from the bathroom, looking somewhat relaxed. Perhaps she'd done a mini-trancing session.

"This isn't about me," she said at last. "It isn't even about C de Baca. It's about New Mexico."

"New Mexico?"

She then listed seven bills, primarily involving women and children that she felt C de Baca was on the wrong side of. The depth of her knowledge astonished me. If she wasn't so flaky, she would have been an amazing policy wonk.

I had a vision of Lia on *This Week in Washington*—without the flower or the streaks in her hair of course.

"C de Baca is such a hypocrite," she continued. "He'll ruin this state and I love it here. It's my home. It's where I was born. It's where I want to raise a family. He's going to ruin it for me and my children."

I looked into her big brown eyes. To her it really was a crusade. Lia hated everything that C de Baca stood for, from Article Seven to banning fugu. She hated phonies and wanted to protect the innocents of the world from them. She was a veritable Hispanic Holden Caulfield, but she wanted to be a pitcher and not a catcher.

Lia undressed and changed into one of the t-shirts on the floor. The shirt said WORLD'S MOST DANGEROUS PLACES, with a picture of a skull with sunglasses.

"What happens next?" she asked as she snuggled next to me.

I hadn't entered my appearance on her case yet, so there wasn't anything wrong with a snuggle, I reasoned. I was just a guy who checked on the case for her; I wasn't her lawyer.

"Next up is your arraignment."

"I was already arraigned in jail."

"That was for the lower court when it was an 'open count.' Next is in District Court on the charges they indicted you on, the second degree murder, the conspiracy, and the tampering."

Then she hit me with it.

"You'll be there for my arraignment, won't you?" she asked. She had forced herself to wake up.

I felt the walls close in, just like they had in the jail.

"You can get the public surrender," I said weakly. "I mean public defender."

Lia pushed me into the bed, her hands on my chest. I never knew that her hundred or so pounds could feel so heavy.

"I was just a number to him at the Metro arraignment," she said, wide, wide awake. "He was already telling me to plead guilty. You're the only one in the world who believes in me. You're the only one in the world who really knows me!"

She now hugged me so tightly that I could barely breathe. I imagined Lia in her red jail jumpsuit. She wouldn't last a week in jail. If they stacked a bunch of charges on her, she could be there for life with women like Knock Out Noriega as a bunk-mate.

I felt the air let out of my body. The air flowed away from my brain toward parts unknown.

"Just for arraignment," I said. "After that we'll see what happens."

She kissed me—not an erotic kiss, but one of gratitude.

"I love you so much," she said.

I didn't know whether I had been formally retained yet; the canons of ethics were murky here.

"If I'm your lawyer, we have to keep it professional from now on."

She nodded. "For now. Are you breaking up with me?"

I looked into her eyes again. I didn't answer. Was I trying to have it both ways?

I slept on the couch. I dreamt about an ad campaign for teenagers to dissuade them from sex. A nubile teen girl appeared and said, "If you're thinking of going all the way; just imagine that you're defending your girlfriend on murder charges!" You've heard of "Presumed Innocent?" Perhaps there could be a sequel, "Presumed Abstinent."

I tossed and turned some more. I knew I would have to ask Lia one more thing. There was an old criminal defense lawyer's quip. The presumption of innocence is green.

When I woke up, I asked Lia. "Are you going to be able to pay me anything to represent you? Costs alone will be—"

She started crying. "You mean you're not going to do it for free? You said you loved me."

Unlawful Entry

EVA SET LIA'S DISTRICT Court arraignment for the Wednesday before Thanksgiving. Judge Kurtz hated surprises, so Eva mentioned that I had better enter by Monday at dawn.

Monday morning I woke in the darkness and stared at my computer screen. Lia would be much better off with the public defender. They knew the judges. I did not. They would get free discovery. I would have to pay for it. They would even get free mental health experts.

I took out an old Entry/Withdrawal of Counsel and began to delete the name of the old client and type in the name Ophelia Paz.

I waited until eight o'clock and called the District Attorney's Office to get an idea about the cost of discovery. A clerk told me that it would be ready soon. Since I was a private attorney the copies alone would run over three hundred dollars.

"Just for this batch," the clerk said. "There's a lot more coming."

That pretty much finished the last bonus check.

I tried to calculate how much money I would lose by representing Lia. I would have to stick with Joel, just to have money to pay the rent, or pay for the copying. That wasn't even counting witness fees. I usually did one pro bono DWI a year, often for a stripper. Ironically, the strippers usually charged more for a few VIP dances than I charged for a DWI.

A murder case was different. I calculated the amount of witness interviews, trial preparation, and the costs of discovery. Witness fees alone on a private case were almost a hundred dollars a pop. Some attorneys charged over a hundred grand for a murder, and then billed the client for the copying on top of it. Lia wanted me to do a murder case for free.

I stared at the screen for another minute. I remembered Lia back at the unit as the women shouted broomstick. If I was any man at all, I would protect Lia. If I was any man at all, I would keep my promise to her, come hell or highwater.

I hit "print" and then e-filed the entry at the District Court website.

I sure couldn't do this alone, especially since I would have to keep going to Santa Fe just to pay the bills. I was crazy enough to do something for free. What other attorney could possibly want to help?

Like a Hurricane

THE DA'S OFFICE WOULD allow me to do one, and only one phone witness interview before the arraignment. I would have to do the interview while driving to Santa Fe on Tuesday morning. The witness's name was Katrina Griego, Lia's neighbor. She had made the 911 call.

"How am I supposed to make a decision on arraignment based on one interview and no discovery?" I asked.

"Welcome to Albuquerque," the receptionist replied. "Lawyers here do that every day."

The phone interview was a three-way: the prosecutor was in his office, while Katrina called in from home. I didn't catch the prosecutor's name, but it wasn't important, as he was just a stand-in. As for Katrina, she was a stay-at-home housewife. A soap opera blared in the background.

"Katrina?" I asked when all parties were on the line.

"If you make a hurricane joke I'll kill you," she said. "It's not funny. People died."

After we got through the introductory stuff, I got to the point.

"How do you know Ophelia Paz?"

"She's my neighbor."

I couldn't resist asking, "Does she live with anyone?"

"She lives alone, has for a couple of years."

"Are you sure?"

Katrina thought for a while. "I don't really know her. There's a back door to the bike path in the arroyo, so it's not like I see everyone who comes and goes. I do know that she leaves the lights on a lot."

That didn't answer anything one way or another. I still hadn't dismissed the wig idea, but the mystery of Lia's mom would last until another day. Time to shift gears, literally. My car had now hit the big hill by the casino.

"What did her front yard look like?" I asked.

"She had all kinds of anti-C de Baca signs in her yard."

I took Lia's defense. "It's not against the law to have signs, is it? There is a first amendment."

The prosecutor figured he better say something. "That's not really relevant. I'll stipulate that there's a first amendment."

I continued. "So what happened on election day afternoon?"

"I was getting ready to go out and vote."

"Did anything happen around four o'clock?"

"It rained like crazy. I'm talking like cats and dogs."

I wanted to make the joke about stepping into a poodle, but wisely refrained. I had now passed the Santo Domingo rest stop and was headed toward the Rio Galisteo.

Katrina continued, "Portia Smith C de Baca knocked on my door, pounded on it. She probably wanted to get out of the rain."

"How did you know it was Portia Smith C de Baca?"

"She identified herself. 'I'm Portia Smith C de Baca, my husband's running for governor.'"

"But she didn't show you any ID, did she?"

"She handed me a flyer with a picture of her and her husband. Besides, there was this big billboard across the street. I mean, I could see her face from my porch."

A semi nearly cut me off. Shit. I passed over the Rio Galisteo, which was running pretty high for this time of year.

"With all the rain that day was Portia wet?"

"Some. Portia didn't have an umbrella, but she was wearing a rain poncho and my porch is covered."

"What did Portia say?"

"She told me she was looking for a house that had all these signs in the yard about her husband. It was raining so hard, she must not have seen them. So I told her to look across the street and I pointed to Crazy Girl's house."

"Crazy Girl?"

"That's what I call my neighbor across the street. Crazy Girl has all these signs about C de Baca in her front yard. I think she's obsessed with the dude."

"Obsessed?"

"She handed out fliers about C de Baca all the time. I wish I had some, but I threw them all away."

I would have loved to have seen those fliers. But something confused me. "Portia was looking for the house with the signs?"

"I guess so," Katrina said.

"Why would she be looking for the signs?"

"I don't know."

The prosecutor laughed. "Beyond the scope of this witness's personal knowledge."

He was right. "So what did Portia do next?"

"Portia excuses herself and heads over to the house across the street. On the way, she called someone up, and started chattering away."

Note to self: Get Portia's phone records. Katrina kept talking over an ominous blast of soap opera music from her TV set.

"Portia pounds on the door, like she wants to bust it down. Crazy Girl answers. Portia goes inside the house."

I had now passed the La Bajada rest stop and was headed downhill.

"So you really don't know what happened inside, do you?"

"No, I don't."

I had scored a minor point. A very minor point. My car now ran more smoothly.

"Then what happened?"

"I didn't see anything more. I went to the bathroom and freshened up. Then I went out and voted. I won't say for who."

"So you didn't see Portia get killed?" I asked. I felt ready to do another victory dance.

"She was killed inside," Katrina said. An ad for a laxative sounded from her television.

"As far as you know," I said. "That's beyond the scope of your personal knowledge."

The prosecutor really should object, but apparently he couldn't remember which of the fifteen or so objections he should go with.

I kept going before he could find one. "What happened next?"

"I saw a man come by and pick Crazy Girl up." She gave a vague description of a man who matched Stone's characteristics, the man I called The Werewolf.

I was almost in Santa Fe. I would have to wrap this up.

"Are you sure you didn't see Portia leave with them?"

The three worst words in cross-examination: "are," "you," and "sure."

"Yes, I'm sure."

"You mentioned the bike path behind the home, on the edge of the arroyo. Could someone go out that way?"

"Calls for speculation," the prosecutor said.

I kept going. "Then what did you do?"

"I saw on TV where a woman was found in the arroyo a few miles down. So I called 911."

I stopped in Joel's parking lot when the prosecutor played the 911 tape.

"That woman they dragged out of the ditch looks like Portia C de Baca," Katrina said. "I saw her go into my neighbor's house and I didn't see her come out. That house is right next to the ditch. Maybe she threw her in."

Shit. I said to myself. "Pass the witness."

* * * * *

The unknown prosecutor asked a few questions. His supervising attorney had probably written them for him. He read each question stiffly.

I grew impatient. I had to get inside my office and get to work. I kept my engine running.

When the prosecutor finished, I did a reasonable-doubt re-cross about how Katrina didn't watch the house the entire time, and so on, but it wasn't enough. Like her namesake, it would take awhile to recover from Katrina.

I turned off my motor. It took a few seconds to die. As I walked toward the office, slowly switching from harried defense lawyer to big time civil dude, I realized that I didn't really know anything. Lia could be innocent; the "real killer" could be her mom. The killer might even be The Werewolf, or perhaps the person who had made her make the promise not to "tell" over the phone. All the prosecution had was circumstantial evidence.

Then again, circumstantial evidence had convicted people before.

That afternoon, Joel agreed to let me off work on Wednesday for Lia's arraignment. I was vague, and said something about a mandatory court hearing from "before."

"You will come in on Thursday," he said, a statement, not a question. "If not, don't bother coming in on Friday."

"Thursday's Thanksgiving."

"I see," he said.

Even he took Thanksgiving off, but probably not the entire day. I could see him proofing a brief over pumpkin pie.

As for me, my parents were due back from their world tour Wednesday afternoon. My mother would attempt the impossible—making the perfect meal while suffering from jet lag. She'd been all over Asia for a month, amassing the cooking secrets of the Orient. Jet lag or not, the meal would be magnificent.

If I missed dinner, she would not let me live. I was still more afraid of my mother than my boss.

"How about coming in on Friday?" he asked. "It's the end of the billing cycle, and you've been a little light this month."

The Friday after Thanksgiving was technically "Presidents' Day." The state of New Mexico had moved the national February holiday to November so state employees could have another day with their families. The powers-that-be figured one extra day with their families would scare state workers back into working harder in December.

I shouldn't have to work on Presidents' Day even if it was in November. I didn't want to piss off the spirits of Abe Lincoln and George Washington, especially with their friendly faces in my wallet. Then again, I didn't like the sound of the words "little" and "light."

"I'll work a full day on Friday, no matter what. And I'll do my best to get out of the case down in Albuquerque."

After I hung up, I looked at my wallet.

"Sorry to miss your birthday, George," I said to a dollar bill. I took out a five. "You too, Abe."

I picked Lia up from her home for the Wednesday morning arraignment. Needless to say, her mama wasn't back yet. Lia wore a gray flannel suit and she looked more like a lawyer than a criminal. She wore a white carnation in her hair, white presumably for innocence.

When I went to District Court, I always parked at the bank across the street for free and had my parking validated, sometimes without actually doing any banking. It made me feel like an insider, someone who knew the ins and outs of the courthouse.

But Lia told me that I shouldn't park at a bank if I wasn't actually banking. It was like stealing. My God, the woman was charged with murder, and she was lecturing me on the ethics of parking. I didn't know whether to laugh or cry.

Just to make her happy, I ran into the bank and checked my balance. My last paycheck from Joel hadn't cleared yet. The ten-thousand dollars I had paid to the bondsman had cleared immediately, of course.

I had to pick up the discovery from the District Attorney's office. I made Lia wait outside. The clerk was very nice when she told me that the discovery wasn't ready, and besides, I needed to pay them the three hundred dollars first. I checked my pockets. I must have left my checkbook at the bank.

We then hurried to the courthouse. As we approached the building, I saw Luna Cruz arguing with a woman in the cafe's covered patio. Luna wore spandex biking gear that left little to the imagination in the cold November air. She was drinking a smoothie. The other woman wore a sweatshirt and drank coffee, but this was no coffee break. The argument grew heated. The two women looked like two softball players arguing over a call.

When we got within earshot, I realized that Luna was taping the argument. The other woman's sweatshirt read APD for Albuquerque Police Department. The officer looked like Luna on steroids. This must be business.

The officer had mellifluous Spanish accent, and sounded like she was a DJ on a local Spanish language station playing *la musica romantica*. When she used the "gaze nystagmus," it sounded musical. Gaze nystagmus was a field sobriety test used by cops. They would wave a finger, or a light, and if the suspect's eyes couldn't follow the light, the cops suspected alcohol was to blame.

Luna didn't let the voice get to her. "Gaze nystagmus cannot be used as substantive evidence, just as probable cause according to State v. Torres."

"You win," the officer said, then shook Luna's hand. Luna stopped the tape recorder. The two women then hugged. The hug had familiarity to it, as if they'd known each other for years.

"Dan, right?" Luna asked as we walked by the porch.

"Luna?"

"We were doing a pre-trial interview on a DWI. I just convinced Officer Nunez here to drop a DWI to a careless driving."

I recognized the officer from a few MVD hearings from back in the day. She was one of the best, but apparently she had met her match in Luna Cruz.

The officer grimaced. "She played nasty with the gaze nystagmus."

"You remember, Lia?" I was about to add "my girlfriend," then "my client," but I just let it be.

Luna smiled. She had to know what was happening, but she pretended otherwise to make the moment bearable.

"You showing her around the courthouse?"

"Something like that," I said.

Lia stared at Luna. And why not? Luna was a role model—successful, strong and sexy. Perhaps there was more to it. Luna was only a few years older than Lia, but Lia looked at her as if she was the mother she no longer had.

"Maybe you can help Dan out with my case." Lia said.

Luna raised her eyebrows, then said something my own mother used to say a lot. "We'll see."

Purple Arraign

INSIDE, AT THE COURTHOUSE metal detector, I beeped like crazy. The guards inspected my ancient phone as if it was about to transform into an AK-47. Lia had to take off all her jewelry, even her belt, before the big guards finally waved her in.

I deposited Lia in the courtroom on the third floor. The jury box held a school principal who had embezzled millions, a city official who had raped his secretary, and of course, the developer who had walked on ten prior DWI charges.

We were ninety-eighth out of ninety-eight on the docket. The judge could quit right at noon, approximately number forty or so, take lunch, and then keep us here for the next fifty or so until late into the night.

If I filled out a "Waiver of Arraignment," maybe we could get it signed by the judge and be on our way. I told Lia to stay put, and hurried to the judge's office where Eva studied the docket with Rachel Santini, the bailiff. Rachel looked like a hostess at the coolest club in Miami, as opposed to a bailiff here in Albuquerque. Despite her appearance, Rachel was strictly professional.

A few other lawyers chatted up Eva. One mentioned a trial in Tucumcari. Another mentioned a competency hearing in Carlsbad, a third talked about his dying mother in Maryland. All of them desperately needed to be put on the docket first.

Eva ignored them. She saved her smile for Mitch Garry, the famed old cowboy who now did death-penalty cases all over the state. He was the guy you wanted if you were really, really guilty, when it came down to life in prison or lethal injection. Thankfully Lia wasn't at that stage. Yet.

Without another word, Eva let Rachel move Mitch's case from ninety-seventh to second. Mitch left with a smile and a tip of his cowboy hat. She then politely moved up the other lawyers to third and fourth respectively. Time to strike while the iron is hot.

"I've got a Waiver of Arraignment form," I said. "Can we get this off the docket? Or at least get me to fifth?"

Eva smiled at me, a motherly smile. "*Danika,* Which case do you have? Please don't say you're here on Ophelia Paz."

"Bingo," I said. "Can I just leave a Waiver of Arraignment?"

Eva frowned. "*Ur isten.* He won't sign it. The case is a *kataztrofa.*"

I assumed that meant catastrophe.

Several probation officers came in, trying to move their cases up as well. The probation officers tried to dress as professionally as the lawyers, but on half the salary. In the crowd, I was pushed up against the desk.

Eva barely looked at the probation officers. They had even less pull in this building than lawyers. To make it worse, two secretaries came in from down the hall, asking for a donation for the courthouse Christmas party. Then a beefy police officer entered who needed the judge to sign a warrant right away, or the criminal was heading to Rio. Ten people now stood in an office that could comfortably hold five.

My claustrophobia kicked in, the walls closed tighter and tighter. I hyperventilated, trying to find the one clean breath of fresh air in the crowded room. I put my hand down on the table to steady myself.

"*Danika,* are you all right?" Eva asked. "You look like

you're about to explode." She felt my forehead like my mother used to do.

"I've got cat scratch fever," I said.

"Your head is burning up. I'll cut you a break for medical reasons. It's Thanksgiving. I have just a bit of the holiday spirit. You can go third, right after Mitch. *Viszlat!* That means good luck."

"I'll need it."

"Is your *anya* in town?"

"My mother? My parents should be back sometime today. I guess. I haven't heard anything yet, which has me kind of worried. I think we're doing Thanksgiving tomorrow."

I stared at a thick pile of papers on her desk.

"My manuscript," she said. "But I'm stuck now. I don't know what happens next."

"Are you going to come see me have my moment of glory on behalf of the fair Ophelia?"

"No," she said. "By the way, your discovery is waiting over in that box."

"My discovery?"

She pointed to a big box in the corner. It was Lia's case file. Apparently Eva had copied the court file with her own card and put it in the box. She had just saved me from paying three hundred dollars to the prosecutor.

"As I said, you're like a *fiam*, a son, to me."

Since I had left the courtroom, three television camera crews had set up in the gallery. They scrambled to get good position, like bridesmaids chasing a bouquet. That was not a good thing for me—or my client. This would be the first footage of Ophelia Paz. The image of her would become the "B-roll" the stations used when describing the case.

A few years back, when I did a televised interview on an embezzlement case, I discovered that I had a little bald spot. The cameraman had deliberately focused the bright lights of the camera right on it, so it looked like he was interviewing the top of my head. You could practically see into my cerebral cortex. Rogaine hadn't really helped. My nightmare was ending up old, alone, poor, bald, and with a restraining order. I was on my way there.

From my past experience, I knew to sit in the left corner, where I could guard Lia from the right. That would protect both her and the top of my head.

The cameras suddenly turned toward the front door as Governor-Elect C de Baca entered like a conquering general. C de Baca was far bigger in person than I had expected. He had been a linebacker at New Mexico Highlands University, a small predominantly Hispanic state school in northern New Mexico. His brother Xavier trailed behind. X was even bigger than the governor-elect. He looked more like a bodyguard than a brother. X escorted C de Baca to the front of the gallery and sat him down. Then Xavier came over to me.

"Dan the man," he said. "Don't worry. We're still cool."

"Thanks, X-man," I said.

I tried to read him, but couldn't. He obviously wanted to tell me something, but hurried back to his brother without saying another word.

Suddenly the door at the rear of the court opened. Rachel and the Judge entered.

"All rise!" Rachel shouted.

Judge Kurtz then rolled in on his wheelchair and hoisted himself up to the bench, grimacing slightly in pain. The grimace looked even worse than usual. I am sure that he wanted to get court over before the holidays, even if he had to lock everyone up to do so.

And here I bitched about a bald spot.

The judge gave a cursory nod toward C de Baca. He hadn't voted for the man. Everyone knew it. They weren't friends in the best of times, and now was certainly not the best of times. Kurtz would retire next year, so he would gain nothing by being nice.

"Be seated," Rachel said.

The first hearing went badly. The judge sent a young sex offender to seventy years in prison. Seventy years meant seventy years, no good time. He would probably die of old age if the inmates didn't kill him first. The offender cried uncontrollably as they led him away.

The judge shook his head. "Cowboy up," he said. "No crying in prison, son."

"Cowboy up," I told myself. Unfortunately the last cowboy movie I'd seen was *Brokeback Mountain*.

Attorney Mitch Garry walked up to the podium. This guy was born cowboyed up. The small man next to him, his client, looked like a Martian. The man had tattooed every inch of his skin purple, with some blood red highlights. Mitch only got them if they were really, really guilty. Mitch mentioned something about his client being a victim of "mistaken identity."

Mistaken identity? Could there actually be another person in this world tattooed entirely in purple?

Mitch pled the Martian not guilty in his inimitable folksy style, almost like he was bringing in a prize sheep for the FFA show at the State Fair. He kept extolling his client's virtues, and then had the guts to ask that his triple-murderer with a purple face be released on his own recognizance.

"Your Honor, he's not a flight risk. All his other crimes also took place within the county," he said with a straight face.

The judge disagreed. Man, I was just an amateur next to a guy like Mitch. He was a real lawyer. He had probably gone to law school to save the world. I had gone to law school due to parental pressure.

Then it was our turn. Lia looked at me expectantly. I knew I would have to top the best lawyer in the state, in front of the governor-elect and three cameramen.

Lia and I walked to the podium. The prosecutor was a young man who had just been promoted from the Metro Misdemeanor

Division. Speaking of cops, I was surprised that Officer Tran showed up in the back of the room. She wore a long APD blue jacket over a skimpy outfit, as if she were a flasher. She must have just come in off a sting.

She came up and stood between myself and Fresh White Meat. He glared at her. Officers never showed up at arraignments. Whose side was she on?

"Did you find out anything about the mom?" I whispered.

"An illegal woman fleeing *into* Mexico died south of Deming about the time of Lia's senior year in high school," Bebe whispered. "I can't confirm anything yet."

So perhaps my outlandish theory might be correct after all. I looked at Lia. Could she be delusional? I didn't have time to ponder as the judge took control.

"Officer Tran," the judge said with a snarl as he glanced at her outfit. "Are you here to entertain the troops? We haven't seen your smiling face in a long time."

He said the words "long time," with the slightest hint of an Asian accent, as if mocking her.

"Your honor," she said. "I have some important information regarding this case that would go toward conditions of release and I came here while still on duty."

"Let's get through the arraignment first. Counsel?"

I slipped into a drawl, just like Mitch. My drawl still had elements of the Maryland suburbs of DC and the Ivy League.

"Your Honor, Dan Shepard for Ophelia Paz."

I should have waived a reading of the charges, but I needed time to think, even if it pissed off Judge Kurtz.

The prosecutor began reading in a monotone. There were a lot of charges.

"My client enters a plea of not guilty," I said, too scared to be folksy anymore. "She has no criminal record before this court and I've already posted, I mean the defendant has already posted a $100,000 surety bond. I ask that you continue her on the existing conditions of release."

Lia chose that moment to begin talking about being "Totally Innocent." Her face was flushed, and was nearly as purple as the tattooed man.

"Please be quiet!" I said to her.

The judge caught it. "Who's the lawyer here, you or her?"

"I am, Your Honor," I said.

I expected the prosecutor to say something, but he turned back and nodded toward C de Baca.

"Your Honor, the husband of the victim, Governor-Elect C de Baca, has something to say about this matter, about this woman."

C de Baca walked up, slowly. Machiavelli had said that it is better to be feared than loved, and C de Baca lived by that credo. He wasn't governor yet, but he was a prince. He nodded at a few of the inmates sitting in the jury box. A few of them knew him from the old days.

"He can't talk!" Lia shouted. "He can't talk!"

The judge banged the gavel down. "If she says another word, I'll hold you both in contempt."

I grabbed Lia's hand and held it tight. Her mouth was about to open. I actually put my hand over it.

"Your Honor, this woman murdered my wife," C de Baca said. "I do not feel safe with her still on the streets. The community is not safe with her on the streets. I want her behind bars without any chance of release, ever."

Time to fall on the grenade. "Your Honor, she has not been convicted of anything yet. There is a presumption of innocence."

"You are correct," the judge said. "*Mister* C de Baca, you are to say 'allegedly murdered.'"

"That's *Governor Elect* C de Baca. Before Ms. Paz *allegedly* murdered my wife, this woman had a long history of harassing my family and me. I will not use the word 'allegedly harassed,' because there is air-tight proof of it. I do not want to go into details now, but I will be releasing them shortly. I believe she is a danger to the community, and a danger to herself."

A danger to herself? I looked at Lia. She was about to open her mouth.

"Your Honor," I said, before Lia could say anything. "There's been no proof of that. She is innocent until proven guilty beyond a reasonable doubt."

"This is not a question on the ultimate issue," Fresh White Meat said with a smile, as if I had walked into a trap. "We're just addressing conditions of release."

"That's why I'm here your honor," Bebe Tran said.

God, I wish I knew what she was about to say, but hopefully she would say that APD had just found some exculpatory evidence and this whole thing would go away.

C de Baca stared at Bebe Tran. She certainly hadn't cleared this with him. She moved to the microphone, tugging slightly at her skimpy clothes.

"Make her stop!" Lia whispered. "Make her stop!"

The judge frowned. "I need to know everything relevant about this case before I render a judgment on conditions of release. Officer Tran is always welcome in this courtroom when she has clothes on. The court will still take judicial notice of her inappropriate outfit, if outfit is the right word for it."

He said that with a slight titter, and there was a glimmer in his eye, as if he was using judicial notice as x-ray vision.

"Your Honor, for the record, I'm Officer Bebe Tran with the APD Crisis Intervention Unit. I must apologize for my appearance, as I was out on assignment when I heard about Ms. Paz appearing in court. As you know, our unit was formed after an officer was shot by a mentally ill man several years ago. Our unit deals with the potentially dangerous mentally ill, and by law we must attend all hearings where people on our list appear."

Our list? I looked at C de Baca, who kept a stone face. He met my eyes. I immediately turned away. I would lose a stare down with him in an instant.

"Make her stop," Lia whispered again. "Please, make her stop."

"It's too late."

The judge looked at us, then motioned Bebe to continue.

She nodded. "Our unit has kept a file on Ms. Paz for several years now. "

Several years? Oh shit! Why didn't she tell me that? Lia had never told me anything about being on a list. Bebe suddenly didn't seem so friendly. Was Bebe supposed to say something about Lia being innocent and "not a danger to herself or others" right about now? What happened to the part where she said we have proof that Lia was innocent?

"Ms. Paz has a long history of 'acting up' in public," Bebe said. "We have concerns for her safety and the safety of others. We have very real concerns about her competency."

Lia's grip tightened on mine. My fingers went numb. What the hell was going on here?

Lia whispered to me, "It's a set-up! I know that woman. She hates me. She works for C de Baca! She's part of a conspiracy!"

As Lia kept whispering I realized that I didn't recognize her. Her eyes were wild; her whole body vibrated.

"Your Honor," I said. "May we take a recess while I consult with my client?"

"Mr. Shepard, I have many other cases on my docket; we will finish this case *now*. My secretary made a special dispensation for you. Against my specific advice. She may treat you like her long lost son, but you are no long lost son of mine."

Out of the corner of my eye, I saw Luna come into the room and squeeze into the back. I certainly didn't want to make a fool of myself in front of her. I would have to take control, right now.

"We have nothing to lose by doing a forensic evaluation of Ophelia Paz." I said. No big deal. I didn't know much about how forensic exams work, but Lia went limp, as if I had betrayed her.

"Are you sure?" the judge asked. "That is a serious commitment of judicial resources. A forensic evaluation could cost thousands of dollars, and as you know, *Mister* C de Baca intends to cut funding of the mental health system."

I looked at Lia. "Don't say I'm crazy," she said.

She sure looked crazy when she said that. Then she mumbled something I didn't catch about her mother.

That did it for me. "Yes, I am sure," I said.

Fresh White Meat leaped in. "We ask that she be put into custody immediately."

The judge nodded to the deputies who approached us.

"Custody?" I said. "I thought you would do an *outpatient* exam."

"Mr. Shepard, when you said you wanted a forensic exam, to me that means a thirty to sixty day commitment to the New Mexico State Hospital."

A big guard approached us, handcuffs out. He looked like he wanted to lock me up, too, just for the fun of it.

Lia looked as if she was about to faint. God, I hoped she wouldn't vomit again. She kept whispering something over and over again.

I had to do something. Had to buy time. What had I just done?

"Your Honor," I said, all folksiness gone. "Tomorrow is Thanksgiving, and the state hospital will be unable to take her until next week at the earliest. I ask that we recess this hearing until I've had more time to research Officer Tran's allegations. And I ask that Ms. Paz be permitted to remain out of custody. Thanksgiving is a very special holiday, as you know."

The judge must have been a speed-reader, because he had already made it through the file.

"I have some very real concerns here, Counsel," he said.

"Your Honor, it's Thanksgiving," was all I could say. Lia's sweaty hand tried to grip mine, but I pushed it away to avoid the appearance of impropriety. She now whispered something to herself, a real whisper. Three words, over and over again.

She pulled on my jacket, wanted to whisper something in my ear. I bent down.

"I love you," she said and squeezed my wrist. So that's what she had been whispering.

"What?" I whispered back to her.

"I love you."

I copied Han Solo in *The Empire Strikes Back* and just replied "I know." Ain't no love in Judge Kurtz's courtroom.

"Counsel I'm still waiting for your alternative to her immediate incarceration."

"I will personally vouch for her," I said. "In fact I will stay with her the entire time she's out of custody. I will put my own reputation as an officer of the court on the line."

"I want her locked up right now," C de Baca said in his gangster voice, his anger getting the best of him. "She's a threat to the community. A threat to my family. A threat to herself. I do not want to be afraid over the holidays, and I have doubts that her lawyer can adequately protect me and mine."

"I'll give you my word," I said.

Judge Kurtz smiled at C de Baca. He certainly didn't mind pissing off the governor-elect in the few days before the man had any real power.

"I'll give her until Friday afternoon to turn herself in to the state hospital in Las Vegas, New Mexico," the judge said at last.

"For how long?" Lia asked.

The judge frowned. "Till she's done. That's what you want, isn't it counsel? The defendant is to remain in state custody in the hospital until we have a forensic report on whether she is competent to stand trial or whether she was insane at the time of the incident."

He looked at me directly. "I ask you again. That's what you're asking this court to do, right, Counsel?"

It was too late to back down now. "I guess so."

Lia looked at me. She hit me hard in my side with the turquoise knuckle-ring. "I'm not crazy," she whispered.

I grimaced from her blow.

The judge frowned. "This isn't some dodge to keep your client out of jail, is it?"

"I'm not a dodger, Your Honor."

That sure didn't sound right. I was no Angel or Red Sock either, but I certainly couldn't offer my theory that Lia's imaginary mother had done the killing.

The cameras kept rolling, preparing to get the infamous "two-shot" of Nervous Defendant and Stone-Faced Lawyer walking away from the bad news. I had learned to always have a smile on my face, even if the judge had just sentenced my client to death. I tried to contort my face into a smile.

Fresh White Meat had a transport order form already prepared. I signed it. I had to bring it to the judge for his signature.

"May I approach your honor?"

"You may."

Just as I made it to the judge's bench, the worst possible thing that could happen, happened. My phone rang, and played out Beethoven's "Ode to Joy," the default setting that I had never bothered to change.

All eyes tuned on me.

"Answer it!" the judge said.

Ode to Joy. There was no joy in the courtroom at that moment. Reluctantly I picked up the phone.

"Hi, Dan." It was my mother. "We're back!"

"Hi, Mom," I said.

The judge stared at me with daggers inches from my face.

"I'm starting dinner for tomorrow this very minute," she said. "Are you bringing your new girlfriend? We can't wait to meet her."

"Mom, are you sure?" I whispered into the phone. "Isn't there someway we can just take a rain check this year?"

"We'll see," she said.

Act II
Luna

Psycho Killer, Qu'est-ce que c'est?

LIA AND I HURRIED outside to the courthouse steps. People in cowboy attire were holding a land auction, and apparently some livestock came along with the land. There weren't any livestock there on the courtroom steps, but the cowboys sure smelled of it. The auction was a legacy of Albuquerque's cow town past. Personally, I felt like a cow stuck in a pen, ready for slaughter.

I took Lia to her house to get more of her things. The turquoise McNugget was gone, as was the picture of her mother. That couldn't be good. I didn't see any bloodstains on the floor, either. Had CSI-Albuquerque already started taking tests? Her computer had not magically reassembled itself, either.

"A lot of my things are missing!" Lia shouted with dismay. "They took what I was going to wear to your parents' house for Thanksgiving!"

"You still want to come to Thanksgiving?"

"You have to take me. It's the law," she said. "You meant what you said about being responsible for me, for vouching for me, right?"

"I guess so."

She was right. I could not leave Lia alone or I would get arrested. I had given my word to the judge.

My mother would not accept any excuse for my absence whatsoever. Lia showed me a few potential Thanksgiving out-fits. The first, a pink sweater combo, made her look like a pre-teen. The second, a black number, was fine, but she kept asking whether it made her look fat.

Fat? I didn't care whether she looked fat. I just hoped she didn't look crazy.

We settled on a third choice, a conservative charcoal sweater and long black skirt. Not only did it make her look thin, it made her look sane.

"Let's get out of here," she said, changing back into her arraignment clothes. "This doesn't feel like home anymore."

It was about five o'clock. I wanted to minimize the number of hours I'd be stuck with Lia alone, so there was only one place to go. The gym.

Midway Sports and Wellness faced the arroyo, a few miles downstream from Lia's place. It was so close to her house, in fact, that some of the stationary bike riders on the second floor might have seen Portia flow by. The concrete was now dry, and a few kids skateboarded down the arroyo, doing tricks on the sloping walls. I couldn't imagine the raging waters rushing through election night.

I had Lia fill out the guest form at the entrance, and sign the standard legal release of liability. After we changed, I bought Lia a one-hour massage, so she could unwind.

Then I ran into "Gollum," a regular, who looked like the character from *The Lord of the Rings*. Gollum had hit the wrong side of sixty. I don't remember whether the original Gollum was a man or a Hobbit, but considering the amount of hair on this Gollum's feet, either could be possible. He wore oversized workout attire as he flirted with a teenaged staffer. Rebuffed, he turned away and headed outside, into the darkness.

I had a moment of terror. Would that be me at sixty-four? Alone and pathetic, on the edge of a restraining order?

I looked down. My feet were already getting hairy.

Panicked, I charged upstairs. After changing, I hit the cardio section and read Bebe Tran's report while exercising on the Nordic Trek 9000. It was a simulation of a cross-country skiing experience. There even was a fan blowing cold air. The Nordic Trek 9000 required using two hands, but I had learned how to turn the pages while trekking. It made me feel like an intellectual Viking.

A woman on the machine in the front row trekked faster than anyone else. She stopped for a second and reached down to get a water bottle. We made eye contact. It was Luna Cruz. She wiped sweat from her face, or was it a tear? She quickly forced herself to smile. She then trekked even faster.

I forced myself to look through a sheaf of papers from Lia's box. I had picked up a Confidential Albuquerque Police Mental Health File on Ophelia Paz, a.k.a. Lia Paz. Each page contained a different police report, dating back several years. It was a miracle that Lia had escaped prosecution, but all of her incidents were minor: trespassing, disturbances, that sort of thing. Almost all involved campaign work. Nothing had ever gone to court.

I then turned to the report detailing the final incident with Portia Smith C de Baca. I was surprised to find that a sign outside her home had read, C DE BACA MOLESTED ME!

The governor-elect molested her? Some sign. Can you say motive?

There were several possibilities. Lia was innocent and her mother, the killer, was trying to avenge her daughter's shame. Or, Lia was an obsessive and still had a thing with C de Baca after all these years. Worse, Lia was delusional and had imagined the whole thing with her mother and C de Baca.

This was the woman I was taking to meet my mother on Thanksgiving? It was too much. I lost my balance and the Nordic Trek 9000 started to shake as if the mighty Thor himself pounded it with his hammer. I put too much weight on the right side. Next thing I knew, Thor threw me up into the air. Pages scattered in all directions. The cardio section at Midway held several of the most up-to-date machines. Unfortunately, some of the machines, including the Nordic Trek 9000, were set right against a railing. On the other side of the railing, twenty feet below was the club's basketball court. Many of the lawyers who worked out at the club salivated over an inevitable lawsuit stemming from someone falling over the railing to the court below. But you would have to be a complete idiot to fall over a railing, right?

I did hit the rail, but luckily bounced back toward the Nordic Trek 9000 and immediately got a splitting headache. Maybe the mighty Thor had pounded me one to the right temple.

Luna got off her machine and hurried over. "Are you okay?"

"Not really." I said.

"What's the matter?"

"My girlfriend is mentally ill and I'm taking her to meet my mother tomorrow. What does that say about me?"

"You're human," Luna said. "You really need to take a break. I mean, you look like death warmed over."

We sat for a while on the exercise mats leaning against the back wall. She wanted to make sure I was okay.

"My dad was a doctor," she said. "So occasionally, I actually feel a need to pretend to care."

"Are you pretending?"

I felt a tinge of nervousness. The massage room was less than twenty feet from our location. What would Lia think if I was here talking with this goddess in black?

Luna checked my head and found only a small bump. She got a bag of ice and made me hold it to my forehead. Then we talked for twenty minutes.

"Enough about me," I said.

We talked about her stuff for the next twenty minutes. Her last boyfriend had left her high and dry.

"You're a good listener," she said to me.

That wasn't totally true, but I didn't want to dissuade her.

"I can be. One side effect of being a criminal defense attorney is that you actually have to give a shit about people."

"So why are you still with her?" she asked. "Because you give a shit?"

I tried to break the tension with a joke. "You know the old Woody Allen joke about the guy who goes to a therapist complaining that his girlfriend is a chicken?"

Luna played straight man. She knew it of course. "So the therapist says why the hell do you stay with her if she thinks she's a chicken?"

"Because I need the eggs," we said in unison.

"Jinx," she said with a smile.

I didn't know if I wanted to be jinxed.

The door to the massage room opened, and I hurried into the changing room before Lia could see Luna and me together. I wanted to avoid the appearance of impropriety, even though no impropriety had occurred.

Yet.

After a shower, I went downstairs to find Lia in the lobby. She was watching TV with a crowd of racquetball players who were waiting for their courts to open. Someone switched the station from the Lobo game to Channel 8's local news, just as a clip Lia's arraignment came on. A racquetball player stared at her in abject horror.

Lia buried her head in her hands. "I'm innocent," she said to no one in particular. "And I'm not crazy, either."

"Let's go, Lia," I said, coming to her rescue. "We need to get a good night's sleep before we meet my mother tomorrow."

I slept on the couch that night. Well, I tried to. I was more nervous about Lia meeting my mother than for her arraignment. There was no way out of it. My mother expected me to produce a girlfriend. For the last five years I had come up empty handed.

On those other occasions, relatives and friends would whisper something in her ear and my mother would say something along the lines of "He's trying."

Lia was all I had at this moment. I sang along with the Talking Heads song "Psycho Killer." The singer David Bryne and I sang together, *"Qu'est que ce?"*

I looked at her. If she had killed Portia, it was under conditions so specific that they would never be repeated, right? I mean, who else could I take to meet my mother tomorrow?

Sleigh Ride to Hell

WE WERE SOMEWHERE AROUND Bernalillo, on the edge of the desert, when the anxiety began to take hold. Unlike Hunter S. Thompson, I chugged Mountain Dew Code Red rather than Jack Daniels, but caffeine could be a drug, too. My misgivings about this Thanksgiving increased with every mile. Lia looked relaxed, like a kid on the way to Grandmother's house, and the horse knew the way to carry the sleigh. I, however, was on the sleigh ride to hell.

"I can't wait to meet your parents," she said. "Could your mother be a character witness for me? She's so powerful. That would keep me out of jail, wouldn't it?"

I didn't bother to reply, and instead stared into the middle distance of the interstate. Then the phone rang. It was my mom.

"Is your girlfriend Luna Cruz, the lawyer?" she asked.

Every time I had mentioned Lia, I had kept it vague.

"No, she's *Lia Paz.*" I was about to say "Lia Paz, the criminal," but I stopped. "She's into politics."

"I'm just dying to meet her." She hung up.

Hopefully Mom wouldn't do a Google search on Lia before dinner. No, she'd be too busy making the best Thanksgiving meal of all time and wouldn't want to risk getting gravy on her computer.

My mom needed grandchildren like a junkie needed heroin. It had been a dry spell before Lia. If I had ovaries, in my mother's eyes they'd be dead by now. Athena Shepard would see Lia as her last chance at a legacy.

"You're in a rut, Daniel," Mom had said all summer. "And it is bothering us. It's killing us. Are you sure you're not gay?"

"I'm not gay, Mom," I said.

"If you are, we can set you up with Serge, this amazing gallery owner who's got a show coming up. The two of you could then do one of those *in vitro*—"

"I'm not gay, Mom."

She had been happy that I got the Santa Fe job, but it wasn't enough. A woman had to validate me, so I could validate my mother.

I remembered when I represented Jesus Villalobos, an accused murderer. What was the difference between him and Dan Shepard, Ivy League lawyer?

My client's mother was proud of him. He had a wife.

Lia had overdone it a bit with her clothes. She must not have had time to coordinate her purple flower with her charcoal outfit. What was that Woody Allen movie, *The Purple Rose of Cairo?* The one that was a flop?

As I ascended La Bajada, stuck behind a beat-up pickup truck, I tried to reassure myself. My parents had stopped the local papers while they were gone. They never watched local news. They were too busy and too jet-lagged to call their friends. Lia was still the nice girl I had told them about, not a psycho killer, well *alleged* psycho killer.

Mom called again as we hit the turn-off for the Old Pecos Trail exit into Santa Fe. When my mom said "Real important question," I thought the jig was up.

"Is Lia allergic to peanuts?" she asked. "We've got this special Thai recipe for the sweet potatoes."

"Are you allergic to peanuts?" I asked Lia.

"No. I love peanuts."

"Peanuts are cool," I said into the receiver.

"This meal will be the best yet," my mother said. "There will be some major surprises."

Lia had gone through every emotion on the drive. At times she vibrated with fear. Other times she looked eager. Maybe she missed her own mother and hoped to be adopted by mine.

Before I knew it, we hit the road to the ski area north of town. Except for the adobe solar houses, it felt more like Colorado than New Mexico here. Majestic pines and aspens lined the road as opposed to Albuquerque's scraggly saber yuccas. Trees just grew bigger in Santa Fe.

As the trees grew taller, we passed Ten Thousand Waves, the new-age health spa that was built like a sprawling Japanese wooden palace. A Samurai could come after a hard day at the office, a geisha or two at his side. Lia had once treated me to a great massage here with magnets or hot stones or perhaps hot magnetic stones. We then took a dip in the clothing-optional pool. Luna had stayed in her bathing suit of course. I did as well. I had felt an unfamiliar emotion that day—happiness.

Lia had wanted to meet my parents on that trip; they were less than a mile away. But I wouldn't have it.

"We'll wait until the time is right."

Was the time right now?

"Thank you so much for bringing me," Lia said. She kissed me on the cheek. "I had nowhere else to go. Thanksgiving alone would be so depressing. I don't know if I'd survive. I miss my mama so much."

I wanted to ask her about everything, but I couldn't. "Don't ask, don't tell" and all that. My frustration level stood higher than a Santa Fe pine. I asked Lia to tell me about trees instead, and she gladly talked about evergreens versus deciduous.

We finally took the turn-off into a gated subdivision set into the woody foothills of the Sangre de Cristos. After my parents had bought the place, a nearby Indian pueblo claimed the subdivision was their sacred ancestral burial ground. The case was still up in the Federal courts; my mom was the landowners' lawyer. Their property was probably the only place in Santa Fe that had actually depreciated over the years.

We pulled up to the driveway. My parents had been lawyers in Washington and had lived for years in a redwood house in a leafy suburb in Maryland. They were the epitome of a D.C. power couple, yet they had drunk Santa Fe style like it was the fountain of youth. Their money did not go as far as they expected in terms of house size, but they more than made up for it with the bells and whistles.

"It's beautiful," Lia said. "You are so lucky."

"I wouldn't use the word lucky."

I wanted to drown myself into the tub back at Ten Thousand Waves.

Red Hot Chili Pepper

WE HURRIED TO THE tasteful redwood door and knocked. My dad answered it. I had correctly predicted that he'd wear a sweater from the Bill Cosby collection, and I had matched it.

I remembered when I was in law school and Dad was doing a trial in Cleveland in the middle of winter.

I had said, "Why the hell are you in Cleveland?"

"I'm in Cleveland so you can go to a private law school."

I felt guilty that I wasn't smart enough to get a scholarship to Georgetown and had to ask him to help pay tuition to American University Law School in D.C. I hadn't bothered to apply to the University of Maryland, where I would have received in-state tuition. Back then I thought I was too good for Maryland. Hah!

A few years later I graduated and worked as a public defender, and Dad developed cancer. That was the reason I left the public defender's office; I knew I'd have to pay my own way. For the last few years, I had failed at that. Dad liked that I now worked for Joel, a real job at last.

Dad had made a full recovery from cancer, but had never been quite the same. He was . . . slower. I gave my dad a big hug, and he smiled.

"What took you so long?" he asked.

"Traffic was a bitch," I said.

"You always say that."

"I do."

"You must be Dan's new girlfriend," he said to Lia.

I looked at him for a moment. Had he read the papers? Or checked out the 'net? He looked too tired to have checked out much of anything.

We had it down to a routine. I knew exactly what my father would do next.

"Could you come over here and help me move the rock?" he asked Lia.

The house had been built around a big igneous rock the size of a grand piano. The rock lay in the TV room. The contractor said that it would be a nice "naturalistic touch," and my dad did not want to spring for dynamite, so they had left the rock right there as a conversation piece.

For the one-hundredth time, my dad bent down as if he wanted to move the boulder. It was his little test. Most people didn't even bend down. Lia bent all the way down and gave it the old college try. The rock actually shook. Lia had the strength of Arthur grabbing Excalibur. If Lia could move the rock, then she would be queen and I would be forced to marry her. The shaking intensified.

We both looked at her with amazement. Lia huffed and puffed with real exertion. Her side of the rock was now a full half-inch off the ground.

"That's enough. I changed my mind," he said with a smile. "We'll let it stay here."

Lia still didn't get it. "Well, if Dan helps maybe we can move it."

Before Dad could answer, we heard a scream in the kitchen—a blood-curdling, horror-movie scream. Then a pot flew out of the kitchen and hit one of the wooden support beams.

"Is something wrong?" Lia asked. "Is there a ghost or something?"

Neither my dad or I moved. We knew that sound intimately.

"I fucking burned my finger!" the voice said from the kitchen.

"Who's that?" Lia asked. "Did someone break into the house?"

I just smiled. "That's my mom."

"Don't worry," Mom said from the kitchen. "I'll live!"

We hurried to the bright airy kitchen that had a view of the deck and then down to the adobe of Santa Fe below. Athena Shepard had already rubbed burn cream on her finger, and put on a band-aid to avoid infection. She kept a well-stocked first aid kit in the spice cabinet. My mom dressed immaculately of course. She might have bought her outfit in Hong Kong, because she had the look of a dragon lady. Well, if the dragon only ate organically grown food seasoned with tarragon and chipotle.

Mom sized Lia up, and nodded. She then frowned as she looked downward. Lia clearly wasn't tall enough. My mother wanted tall grandchildren. Lia was also a few pounds too heavy, but at least she had childbearing hips.

She shook Lia's hand. "So nice to meet you. Dan hasn't really told us much about you."

"Nice to meet you." Lia was obviously self-conscious. "I need to freshen up in the bathroom," she said.

"I talked to Joel," my mom said as Lia searched for the bathroom.

"Oh?" I panicked.

"I'm working on this top secret project that I'm bringing to your firm," she smiled. "I saved your ass in Santa Fe."

"Thank you," I said. "I guess. What do you think of Lia?"

"Jury's still out."

She got back to work. The kitchen was a mess, as if a suicide bomber had ignited himself next to the sweet potatoes. Mom put the same energy into her Thanksgiving meal that she had put into her briefs when she was a champion lawyer who convinced the Supreme Court about tax-free municipal bonds truly being tax-free.

She had left pots everywhere, and all but one was filled with enticing aromas. Apparently she had punished the offending pot, the sweet potatoes, or was it carrots? An orange mass lay on the floor.

Lia appeared from her freshening just then, and did the perfect thing.

"Let me help," she said.

She grabbed a sponge and wiped up the mess. Lia resembled a dog digging for a bone, and had her ass facing up toward my mom.

"Thank you," my mom said to Lia's rear end, which literally shook in front of her as Lia washed the floor. "I see we're getting a look at your best side, Lia."

I looked at my mom. Nothing on her face indicated that she had seen the papers or the Web, or knew that the ass in front of her belonged to an accused killer.

Mission accomplished. Lia got up and put the sponge in the sink and gave my mother a polite hug.

"Well so much for the Thai peanuts," my mom said.

"I can live without peanuts," Lia replied.

We waited in the living room and heard more swearing. The asparagus tried to make a run for it, the vinegar flooded, and there was more burning of God knows what. What was she making in there? A bomb?

Lia watched television. She was too nervous to say much and pretended to care about the Dallas Cowboys as I caught up with my dad. He was very interested in my job with Joel. He wanted to make sure that I took it seriously.

"You're not getting any younger," he said. "It's time to make something of yourself."

"I'm trying, Dad," I said. "I'm trying."

Was I trying hard enough? And what the hell was I making?

"Don't worry, I have faith in you, Dan."

Thankfully, dinner was served before I had to justify his faith.

My mother had changed her clothes, even though I had never seen her leave the kitchen. Did she have a spare closet in the refrigerator? This outfit was totally Santa Fe: layers of scarves draped over a mustard colored sweater. Dijon mustard color to be precise.

The meal did not need sweet potatoes and only the top half of the asparagus spears appeared to look like a work of art. For one brief moment I saw fear in my mother's eyes; she desperately wanted a successful verdict on the meal. She even looked at Lia in anticipation of her ruling. Had she poisoned Lia? Or perhaps she had slipped in a fertility drug or a contraceptive pill, depending on what she thought of her?

Lia took a bite of the turkey and smiled as she savored the complex tastes from several cultures. "Delicious."

We all dug in. Wow!

"Best meal ever," I said.

It really was.

"You cook much better than my mother," Lia said.

I grimaced.

Once satisfied that her winning streak continued, Athena quickly went into lawyer mode.

"Lia, so where are you from?" she asked at the end of the meal.

"Albuquerque for most of my life. I was born in Deming, near the border."

"On this side of the border," I added.

"Your mom and dad, are they still alive? Still together?"

My stomach tied itself in knots.

"My father's dead. He used to work in a hospital in Deming, then he worked for the City of Albuquerque."

That was vague. Working for the City of Albuquerque could mean anything from meter maid to mayor. He was dead, so my mom didn't press. Hopefully my mom thought he was a doctor, as opposed to a tech.

"My mom—"

Lia thought about it. My stomach tied the knots even tighter.

"I saw a picture of her mom standing by the pyramids in Chichen Itza," I said. I knew my parents had been there last year. "She's from there."

"Chichen Itza?" my mom said. "I just love Chichen Itza."

Lia jumped in. "Chichen Itza was built by the Mayans in the early classic period, around the year 600."

Mom and Lia then conversed for ten minutes about the ruins. Lia knew her ruins, all right. By the time Lia had finished, my mom thought that Lia had built them herself. My dad brought some pictures to the table, and Lia gave some fun facts about the heights and weights of each pyramid.

"You don't really look Mayan," my mother said.

"I'm not full blooded."

My mom then resumed the interrogation. "Did you go to Albuquerque Academy?"

"No, *Burque* High School . . . Albuquerque High, the one downtown. But I didn't graduate. I got my GED."

My mom nearly wilted. GED might as well have been STD, a sexually transmitted disease. Lia looked like she wanted to go into the whole story about C de Baca and her back at Albuquerque High.

I jumped in. "Lia had a medical problem."

"Like Mono? I had Mono when I was in high school. I was out for a whole year, but I still graduated with my class."

"Sort of." I said, holding onto Lia's hand for dear life. My mom didn't want to pry further on that one. "I admire people who overcome illness."

She had a more important question to ask. "You did go to college? Out of state?"

"I stayed in state. I had a lottery scholarship."

"A *scholarship*?"

Scholarship was a magic word to my mother. Maybe Lia was a Rhodes Scholar or a Fulbright. Since my parents were transplants, my mother wouldn't realize that it only took a 2.0 from a New Mexico public high school to get a lottery scholarship.

"Did you go to UNM?"

When Lia said nothing, my mother pressed. "New Mexico State? Dear God, I hope you're not an Aggie. What is an Aggie anyway? Is it a kind of a ram or something?"

"It's short for Agricultural," Lia said with authority. "It was the land grant college. Kind of like Cornell is the land grant college for New York."

Lia pointed to the Cornell pennant on the refrigerator. My mom had gone to law school at Cornell. Good answer!

"I didn't go to NMSU," Lia said. "I went to New Mexico Highlands in Las Vegas. The Las Vegas in New Mexico. There's one in Nevada, too."

Highlands was certainly not Harvard. Athena frowned. "I know where Las Vegas, New Mexico, is, dear," she said. "They're doing an expansion of the state hospital there, and I'm handling the permitting."

"I'm going up there tomorrow," Lia said.

My heart skipped a beat.

"Then I might see you there," Mom replied.

I didn't know that my heart could skip two beats in a row. I had never fainted before, but this could push me over the edge.

"This gravy is amazing!" my father said, coming to my rescue. He liked Lia now, because she had liked his pictures of the Mayan ruins. "What's in it?"

Mom smiled. If you want to change the subject, get her talking about cooking. She supplied the details of how she found the recipe and the special hot pepper that she had to order from India. "I forgot its name."

"Naga jolokia?" Lia asked. "That's the hottest pepper in the world. My mom told me about peppers."

"They impounded the *naga jolokia* in customs at the airport," my mom said with a resigned smile. "You can't ship it here. Apparently it's on a Homeland Security list, so I had to improvise."

After another awkward pause, but I filled it with my usual joke about the wild rice being "way too wild." Mom then asked Lia about politics.

I looked anxiously at Lia, just as I had when she met with Governor Mendoza, but she passed with flying colors. She knew even more about politics than she did about peppers. She was most passionate with issues involving children, and Article Seven of the Children's Code.

"I see your point on the Children's Code Amendments," my mother said.

"C de Baca wanted to repeal section three, but I think it will die in Committee," Lia said. "He doesn't have the votes."

My mom nodded. I even nodded. Dad looked up from his reverie and he nodded, too.

The meal was finally over and I had survived without throwing up. I went back to the kitchen, and brought out the Lithuanian pumpkin pie. We were stuffed, so no one took more than a polite bite of the pie. I quickly cleared the table. It was part of the deal. I never had to cook at my parents' house as long as I cleared the dishes.

Mom then brought out coffee from Afghanistan, a Tora Bora blend.

"Is it decaf?" my dad asked.

"Of course," Mom replied. "I think the last thing this family needs is caffeine."

"I would have liked caffeine," I said. "We've got to get on the road back to Albuquerque."

My mother nodded. It looked like we would survive the meal without incident, but then she looked at Lia again.

"I saw you both on TV."

I nearly fainted right there. Lia looked blank.

"Oh?" I said. "What did you see?"

"I couldn't sleep after your father nodded off, and they replay the news on Channel 8 late at night. The Rogaine does seem to be working wonders on you."

"Uh, thank you, but could you hear what I was saying?"

"Oh, no. I had the volume off so I wouldn't wake your father."

"You didn't miss much," I said.

"It must be hard defending that horrible woman. The one who killed Governor C de Baca's wife . . . ."

"Which woman?"

"You're defending that Asian woman, right?" My mother looked at Lia. "And it was nice of you to help him out. He's so disorganized sometimes."

Suddenly it hit me. Mom thought Lia was acting as my paralegal, and that Bebe Tran in her tramp outfit was the criminal.

"It certainly is hard," I said.

"Do you like criminal law?" Mom asked Lia.

"Not really," Lia said. "Not so far."

I almost expected my mom to ask for Lia's case plan right there and then. Instead, Lia began rocking back and forth. I recognized what she was doing because she had done it at the arraignment. Was this Siberian trancing?

Lia mouthed the words "I love you" as if it were some kind of *mantra*. She reached for my hand under the table. I grabbed it. She calmed down, but only a little. I had maybe an instant before my parents caught on. I thought about spilling something on purpose. But there had been enough blood, I mean gravy, spilled tonight.

My dad rescued me again. "Speaking of Asia, maybe we can see the video from Malaysia."

"Sounds great," I said.

Setting up the display onto the big screen was excruciating, as my dad's portable technology was in an abusive relationship with the electronics at home. When we finally saw the video, it was mixed with video from other trips. There was a five-minute stretch of my dad taking a picture of the *Champs Elysee*. I mean a close-up of the pavement itself.

"We really, really have to get going," I said, glancing at my watch. "She has to get up bright and early to get up to the Mental Health Center to umm . . . meet with her client."

I squeezed Lia's hand tightly. She stopped muttering.

"I've got a lot to do tomorrow," she said. "It's a big day."

I got up, hurried to Lia and pulled out her chair to at least pretend that I was a gentleman. After we got our coats, my mom went over to Lia. I thought of all the movies where the drug-dealer instantly whips out a gun and kills someone. My mother merely whispered something in Lia's ear.

Lia didn't hear her at first and leaned closer.

I started shaking. I felt shocks going up and down my body.

Lia then smiled a smile that I couldn't read.

"I'll wait for you outside," she said to me.

"I'll wait outside with Lia," my dad said.

After the door was safely closed and Lia was out in the sound proofed car, Mom looked at me. "Jury's back."

"The verdict?"

"I had my doubts at first, but I really like her. This one could be really special."

"Special?"

"It's obvious. Do you know why?"

"Umm . . . no."

"She's the first one who loves you. Really loves you. You can see it in the way she looks at you."

"Oh."

She hugged me tight, a real hug. "Don't let this one get away."

"Sure."

"You're not getting any younger. Your father really wants to see you married before . . . ."

"We'll see what happens," I said.

"You seemed very nervous all night," she said. "Are you sure you're not gay?"

Outside, my dad hugged Lia As long as I had a real job, he was happy that I had someone who seemed to love me. Now that Lia was safely in the car, I saw a weariness in his step as he walked back toward the door. Was this his final hurrah, the trip around the world? It looked like it had killed him.

Mom walked to the car with me.

" Lia and me . . . it all depends," I said.

"On what?"

I was about to say on whether she's found competent, but I just smiled. "It just depends."

But what would my mother say if she knew the truth? I shuddered to think about it. I went out and got into the car with Lia, who was positively giddy.

"What did my mom say to you?" I asked.

"She said that I had her blessing."

"Blessing? This isn't the old country."

"She said that I had her blessing. If we got married."

She looked at me expectantly.

"Let's just get through the competency hearing first," I said.

"I'm not crazy," she said. "You're crazier than I am."

I didn't disagree. "I bet my family is crazier than yours."

"Just don't ever say I'm crazy," she repeated

Vegas, Baby, Vegas

I DROVE FOR A few minutes without saying anything. When we had safely passed Ten Thousand Waves Lia interrupted my concentration.

"Did your mom say anything else?"

I told the truth. "My mom thought you were pretty special."

"Special like 'special ed?'"

"No, special, as in someone she could see her son marry."

Lia positively beamed.

Lia slept at my house per the dictates of her conditions of release. I gave her the bed again, and slept on the couch. I woke up in the middle of the night and I looked at the bed. Lia slept there, looking as innocent as a newborn. My God, I almost wanted to use a video of her sleeping there as my entire closing argument.

"Ladies and gentlemen of the jury, just look at her. Could this woman really be a psycho killer?"

What would my mom think if she knew the real deal about Lia? She would find out eventually. Assuming Lia was found not guilty we could then save money on the wedding and have the same judge perform the ceremony right then.

I awoke before dawn to a freezing apartment. It was either too hot or too cold in there. I should have slept with Lia, if only for warmth. To freeze my emotions, as well as my libido, I took a cold shower and reminded myself that the day after Thanksgiving was technically President's Day. I felt like Washington taking a bath in the Delaware.

I then woke Lia.

"Do we have to go?" she asked. "Couldn't we just run away together to Mexico?"

I thought about it for a moment. Dan Shepard on the run. We could hit the border by noon, then drive further south into Mexico. We could make it to Acapulco in a couple of days.

Acapulco? I nearly had a heart attack at my parents' house in Santa Fe. I wasn't cut out to be a fugitive. Neither was Lia. Then again, perhaps she might have inherited some border crossing skills from her mom.

We had to get on the Interstate soon so I could make it to work in Santa Fe by nine. I figured we'd stay until three, then I'd take her to Vegas to check her in before the end of the day.

When I arrived in Santa Fe I dropped Lia at Fidel's organic coffee shop. Fidel's was within sight of the office. I figured there was a same-parking-lot exception to Lia's conditions of release.

"Stick to decaf," I said with a smile.

I hurried across the parking lot and was actually on time for a change. I even arrived before Joel, perhaps my biggest success of the year so far.

Half an hour later, Joel came into my office.

"You still haven't totally caught on here," he said. "I understand you're very busy right now with your *other* case. Did you really think I didn't know?"

I stayed silent. "Are you firing me?"

I had a moment of panic. What would I tell my dad?

"Not yet."

I waited. He handed me another contract to sign.

"I want you to be a staff attorney," he said.

"Staff attorney?"

"You'll get to choose your own hours, as long as you give me thirty hours a week."

"I appreciate your understanding," I said. This was actually the best possible thing. I could cut down my hours when I'm stressed, then rock on back when I was ready. And I could still tell my dad I was a big time Santa Fe lawyer.

He handed me a brochure with a mountain on the cover.

"Thanks to your mother, we've landed a major client. The Barkoff Corporation is developing a major new resort property in northern New Mexico. The resort will also include a nature preserve for endangered species. They want a law firm that knows how to do environmental compliance with the Feds, as well as interface with the public."

Developing an environmentally aware winter resort? With a nature preserve? Cool!

I opened the glossy brochure. It would be amazing, almost the size of Vail, yet the company had committed to the highest in environmental values. The nature preserve would protect endangered species of mountain lion. Mountain lions? Cool!

The money would be staggering. One lawyer friend in Aspen received a million dollar fee just so his client could flush a toilet in a national park. It wasn't the greed that got to me. Developing a major ski area was sexy. Saving an endangered mountain lion was sexier. In college, at Brown, I was a Natural Resources major. Environmental law was my focus at American University Law School, specifically land use development. I had always wanted to be the good guy for the evil developers.

My knees wanted to slalom though the parking lot I was so excited. Ski areas were so much easier to deal with than criminals. Joel had me do some "background" research on the company over the Internet for the rest of the day, billing all of it at the higher rate. I was hooked. Jeff Barkoff, the president of the company, even e-mailed me and asked some fascinating questions about environmental statutes and Indian law. We then talked skiing for fifteen minutes, all on the clock. My aggravated burglars back in Aguilar certainly had never skied the Kachina Ridge at Taos. This was the type of work Ivy League graduates were supposed to do. For the first time in a long time I felt like an intellectual, like the real big time lawyer my parents wanted me to be.

Joel smiled at me, when I left.

I smiled back. "See you Monday," I said.

Lia hadn't done decaf at Fidel's. She had gone with the triple espresso and was triply wired. As we drove, the Interstate zigged and zagged gently through rolling hills, lush with junipers and pines. The north-facing sides still had snow, like Vermont with adobe. The south-facing sides were more arid. Not quite Arizona, but close. We passed a few nice little villages off the highway: Pecos, Glorieta, and Romeroville.

Glorieta Pass was the site of New Mexico's one civil war battle where Union forces stopped Confederate and Texan forces that were trying to conquer New Mexico for the South. A Confederate flag even flew over Santa Fe for a while. The Union victory was called the Gettysburg of the West. The area was key to the almost-forgotten New Mexico campaign.

Lia had a brief breakdown near Glorieta.

"I'm not crazy," she said over and over again.

"This is just an evaluation that will help us with the case," I said, trying to calm her down from her own mental cannonballs.

I shifted the subject to her happy memories of the town of Las Vegas; her college days at New Mexico Highlands. It wasn't that different from my days as the Ivy League underachiever at Brown, but I was smart enough not to say anything.

"Highlands is the Mustangs, right?" I asked.

"The Cowboys. *Los Vaqueros*," she said with pride. "Highlands was founded as the New Mexico Normal School in 1893."

It was hard, but I resisted the joke about normal.

"You seem to be taking this well," I said instead.

"I kinda know what to expect," she said. "I meant I've been committed before. In high school. A civil commitment. I spent a year here, you know."

A civil commitment? For a whole year?

"Please don't ask me about it." Lia closed her eyes and that was it. The topic was off limits. For now.

We took the first exit to Las Vegas and headed toward the east part of town, toward the foothills. No one could ever confuse the two Las Vegases. The architecture here wasn't really adobe, more Victorian, as if it had been settled by the English rather than the Spanish. Well, maybe like the English prisoners of the Spanish. Several signs announced welcoming local churches. This Vegas was a moral town as opposed to Sin City.

We made our way to the state hospital outside of town on Hot Springs Road, a rural road in the foothills to the north. God, I'd sure love to drown in a hot spring right now.

As we parked, I saw my mother coming out of the hospital with a file. Semi-retirement suited her well. Hopefully she wouldn't see us.

Too late.

"Dan!" she shouted.

I only had to fool my mom for a few moments. Lia had dressed nicely and could almost pass for a young lawyer. Well, maybe a young legal secretary. Compared to the people escorted by police, she sure didn't look, well . . . crazy.

My mom smiled at us and looked at Lia.

"You'd better take off your jewelry," she said. "The metal detectors are pretty sensitive in there. They almost didn't let me in with this belt."

"I got a feeling they'll let her in," I said.

"I was a little tired yesterday with the dinner and all and I was slightly confused why you were coming here to the hospital. Did you say you had a client here?"

Lia was about to say something, but I held her hand tight.

"Yes," I said. "A big case."

"Well your client is in good hands with the two of you," my mother said.

She could make me feel like a million bucks sometimes. She gave me a hug. Then she gave Lia an even bigger one.

"Got to run," my mother said, and headed out.

I smiled. I was going to make it! My mom began fiddling with her keys so she could open her car door. She could never find the right key.

Dr. Mary Ann Romero, who was a director at large of the hospital, emerged from the building into the parking lot. She was a tall imposing woman who had never taken shit from anyone. We had a history, of course. She had testified for me in a few cases and seemed to travel to all the mental health hot spots in the state.

My mother still hadn't found the right key. She smiled at Dr. Romero. At first my mother thought that Dr. Romero had a question for her, so she hesitated.

Dr. Romero nodded back, then focused on Lia.

"It's good to see you again Lia," she said. "Please, come with me."

I was about to follow, but Dr. Romero waved her hand. "Just her."

She took Lia through the doors and the doors clicked shut behind them both.

I wondered if I would ever see Lia again. I wondered if I wanted to. My mom came back over to me.

"Why did they let just her in and not you?"

"She's been here before," I said.

Dan Shepard's Disease

As I LEFT LAS Vegas, southbound on I-25, I couldn't help but remember my own interaction with New Mexico's mental health system. About two years ago I lost a job at a private firm because I couldn't figure out that firm's complicated billing system. I always rounded down, and never billed my daydreaming time. I had lasted only two weeks. My boss actually asked if I had brain damage when he fired me.

Paranoid, I sought out an MRI, forgetting that I no longer had health insurance. The MRI nearly caused a claustrophobic attack while I was in the cylinder. I felt like I was in the coffin of the future, about to be ejected for burial into outer space.

After twenty minutes, the machine had revealed no brain damage. Unfortunately, a few weeks later I received a bill for a thousand dollars that was not covered by insurance. I had a worse panic attack when I had to ask my parents for the money.

I had found a free counseling service at a local mental health clinic. I went once a week and sat there with the other indigent patients. I had met Dr. Romero during her rotation through the clinic. The woman sure got around.

Dr. Romero enjoyed having an intelligent client for a change. Eventually she decided that my particular case was so unique that the entire department would interview me. I remembered Lou Gehrig. If you suffer from a rare disease, you should get to name it. "Dan Shepard's Disease" would be a heady cocktail of low self-esteem, guilt, paranoia, claustrophobia, fear of commitment, sexual dysfunction, and Oedipal rage with a nice twist of narcissism on the side.

When I woke up the morning of the evaluation, I didn't know what to wear. I had read enough forensic evaluations to know that the evaluator always looked at the patient's appearance noting whether they were "appropriately dressed." What's appropriate for a depressed lawyer with learning disabilities? Would they look at my Jerry Garcia tie like a silk Rorschach and ask, "What does it mean to you?"

After a dozen minutes of angst, I finally went with jeans and a black shirt from the Gap to look more like a Hollywood screenwriter. Well, a depressed Hollywood screenwriter. No tie. I added a nice black jacket to look more like a hot young producer, or perhaps a hip comedian touring the heartland.

Out in Hollywood, all the successful writers had at least two therapists. I would have ten in one day! When I arrived, it was quite hot so I left the jacket in the car. I didn't want to out-dress my evaluators. Dr. Romero made me wait in the lobby with the rest of the patients. I purchased a Diet Mountain Dew from the vending machine. The caffeine made my arms shake like I was coming down off Diet Methadone.

Right before my nineteenth nervous breakdown, Dr. Romero finally called me into the cramped meeting room. It felt more like a faculty lounge at a junior college then a medical examining room. With the exception of Dr. Romero, they all were young grad students. Two students munched on a massive order of McDonald's Chicken McNuggets with sweet and sour sauce. I was hungry myself. Could I ask them to share?

For a moment, the only sound was McNuggets going through the digestive track.

"You probably wondered why I called you here," I said, trying to sound funny.

No laughter. More McNugget munching.

Dr. Romero then presented my case. I was a thirty-something male with depression, inability to forge meaningful relationships and had trouble living up to my parents unrealistic expectations.

"The patient wishes to address the group," she said at last.

The patient? I had a moment of stage fright. I then mumbled a few moments about my birth and childhood and quickly got to my first issue.

"My dad yelled at me for not being able to tie my shoes."

"Did he beat you?" Dr. Romero asked.

"No, of course not."

They looked bored.

"My mom is disappointed that I'm not married yet."

"Wow, mommy issues," a student laughed under her breath. "How so not original."

My God, last month's case study was probably fed human flesh by his father. Dr. Romero looked away, self conscious that she had brought in such a boring specimen.

I then discussed the anxiety of the wait list for an exclusive private school in Washington D.C. as a formative experience. I tried to be profound.

"My whole life has been one big wait list," I said.

For some reason, one student perked up. She looked like a nice Jewish girl. She wore old clothes, and expensive old jewelry as if she came from money. I think her name was Nancy. Under different circumstances, I could have dated her.

The Nancy nodded, as if she too had been wait listed. Then she muttered something about getting into Harvard. When I had done stand-up, I had looked for one friendly set of eyes. I had just found them.

Under other circumstances, Nancy would have been my target at a party. I looked straight at her. I mentioned every wait list, talked about parental pressure and over-sleeping for the communications class.

"I got a B minus instead of a B. I should have made it into Georgetown Law School. I'd be doing international environmental law right now," I said.

Amazingly the other students nodded as well. They related to me in spite of themselves. They had stopped looking at me as the patient; I had become their cool colleague.

I ducked most of the questions and went into my funny stories, like going to the female jail with my zipper open. My evaluation had now become a stand-up act. They particularly liked my story about proposing to a client on behalf of his girlfriend.

"When he asked, 'Do I still have to go to prison if I get married?' I replied, "Marriage is not an alternative sentence.""

The group all laughed out loud.

After about an hour, Dr. Romero glanced at her watch. She was a state employee after all.

"I think we've got all we need," she said.

"But I'm just getting started," I said. "We haven't even hit my law school issues from the 'D' in my State and Local Government class. I'm still traumatized."

The students smiled. I looked at their notepads. Other than a few scribbles from the beginning, no one had taken any notes at all.

"Thank you, Dan," Dr. Romero said.

They excused me and then talked about me behind closed doors. I wanted to wait them out and buttonhole them, just like "polling a jury" after a guilty verdict.

I sat in the lobby for a moment and grabbed another Diet Methadone. As the green liquid flowed directly into my brain, something hit me—I had been so eager to entertain that I had failed at the true mission. I hadn't gone deep into my issues, and I never figured out why I had fucked up my life so badly.

A guard came over to me. "Son, you really need to move on," he said. "The show's over."

The next week, Dr. Romero called with bad news. There was an internal dispute with the financial department. I wasn't considered indigent enough, so I had to stop treatment. I never even found out what my diagnosis was.

Needless to say, "Subject of a case study" didn't go on my resume when I applied for a job with Joel.

Back in the present, the highway passed a hamlet called San Jose. This San Jose was a far cry from the high tech hub of Silicon Valley. It was a collection of adobe homes with tin roofs. I don't know if they had calculators out here yet in this neck of the junipers, although one could buy a thousand square foot home for ten thousand dollars. Unfortunately, you could sell it ten years later for only nine thousand dollars.

I had to stop making jokes about everything. I had my chance to find out about myself when I went to the clinic, but instead I turned it into yet another joke. I started to cry. My whole car became one big teardrop. I had lost something in the Las Vegas hospital parking lot today, lost something in the hospital back in Albuquerque then. I wasn't sure what it was.

God, I hoped Lia didn't blow her chance like I had. I knew one thing for sure. Dan Shepard's Disease was incurable.

Turquoise Curtain

I SPENT THE WEEKEND pouring through Lia's box. I was amazed at how little I learned for three hundred dollars worth of copies. There were no medical reports, and even worse, the witness statements were handwritten. I would have to interview the witnesses myself to decipher what they had said.

The next Monday at work, Joel asked if I'd like to sit second chair, well, third chair, at a hearing for the Barkoff people. Santa Fe District Court was on the north side of town, just a few blocks from the plaza. It could almost pass for an adobe Mercado, except for the metal detectors. The snow had mostly melted on the warm day, but the few white tufts that were left made the courthouse look rustic.

I carried Joel's briefcase as we walked past the second-floor courtroom. The crowd was about fifty percent Anglo, and fifty percent Hispanic. One woman talked about her acupuncture sessions as part of her DWI probation.

"The reason I failed the walk and turn test is because of bad *chi*," she said.

I smiled. Even the criminals were more sophisticated here.

Our courtroom could pass for a mixed media gallery with its delicate shades of teakwood around the benches.

"Are you doing the hearing?" I asked Joel.

"Oh no, they wanted the best lawyer in New Mexico. It's the person everyone gets for big cases."

"Mitch Garry?"

Joel laughed. "I think you might know her."

I shouldn't have been surprised that my mother was the heavy hitter, nor that she was late. The court waited for her, rather than vice versa. When she finally arrived, her black suit with gold trim gave her more gravitas than the judge himself. She was like the black hole of the law; she sucked the opposing energy completely out of the room.

The issue involved adding ten pages to a brief, but tens of millions of dollars were at stake. When the case was called, I learned what the word "brilliant" really meant. She managed to make "collateral estoppel" sound sexy. She even cited the magic case I had found for them, made it a point to cite the "good work of someone on our team."

Why couldn't I have inherited even a tenth of that legal talent?

Sure enough, the judge ruled that we were able to add an extra few pages to the brief. The client was ecstatic. Civil law can be fun sometimes.

I expected my mother to hug me in triumph, until she said the ominous words, "Dan, I know about Lia. Why didn't you tell me?"

I expected her to yell at me, to swear and ask how I could bring a mentally ill murderer into her house. I expected her to disown me. I would then tell her that Lia was innocent, and this was about justice. Once I vindicated Lia, I would show her.

When I said nothing, my mother turned and walked back to Joel. At first I thought they were talking about me, until Joel took out a few baby pictures. "You must be so happy," she said to him.

I slinked out the side door. Had I just been disowned?

Estrogen Alley

I TRIED TO CALL my parents, but they didn't pick up. I spent the night in Albuquerque and read through Lia's box again, hoping to find something I missed. No, there was nothing here. Or perhaps my emotions had gotten the best of me. Every time I read a police report, my gut tightened. I was in too deep with Lia. I needed a fresh eye. And fresh air. I wouldn't win Lia's case here in my messy apartment that reeked of spilled coffee and dirty underwear.

I would have to be pro-active. First I would have to find an office in Albuquerque, just to do witness interviews in a room that didn't smell. Hopefully, I could find a criminal defense lawyer to help me with the case.

I glanced through the *Bar Bulletin* online. Converted bungalow offices in Albuquerque were far cheaper than Santa Fe "office condo villas." Most criminal lawyers had converted houses in the old Barrio Wells Park neighborhood—the BWP—between downtown and the freeway. A famous Albuquerque boxer had BWP tattooed on his chest. If your neighborhood has its own gang tattoo abbreviation, it probably was a bad sign.

I saw an ad "Office with Secretary" listed, with the tag "Call Luna or Jen."

Luna? I called immediately. Jen, the secretary, picked up and asked me to come by as soon as possible. The office was "in play," whatever that meant. They were working through weekend.

Luna's office was a small adobe building near the courthouse. Inside, the office was eclectic. Unlike Santa Fe, they certainly hadn't used a designer. Diego Rivera paintings clashed with movie posters for big blockbusters—the sublime and the ridiculous. I loved it immediately.

Unfortunately, they were not alone.

"You both have kids?" I asked.

Her secretary, Jen, introduced me to her two-year-old daughter Denise, and pointed to Luna's one year old, Sacagawea. Jen sat at the front desk, holding Denise. Luna sat at the back desk with Sacagawea. Both babies cried simultaneously.

Two phones rang a half second apart. The crying and the phone ringing formed a symphony.

Jen picked up one line while holding onto the baby. She somehow managed to quiet the baby, set up a deposition, and change a diaper—all without missing a beat.

Holding a now quiet Sacagawea, Luna said, "You sure want to rent space here in Estrogen Alley?"

"Well, more than that, I need help with Lia's case. You probably know it's not just a zoning case."

"Duh," said Jen.

"What do you want from us?" Luna asked.

Before I could answer, the phone rang again and Jen picked it up. "They're ready for the phone interview."

Jen hurried over and took the baby from Luna. I watched in amazement as Luna switched from Mother-of-the-Year to Hard-Ass-Lawyer with the twitch of an eyebrow. She put the call on speaker phone so she could take notes. She cross-examined a cop who had been sent to the Middle East with the Reserves. I could hear gunfire over the speaker phone on the other end, and

Luna hit him hard with question after question about his recollections. He probably couldn't wait to get back to the green zone.

After Luna finished, she called to Jen.

"I need a motion in limine and a motion to dismiss," Luna said. "We put the fear of God into that cop."

"I'll just fix up the one from the Mayhem Moreno case last year," Jen said. "I'm amazed that guy keeps hiring us. We've got to start charging him more."

Jen typed out the pleading, then cut and pasted a masterpiece in a matter of moments before bringing it to Luna to sign. They were better than a pit crew at the Indy 500, because a pit crew never had to change a diaper during a race.

Jen laughed. "Just think how much more fun this would be if the client was actually paying us. He's still five months behind."

Luna sighed. "Why do I have to be so good at something I hate? Why couldn't I have been a singer or an Olympic champion, something like that?"

There was an awkward silence. Jen looked away, slightly embarrassed by Luna revealing too much of herself in front of a relative stranger.

I tried to break the silence. "Well, you girls are really good," I said.

"We're not girls," Jen said. "We're geishas."

Jen had a poster over her desk of an animated television show called *Laser Geishas*.

"Laser Geisha Pink!" Jen called out.

"Laser Geisha Blue," Luna answered.

"How many times do you do that a day?" I asked.

Jen shrugged.

Luna finally had a quiet moment. "I ask again, what do you want from us?"

It would be good to have the Laser Geishas covering my back.

"I need your help with Lia's case. I need to do some interviews here, and I also might have to ask you to help when I'm
stuck in Santa Fe. I can pay a little for renting the office and
some costs. I haven't done a murder case in a long time so I need
some moral support, too."

"State v. Ophelia Paz," Luna said, shaking her head. "Is she
still your girlfriend while she's in Vegas?"

"No," I said. "The whole relationship is on hold until a court
determines whether she's competent. I mean innocent."

Luna shook her head. "I don't know."

"Ophelia likes you," I said. "You're her role model."

"Luna was my role model once, too," Jen said. "Not no
more."

"So *the* Dan Shepard needs my help," Luna said. "The
famous Rattlesnake Lawyer."

"I haven't been the Rattlesnake Lawyer in a very long time."

She laughed. "I heard about that big case you did way back
when. That Jesús Villalobos case. You waived closing argument
in a murder case. You had balls."

I looked down. "Still there."

Luna thought for a moment. "You can use the office, if you
need to. Pay what you can. As for my helping with the case,
we'll have to see about that."

Two Out of Three Ain't Bad

LIA CALLED EVERY NIGHT and asked the same question: "What's going to happen?"

Each night I gave her the same answer: "I don't know."

Aggravated, I pestered the DA's office every day for the next three days. No one returned phone calls over there. The nice receptionist actually mentioned a getting restraining order against me for my telephone harassment. After my next check cleared, the DA finally overnighted the next round of Lia's discovery. Unfortunately, they sent it to Joel's Santa Fe office, which was still my official address listed in the bar directory.

Joel was pissed when he saw the big box come by special delivery.

"You better do this on your own time," he said. He looked as if he wanted to shred the entire box right there.

I hurried back to my workspace at the firm's library. I knew I was supposed to study a treatise called "Eisenberg on Easements." Unfortunately, Lia's box called my name in a soft, alluring voice.

"You're so brilliant," the box said.

Easements reminded me that *they* paid my bills, not Lia, so I managed to find a good citation or two for a brief before I delved into the box. Just as I was about to open it Joel walked by, so I quickly switched back to Eisenberg. Once the coast was clear, I had Jen call the DA's mean receptionist to set up the first round of witness interviews. I didn't want to piss her off by calling myself.

"Make them for next week," I asked Jen.

"I'll try," she said. "Remember, I don't work for you."

"Not yet," I said. "Are you going to have a nursery when I'm there?"

"I can't make any promises," she said. "Babies will be babies. Mothers will be mothers."

I hung up before Joel walked by again. This time he smiled.

"I just heard from Barkoff again," he said. "It looks like the ski area is up for its environmental review. I'll have you work on that next week. Isn't that exciting?"

"As a matter of fact, yes."

An environmental review sounded like a lot more fun than stressful witness interviews on a criminal case.

Happy, Joel even trusted me with a mediation that afternoon. Rhiannon Goldstein Manygoats had a dispute with her contractor over an unfinished drywall project for her gallery. We met at a private mediator's office on Canyon road. The mediator actually lit incense and asked Rhiannon to talk about the "real issues" behind the dispute.

Rhiannon surprised me with her reply.

"Don't fuck the help and then blow him off," she said.

The embarrassed contractor vowed to finish the drywall job that afternoon free of charge.

I savored my little triumph. And yet every moment I spent away from Lia's case, I felt guilty. I missed her. I had fucked her then I had blown her off. I now had to fix the drywall in Lia's life.

That night Lia told me about her roommate, a dual-diagnosis schizophrenic Navajo named Heidi Hawk who was up for a diagnostic on an embezzling scandal. I had represented a Heidi Hawk in Aguilar, a paint-sniffer. I wondered if they were the same person.

Lia said that this Heidi Hawk had also worked as a janitor in a Crater County truck stop, then moved into a job as a clerk in District Court. She'd had some involvement in the courthouse construction scandal, and the stress had pushed her over the edge.

Lia also mentioned that every night Heidi said the words she needed to hear: "You're not crazy, you shouldn't even be in here."

The hospital hadn't started doing the testing yet. The staff was beyond overwhelmed just to maintain order, without doing any diagnostics.

"I keep telling them I'm not supposed to be here and they agree," Lia said. "Every bed on the diagnostic side costs a whole lot because they provide medical attention, security and then they have to do all the testing. C de Baca is going to cut their funding, so everybody here is on edge. I think the staff is more nervous than the residents."

The back-up on getting evaluations done ran all the way to Albuquerque. Plus, therapists charged more per hour than attorneys, and I remembered Judge Kurtz's comment about wasting judicial resources.

"Maybe I shouldn't have sent you up there," I said. I had a moment of panic, suppose the judge got pissed at me for wasting a bed in Vegas?

"Just remember that I love you," she said. "I love you. I love you. I love you."

I didn't know what to say. If she wasn't competent to stand trial for murder, could she be competent to love? I didn't know. It was almost an existential question. Was I one of her delusions as well, possibly like her mother? I didn't feel that she was my girlfriend any more. I knew I should tell her that we were "taking a break." I had sorta done that already, when I said I was her lawyer, right? Then again, it would be uncool to break up with a woman while she was in a mental hospital. I once had a girl-friend with a broken foot who I drove around for a week and didn't break up with until she could walk again. This was like a really big broken foot, I guess.

"Well?" she said.

I didn't tell her I loved her back. I wasn't sure. I knew I missed her. I knew that I desperately hoped she was found not guilty. I knew I had this strong feeling in my gut, but perhaps it was more concern than love—the same concern I felt for a wrongly accused client, multiplied a thousand fold. That wasn't love, was it?

Like an old song said, *"Two out of three ain't bad."*

"Good luck up there," was what I said instead.

Fresh White Meat Redux

THE NEXT MORNING I called in sick to Joel's new secretary, Victoria Scarborough. Victoria was English, which was the second best type of secretary one could have in New Mexico. The best was European and classy, like Eva, of course. A secretary like Jen, who was going to law school, was great, too. The only thing worse than having a bad secretary was having no secretary at all. Like me.

In typical Santa Fe style, Victoria was an acupuncturist on the side. Apparently there were more acupuncturists in Santa Fe per capita than in China, so she now answered phones to pay the bills.

"I can't come in today," I said.

"Well that creates a bit of wicket, doesn't it?"

"Joel said I could pick my hours, as long as they add up."

"Well, no one's here," Victoria said. "Joel is on a plane to Switzerland. He'll be gone for a spell."

"That's good, I guess."

"Not hardly," Victoria said with ice. "You were quite the wanker on one of your last briefs. He's trying to save the client. He quite cares about you and doesn't want to sack you. Are you sure you can't make it today? I need someone to review a few forms before they go out."

The moment of truth. I couldn't leave Luna with the witness interviews just yet. I had started to like working with Joel. Lia wasn't paying me. Joel was. I thought of my dad. I couldn't burn my bridges yet. I glanced at the blank walls of my house and I knew I couldn't quit my day job. I wasn't ready to make that leap of faith.

"I'll make it up there by the end of the day," I said.

"I suppose that will have to do."

I arrived at the Law Office of Luna Cruz a little early and found that the DA's office had sent the junior prosecutor I called "Fresh White Meat" to cover the case.

My God, he could be me at twenty-six. He was a Clark Kent look alike, with a green kryptonite necktie. He had probably hoped to be a senior partner at a big firm by now, but he still hadn't figured out to tie his tie in a proper double Windsor, and it clashed violently with his wrinkled brown suit.

"Fresh white meat," I said to myself.

"What?"

"Nothing," I said. I had better to learn to stop talking out loud or I would get myself into trouble.

"I've heard a lot about you, Mr. Shepard," he said as if I were a grizzled veteran from the last war. When did I become *Mister* Shepard?

Fresh White Meat made it a point to ask for the witness fees up front. Budget cuts were hitting the DA's office, too. I wrote a check, praying it would go through. He then excused himself, and went into the conference room where he poured over handwritten notes as if this little deposition was a Supreme Court case.

Luna's big brown eyes danced in the florescent lights. I had dressed for the occasion, wearing my Hollywood power suit, all black, but to balance it I wore my light-hearted Nicole Miller vintage tie that showed scenes from old Route 66. Luna stared at the tie, as if trying to find her hometown of Crater, New Mexico on it.

Normally I would have saved this ensemble for court, but I had wanted to impress Luna. She wore a black suit that looked like a slightly less expensive version of my mother's black one from court in Santa Fe.

"Nice tie, Mr. Shepard," she said with a smile.

A tiny silver cross dangled around her neck, although somehow she didn't strike me as the religious type.

"I like your outfit as well," I said. "Black suits you. Nice cross, Ms. Cruz. Or is it nice cruz, Ms. Cross?"

"Whatever. Your girl Ophelia called me by the way."

"Lia called you?"

"She begged me to help you with her case. She kept saying you were brilliant, but she wasn't sure you had much experience in this sort of thing and felt you were a little distracted. She then went on about how brilliant I was."

"What did you tell her?" Lia's sudden lack of confidence hurt me a little.

"I told her I'd help a bit, for now. I haven't been called brilliant in awhile."

Before we could talk more, her phone rang. She frowned and hurried into her office to take the call. Jen snorted.

I looked at Jen, who was engrossed in an Internet gossip site. "You don't like me much, do you, Jen?" I asked.

"It's nothing personal," she said. "You just seem to like Luna a lot. I can tell. She won't admit it, but she likes you. She thinks you're funny."

"Do I amuse her?" I asked. "Funny how?"

"That's a line from *The Godfather*, right?"

"*Goodfellas*, actually."

Jen frowned. "I never get those things right. Well, she's very lonely right now. She needs a male presence in her life."

"I can be a presence."

Jen scowled. "Luna's totally been through more things than you can possibly imagine. So have I. I don't want to see anyone hurt her."

"I said 'presence.' I'm not going to hurt her. I'm not interested in anything more."

"Oh you are, you just don't know it yet."

Nystagmus Girl

IN LUNA'S CONFERENCE ROOM the State went out of its way to provide the most worthless witnesses possible. The first few officers deposed took the dispatch. The next tagged evidence at the lab, and the third merely drove Officer Tran to do the arrest. One cop said he asked Lia for a statement.

I was excited. "Did she say anything?"

"She exerted her fifth amendment right. She said she had a lawyer who was—"

"Brilliant," I cut him off. "No further questions."

Nothing much happened until Officer Nadia Nunez from the APD Field Services Bureau arrived. She was the officer Luna had interviewed outside on the day of Lia's arraignment. Nadia and Luna had a long history. From the minute I saw them at the courthouse, I sensed it was personal. Could the two of them have been . . . together? Nah. Both women were straight, as far as I knew.

Nadia dressed in a crisp blue APD uniform. She had her case notes with her, but didn't look at them. If she had a degree, she easily could have been a better lawyer than I was.

Luna made it a point to be inside the room for the interview. She stared at Nadia, and then moved closer to me, as if marking her territory. Nadia was also mad at Fresh White Meat because he had lost a case she had investigated. I could kid myself that she was flirting with me, but she played a deeper game against the other two.

Thankfully, Nadia's role in the case was limited, and she was very easy going. To her, this was a game rather than a deposition. She had taken the pictures of the crime scene and went over her findings in a big DJ voice. She showed us photos of the bloody stone, drag marks, and blood stains in the back yard.

Nadia also talked about what she didn't have. Due to the moisture of that November day—and a lab error—she didn't have fingerprints. Nadia was honest and just got the data; she didn't theorize.

She must have said, "I can't answer that question, Daniel," ten times. She then added, "The criminalistics report will come soon, and should provide some answers. The medical report will provide the rest."

As for Lia's psychological profile: "You'll have to talk to Officer Tran about that, Daniel."

Nadia's professional facade crumbled briefly when she muttered "That ho," under her breath. Officer Tran was obviously not too popular in the APD these days. But Nadia quickly resumed her tough cop role. She made eye contract whenever she used my name, but she made it a point to look to Luna first, to make sure Luna knew. I liked hearing my name, especially in her voice. I finally made it to my last question.

"So you really don't know who killed Portia, do you?"

I expected her to go on about the lab, or the hospital, but instead she smiled.

"You got me, there, Daniel," she said. She then looked to Luna and added, "This one's even better than you are."

"Better how?" Luna asked out loud.

Androids Make Better Lovers

THE FINAL WITNESS FOR the morning was the EMT, Rutger Macaron.

I asked first about his name. He said his mother had loved Rutger Hauer in the movie *Blade Runner*. This tough Hispanic man with bleached blond hair could indeed pass for a replicant, the android version of the perfect man. Rutger was the one who fished the body out of the ditch, a few miles downstream from Lia's house. Rutger's tattooed left bicep was bigger than my head. The tables were now turned. I found myself jealous of him as he smiled at Luna and ignored eye contact with me.

Luna smiled back.

Rutger put a shiny DVD on the table, as if it was his acting "reel." We clicked on the TV to find there was a disc already playing: the ever-popular Barney the dinosaur. I couldn't seem to manage the disc swap. Rutger smiled, then with a few strategically placed taps, got his video to play.

Luna smiled.

Rutger narrated the action as if it was an extreme sports video. For some reason, he adopted a faux Australian accent. That afternoon had been brutal because of the storms. He was already on call, going from accident to accident. It was their seventh save of the day.

"It's what I do for a living," he said. "Day in, day out."

"Cool." This from Luna.

A news helicopter picked up the action as a tethered Rutger descended into the whitewater of the arroyo. Luna could not take her eyes off the damn bicep as he pointed to the action on the screen. After tethering himself, he had dived in to get the body, which was wedged in a grate. He had picked her up, and tried in vain to give her mouth-to-mouth.

His rope was nearly broken, cut by some debris, and he was almost swept away by the strong current. But with pure force of will, Rutger swam against the waves with Portia Smith C de Baca's body in his iron grasp. Fresh White Meat smiled. He knew how well this stuff would play to a jury. So did I. To top it off, Rutger was able to make a positive ID of Portia. He had seen her before.

I had only one question. "Was she dead when you got her out?"

Luna looked at me as if I was pulling Superman's cape off. "I'm sure he did his best to save her."

"He's not on trial here," I said. "Lia is. So was Portia still alive when you grabbed her from the water?"

"She wasn't breathing," Rutger said.

"You don't know how she died, do you?"

"You'd have to ask your client about that," he said with a smile.

After Rutger left, Luna said, "That was fun. You've got potential."

"Thanks," I said. "Potential for what?"

"This could be the start of a potential friendship," she said.

"Don't you mean beautiful friendship?"

"Sorry. Rutger's beautiful. You're not."

Pearl Harbor Days

MORNING WITNESS INTERVIEWS OVER, I had to get to Santa Fe by two o'clock and put in a few hours of paid work. Over the next few days I learned the details of our big deal; it was basically a trade. Barkoff had land near the freeway. The tribe had land in the mountains. The tribe would get the land near the freeway to build a casino and Barkoff would build the winter resort on the old tribal land in the mountains. Deals like this were happening in New Mexico every day.

I liked my Santa Fe routine. We had an Indian summer, excuse me, a Native American summer, the next few days—a wonderful December warm spell with sunny days in the fifties. The dry air and desert sunlight made it feel much warmer on my skin and I didn't even wear a tie or a jacket. But when I descended back to Albuquerque at night the thicker air depressed me. Life without Lia was fine in Santa Fe, but it was terrible in Albuquerque. In Santa Fe, I could bill all my research. I could work for Lia and do it on Joel's dime.

The firm had represented Rhiannon Goldstein Manygoats. She had been at the Governor's party, and she had been the one who said she wanted C de Baca dead. So I checked our own data bases on her. Turns out she was on the board of the Agua Caliente Land Trust, and connected to the famed "Agua-gate" scandal that had tripped up Governor Mendoza. She was also involved in a questionable land transfer.

Rhiannon Goldstein Manygoats was leaving Joel's office as I arrived that morning. She blew me a kiss and her kiss smelled of wheatgrass. She handed me a personal invitation to the big "arts crawl" happening in a few weeks during the session.

"I thought you were leaving once C de Baca was in office."

"Who knows, repression might be good for the gallery," she said. "Lord knows he's ruined my real estate business!"

There was something about Rhiannon that bothered me. She had ties to the campaign, hell she had ties to half the land deals in New Mexico. At the election party, she had said she wanted C de Baca dead. As a client, I had access to a lot of info about her on the firm's computer files.After doing a little research, I found my hunch was correct. Rhiannon was a trustee of the Agua Caliente Land Trust, the scandal that tripped up Governor Mendoza. When C de Baca made Agua-gate a campaign issue, she had millions stuck in a trust account pending final resolution of an investigation. With C de Baca firmly in power, she would probably never see any of that money.

Could Rhiannon have a connection to Portia's murder? Maybe a blackmail scheme gone wrong, something like that? She easily could have made it up to Santa Fe in time for the party. But did she have a link to Lia?

I could not get the wheatgrass smell out of my head.

I looked up Lia on the public records websites. Lia was indeed born in Deming, New Mexico on the year she had stated. There was an amazing irony. I noticed that Deming was in *Luna* county. That would make her Lia from Luna.

I even found a copy of Lia's birth certificate, which had been uploaded. Records were often primitive in the bush, as I sometimes called the outlying areas. The certificate, I saw, had a notation. The clerk had typed in that he didn't believe the birth mother gave a real name, as she was an illegal alien, so he called her "Jane Doe."

Shouldn't it be Juana Doe? No, as much as I hated to say it, the most likely theory was the murderer was Lia's mother, whatever her name really was.

Like the warm December weather, my Santa Fe honeymoon couldn't last. Joel was as warm and cuddly as the Matterhorn when he returned from Switzerland the next week. I had made a major mistake on the Federal easement restrictions. I had missed citing the new amendments to regulations that had taken effect in July. Joel kept mentioning my "learning curve." My briefs sometimes had tabs and capitalization mangled when I e-mailed it to the client, and the client said that it reminded her of something by poet ee cummings.

Complicating matters, Lia had gained an additional privilege: she could now call me at precisely one-fifteen in the afternoon, in addition to her eight o'clock nightly call.

"I hope you're talking to a client," Joel said, noticing my impassioned voice as I tried to comfort Lia while typing a brief on the latest amendments to the Endangered Species Act.

"I am," I replied.

As he walked away, I wondered if I was on the endangered species list. I then told Lia for the tenth time that no I didn't know what would happen.

It was now December 7th, a day that would live in infamy. A secretary from the DA's office called me in the morning to set up interviews with the criminalistics folks. Finally!

Unfortunately, I would have to do those interviews that afternoon, before everyone went to their annual conference in Maui.

"How about Officer Tran?"

"You have to make your own appointment with her," she said. She gave me a number.

"I'll call back to confirm." I was up to my neck in environmental statutes.

What would I do?

I called Luna.

"I need a favor," I said. "Could you do some witness interviews for me?"

"I don't know," she said. "I'm pretty busy."

Time for flattery. "Luna, I saw you manhandle Officer Nunez during that DWI interview."

I wasn't sure if I should have used the word manhandle.

"So?"

"Well, it's clear that you know a lot more about this sort of stuff than I do. Besides, you're so brilliant."

Did I just use the word brilliant? Well, it worked for Lia.

"Okay. I need to justify my existence," Luna said at last. "I'll do them. What the hell."

"You are the greatest!"

"You owe me," she replied.

I hung up after I gave her the phone numbers. I decided to call Officer Tran myself. Interviewing medical personnel was boring, but interviewing a cop, especially one like Bebe Tran stirred my blood. And besides, Officer Tran was key to the case. As an officer in a mental health unit, she probably knew more about Lia than anyone else on the force. I left a number on a pager.

I finally finished going through most of the statutes. When I walked out to my car, I realized that the brief December lull was over; winter was coming back in earnest. It even looked like snow.

When I was halfway home, Luna called.

"Meet me at the gym when you get back into town," she said. "I've got something to tell you."

Chlorine Dance

THE SNOW BARELY DUSTED as I arrived at the gym in Albuquerque. Luna was already in her black workout clothes. The girl did like black. Luna didn't wear much make-up, and had her hair pulled back. Her hair seemed a little grayer tonight. She had already lifted free weights before I arrived. Her lean arm muscles glistened slightly with sweat. I wondered if I could bench more than she could. I hoped so.

"I'll save a stationary bike for you," she said, "if you think you can keep up with me."

"I can keep up with a stationary bike," I said. "How about the Nordic Treks? We can pretend we're skiing on the side of a fjord or something. How do you say fjord in Spanish?"

"*El fjordo,* I guess. Or *La Fjorda.* I don't know whether fjord is masculine or feminine. Despite my surname, my mom was Jewish, and I only took a semester of Spanish."

"I would assume masculine," I said. "Fjords jut into the land."

"Let's just say it would depend on your perspective. And whether it is the land or the sea doing the jutting."

As we trekked in place on the machines, we talked about everything except the case. I had run cross country in college, well, ran on the "C" team. Luna pretended to be impressed that I had once completed the Marine Corps Marathon in D.C. in under three hours and thirty minutes, which would make me faster than Oprah.

"Didn't you try out for the Olympics in something?"

She talked a little about trying out for the triathlon and failing utterly in front of fifty thousand people. I sensed it was a sensitive subject so I switched gears. I found that Luna could have an articulate conversation and keep up with my literary allusions while taking the Nordic Trek 9000 to its maximum setting. I couldn't help but hum the song from *Apocalypse Now*.

"Wagner?" she asked. "The Valkeries song. Are you saying I'm a Valkerie?"

"You're kicking ass on the Nordic Trek. If the Valkeries were alive today they'd be waltzing on the Nordic Trek."

She laughed. "They've got a hot tub downstairs and I think they've actually sterilized it tonight."

"Sounds good."

She got off the Nordic Trek. "There's something I need to talk to you about. Why I called you."

"What's that?"

"How Portia died."

The communal hot tub was outside in an adobe enclosure under the moonlight. It was very cold outside and the air was thick, as if it the light dusting of snow could turn into a blizzard. I hurried to the hot tub. It was co-ed, so I wore my gym shorts, which could pass for swim trunks in a pinch.

PLEASE SHOWER BEFORE ENTERING a sign read.

I took the world's shortest shower, then jumped in the tub. Moments later, Luna came out and threw off her towel. She wore black of course, and filled a bikini very nicely indeed. The material could almost pass for leather.

The gray streak in her hair glistened in the moonlight, as if it was sterling silver.

"*So go and wear that touch of gray, kinda suits you anyway,*" I sang the old Grateful Dead song to myself. "*Cause it's all right.*"

Luna was a woman. Lia was a little girl.

Luna smiled. I had pumped myself up pretty good on the Nordic Trek; Thor himself would have been proud. Luna dipped her foot in, and then stopped. She pulled back as if it was acid.

"Are you afraid of pools?" I asked. "Chlorino-phobia?"

"Sorta," she replied. "I'm not afraid of regular pools however, but once those jets start going I get kinda paranoid. Seriously. My best friend dunked me in one a few years ago. Nearly drowned me. On purpose. I can't stop thinking about it when I get into one of these things."

Her dead-eyed stare indicated that she was serious.

"This will be the first time I've taken a plunge in years."

"I promise not to dunk you," I said. "And I will fight off any one who tries. So take the plunge."

She descended like Botticelli's Venus taking a break from posing, entering slowly, then sitting up against a jet. Luna purred as the jet worked like a vibrator on her shoulder.

"Alone at last," I said. "You wanted to tell me something."

She waited a moment before beginning. "The medical report is inconclusive and incomplete. It's still being evaluated. "

"Still being evaluated?" That sounded suspicious.

"Welcome to New Mexico, the land of medical *manana.*"

"Do they have any theories?"

Luna pantomimed each option as she talked.

"First, someone could have hit Portia in the forehead with a stone, like a brass knuckle. A bloody stone was found on a table. No one knows how it got there. Second, someone could have grabbed Portia's head and jabbed it onto the stone. Or finally, Portia could have accidentally fallen and her head just happened to hit the stone."

"Sounds like reasonable doubt."

"But not *all* doubt. I used to be a prosecutor. When was the last time someone accidentally fell in your house, hit their head and then dragged themselves out to rushing waters in an arroyo?"

"That would be never," I said. "When will the report be complete?"

"When the powers that be decide how they want the report to look," Luna said. "I get the feeling that there's some major political pressure."

"Shit." Autopsies could be political all right.

The jet kept working its magic on her left shoulder.

"Some good news. Lia's fingerprints were *not* found on the stone. No fingerprints at all were found on Portia, due to the water. Some bad news. All of the blood found at Lia's house was a positive match to Portia."

I hated words like "positive" and "match."

"It was unclear whether Portia was dead when she was thrown into the ditch," Luna said. "She was almost certainly dead when Rutger pulled her out. Other than the gash on her forehead, there were no defensive wounds on her body."

" Rutger isn't such a big stud," I said. I flexed again.

It started to snow. She looked great with snow in her hair. Unfortunately, Gollum appeared at the edge of the hot tub just then and got in.

No shower, of course.

Luna laughed as Gollum told her some amusing anecdotes. She was as nice to him as she was to me. She had a good heart. Finally, she got out of the tub. I tried not to stare at the effects of the cold weather on her bikini top.

"I've got to pick my daughter up from daycare."

Gollum stared at her as she left.

"Do you like her?" he asked. "I thought you already had a girlfriend."

I got out and shivered in the cold night as I grabbed my towel. The cold froze my brain. I didn't know what to think any more.

I couldn't help but think that Luna had never killed any one. As far as I knew.

By the time I made it to the car, it had stopped snowing. Albuquerque was hardly a winter wonderland after all. My phone rang. At first I thought it was Lia, or hopefully Luna, but it was Officer Bebe Tran. She worked swing-shift and could meet me when she was done, around midnight. Tomorrow she was going home to visit dying relatives in Vietnam until after Tet. Tet in Vietnam apparently was like Christmas, Thanksgiving and Fourth of July all rolled into one holiday.

"When's Tet?"

"January," she said. "If you want to meet, it's now or never."

I had a little time to kill, so I swing by the apartment first, only to find my cable had been disconnected. I had let a lot of my Albuquerque bills slide.

Lia called. Eight o'clock sharp. I'd almost forgotten. Lia told me how lonely she was and how much she missed me.

"I miss you too."

"I want you" she said. "I want you. I want you. I want you."

I didn't respond. I knew I wanted something, but I wasn't sure what.

Lia kept on talking a mile a minute. She'd begun telling me that the hospital had screwed up. Instead of testing her for competency, a doctor had given her a sex-offender evaluation.

"A sex offender evaluation?" I said into the phone, startled.

Lia continued talking about the questions they asked—about losing her virginity, starting fires, bondage, pornography, etc. . . .

Before I could ask Lia another question, the connection was lost. Then my cell rang again.

"Lia?"

"It's me, Officer Tran," she said. "It's kind of light right now. We're setting up on Central Avenue, right off Louisiana Boulevard. I can meet you now if you don't want to wait up. I might have to do a double shift anyway, so I can get you in early."

Tet Offensive

THE NEIGHBORHOOD BY THE state fairgrounds was called the "War Zone," and I couldn't help but think of an adobe Baghdad, or perhaps Saigon in 1974, as many of the signs were in Vietnamese. It was an uneasy mix of Hispanic, African American and Latino combined with the stray smell of horse shit from the rodeo grounds.

I'd had one bad experience in the War Zone. I'd had to meet a client here to pick up his hundred dollar retainer payment. When I arrived, he had mumbled something about "getting the money from his mother," then disappeared into the darkness.

He had left me with a friend, Tyrese, who dressed entirely in blood red sweats. Tyrese babbled on about his potential million dollar law suit against the police for roughing him up ten years ago. I didn't know what the statute of limitations was, but I knew it was shorter than ten years. To make it worse, he had never gone to the hospital. I had to politely tell him the bad news about not having a case.

I then had to wait with Tyrese out on the street. If I left, I would never, ever see my hundred dollars, and my phone would be disconnected. Several low riders had driven past me that night. A few flashed gang signs, which I failed to correctly flash back. I hoped it wasn't a set up.

The client had returned thirty minutes later, twenty dollars short. I told him not to worry and got the hell out of there.

I was not happy to be back in the War Zone. Why couldn't this meeting be in Santa Fe at Joel's office?

I spotted Bebe as she walked down Central Avenue with an exaggerated swivel. She waved me away with the long nails on her delicate hand and me flashed a sign by holding up both hands—ten minutes. Or perhaps ten dollars.

I parked a block away on Central walked up the street. Bebe lured a cowboy driving the world's dirtiest pick-up truck. Within moments, he was on the ground whimpering. Sirens were everywhere.

How can guys be so stupid? They sent him away in a paddy wagon with a number of other losers.

Bebe pointed to a small nearby Vietnamese restaurant called *Café Tet*. The restaurant had once been a Mexican joint, and the few Vietnamese posters in the window did little to create any Asian ambience. Inside, two Vietnamese men in their twenties wore faded Dallas Cowboy jerseys with former Cowboy star, Dat Nguyen's name on them. They played an angry game of pool in the back of the restaurant. One had a white uniform, the other blue. They bet a large bill on every shot.

The men knew Bebe and she spoke to them in Vietnamese. Both Blue and White then slapped down hundred-dollar bills on the table. For some reason, I had a vision of the Russian roulette scene in *The Deer Hunter*. I didn't know whether I was Robert DeNiro or Christopher Walken in the scene. Walken was the one who blew himself away.

Bebe let her blue police jacket slip open a bit, revealing the red lingerie that she used as a lure. She wore a push-up bra. I didn't know whether it was genetics or construction that pushed things up so high. She put her I-phone down on the table.

The pool players mumbled comments in Vietnamese under

their breath. Blue slapped down another twenty, White matched him.

I was about to turn on my tape recorder when she grabbed my hand.

"This is off the record," she said. "I can give you a lot more."

"Sure," I said. What more could she give? "Officer Tran, does your unit regularly monitor Ophelia Paz?"

"You know, you can call me Bebe," she said. "But yeah, you might say I was a regular visitor to her house."

"Why?"

"She was one of our regular stops on our rounds of the crazies. She's on our list."

"How do you get on the list?"

I worried for a second that I might make that list someday.

Bebe smiled. "Ways too numerous to mention. If Lia didn't like someone, or if someone got in her way, she would put up signs and protest them. You heard of the Million Man March? This was one crazy girl march. She even protested me."

"What happened?"

Bebe closed the jacket tight. Showtime was over.

"When I was a trainee at one of the substations, she came in to report C de Baca had raped her. Back in high school. Kinda past the statute of limitations, if you know what I mean. I told her that I wouldn't forward her complaint to the prosecutor."

I thought about my potential client with the ten-year-old claim. I nodded. "So what did you do?"

"I didn't take her report and told her to kindly remove herself from the premises. I did everything by the book."

"She didn't like that."

"She protested me. I mean a real live protest—she marched in front of the substation holding a sign: TRAN UNFAIR TO VICTIMS!"

I shook my head, more in resignation than in shock. I could easily picture Lia protesting a police station.

"Why didn't you charge her with disturbing the peace or something?"

"My supervisor believed Lia's internal affairs complaint that I acted in an 'unprofessional manner.' I had to stay a police trainee, at police rookie wage, for an extra year. I'm still at a rookie wage after all these years due to various Ophelia Paz complaints."

Bebe let her jacket open a little.

"Do you think I like standing out in the cold like a ho? Excuse me, standing outside as a 'rookie ho.' It's because of your little girlfriend and all her stuff. We've got some scores to settle, she and I . . . ."

Yet it wasn't rage in Bebe's brown eyes, it was sadness. She acted like a real whore having a moment of clarity, realizing that this life was no life for her anymore.

Time to move on.

"According to your files, what's Lia's diagnosis?"

Bebe did her best to sound like a therapist. "She's bi-polar. Ninety-nine percent of the time she's normal, but when she gets stressed, I think she could kill. Like she did with Portia Smith C de Baca, *allegedly.*"

"You're not a psychiatrist, are you?"

"Actually I am. Or will be. That's my undergrad degree here at UNM. Forensic Psychology. I'm trying to get a joint JD-MD at Stanford or UCLA. Let's just say I'm from an over-represent-ed minority at those schools, so I have to do whatever I can to get in. Police work looks good on a resume. A girl's gotta do what a girl's gotta do."

"There's a muddy line between the things you want and the things you have to do," I said.

"Sheryl Crow," Bebe said. "*Leaving Las Vegas.*"

I could learn to like Bebe. "What about Lia's mom?"

"I don't know one way or another," Bebe said. "Her mom might be dead. Or her mom might just be real good at sneaking around."

"You don't like Lia, do you?" I asked.

"I worry about her," Bebe said with genuine regret. "As I mentioned, the protest wasn't the only time we dealt together. She did another internal affairs complaint on me about two years ago. It took a year to throw it out. Stanford found out and they rejected me outright. Police work makes you stand out from the pack, but unfortunately, brutality does not look good on a resume."

"Brutality?"

Bebe looked too small to be brutal.

"I dragged her away from a sit-down demonstration. She said that I sprained her arm, and made another internal affairs complaint on me."

There was a beep on her I-phone. She texted a quick reply.

Bebe took her APD coat all the way off to reveal her sexy decoy costume. She had a great figure despite her petite frame, or maybe she had creatively used underwire to make mountains out of molehills.

"If you ever need anyone to testify that Ophelia Paz, a.k.a. Lia Spaz, is mentally unfit, I'm your girl. We're on the same side here. If Lia killed C de Baca, I can pretty much keep her out of prison with all the stuff I've got on her on competency. If that's what you want."

"Cool." I smiled back at her. Maybe we really were on the same team.

She glanced at a text message and frowned. She let out a sigh.

"Just talk to me for a moment," she said. "It's warm in here. I don't want to go back out there again in the freezing cold and pretend '*me so horny*' for obese drunken idiots from Podunk, New Mexico. Aren't you supposed to ask what's a nice girl like me is doing in a place like this?"

"What's a nice girl like you doing in a place like this?"

"I was born in Hanoi. My father was a dissident. My mom did what she had to do to survive while he was in prison. When

I was seven, we moved to a refugee camp in Arkansas, of all places, as a political refugee."

"Arkansas?"

"It was worse than Hanoi. You wouldn't believe what they'll fry up in Arkansas and call dinner."

Bebe was the best student in the camp, and had always dreamed about being one of the expert witnesses she saw on TV, and in the movies.

"I want to work with torture victims and do war-crime prosecutions in the World Court. My mother and father were tortured in Vietnam, so it's personal."

Wow. My parents were stuck in traffic on the beltway once back in D.C. I was spellbound. To see her dressed like this, like a discount Madam Butterfly, partially because of Lia, hit me right in the gut. This woman should be arguing in the World Court, not decoying here in the War Zone.

"Do you like being a cop?"

"I hate APD. They say I have a bad attitude."

I didn't want to bring up Officer Nunez's characterization of Bebe as a "ho."

"Are there any Vietnamese cops you can hang with?" I asked.

"I'm the only Vietnamese female cop. The wives won't let the male Vietnamese cops work with me. They're jealous."

"You seem lonely. Do you have family here?"

"My mother's in jail. She says she knows you. Thuc Doan Le from D-9. My own mother's on the crazy list. Think how that makes me feel."

I remembered the little Vietnamese woman from the unit. Bebe had come from that? And I thought I had mother issues. Time to change the subject before she became completely depressed.

"So what are you working on now?"

She described her duties. APD's Mental Health Unit had only two and a half officers, and she was the half. The rest of the time she was stuck in Vice as a decoy. She was just too darn good at what she did for them to let her leave, especially now that they kept her at a trainee wage.

Bebe described the sliminess of standing out in the cold and affecting a fake accent. She leaned against me and took my hand.

"I suppose I could quit this and do nails like my sister," she said.

She would have been great at nails. I enjoyed Bebe's touch as she examined both of my hands, like a faith healer with a magic touch. If this was what a manicure felt like, I would break down and get one. What was the hell was she up to?

Bebe stared at another text message on her I-phone. She shook her head. She really didn't want to go out there.

"Please keep talking to me," she said. "We can pretend it is court business."

I would never get a chance like this again.

"Do you have any funny stories about your job?"

She told me about a few elaborate stings they had done on a dirty accountant. I think I had heard about it. They had busted the guy on soliciting, and then were able to use leverage to get him to roll on some of his big drug clients.

"I felt sorry for him, but he shouldn't be cheating on his wife with me."

"Cheated? How far do you actually go?"

"People think that cops can't get naked, or can't actually have sex with them."

I stared at her. "You *can* have sex with somebody?"

She laughed again. I couldn't tell if she was kidding or not. She kept touching my hands with her long nails. I had long since left lawyer mode.

She sighed again. "I hate doing this. God, sometimes I'm worried that I really am a discount ho like my mother."

Her phone beeped. Another text message. She didn't even glance at it. But the beep stirred something in her. Maybe it was a memory of her father, or just a sudden breeze as the door opened to let in the December wind. She glanced at Blue and White in the corner, then a tear fell. She immediately caught herself.

"I didn't want you to see that. I'm not as tough as I pretend to be."

"It's all right."

"I don't know what I'm going to do anymore. Your girl, Lia, ruined me. Really. She sent a copy of the disciplinary complaint to some of the schools I applied to. Each application costs like a hundred bucks and I lost it all. I've got to find more psych PhD programs soon. Deadline's coming up and I might not be able to make it. I can't keep doing this."

She covered her face again. She was actually crying. Her I-phone rang again. This time, she took it.

"*Me so horny,*" said another cop, his imitation of the legendary Papillion Soo Soo in *Full Metal Jacket* roaring through the ear piece. "Get your ass out here and love someone *long time*. We have a quota to fill."

"Give me a fucking minute," she shouted, keeping her hand over her face, wiping away the tears. "Personal time, okay?"

She hung up the I-phone and wiped away another tear. She said nothing for a long minute as she tried to force the tears to stop. The tears kept coming.

Bebe said, "God, I want to quit so badly, but I can't fucking afford it. I'm so broke. Who ever thought I'd go to the police academy to learn forensics and end up as a trainee ho?"

Her profanity surprised me. She was serious. Dead serious. She looked at me, her eyes still moist from tears. I wanted to rescue her so badly and get her ass into Stanford where it belonged.

"Do you need money?" I asked.

"You would help me out?" she asked. "Besides, I really like you. Once this case is over, maybe we could be friends. I'm sure you could help me with the law stuff. We could stay in touch."

Blue and White vanished suddenly, their pool cues left on the table.

"We have a lot in common," she said. "I don't meet many smart guys like you on this job, that's for sure. We could hang out."

Other than Lia, no one had called me smart lately. "Hang out?"

"I'd like that," she said. "Maybe we can be together."

"Together?" I asked. I wasn't sure what she met. My white knight impulses now bubbled to the surface. This was a woman worth saving.

"I just need a little help. Please help me out, Dan. Please. No one would have to know."

"A little help?"

"Just a little loan," she said.

I reached for my wallet. "How much do you need?"

"Just a hundred for a new application to Stanford."

I actually did have a hundred from an ATM stop I'd made earlier. I took it out of my wallet. I noticed my hand was wet with sweat as I handed her the money. At that time, I knew I was supposed to say that this was a loan, purely intended for her Stanford application. I didn't say that. Didn't say anything.

She took the money with those long nails and laughed. Her tears vanished, as if they'd never been there.

"Good news," she said. "I just made another bust."

"Who?"

Within seconds, strong hands came from nowhere, and jammed my face against the dirty floor. Dollar bills floated out of my wallet and into the air. Someone grabbed my hands and jammed them behind my back at an angle beyond what nature intended. I heard the sound of cuffs.

Bebe's high heel now squeezed against my back into a pressure point, like an acupuncture needle. The rest of the APD Vice Unit joined her, guns drawn.

Blue and White returned for the big finish and now laughed in the distance. Blue handed White a thick wad of cash. Apparently they had bet on me succumbing to Bebe. White had won.

Bebe stood on top of me. "Well, good news for me," she said. "That's quota for the night."

"The money was for you to go to school. By 'hanging out,' I just meant you know 'hanging out.'"

Really? I wasn't even sure I knew what I meant. I claimed that this was a 'white knight' impulse, but was it?

"You think a jury will buy that?" She moved her heel and let my face fall to the floor. "Oh wait, it's a city code violation, you don't get no jury, just a judge."

My claustrophobia kicked in immediately. I was in a dirty coffin, I couldn't move . . . for the rest of my life, for the rest of my afterlife. How could I be so stupid? As I stared at the floor, the entire case flashed across the pine floorboards. I could probably beat the case on entrapment. She had lured. I was indeed doing a client interview, asking for information. I had given her the cash, but there was no *quid pro quo*.

Then I realized that neither quid, pro, nor quo really mattered. I was a somewhat prominent lawyer. The video would show me handing cash to an attractive Vietnamese woman dressed like a prostitute. The audio was ambiguous. Hell, the whole thing was ambiguous.

I knew I would make the front page of the papers. My mugshot would run one more time in the metro section, even if I got off. I would never get a female client again; certainly never get a juvie. I didn't see getting many big banking clients either. Effectively, I would be finished as an attorney in New Mexico.

Bebe said nothing for a few more moments, then laughed again.

"Nobody would believe that you just wanted to hang out for a hundred dollars with someone dressed like me. I think we even got a close-up of your hard-on."

The coffin walls closed even tighter. I heard the police radio chatter, some chatter back on this end, then nothing.

All of a sudden the cops started laughing. Bebe Tran bent down and unlocked my handcuffs. One cop gave her a twenty.

"Got you." Bebe smiled with triumph. She smiled at Blue who now had White's money. Those bastards had bet on me again.

I got up and shook myself off. I was about to say something.

"I'm keeping the vid," Bebe said. "Lia's crazy if I say she's crazy! So do not fuck with me, or I will bust you for real."

I took a breath. "Was all that talk you were giving me for real?"

"I did not lie to you once," she said. "Your bitch really kept me out of Stanford. I really do need the money, but I can't take it from you. Appearance of impropriety, and all that. I'm just here to protect and serve."

"Protect and serve who?"

She walked back onto the street. "I guess that depends on you."

Winter of Our Discontent

I DON'T REMEMBER THE next two weeks of December. The glorious Indian Summer had long since ended. Now was the winter of our discontent, although technically it was the late fall of our discontent. The sun hadn't risen yet over the Sandias when I woke up each morning, but somehow I was always late by the time I made it to Santa Fe.

Joel had me sit in the library on a plastic chair. A new associate was in my old office. The research for Barkoff was stimulating, but I hadn't done land use law in years. Like struggling up La Bajada, I kept wheezing to make it to the top of the learning curve. I either rushed my work and screwed up, or took too much billable time to make it perfect.

Joel was more disappointed than mad at my failures. I tried to explain that I had been a criminal lawyer all my life, and didn't know an interrogatory from an asshole. He was disappointed that I used "can" instead of "may" in my memos, for example, as if I should have known better. I was a lawyer. I was a writer. But, I wasn't the best legal writer.

The one good thing about staff attorneydom was that Joel no longer cared if I left at three in the afternoon. He stayed occupied preparing for the environmental review of the ski area and only checked my memos every few days.

* * * * *

Most days, I'd make it back to Luna's office in Albuquerque by four or four thirty, depending on traffic on I-25 and whether or not there was a prison break, or an accident under the Paseo del Norte Bridge. Luna and I talked at her office as we worked to put Lia's case together. Luna told me a little more about herself, about her job as a junior prosecutor in Crater County. What happened there could be a novel.

She then told me how she became the District Attorney of Crater County, then lost a near unanimous recall election and became a defense attorney in Albuquerque. She didn't tell me what had happened to the father of her child, or even who it was. She was very much alone right now and not too happy about it.

"I never thought I'd be a single mother like the bimbos I knew back in high school," she said. "I used to laugh at them. I was going to be different."

After twenty minutes of Luna, I would hurry across the street to Albuquerque's District Court, and personally file my motions with Eva before she left for the day. She often wrote in the corrections, adding lines for signatures, which I usually forgot.

Other than my time with Luna, the five minutes with Eva were the highlights of my day. She was like the mom I never had. She laughed at my silly jokes, and as a foreign film buff, she even got some of my more obscure movie references. Eva didn't judge me for my failures, or my indecision, as I felt my own mother had. And as a former nurse, I knew Eva would try to come up with a cure for whatever ailed me.

My nights were spent talking to Lia. One night, she asked about Bebe Tran and I nearly froze. Lia gave her perspective on Bebe, which was that she hated Bebe as much as Bebe hated her. I didn't know whom to believe. I had tried to set up more wit-

ness interviews, but the D.A. wouldn't set anything until after
the competency issue was settled.

As for the evaluation, the tests had finally begun in earnest.
I grew nervous when Lia told me that she didn't get along so
well with Dr. Romero. She kept asking me what to say to the
doctor.

I didn't know. I wished there were Cliffs Notes for competency tests. I told Lia to tell the truth, but I didn't know if that
was the best thing either.

One day Luna was in court, so I had more time to spend with
Eva. I now felt torn between Luna and Lia.

"*Danika,* you definitely should go with Luna instead of
Ophelia," she told me. "You and Luna have so much in common."

"What? What do we have in common?"

"You don't really want to be *ugyved,* lawyers," she said. "I
can tell. But that doesn't mean that you both aren't good at what
you do, *Danika.* And you both have heart, a lot of heart."

"How about Lia?"

For some reason, whenever I mentioned Lia, Eva would
shake her head and call her by her full name. "*Hagyd Beken.*
Stay away from Ophelia."

"Should I get out of Lia's case?"

"You can't, *Danika.* Once competency is raised, judges
around here won't let you get out of a case until the issue is settled. But Judges hate the *orult* cases where the defendant might
be crazy. They clog up the docket and sometimes they never,
ever end."

I stared blankly. Hungarian was a difficult language.

"*Orult* means crazy," she said, understanding my blank
stare.

"I have a feeling that case will end, one way or another."

"You never should have said Ophelia is *orult,*" Eva said. "I have a bad feeling about that. The judge got a nasty memo from C de Baca. When C de Baca is *kormanyzo,* governor, he'll be signing all our paychecks. One way or another."

Holly Jolly Hell

BY DECEMBER 21ST THE days were short and the nights had grown very, very long. I had a bad case of bah humbug until I received a green and red Christmas invitation with a Las Vegas, New Mexico postmark. Inside, I found a primitive-looking picture of Santa Claus flying over a New Mexico landscape. Santa was about to land on the chimney of a vaguely adobe building. The style was abstract. Picasso in prison.

It took me a moment to recognize the building; it was the state hospital in Las Vegas. Lia had invited me to the state hospital's annual holiday party for families. This was the only party I'd been invited to all winter. Joel hadn't even invited me to the firm's party at his house. At least I had a date to one Christmas party, even if she was a resident at the asylum.

When I arrived in Las Vegas on Christmas Eve, the hospital's peculiar mix of industrial angst and adobe charm was now covered with holly and jingle bells. The plastic angels on the barbed wire on the roof looked like they, too, were in bondage.

I shouldn't have been surprised to wait in line to be frisked by an armed guard as I entered the hospital. All the presents were opened, and wanded, too. I felt guilty because I didn't even think of bringing a present.

The party was held in a converted activity room, Multi-purpose Room B. Multi-purpose Room B could pass for an elementary school classroom, considering the drawings on the wall. All the tables were bolted down, and the television and stereo had been smashed. I wondered what the residents had been watching that had upset them so much.

Today all of the visitors were greeted by a choir of residents. They were quite good. At first glance, I thought they were the real Whitney Houston, Britney Spears, Lindsay Lohan and Paula Abdul. Why not, all of them could be residents here. I soon realized that the choir was really comprised of residents in drag.

I waited with the families before they brought the rest of the residents out. They looked like the families of the prisoners I had seen at MDC in Albuquerque. I even recognized the kid I had stared down at MDC when Lia was released. He still wore his Albuquerque Isotopes jersey.

Isotope was out of his element. He said nothing, but he clearly remembered me. His anger at me yelling at him at the jail had not reached its half-life yet.

This was a hospital for the criminally insane, as well residents like Lia, who were in for an evaluation. Many of the other residents looked like hard-luck cases. If they hadn't been charged with a crime, they'd be out in the New Mexico night, panhandling for change, or playing guitars and singing. Others looked surprisingly normal. I even recognized a lawyer who now was a resident. There but for the grace of God.

The residents were in surprisingly good spirits. One of them hugged me and I hugged him back. He smiled.

"Merry Christmas," he said. "Are you Jesus?"

"I don't look a thing like Jesus. I think you're confusing me with someone else," I said. "But Merry Christmas right back at you."

Lia and the other residents from the diagnostic wing came at last, accompanied by an elderly guard who seemed more like their grandfather. Lia wore the same clothes she had when she went in, but the staff had let her wear a sprig of mistletoe in her hair for the season. She had gained a little weight.

The food at the party was excellent. Supposedly a famed English chef from Taos had freaked out in his kitchen. He was here pending his own diagnostic on aggravated assault with a kitchen knife. I didn't care. The man could make a mean posolé with pear salsa.

Over sips, Lia introduced her roommate, the legendary Heidi Hawk.

"I've heard so much about you," Heidi said. "Do you remember me?"

She was indeed the paint-sniffer I had represented all those years ago. She'd since moved to Crater, and then to Albuquerque. Apparently the stress of her days at the grand jury division had pushed her a little over the edge.

"You saved me that time. If I hadn't gotten off drugs, I'd be dead, instead of here. And here, I'm on honors."

"Good for you," I said. Seeing her here on an embezzling rap didn't exactly make me proud.

"Lia can't stop talking about you," Heidi said. "We love her here."

Lia blushed, then introduced me to the entire female ward. They all smiled and hung on her every word. In the ward, Lia was everyone's friend. The friendly staff treated her like one of the family and Lia positively glowed.

"She's the granddaughter I never had," the elderly guard confessed as he gave her a Christmas hug. "My real grand-daughter's in prison for meth."

Lia whispered to me, "Just because I like it here, doesn't mean I'm crazy. I'm trying to impress them with how I am so not crazy!"

"Sure you're not," I said.

I picked at the bowl of piñon brittle flavored with cashew nuts and green chile that was beyond delicious. I resisted any jokes that involved nuts.

"I don't know why I'm so hungry these days," Lia said. "Am I getting fat?"

That's a question no man can answer correctly. "You look fine," I said. "Maybe it's just your meds affecting your appetite."

"I'm not on meds," she said. "I told them I didn't want them, and they can't force them on you without your consent. It was a law passed in the last session. House Bill 651, the Mental Health Bill of Rights Amendments."

I didn't know if Lia's lack of medication was a good thing. At least she still had her memory. We sat on a couch and talked. I didn't want to hold her hand. It was almost like a church social event. Physical contact was discouraged.

Lia told me she had adjusted to the routine of the hospital. She had become the pride of the unit's art classes. They still weren't done with the diagnostic tests, as Dr. Romero was only here on Fridays. So Lia painted landscapes and wrote poetry. She had always loved to paint and had done the cover of the Christmas card, a very big honor. She pointed to her paintings on the wall. She had drawn a lot of sad women standing alone in the mountains looking at the sunset. Georgia O'Keeffe meets Sylvia Plath. One sad woman stared at an angel hovering over Sandia Crest near Albuquerque. Oh my God, the angel had my face.

"You're my angel."

I had never been an angel before, and felt uncomfortable that the people in Multi-purpose Room B would look at my face every day. Perhaps that's why the man had confused me with Jesus.

I turned away from my face, and looked at Lia. She really did think of me as an angel.

There was so much I wanted to ask her, but she was so happy right now. I didn't want to spoil the moment. I was her lawyer. I couldn't really love her anymore. I looked into my heart but wasn't sure what I felt. She was my client now, with inevitable appeals that could last a long time.

Part of me wanted to officially break up with Lia right then.

But I looked into her eyes, then around the room. Even the most downtrodden psychopathic killers received healthy doses of yuletide cheer from their families. I didn't have the heart to break up with Lia here, especially under the mistletoe. I would be the Grinch who stole Crazy-mass. I'd have to wait until after New Year's.

Just then I heard something. It sounded like footsteps on the roof. My next thought was that it was a jail-break. The noise grew louder. The residents started a slow clap.

"He's coming!" Heidi said.

He's coming? Who would come to an insane asylum on Christmas Eve?

The clapping grew louder, and the pace increased. The lawyer/resident stomped his feet into the "We will rock you," chant. The others joined in. Somehow the residents kept a perfect beat.

"He's almost here!" Lia shouted.

"What's going on?" I asked.

"Don't you know?" Lia asked. "He's coming!"

"Who's coming?"

The room reached a frenzy; the clapping and stomping were deafening. I was indeed being rocked. Was this some kind of mass delusion?

"Do you believe?" Heidi asked Lia.

"I believe," Lia said. She looked at me.

"I guess so," I said.

The energy in the room had now hit the level of pandemonium.

"Do you believe?" Lia asked again.

"Yes, I believe," I said.

"He's here!" everyone yelled. "He's here!"

"Who's here?" I asked.

Then I heard a knock on the door.

"Ho ho ho."

Oh my God! It couldn't be.

Then again. "Ho, ho, ho!"

The elderly guard opened the door. "And now for the man we've all been waiting for. . . ."

"Ho, ho, ho!" My God, it was him! Sure enough, Santa Claus entered the room, much to the delight of all present.

I heard a guard whisper to another that it was Jimmy, one of the residents from another wing who was in on a lifetime commitment after a murder, but I didn't want to know that, not tonight. To everyone in the room, including me, he really was Santa Claus. They might boo Santa in Philadelphia, but not here in Vegas.

Some children of the residents were in the room, and they rushed to sit on Santa's lap. Lia did too, then hurried back to me.

"What did you wish for?" I asked.

"What do you think?"

I surprised myself by finding a tear in my eye. I didn't much believe in Christmas, but yes Virginia, there was a Santa Claus.

"Say it," Lia said.

"What?"

"That you love me."

Before I could say anything, a buzzer went off. Apparently one of the residents had tried to escape.

"We're in lock down!" the elderly guard said. "Everyone back!"

There was an audible groan.

"Does that mean Christmas is canceled?" the young boy on his lap asked.

"You can't cancel Christmas," Santa Claus replied.

The kid began to cry.

"Let's get moving people," the guard said. He had a billy club.

The residents formed an orderly line and headed through the door back to their cells.

I waved at Lia and mouthed the words "Merry Christmas."

The End of the Trail

I RAN OVER SOME mistletoe in the parking lot. By the time I hit La Bajada and began the descent toward home, I was in full Humbug mode. Why hadn't I broken up with Lia? Why was I still on the case? Why didn't I tell her that I *didn't* love her?

I didn't get any other Christmas-party invites, and my parents were out of the country again. They still weren't talking to me because I had brought an accused murderer to their home for Thanksgiving. Had Lia only been up for insider trading, it probably would have been cool. But Joel let me take Christmas Day off, and I watched football. I always cheered against schools that had rejected me, so I was very happy to see Michigan, Duke, Virginia and Stanford all lose badly. I was especially glad to see Stanford lose, because of Bebe.

I had to work December 26th to make up some lost hours. Joel didn't talk to me; he was on the phone all afternoon. When I told him I needed to leave a little early, he actually smiled.

I arrived at the District Courthouse in Albuquerque right before five. Except for Eva, the building appeared empty.

"I feel terrible that I always dump on you," I said as I entered her office.

"Back when I was a nurse, everybody dumped on me. That's why I left."

"Being a secretary can be a dump, too."

"You're so funny, *Danika*. Why are you still alone at almost forty? You should make your choice and settle down. How's your *orult* girlfriend, Ophelia?"

"She's my client, not my girlfriend."

I tried to make a joke out of it. "I'm hiring a forensic psychologist to do a competency exam, and ask her if she understands the difference between love and law."

Eva laughed. "I don't know. I think you're more *orult* than she is."

"You might be right. No more criminals. I'm done with involuntary manslaughterers. Know any cute aggravated burglars?"

Judge Kurtz wheeled into the office and gave us both dirty looks. I guess a few other people were working this late in the afternoon over Christmas.

"I can arrange for you to spend some time with the aggravated burglars if you keep this up," he said. "There's a room over in the jail called the Honeymoon Suite."

"I'm going to use that Honeymoon Suite line in my book," Eva said. After the judge left, Eva smiled. "I have an idea."

On December 27th, Joel asked me to stay past five. I had to finish reviewing more environmental statutes for him and put them into a notebook.

Joel had said, "I want that notebook to be so complete that a six-year-old could pick it up and do the case."

I noticed a new lawyer sitting in the library. He didn't look much older than sixteen. Seventeen tops. Joel glanced at my work and told me that he liked my trial notebook. We then went over all my work on the Barkoff cases. I apologized that I was taking a little longer to conquer the learning curve. I vowed to do better.

He frowned. I didn't say anything. I knew what was coming.

"This is not working out," he said.

"I thought you liked my work."

"I liked your work when you were working, but you are always busy working on your own case."

I must not have done as good a job of juggling as I had thought.

"So what does that mean?" I asked, even though I already knew.

"It's time to terminate our relationship. I'll send you a check forthwith."

For a minute, the only word I heard was "forthwith." Who the hell said words like forthwith? It took me a second for it all to sink in. "What about the trial notebook?"

"Someone else will be able to do the trial. Thank you."

He looked at me. "You could have gained the skills, but I could see your mind was on something else. I let you work only thirty hours a week, and you couldn't even give me that."

They had once called me a baby lawyer when I was back in Aguilar. Now I wasn't even a baby lawyer any more. I was an aborted lawyer.

I was about to beg, but I knew it was too late.

He was right.

I didn't bother to say goodbye to Victoria. Shit, I had at least expected to last until after the New Year. The wind from the Sangre de Cristos whipped right through me as I walked away.

"Get the hell out of here," the wind yelled. "You don't belong here."

God had given me a chance, a real chance at financial independence, a real chance at Santa Fe and all it represented: My mother's love. Money. Power. Intellectual fulfillment. Self-esteem. I had blown it. Badly. And for what? An accused mentally ill murderer? Santa Fe had just spit me out on my ass.

There was construction on St. Francis Drive, so I had to

leave Santa Fe via Cerillos Road to the west. I had been pushed out of the adobe bubble and now had to drive out on the other side of the turquoise curtain, as if I was using the service entrance. I had always avoided Cerillos Road and now I remembered why. This was the ugly part of Santa Fe, the part that looked like . . . well, it looked like Albuquerque. I passed CITY DIFFERENT PAINT AND BODY, and CITY DIFFERENT PLUMBING, and they didn't look so different after all. Even an adobe Wal-Mart was still a Wal-Mart.

Joel had just stepped on my rose-colored glasses, and I needed those glasses for the drive home. On the interstate heading southwest, I headed directly into the sun. I tried to squint, tried to see the road by looking at the white line to my right, but even the sun laughed at me right now.

I had a moment of guilt as I thought about my dad. I had let him down. I had let my mom down. I had let myself down.

A car honked. I had veered out of my lane. I went back into my own lane, and slowed slightly. I still hadn't made up my mind on the whole life-thing when my phone rang. Was it Lia? Was it Joel changing his mind? Was it my dad dying?

It was Eva. "I need you in the judge's office first thing tomorrow morning. It's very important. Can change your work schedule in Santa Fe?"

"That won't be a problem," I said.

Lia called that night but I didn't take her call. I couldn't tell her that I had been fired. I couldn't tell her that maybe her brilliant white knight wasn't so brilliant anymore.

The next morning Eva's office was empty and the judge's door was closed. Then Luna walked in and nodded at me. She wore spandex, as if she had just detoured from an early morning marathon. Whatever it was, this must be important.

"What are you doing here?" we asked each other.

Eva came out from the judge's office as if she'd been monitoring us from inside. "I've got two tickets to Governor Mendoza's Farewell New Year's Eve Party."

That was a big deal. It was the biggest party of the year.

"But there's one condition," she said. "Luna, every morning I hear you complain about being so lonely. And *Danika,* with you, I hear the same thing every afternoon."

Luna and I looked at each other.

"What are you saying?" Luna asked.

Eva smiled. "You two can go to the ball, but only if you go together."

Luna and I both blushed. We were about to protest, but I looked at Luna and smiled. It took her a bit longer, but then she smiled too.

"Is Luna, Cinderella?" I asked. "I know I'm no Prince Charming."

"Don't sell yourself short," Luna said.

Hugology

LUNA PICKED ME UP at dusk on New Year's Eve. She had the nicer car, after all. I felt a bit of anxiety returning to Santa Fe, as if the entire city would laugh at me.

Luna was dressed to the nines in the beautiful Acoma dress I had seen her in the first time. God, so much time had passed since then.

"We're just going as friends, right?" she asked.

She looked to be even more nervous than I was.

"Just friends," I said, and gave her a hug, just in case.

"I'm a hugologist," she said. "I analyze hugs."

"So what does that hug say?"

"You better keep that thing in your pants."

Outside, it was cold; more snow was on the way. What was it about this year? So much for global warming. This year New Mexico had received more snow than Minnesota.

After a few moments of silence on the interstate, I dropped my little bomb.

"I got fired," I said. "Do you still want to be seen with me?"

"I've pretty much been fired from every job I ever had," she replied. "There are times I wish I could fire myself."

"Me too, but I thought you were this amazing lawyer."

"Amazing? I'm amazing at closing arguments and cross-examining cops. I'm amazing at understanding my client's complicated issues and coming up with a strategy to help them. But I'm disorganized. I'm moody. I get bored doing this every day when I would rather be running in the mountains. I lose my patience with clients who expect me to produce a miracle out of my ass every time. I have Jen to help me and she, *is* amazing, when she isn't running off with yet another bad boyfriend, which seems to be every other week."

"Ouch," I said.

"And you know the worst thing? I've become a sucker for lost causes."

"Well, maybe I can help you out with that."

She considered my offer, but didn't respond.

As Luna drove up I-25, I thought of the Pueblo Indian Revolt of 1680. The Spanish had already conquered New Mexico, but the Natives under a charismatic leader had pushed them back. I felt like the Spanish must have after they were expelled. They had probably come up this same route to re-conquer Santa Fe.

My stomach churned as we exited onto St. Francis Drive and headed into Santa Fe, as if expecting an ambush. It was quiet, way too quiet.

We stopped for dinner at a chic Italian restaurant in the Sanbusco Center near downtown. I had thought Sanbusco was a great Spanish explorer, but Luna explained that it stood for Santa Fe Builder's Supply Company.

"I think they're a wholesaler for drywall," she said. "Sorry it isn't more sexy."

The cappuccino machine was broken at the restaurant, and we needed to be hyped for the rest of the night and the long ride home, so we ended up next door at a chain bookstore that had a café.

"I know I should support independent bookstores," she said. "But the chains just have better selection. And better coffee."

An author in dark clothes sat in front of the store, pimping his book as if it was the finest girl on the corner. I laughed. An author doing a signing on New Year's Eve, talk about a loser.

Luna went over to him and slapped him in the face. "You bastard," she said.

She turned around and the author looked at me with a mischievous smile. I bought his book.

"Dude, sorry about her," I said. "She must have confused you with someone else."

"She knows who I am," he said. "Do you?"

"Not really."

"She and I go way back," he said. "This is my third book since I met her."

I didn't quite understand what he meant. He seemed to know who I was as well.

"But in the future, never slap an author," he said to Luna. "Bad things can happen."

Governor Mendoza's party was at the Hotel La Fonda. The hotel's nickname was actually "The Inn at the End of the Trail." The Old Santa Fe Trail had run from Franklin, Missouri to its end, right here at the plaza. I don't know if the old cowboys would have felt comfortable at the La Fonda. It was now a haven for mildly rich New Yorkers and Hollywood types who were in town soaking up local art and culture.

The La Fonda's architecture was a tip of the hat to the multistoried masterpiece that was Taos Pueblo. It was far more touristy than the upper-crust Eldorado. This was the fake Santa Fe.

We weren't ready for this trail to end, so we walked around the streets of downtown. a little longer. We didn't hold hands, but we did an odd bumping as flirtation. Each bump lingered more than the one before. We passed the hotel and walked all the way to the Cathedral Basilica of St. Francis of Assisi. Luna looked at the old cathedral, and silently prayed.

"What are you praying for?" I asked.

"I don't know."

I'd pray, but my job isn't coming back from the dead. I did not know if I wanted it to. I then reconsidered and prayed for Lia. It couldn't hurt.

For no reason at all, Luna gave me a hug. It was a hug I could not read.

"Are you ready?" she asked.

"Honestly? I don't know."

Party Politics

FOR A NEW YEAR'S Eve party, it was a remarkably glum affair. Everyone dressed in black, not to be stylish, but as an expression of his or her political outlook. I recognized many of the people from the election party: Rhiannon Goldstein Manygoats, and a few Sikhs named Khalsa. I think all Sikhs were named Khalsa. I also shook hands with some of the Navajos in their suits and bolo ties.

Joel was there with his new protégée, the teenager. They ignored us. Everyone did. No one wanted to celebrate the end of this year, the end of this term.

Luna and I sat at our own table and nursed our single Michelob Ultra for the night. She told me she watched carbs, so I figured I might as well follow her lead. We certainly didn't want to risk drinking and driving, or even drinking and dancing. We didn't want to have to defend each other.

"Whenever I sleep with someone, something bad happens," she said out of nowhere. She still looked glum after seeing the author in the bookstore, as if he was responsible for her misfortunes in life. I knew not to ask her about it.

"Hey, the last woman to sleep with me is in an insane asylum," I said.

"I'm not in an asylum. This week at least."

"Are you about to sleep with me?"

"Don't get too excited," she said. "I'm not as crazy as your last girlfriend, as far as I know. Well, as far as you know."

Eva waved at us from across the room and hurried over. She wore a black suit identical to my mother's courtroom outfit but accented hers with a scarf and hat that gave it a more European look.

"You two make such a perfect couple," she said.

"We're just friends," we said at the same time.

"Jinx," we both said.

Eva laughed. "*Danika,* I still got it," she said. "As a match-maker at least. *Sok szerencet.* Good luck to both of you."

After Eva left, Luna and I talked about our past relationships. This was always dangerous for me. First I told Luna that I had loved a reporter named Amanda who had broken my heart. My next girlfriend, Veronica, lasted a few years but she outgrew me, which wasn't hard.

"I'm on a schedule," Veronica had said. "Either you're on it, or you're not."

Once Veronica got her law degree, she married an entertainment lawyer in Hollywood, and they started their own firm. I had sent a script to them, to see if they would help me get representation, but they had rejected me.

"No one wants to read about Hispanics in New Mexico," Veronica had said. "Especially when it's written by a rich wimpy white boy."

I didn't tell Luna about the model who wanted to collaborate with me on a script about her life. No one would believe that a beautiful woman would drive across the country to see me, and then ask me to take her shopping for drapes at Target. I had been hoping for something more than drapes.

A mariachi band started playing. Their sheer exuberance got everyone out onto the dance floor, even the Sikhs, who had surprisingly good rhythm. I recognized the singer's voice immediately and a shiver went through my body. Her name was Anna Maria Villalobos.

More than ten years ago I had represented her then fiancé, Jesús Villalobos, in my first murder case. I had actually been the one to propose to Jesús on her behalf and had been best man at their wedding.

The skinny girl had grown into a beautiful woman. She had the big voice of an African American diva roaring out of a tiny Latina body. Anna Maria had made it to the Hollywood round on *American Idol*, and should have won but had been thrown off before the finals because of an undisclosed scandal.

She still had the same ring on her finger, so true love had lasted. Unfortunately, her true love languished in prison on new charges. I thought I had saved someone. I guess I had failed after all.

Somehow the band magically gave both Luna and me rhythm. Anna Maria smiled at me from on stage, and blew me a kiss. During one song, she came over to us as we danced, mike in hand. She sang her heart out just to us in Spanish. Even though I couldn't understand the words, I sensed the emotion welling in her with each note. Luna sensed it too.

No, I didn't love Lia in the same way that Anna Maria loved Jesús. No one could. Anna Maria had stuck with Jesús for ten years now, and I wanted to dump Lia after only a few weeks.

As I looked at Luna dancing with me in her black dress, something hit me. Maybe it was the music, maybe it was the altitude taking the oxygen away from my brain. Or perhaps it was seeing a ray of hope in her big brown eyes during the darkest week of my life.

I knew one thing.

I could love Luna with that intensity.

She was the perfect woman for me. Even her flaws were holes that I could fill. But could Luna ever love me back? I was hardly the perfect man.

A drunken reveler stumbled over Luna and she lost her balance and fell to the floor. Her dressed accidentally hiked up to show a long, perfect leg.

I laughed out loud.

"What's so funny?" Luna asked.

I thought back to my mother cooking in the kitchen and burning her hand.

"You remind me of my mother," I said. "Believe it or not, that's a compliment."

Luna recovered nicely. After a set of thumping *Tejano* numbers, Anna Maria came over to our table where we talked about old times. I did buy her CD; it was the least I could do. I made her autograph it, and she signed it To DANIEL, WHO SAVED MY LIFE.

I felt good about that. I had saved a few lives in my time, but hers was the one I had valued most of all.

Anna Maria gave me a hug, then went back to the stage. She looked back at Luna, and pointed to me.

"This one has a great heart."

Luna smiled. "I've never met a lawyer who saved a life before," she said. "With the exception of Jen, most of my clients hate me. When I was a prosecutor, *everybody* hated me. I only got one vote in the recall election."

"I would have voted for you," I said. "I can try to save your life too."

She laughed. "I need that right now."

Anna Maria did another set in Spanish, a romantic set. Her Spanish version of "Brown Eyed Girl" gave me goose bumps. Luna and I slow danced to "Brown Eyed Girl," with our brown eyes closed tight. I made it a point not to grind, though Lord knows I wanted to.

Later, after a long sad song, Luna whispered in my ear. "I'm ready."

"Ready for what?" I asked.

"I don't know."

We walked to the parking lot to find that snow had already accumulated on the streets.

Luna swore under her breath. "I don't want to drive back to Albuquerque in this."

"My parents are in Aspen," I said. "Do you want to stay at their house?"

She caught a snowflake in mid air with her tongue.

"Just to stay the night," she said. "We're not going to do anything, right?"

There was dread in her eyes.

"I think you could take me in a fight if I try anything," I said.

She didn't say anything, just nodded. When we got in the car, I told her to make a left by the church.

I played Anna Maria's CD on the way. Damn, she was good, it sounded as if she was singing right next to us. If she hadn't spent her youth in the small town of Aguilar and married a prisoner, she'd have been a superstar by now. What was it that Anna Marie had done to get kicked out of her big chance with *American Idol*? I told Luna the story of Anna Maria's wedding to Jesús while he was out on furlough from the Boys' School.

Luna laughed out loud. "That's both romantic and pathetic at the same time."

"That's me, romantic and pathetic."

She looked at me. "You're not . . . romantic."

We drove into the foothills toward my parents' house. There was something about this snow. The flakes were dirty, almost like ash. Perhaps there had been an explosion in Los Alamos, at the lab. Luna started driving slower, as if she never wanted to arrive. Then she shivered.

"You okay?" I asked.

"I don't know," she said. "There's something about this snow."

I thought about the night Lia was arrested. It seemed as if so much time had passed since then, although it had been only a few weeks.

We reached the house and got out of the car. Luna leaned in close to me, as if she wanted me to protect her from something.

I fiddled with the house keys. My parents' door was a redwood piece of art, but as a functioning door, it was a piece of shit.

"Hurry up," she said. "I have a surprise for you inside."

Son of Obligatory Sex Scene

WE HURRIED TO THE guest room, but my parents had converted it onto storage for their mementos from around the world. The only functioning bed was in my parent's bedroom, so we started a fire in fireplace next to the bed and put Anna Maria's CD in the player. Anna Maria sang "Strangers in the Night" in Spanish. Luna's heart melted with each "do be do be do."

Luna held my hand and moved closer to me. Instantly I felt warmth. I rubbed her neck to get the friction going. She rubbed my hands. She knew about trigger points.

I leaned closer to Luna and we ended up dancing. I remembered the old joke that people shouldn't have sex standing up. It might lead to dancing like this.

Luna took a deep breath as if gathering courage. Then she kissed me. A real kiss. I felt as if I was in a Greek temple about to fuck the Oracle of Delphi, umm . . . Greek style. Nothing had ever felt so wrong.

I couldn't help myself. I kissed her back. Suddenly I felt warmth all over my body. When I released her, I felt the cold from outside. When I kissed her again, the warmth returned.

"We probably shouldn't do this," she said as she grabbed my crotch. "But—"

She was pleasantly surprised.

"That's all your fault," I said.

She undressed, then slipped under the covers. I caught a glimpse of her utterly perfect body before she slipped the covers on. This woman had dropped a kid a short while ago, yet she had kicked gravity's ass. Yet I hesitated. I had never been so afraid of making love to a woman before. I kept waiting for my phone to ring, or my parents to come home out of the blue.

Anna Maria still sang of love in Spanish. Perhaps it would all work out with the next *do be do be do*.

Luna's breasts were high and firm, I wondered if they were real. She had a few condoms with her that she pulled out of her purse.

"I've been carrying these with me ever since I got pregnant," she said. "I never thought I'd use them."

"Well, you can now,"

She put one on me with her mouth.

I nearly lost it right there. It had been awhile for both of us, and it felt so good to be inside her. It was different from that night with Lia. Lia had attacked me, but here I wanted Luna far more than she wanted me, even though she had made the first move.

And then it was over. Too quickly. And yet somehow, magic kicked in. Moments later I was ready again. This time it lasted a long, long time. And then again. She became loud, passionate.

"You're the perfect woman," I said.

She laughed. "Hardly."

I usually wasn't much of a cuddler, but I held her tight. I did not want to let her go. Ever. Luna shivered slightly and edged closer to me, as if she was frightened of something outside.

"No one's out there," I said. "It's just you and me."

She did not want to let go. She held me as if I would protect her from all the evil in the world.

"I like that," she said. "The whole you and me thing."

"I do too," I said. "You're the hugologist, can you read this hug?"

She said nothing, but held me tighter. "How about this one?"

Then it turned midnight. I looked at Luna, almost waiting for her to disappear. It was almost too good to be true.

I took a deep breath. I had survived another year. Why had we been so nervous? Everything would work out just fine. This next year would be even better than the last one.

This was an absolute perfect moment. Luna squeezed my hand. I squeezed back. Maybe we could do it one more time.

Then, as if on cue, my phone rang. Who would call on a night like this?

It was Lia, of course.

"Happy New Year," she said. "They let us stay up late."

Luna stared at me as if I had just turned into a pumpkin.

"I love you," Lia whispered from the other side of the phone.

What do I say to that?

"Did you hear me," Lia said. "I love you. I love you. I love you."

Luna went into the bathroom, still naked. Oh my God, she was so beautiful.

"I love you, Luna," I said into the phone.

"What?" Lia asked.

"I said I love you too, *Luna.*"

Suddenly it dawned on me. Oh shit. Oh shit. Oh *Shit*!

"Did I say that out loud?" I asked.

"Yes," she said.

"I meant Lia."

"Then why did you say Luna?"

"Just a mistake."

"Is she there with you?"

Suddenly the toilet flushed. It made a loud noise. I didn't know what to say.

"Is she there with you?" Lia demanded. "Don't lie to me! You're my lawyer! Is that fucking skinny bitch there with you?"

I still didn't know what to say. Luna was now back in the room, staring at me.

"Yes, she's here with me," I said.

The phone went dead.

Luna said nothing. She heard enough to put two and two together. If she could have left the house right then, she would have, but the snow had turned my parents' house into our prison cell for the night.

"You just don't get it," she said. Even though it was my parents' house, I let her stay in the bedroom and I wandered out toward the kitchen. She slammed the door behind me.

Dead Spot

I DIDN'T SLEEP AT all that night. Had I blown it with both my client and my co-counsel? Had I blown it as a lawyer and as a lover?

The shame of unemployment hit me fully as the dawn arrived. What a way to start the year. I looked out my parents' bay windows at the snow on the Sangre de Cristos; the sun did not make it through the clouds. We might as well be in our own private Siberia. It was a black-and-white movie out there, a depressing Russian black-and-white movie without subtitles.

I tried to take stock of my life as I stared at the top of the mountains. I didn't want to get out of bed. Ever. But hunger forced me out by nine. I didn't shower. Instead, I put on a pair of my dad's old sweats and made some instant holistic oatmeal my parents had bought in Finland.

"Do you want breakfast?" I yelled.

"Not interested," came the reply.

I heard the sound of the Nordic Trek 9001 from my parent's exercise room. Luna definitely had her own way of fighting stress. My cell-phone rang again. I looked at the caller ID and recognized the prefix for Las Vegas, New Mexico. I almost let it go, but I supposed the healing would have to begin here.

"Lia, I'm so sorry."

"It's Dr. Romero." She was normally unflappable, but today she breathed heavily. "Lia attempted suicide last night."

"How?"

"One of the techs accidentally left a medication cart in the open. We were on a skeleton crew for the holidays. She left your number on the note. It told us we should call you."

I panicked. It was all my fault. All my fault!

"Where is she?"

"She was airlifted to Albuquerque," Dr. Romero said. "I don't know if she's going to make it."

"I'll be there as soon as I can," I said, "but I'm in Santa Fe and the snow is pretty bad up here."

"Please try," Dr. Romero said. "Maybe you can get through to her."

Get through to her? I didn't want to tell Dr. Romero that I was probably the reason Lia was in this position. I mumbled something about trying, then hung up.

"Is something wrong?" Luna popped into the kitchen. She was in my mom's Cornell University sweats, which created all kinds of unfortunate images.

"Yeah," I said. "Lia tried to check out."

"Check out?"

"Suicide attempt. Pills."

Luna shook her head. "I don't know what to say," she said.

"There's nothing to say."

"Can we go home now?" she asked.

I looked at the snow. "I don't know. You're the one driving."

Despite my anxiety over Lia's health, we waited another hour for the snow to begin to melt. Santa Fe had indeed become a Siberia. Luna made it out of the subdivision to the highway where the roads were plowed, somewhat. She had only two near misses on the way. Once we got into Santa Fe proper, the traffic on Paseo de Peralta became Paseo de Alto, stop and go traffic all around. Why was everyone up so early on New Year's Day?

I then remembered. It was the new governor's inauguration.

Governor C de Baca. It hurt to even say the name.

It didn't take long to find the many security checkpoints that were snarling traffic. C de Baca's official inauguration diverted traffic through some tight security.

"What an asshole," I said, breaking the silence.

"He did lose his wife," Luna said. "You can't blame him for being paranoid."

I told her what little I knew about Lia's suicide attempt.

"What am I supposed to say?" she said. "I knew this would happen. It's not your fault. I told you every time I sleep with someone, something bad happens. I'm cursed!"

I didn't know what to say to that one. I felt like Santa Fe itself was cursed. The atmosphere had changed now that C de Baca had taken over New Mexico. Even the snow looked darker. I looked at a private security guard who watched us intently. He looked at me as if I was on the terrorist watch list.

I also heard the distant sound of a parade, but with the wind, the sounds of the marching bands were shrill and out of sync.

We eventually made it out of Santa Fe alive. Despite all the snow this year, New Mexicans still couldn't drive in it. Worse, a truck had jack-knifed at the bottom of La Bajada by the mostly dry Rio Galisteo. Both directions of the freeway had stopped dead. I tried to call University Hospital, but I was in the one dead spot between Albuquerque and Santa Fe. Even satellite phones didn't work here. This was no-man's-land, a dead spot in every sense. Luna stared out the window as if she wanted to be anywhere but with me. Ophelia Paz lay in a hospital room forty miles south of us, but with the traffic, she might as well be on Mars, or perhaps Venus?

A public-safety aide walked along the road.

"Fatal crash," he said. "Prepare to be here for hours."

It was New Mexico, so I didn't bother to ask if alcohol was involved. It always was.

I had to relieve myself, badly. I exited the car, and walked to the bridge over the Rio Galisteo. This pathetic little ditch actually had running water for the first time I could remember. I remembered when I was six, and we were visiting my grandmother for Thanksgiving. We had been stuck in traffic over the Hudson River on the George Washington Bridge, or the Tappan Zee Bridge, one of those. I remembered peeing. A gust of wind nearly blew me over the side. My dad had to run to the side of the bridge to keep me from falling into the Hudson.

Right now, a jump into the Rio sounded like the perfect career move. There was access to the Rio Galisteo below, without climbing any fences. There wasn't much of a current in the Rio, and the fall wouldn't kill me. Yet I felt an incredible weight on me that would push me through the mud down to the center of earth, down to Hell itself . . . where I belonged.

I finished my business, zipped up, and sat on a rock on the edge of the riverbed. Luna came over and sat on the rock next to me.

"Could you turn your back for a second? And keep guard?"

She hurried under the bridge. I didn't know how good of a guard I'd be in a crunch.

"I'm still not talking to you," she said, coming back.

She sat back down on the rock. I tried my phone again. I couldn't bring it back to life. I couldn't bring anything back to life. We stared at the weak current of the Rio Galisteo. Eventually this creek flowed into the Rio Grande, just like Portia Smith C de Baca's body would have done. My DNA and hers would probably have met in the big dam in Elephant Butte reservoir, or perhaps make it through a tunnel in the dam and somehow end up in the Gulf of Mexico.

I stared at La Bajada to the north. The ridge now looked a million miles high.

"You still love her," she said.

I thought for a second. "No, I don't. I do feel for her, though. She's a human being. Something bad definitely happened to her.

Governor Elect C de Baca, excuse me Governor C de Baca did something to Lia. I don't think Lia murdered Portia in the strictest sense of the word. Either she didn't do it, or she was mentally ill. She doesn't deserve to go to prison."

We stared at the Rio some more. A large black bird flew overhead. Was it a vulture?

"Do you love me?" Luna asked.

I looked at her. "I'm starting to."

"Shorter and better answer," she said.

"Yes."

No, I really didn't love her. Not yet. I wanted to love her. I wanted it with every bit of my heart, but I knew there was something missing and I knew what it was.

"Well, I don't love you," she said. "Not right now. I just can't risk it again. I've been hurt too badly too many times. And I've got a kid. You're certainly no father figure."

That hurt.

We sat for what seemed like an hour, and held hands in spite of ourselves. The electronic gods must have finally smiled on us; my phone rang.

It was Dr. Romero. Lia would live.

I heard the sound of tow trucks up above. The mess would soon be cleared, and we'd be on our way. I wasn't sure I wanted to make it to my destination.

When the traffic finally did clear, Luna drove to University Hospital.

"Do you mind if I wait in the car?" she asked. "I've been here before and it brings back some very bad memories."

She didn't specify why she had been here; whether she'd been a patient or for someone else. She looked like she was about to puke.

I nearly had a freak-out in the parking-lot elevator when the door took an extra second to open. My claustrophobia kicked in, but I stopped myself. I didn't have enough energy to freak out.

The Korean nurse at the reception area, a Nurse Song, took me to Lia's room.

"Luna just called and asked me to help you," Nurse Song said. "My daughter, Jen, is Luna's secretary."

Inside the hospital room, Lia wore restraints over her arms and legs. She looked years older. I walked to her bed, but didn't know what to say. Lia finally recognized me with a nod. She said nothing for a while. I put my hand on her wrist. She moved her wrist closer to me, as much as she could within the restraints.

"I'm so sorry," I said. "Are you going to be all right?"

"I'll live," she said in a weak voice.

"Why did you do it?"

"It wasn't you. Well, it wasn't all you."

"Thanks," I said. "I guess."

We stared at each other for a few minutes. Neither of us could think of anything to say. Nurse Song finally came back..

"Time to go," she said. "Visiting hours are long over. "

I got up to leave.

"You've got to promise me something," Lia said.

What do I promise her? Not to fall in love with Luna? Too late for that. To fall in love with her? That wasn't going to happen either.

"What is it?"

"You've got to save me, Dan. You've got to save me. You've got to save all of us."

"All of us?"

"It isn't just me," she said. "C de Baca is evil. He will ruin the state. Ruin it for kids. Ruin it for women. Just save me from him. Whatever it takes."

"I'm no savior."

"Right now you're all I've got. I can't lose you."

"Just let me be your lawyer from now on. I can't be both."

"Just don't say that I'm crazy," she said. "Ever."

The Dog Pound

I COULDN'T SLEEP THAT night, of course. I listened to Anna Maria's CD over and over. I thought of Luna when we danced to "Brown Eyed Girl." Then I thought of Lia at the hospital, drawing a picture of me as an angel. My brain shifted between images of the two women. My throat closed and my eyes burned.

I tried not to, but I cried anyway.

I hadn't bothered to make a New Year's resolution, but it should have been to be a better lawyer. A real lawyer. That wouldn't be hard; I couldn't be any worse. I was done as a Santa Fe lawyer. I had to be an Albuquerque lawyer, whatever that meant. I still woke up early, expecting to drive north, and felt a depression when I had nowhere to go. I had to keep busy.

The January weather was strange. It looked as if it should snow, but it never did. The week after New Year's, I did a circuit through District and Metro Courts as a way of gaining exposure to the Albuquerque legal community. I couldn't believe they had forgotten me so quickly, but after a few of my dumb jokes, they remembered me all too well. I got a break when a lawyer was run over crossing the street, and he handed me a file before the ambulance took him away.

"Plead the second DWI down to a first," he said from a stretcher. "And get rid of the 'Ag!'"

I quickly learned that an "Ag" meant the defendant blew over a .16 or refused to take the exam. It was a mandatory two extra days in jail. Getting rid of the Ag was a reason for top lawyers to justify charging thousands.

The big lawyers charged thousands, but I only charged my peers a few bucks here and there for hearings. I would double my rate if I actually had to run between courthouses, I decided. I soon found myself standing in for other lawyers in a wide variety of settings. Unfortunately, to make a living in Albuquerque, lawyers had to be in three places at once. After former Olympian hopeful Luna Cruz, I was probably the fastest lawyer in town, doing the Metro to District to MVD (Motor Vehicle Division) dash in record time.

But when it came to Lia's case, I was still on a big, steep treadmill. The suicide attempt had pushed her testing back, and there was nothing I could do to make the evaluation come sooner. Lia had also lost phone privileges, so I couldn't even talk to her.

She did, however, somehow sneak a call to me after hours one evening and I asked how she and C de Baca met.

"He was a football coach at Albuquerque High," she said. "I was a cheerleader so I knew him from hanging out on the sidelines. He was always checking me out. After the season was over and we won the state, there was a party over Christmas break at this girl Brandy Porter's house."

Lia stopped talking and began crying. Really crying.

Then a stern voice came from her end of the line. "Lia, you're not allowed to call anyone."

Then the line went dead. I tried to call her back, but couldn't get through. I called the main switchboard. A receptionist with an Indian accent told me that "Lia had been moved to another facility."

"Could you check on her?" I asked. "Is she all right?"

"I don't have access to that information, sir?" the operator said. "I'm here in Bangalore."

I felt as if I might as well be in Bangalore.

Lia said that C de Baca had molested her when she was in high school. I needed someone to verify that story. I didn't know whether it would help or hurt the competency case, but overall, if someone backed up Lia's claim, it had to be a good thing. Perhaps I could prove she had Post Traumatic Stress Disorder.

The State wouldn't schedule more witness interviews until we had the competency thing settled. I would have to find Lia's witnesses on my own. There was the girl from her cheerleader squad who could possibly back up Lia's story about C de Baca in high school. She shouldn't be too hard to find. Lia had gone to Albuquerque High, and it was just across the street from me. They should have records of Lia's time there.

By January 7th, school was back in session. Albuquerque High, a.k.a " The *'Burque'* High" or "Bulldog City," was known as Albuquerque's most diverse school. It had a large percentage of Hispanics of course, but it also housed the relatively rich kids of UNM professors, some Asian immigrants, African-Americans from the south side, and a rainbow coalition of everyone else who had moved to Albuquerque's blossoming downtown.

When I awoke the next morning I called the school office, but was put on infinite hold. I would have to run with the Bulldogs in person. Unfortunately, when I drove over, I found that the visitor's lot was a long way away from the school entrance on the south side of the building.

It was eight o'clock in the morning, and a few straggling students hurried to avoid a "tardy" on their permanent records.

Someone shouted at me as I entered the building.

"Where's your girlfriend, *ese*?"

I turned and recognized Isotope, the kid I'd seen at the mental hospital. This kid was everywhere. He still wore that stupid oversized baseball jersey for the Isotopes, Albuquerque's triple A baseball team. Up close, Isotope's skin was terrible, perhaps he'd gone dumpster diving in one of the radioactive dumps at Sandia Labs. He looked to be well over eighteen, probably here for the school's famed "return to class" program for felons.

Isotope said he laughed about me with his radioactive gang-banger friends.

"I guess you like that crazy pussy," he said.

An Albuquerque public school policeman ignored Isotope, but eyed me suspiciously. Isotope belonged here, I didn't. The guard directed me to walk though the school metal detector. Security here was as tight as District Court, but the fact that I was an older stranger made me disreputable.

"Why are you here?" the guard asked. "You're not on my list."

High school guards were on the low end of the guard totem pole. And this guard looked the part: he was short, squat and somewhat wooden.

"I'm trying to look somebody up," I said. I quickly realized that didn't sound right. "I'm a lawyer. I'm investigating a case."

I showed him my crumbling bar card, and he escorted me to the principal's office. Damn, where had the time gone since my own high-school days? These kids' parents were my age. Even some of the teachers could have been my kids. Well, I couldn't say I was old enough to be their father, since I had lost my virginity at an extremely advanced age, but that was a story for another time.

When we arrived at the principal's office, a sign over the door read, THE DOG POUND.

The short guard told me to sit in a corner with some students, as if I was Jeff Spicoli from *Fast Times at Ridgmont High*, and had been busted with a dime bag. The principal's office felt, well, like a principal's office. I could see why he called it the dog pound. The students had the big brown eyes of abandoned puppies.

After I presented my bar card to the receptionist and a few vice principals, the receptionist finally indicated that I could enter the principal's office. Albuquerque High's mascot was the bulldog, and Principal Tommy Odelia certainly looked like one. Could a bulldog be a pit bull?

There was an instant gasp of recognition. He was the man I had nearly run over back in November. If he had been a few feet over, I would have killed him. Shit.

"You're a lawyer?" he asked incredulously as he scanned my bar card yet again.

"Uh . . . yeah," I said.

"You drive like a madman. I see you out there every morning. You should clean your damn windshield; you're going to kill someone!"

"I'm sorry, *sir*," I said.

"Well what do you want?" he asked.

"Sir, I'm representing Ophelia Paz, who's charged with killing Portia Smith C de Baca."

The Bulldog chewed on that information as if it was a tasty bone with some nice fatty gristle.

"I can't release any information without a court order," he said by way of an answer. "It's the law. You know that."

"I don't want records," I said. "I just need some information. Off the record."

He said nothing. His eyes made it clear that I had a minute, tops, to make my case.

"You remember Governor C de Baca?" I asked. "Back when he was a teacher and a coach here?"

The Bulldog nodded. He thought for a minute, then smiled, as if he tasted blood. My blood, or C de Baca's? "This is about the girls he molested, isn't it?"

I smiled. Hopefully he was on my side.

"What happened?"

"Let me start from the beginning," the Bulldog said. "The governor and I go way back. Way back."

"Start from 'way back' then."

The principal was surprisingly friendly for a moment. Perhaps it was lonely in the dog pound.

"C de Baca's from the neighborhood, just west of the campus," the Bulldog said. "He used to run around with some bad gangs. He flunked out of school here, back when I was student-teaching. I kept him from going up to the Boys' School at Springer a few times. One time his brother Xavier threatened to kick C de Baca's ass if he didn't straighten up, and C de Baca came to school with a black eye the next day. That worked for a couple of weeks."

I had forgotten about C de Baca's past. The principal showed me a yearbook from C de Baca's first year as a teacher. He had been voted teacher of the year by the students. The quote next to the picture said, "With God, all things are possible. Thank you Albuquerque High for taking a chance on me. I have learned more from you than I will ever teach."

The Bulldog continued. "C de Baca straightened up when he found Jesus through Xavier, then married that rich white girl, Portia Smith. Her dad was a minister at one of the mega churches. I think he's on national television these days."

"Was he married when he was here?"

"No, that came later. C de Baca had found Jesus, but his relationship with Jesus was not perfect. He was always back-sliding, especially when Xavier was out of town. Still, I helped get him hired first as a teacher's aide, and then as a teacher and assistant football coach, back when I was the athletic director. It was weird, but the head coach let him do all the locker-room speeches. You know, the 'Win One for the Gipper' kind of thing."

"So did he win one for the Gipper?"

"That year we went ten and oh. We're one of the smallest schools in Albuquerque; we don't have big money like the schools in the heights, yet we killed them that year. Then we beat Aguilar High for the state title. That was the year they had the kid who murdered Victor Slade, who was supposed to be the golden boy."

I bit my lip. I had defended Anna Maria's husband Jesus on killing Victor Slade. I didn't bring that up.

The Bulldog shut his eyes, remembering the glory days. Those days were long gone here. Those kids out in the lobby sure didn't look like athletes.

He walked over to the bookcase and pulled out a copy of the yearbook for Lia's junior year. It was not dusty and looked as if it was used regularly. I scanned it. Lia had once been in almost every activity, even debate club and honor society. She had been queen of the school. I was proud of her.

The Bulldog continued as I leafed through the pages.

"One day, Ophelia Paz came into the office and said C de Baca had come on to her, said another girl, Brandy Porter, would back up her story. There were three Porter sisters, a sophomore, a junior and a senior—Brandy, Sherry and Margarita. Their nickname was the 'Liquor Sisters,' since they were all named after drinks."

Brandy Porter. The Liquor Sisters. That sure sounded interesting. I leaned forward. "Did you believe her?"

"Lia wasn't a very credible witness," he said with a sigh. "Then there was a change in her over Christmas break. No one knew why."

I realized that most yearbook photos were taken during the Fall semester.

"A change?" I asked.

"That was when he supposedly raped her. The other cheerleaders said she suddenly developed mental problems, and began calling her Lia Spaz. They all said she imagined the whole thing. All except Brandy Porter."

"Could it be Post Traumatic Stress Disorder?"

"We never knew what the trauma was. Lia dropped out in January and we never saw her again. I made C de Baca take a job at another school. On the west side. He got to be head coach in a year or so, they won state, he got on the city council in one of the suburbs . . . and you know the rest."

I couldn't read the Bulldog. I didn't know whether he had believed Lia or not. He looked down at a few current student disciplinary files and made some marks with a red pen, as if drawing blood. He put one file in a box marked EXPULSION.

I had better get him back on track.

"What did this Brandy Porter say?"

Because of alphabetical order, Brandy Porter was on the "P" page with Lia Paz. She looked bi-racial, or possibly tri-racial: Latina, African American and Native. The caption underneath her picture read, HERE COMES TROUBLE!

"First Brandy agreed with Lia. Then she backed off when Lia disappeared. Then she disappeared herself. Never graduated. If she had backed Lia up, C de Baca wouldn't be governor right now."

Time to make my play.

"Can you help me find her?"

He thought for a second. He looked at Lia's yearbook picture, then at Brandy's.

The Bulldog frowned. "This isn't for you. This isn't for Lia. God, I hate that sanctimonious prig, C de Baca. He's going to cut our budget to the bone."

Perhaps Lia was right. This wasn't just about her. Maybe I did need to be on a mission.

"So where is she?"

"Brandy's working at one of the Indian casinos outside of town." He gave me a name. "She came up to me last week when I was playing the dollar slots."

He laughed for a moment. "I once got a lap dance from a former cheerleader. While they're here in Bulldog City I protect them. Once they're out, it's too late."

"Do you have a phone number for her?"

I had asked one question too many. He took the yearbook away from me and slammed it shut. Then he gave me a look that could be described as that of a mad dog.

"I think I violated about half a dozen rules and policies regarding student/teacher confidentiality in the last half hour. You better not call me as a witness."

"Or what?" I couldn't help but say.

"Or I'll have your ass busted for reckless driving in a school zone!" He wasn't smiling. "I mean that. I'll have security show you out."

Isotope and his gang kids stood by the door, and a girl giggled at me as I walked out.

"What a loser," she said.

"This school is the loser," I replied. I regretted the comment instantly but the security guard pushed me out the door, so I didn't have a chance to take the comment back.

Fall Out Goy

OF COURSE I FORGOT where I parked in the lot. Unlike the Subarus and hybrids in Santa Fe, every car in the visitor's lot was a massive pick-up truck or SUV, which blocked the view of my little Saturn.

Footsteps came from behind, but when I turned around I saw nothing. Maybe a dog had ducked behind a car. There was no security in the visitor's lot so I was on my own. The footsteps grew faster and faster, like a pack of wolves.

I walked to a car that looked like mine, but it was someone else's. Where the hell was my car? I was more than a hundred yards away from the school now, almost in another school district. Suddenly, someone jumped out from behind a big pick-up truck.

"You!" I said.

It was Isotope and his three fall out boys about to take me beneath the planet of the apes.

"*Burque High!*" Isotope said as if it was a challenge.

One boy hit me hard with brass knuckles, right in my ribs.

I had taken a karate class for all of a week back in D.C. I swung hard, putting every ounce of energy into a punch to one of the other boys. I hoped to God my punch was hard enough to knock him out.

No such luck. I had grown soft up in Santa Fe; my punches didn't have much power.

Isotope swung at me. "Don't ever dis the 'Burque,' *ese*."

It was almost refreshing. This wasn't part of the big Santa Fe scandal. This was pure Albuquerque violence. I punched hard, but hit only air.

Another fall out boy hit me in the gut. I went down hard to the ground, but I kicked him before he could get near me again. I had worked too damn hard to give up my wallet. It hurt like hell but I got back up. The boy came at me again but he must have been high or on something. He was moving in slow motion. I dodged easily and he fell flat on his face.

He got up and I pushed him into one of the cars, which had a car aarm that sounded if someone just touched the vehicle.

"Please stand away from the vehicle!" the alarm said in a voice that sounded as if it was from a nuclear reactor.

I now had my fists up, ready to go.

"It's so on," I said. When did I start talking like I was in jail? I figured I had to stand strong for another thirty seconds.

At second twenty-nine, Isotope and the boys decided to run. I pretended to chase them, but I had sprained an ankle, and couldn't keep up. They escaped before any security came.

After I gave a report to the police, I limped back to my car. I felt a moment of triumph until I realized that my tires were slashed. I was so very stuck here in Albuquerque.

Don't "dis the Burque" indeed.

Liquor Sister

LIA WAS STILL IN the Albuquerque hospital and didn't call that night. I went there to try to visit but Nurse Song said Lia was still "off privileges." Her little phone call to me had apparently pushed her progress back even further and limited her privileges even more.

"She's doing as well as can be expected," Nurse Song said.

"What does that mean?"

"She's making a full recovery," Nurse Song said. "But her doctors don't want her to have contact with anyone who might upset her."

"*Upset her?* But Dr. Romero said—"

"Dr. Romero doesn't make all the rules."

I walked away in a huff.

The next morning I treated myself to breakfast at a sophisticated bistro known as The Grove, in the East Downtown (Edo) neighborhood and yoga district. The genteel yoga studios mixed with cheap motels, the word's scariest hot dog stand, and a closed fish and chips joint. The Grove hired the most beautiful waitresses in town.

Across the street I watched a woman and a man leave a transient motel and hurry to a fast food kiosk. The man bought the woman a taco. The woman looked every inch the street whore, and I hated to think what disgusting things she had to do for that taco.

Hell, that was the practice of law, doing a lot of disgusting things for a taco.

Inside, the Grove was an oasis from the Albuquerque desert. The place was a "chick restaurant" at lunch, but during breakfast it was filled with lonely aging yuppies like me.

I ordered oatmeal and *Flora Azul* coffee for ten times what I would pay if I made it at home. A waitress I recognized, Bailey, took my order, but a beautiful young Latina brought the food out to me. She looked familiar. Maybe all the recent rejection had killed me but I wanted to prove my manhood by harmless flirtation with a waitress.

"You look like—"

"Luna Cruz," she said. "The famous lawyer, right?"

The woman's accent clearly placed her from Mexico.

"How do you know Luna?"

"She's my sister. I'm Selena."

"How come she doesn't talk about you?" I asked. "And how come you sound like you're from Mexico?"

"How you say, it's a very long story," Selena said. "It's not over yet."

"Has Luna said anything about me?" I asked Selena.

"No." Selena said. "Was she supposed to?"

That afternoon, my bruised body had recovered enough to seek out Brandy Porter at the tribal casino. I had collected a hundred dollars in cash from an attorney over lunch. I didn't know if it was a good thing to have that much money when going to a casino, or not.

I didn't want to look like a "suit," so I went with jeans, and a sweatshirt that said "Brown," my alma mater. Outside of

Albuquerque Academy, most folks in New Mexico didn't realize that Brown was a university. They probably thought I was
advertising the color of my underwear.

The casino could be Santa Fe on steroids. Other than the
Albuquerque airport, it was the biggest adobe building I had
ever seen, seven stories high, which was about as high as an
adobe building ought to go. The packed parking lot was nearly
the size of Disneyland's, but there were no cartoon characters
there to help guide you.

In New Mexico there wasn't much to do besides gamble and
eat. Several people lumbered out of their cars and waddled
slowly to the buffet entrance. As for the gamblers, many New
Mexicans thought that with one push of the spin button they
would become instant millionaires. I hated to admit it, but on
some days of my unemployment, I'd come here too, gambling
penny slots, happy when I won two dollars and fifty cents.
Today, I had some real cash in my pocket.

Inside, the massive main room smelled like secondhand
smoke and spilled soft drinks. Since they were on sovereign
tribal land, casinos were immune from the State's tough smoking regulations. C de Baca had vowed to repeal all smoking
restrictions. As I coughed, I had another reason to hate him.

Unlike most Vegas casinos, this casino had a view to the
beautiful mountains beyond. No one noticed the billion years of
geography outside; most people's eyes were two feet in front of
them on the slot machine. This particular casino also wasn't the
kind of place that the crew from *Ocean's 11*, *12*, or even *13*
would try to rob. Most gamblers played the penny slots, rather
than the nickel or even the dollar machines. There were a few
high-rollers at the tables, but the feel was more Las Vegas, New
Mexico, than Las Vegas, Nevada. Some gamblers looked like
they'd just left the state hospital as they mumbled to themselves
and stared at the machine's video screens.

Off to the side, I heard music coming from a popular rock and roll chain restaurant. The wait staff, largely Native American, danced to the Village People hit "YMCA," spelling out each of the letters in the song. I didn't know whether to laugh or cry.

And yet after a few seconds, the scene grew on me. The dancers had snuck in a few secret moves of their own that made the silly dance somehow magical. Perhaps they had done a rain dance, as it actually started raining outside.

Security was surprisingly tight around the penny slots with several guards dressed in white uniforms with the gaudy tribal logo. I couldn't resist remarking that Tribal casino guards were a step higher up the totem pole. That mixed metaphor wasn't a racist remark, was it?

One guard eyed me warily. He wasn't Native American, but apparently had grown his red ponytail into a political statement of solidarity. I looked too clean cut to be a penny slot gambler, but not dressed well enough for the main tables. I was most definitely too skinny to be here just for the buffet.

I approached Pony Tail and asked him about Brandy Porter. I told him I knew her from *"Burque* High."

"Brandy must be on break," he told me. "She works the non-smoking room and the area around there."

I thanked Pony Tail and went over to the non-smoking room, the only place I could breathe.

While I waited for Brandy, I played the latest penny slots in her designated serving area. There was one machine "Risque Business" that displayed a "Gentleman's Club" with images of dancers on its face. Three dancers on one line activated the "animated strip tease bonus." Sex and gambling. Ouch! I tried that machine but the tiny slot didn't accept my crumpled dollar bill.

I knew if I put my hundred dollar bill in that slot, I could just kiss it good bye.

I found a woman shouting "change" and exchanged the hundred for ten ten dollar bills. Then I found a machine that had a TV show from my youth. It took my ten without complaint and played the theme song as if it was on meth. Every spin brought me back in time to when I watched that show. Life was so good back then. I was hooked after the second spin. I played three lines.

The woman next to me frowned as she watched me hit the spin button.

"Three lines?" She was gambling all forty-five lines, which I thought defeated the whole purpose of penny slots. "How do expect to win if you don't take risk?"

I did win fifty cents on the machine, then lost three cents a spin until a voice asked "Soft drink?"

I turned and barely recognized Brandy Porter from her high-school picture. The years had not been kind. Brandy was an appropriate name; she looked like an alcoholic, a real liquor sister. She was a heavy-set woman; apparently she gained little aerobic benefit from walking around the relatively clean air of the non-smoking room. She looked jittery, as if she chugged the warm leftover cokes on the way back.

No money filled her tip jar, and her luck certainly wouldn't improve from the gamblers in the penny slots. An obese lady in an orange outfit and orange hair didn't even say "thank you" when she was given a Diet Coke. Brandy's sour disposition grew worse with every spin.

I almost didn't want to bother her. This sad woman couldn't know anything, or if she did, she had forgotten after years of this routine.

Brandy stopped by a machine called "Mayan Princess." The Mayan Princess on the machine had streaks in her hair, just like Lia's. The scene on the front looked like Chichen Itza. Brandy wiped up some coke that had spilled on the seat.

"Are you Brandy Porter?" I asked.

"Why do you care?" Even her voice sounded beaten. Her yearbook entry had said HERE COMES TROUBLE! Trouble was now too tired to walk away. "You can play now. I just wiped off the machine."

I had better sit at the machine. I put in a ten and played ten lines at a penny. I did get two "scatter pyramids" which gave me a dollar.

"What do you want?" she asked.

I spun again. I almost got five princesses in a row, which would have given me the "sacrifice bonus." I had better do it again. I knew I would win next time. Or the time after that. I hit spin.

"Sir, what do you want?" Brandy said impatient, yet in no hurry to push her cart.

I forced myself to make eye contact, even if it meant I would lose a potential penny jackpot. I hit spin again.

"What can you tell me about Ophelia Paz?"

Her eyes indicated that I had hit a "machine malfunction" key in her brain. I put a dollar in her tip jar.

"Ophelia was my best friend until junior year. She was a great girl, had a great heart."

I smiled.

"Then she became Lia Spaz. The crazy girl."

Brandy walked away from the Mayan Princess as fast as her weary muscles could push the cart. Then she looked for the next round of players. "Cokes, coffee. . . ."

I got up and chased after Brandy, barely squeezing through the penny slot crowd. God was everybody in this casino overweight?

"What about Governor C de Baca?"

She slowed a little. I put a ten in her jar.

"Who are you?" she asked.

"I'm a lawyer." I didn't know what to say. I just went with "This is official court business."

"This is Indian land, it ain't part of America. You can't come in here without the tribe's consent."

Brandy looked afraid when she said that. She pointed to a

black surveillance camera. Apparently this had happened before. She then pointed to Pony Tail and stared at me again.

I put in forty bucks into her tip jar. I realized I had already spent the rest, one line at a time. Where did the money go?

Brandy frowned. "The last guy tipped me eighty."

She kept walking, served another person, then another. Neither tipped. Who was the last guy?

I hurried over to the ATM machine and got forty more. There was a three-dollar surcharge. Shit.

I tipped Brandy the other forty and she gestured to a corner, next to another Mayan Princess machine. It must be the most popular game in the casino. They were all over the place.

"This is the dead spot," she said. "The cameras are blocked here by the big screen TV over there and the free pick-up truck they're giving away."

Part of me wanted to buy a ticket for the free truck. It was only a dollar.

"Sit down and put in a few bucks. You've got like a minute."

I put a scrunched dollar into the machine. It was rejected, so I had to exchange it for a crisp bill with Brandy. That one worked. Thank God.

The theme song played and I spun. Had I already morphed into a compulsive gambler along with my other neuroses? Time to get to the point quickly.

"Tell me about Ophelia and C de Baca."

"He was one of the coaches. All kinds of sports. He was also my 'Values Clarification' teacher," she said. "'Values Clarification?' That's a like a total laugh. He was like a total horn-dog asshole."

"Do you think he came onto Ophelia at the party at Christmas Break?"

"Something happened. They left the party together. She was never the same after that Christmas. I wasn't like an eyewitness or anything."

"Did she say anything to you?"

"She didn't stop talking. None of it made any sense. And then she disappeared."

"Was she pregnant? Did she get an abortion? Did she—"

"She just disappeared. I heard she was locked up in Vegas. I never saw no kid, but I didn't see her again for years."

"How about C de Baca? Did he come on to you?"

She nodded, then said, "I got to get going."

"I really need your help," I took a gamble. "For Ophelia's sake."

She hesitated, and looked around nervously. "Like I said, something happened to her. I know that. He did it. He screwed her. She's never been the same. I've never been the same."

"Did something happen to you?"

Before she could answer, music emerged from the machine. Sacrifice Bonus. That had to be a good thing.

"You gotta bonus," Brandy said. "You might win big."

Brandy hovered over me and I knew why. If I won the mega-jackpot, she expected a cut. She might even give me all the secrets about Ophelia and C de Baca. I pushed more buttons for the super reward round. My eyes grew bigger with every free spin. Who knows? Maybe there could be a Rattlesnake Lawyer slot machine someday with a 'Litigating for Godot' bonus round.

The machine displayed three altars on the screen for the Sacrifice Bonus. Brandy told me to go with the center box. I touched the center altar.

The machine spurred, and then sputtered.

"Looks like you won two whole cents," Brandy said. "I really got to get going."

She pushed her cart.

I took one more look at the Mayan Princess. I didn't want to quit, but I had to. I got up and left sixteen credits in the machine.

An old lady asked, "Are you done?"

I nodded, then followed Brandy. Needless to say the woman won a "rollover" mega-jackpot. The Mayan theme song now played a triumphant tone.

Thankfully, there was a bit of confusion as the flashing lights went off. The theme song now blared through the entire casino.

The woman actually ran over and slipped me a twenty, for luck. I gave the twenty to Brandy. Twenty bucks bought thirty more seconds of her time.

"Did you ever see Ophelia again?" I asked.

"Four months ago," Brandy said. "Lia and this other dude came and tried to get me to join them. They wanted me to do a TV ad against C de Baca. But I wouldn't do it. They offered me a lot of money."

"Who?"

"He was dressed in black, like Johnny Cash. She called him Joel."

Joel? Oh my God. My ex-boss was in on this too? And I was worried that he would find out about Lia; he knew about her the whole time. Hell, he might have been behind it all. Joel?

"How much did he offer you?"

"Like a hundred grand." She looked down at her tip jar, which was empty except for my bills. "They said it would be tax free, off the books."

"Are you sure it was Ophelia?"

"Ophelia was going on and on about justice for women, justice for children and some weird thing called Article Seven or some shit. She was just as hyper as she had been back then. Trust me, I know Ophelia."

Article Seven sure sounded like Lia. I thought for a moment about Agua-gate, the big land transaction that nearly sank the old Governor, Mendoza. A lot of his powerful contributors had millions riding on the outcome of that deal and would no doubt do anything to see that he won. Once that deal went bad, Governor Mendoza's people lost a big jackpot of their own.

"Why didn't you take the money?" I asked.

"The Pueblo people here told me not to do it if I wanted to work in New Mexico again."

"At a casino?"

"Anywhere. Trust me, if you get fired from a casino, everyone thinks it was for stealing or something. You're like blackballed. Somebody on the other side must have gotten to them."

Before I could question her further, the jackpot song ended. By now, all sorts of casino officials had hurried to the area to take a photo with the big winner. Pony Tail had also come closer.

"I can't talk to you no more," Brandy said. "Or it's my ass. But your girl is in it deep."

She knew she had spent enough time with me; no amount of money would make her stay longer. Maybe it was another chug of Diet Coke, but she had the energy to get her cart rolling at a decent velocity. Before I could catch her, she made a hand-sign at a camera on the ceiling.

Within an instant, Pony Tail was next to me, his big hands on my relatively little biceps. I could fight off three juvenile delinquents. But they were kids. This was a man.

"This is sovereign tribal land," he said. "You are an illegal alien here."

He took me to a side door, opened it, and shoved me out. Then he slammed the door behind me.

I limped back to my car.

I found I still had some change in my pocket. I went to the back entrance and found another Mayan Princess game. As long as I was gambling, and losing, the tribe didn't mind. I did make it to the sacrifice bonus several times, but I always chose the wrong altar.

Breast Litovsk

I CALLED JOEL'S OFFICE from the casino parking lot once my
money ran out. Victoria said he had left early. Apparently there
was an "arts crawl" on Canyon Road in honor of the new legislative session. He was out crawling artistically, I supposed.

"He doesn't want to talk to you," she said in her clipped
British accent. "You've become a non-person, like Winston
Smith in *1984.*"

Non-person or not, I got in my car and headed north. On the
way up, I tried to call Lia at the Albuquerque hospital.

"There's no patient here with that name," the receptionist
said.

"Where is she?"

"I can't release that information," the receptionist said.

Lia must be back in Vegas. Was that a good thing?

I began my arts crawl at the western edge of Canyon Road,
just a block from the Roundhouse. I was winded immediately. I
had lost my altitude acclimation to Santa Fe's seven thousand
feet after only a few days.

Groucho Marks had said that he didn't want to be in a club
that would have him as a member. Well, I had been kicked out
of the Santa Fe club. I had mixed emotions

Snow lingered on the ground amidst a few stray patches of ice. I would have to walk carefully or wind up on my ass, yet again. I walked passed the first gallery, then the second. This street had more galleries than any other street in America. The various mixed media sculptures jutted out of the galleries like angry plants.

I would have a hard time picking out Joel. This wasn't your typical tourist crowd tonight. Everyone was dressed in black with big scarves, and big cowboy hats. Most of the boots came from species not found in nature.

I wandered through a few galleries, featuring strange take-offs on indigenous art. I noticed that even though many of the artists were Native, all the gallery owners looked and sounded like divorced white women from New Jersey. This week they favored dread locks and diamond nose studs. Next week, who knew?

I did find a gallery specializing in animation cells. They had a lot of pieces from *The Simpson's*, including a cell showing the lawyer character Lionel Utz standing next to his building with the caption *"I can't believe it's a law firm."* If I only had three thousand dollars I would have taken it home with me right there.

With my Brown sweat shirt and jeans the clerk could tell immediately that I couldn't afford the piece, so I threw on my messy parka that had every ski pass from every ski area in my life. There are people who look like a million bucks in jeans and a parka. I was not one of them.

I remembered Rhiannon Goldstein Manygoats had a gallery here and found her place a few galleries down: Manygoats Many Media.

Inside the gallery, Rhiannon had a bronze mixed media piece called "Prison Riot," which was an interpretation of the riots by way of Rodin's Gates of Hell. It was up for a silent auction with the starting price higher than a condo—even a condo in Santa Fe.

Rhiannon smiled. She remembered that I had helped her out

with a case when I was at Joel's office. She tried to chat me up about potential real-estate deals, so I played along, playing Mr. Santa Fe Up-and-Comer.

"Sure you don't need a new loft in downtown Santa Fe?" she asked. "You wouldn't have to walk so far to work."

"No," I said. "I'm looking for Joel."

I froze. Suppose she already knew that I was a non-person?

She smiled instead. I had just been paranoid. To her, I was still Mr. Santa Fe, part of her exclusive club.

"I think he's over at the Brest-Litovsk gallery," she said. "They're having an event there. Global warming, I think."

I took a stab at investigation. "You were involved in the Agua Caliente Trust. The trust associated with the whole Agua-gate scandal."

She laughed. "I really had nothing to do with that. They just needed a name on the deed."

"Round up the usual suspects," I said.

"Something like that," she replied.

An old cowboy in a tattered Western hat wrote in a bid for the riot piece. A man in a suit and suspenders like Gordon Gekko from Wall Street immediately followed with a higher bid.

"Are you going to put in a bid?" she asked.

"Maybe next time."

I headed deeper up the canyon. The current of people in black thinned as we went further eastward, away from down-town and toward the mountains. I finally found the Brest-Litovsk gallery, which specialized in the art of Eastern Europe. I wish Lia were here to tell me if Brest-Litovsk was in Russia, Ukraine or Belarus. The building was adobe, but once I crossed the threshold I felt as if I was in Dr. Zhivago's waiting room in Russia.

Many of the Eastern Orthodox icons on the stucco walls looked identical to the New Mexican *santos,* the popular religious icons in this neck of the woods. Someone had mixed the babushka dolls with Navajo storytellers, to the tune of a thousand dollars a babushka. There was also a thousand dollar chess set. As I looked at the board, I thought of the pattern on the floor of the Metropolitan Detention center, and I nearly toppled over a pawn.

Before I could get over to Joel, the owner, a petite woman with a Russian accent, took a look at me and my scummy parka. She mentioned they had a sale on unsigned posters in the back. Did I really look that poor?

I brushed her off and headed for Joel. Joel was dressed in black of course, as was his wife. He looked at thousand dollar water colors of the steppe, as if Grandma Moses had been raised in Vladivostok. He wore a silver Russian cross over his outfit and looked like he was trying to ward off artistic vampires.

Joel was not glad to see me. He reached for his cross as if that would somehow make me disappear. I could be the son busted for pot, asking Dad to bail him out.

I hated him, but I had no choice.

"Joel, I need to talk with you."

"Dan, please. This is not the time. Please don't make a scene"

He tried to brush me away. I wouldn't move. I wasn't afraid of Isotope and I wasn't afraid of Joel.

"*When you got nothing, you got nothing to lose,*" Bob Dylan had said. What were they going to do here if I made a scene? Not sell me a thousand dollar doll?

"You know I can file an EEOC suit," the New Mexico equivalent of a discrimination suit. "You fired me."

"You'd lose," he said. "I fired you for incompetence, not race."

That hurt. "Do you want to risk a lawsuit?" I used my old defense mechanism of humor. "Incompetent people have equal rights too."

I was about to say that I had Dan Shepard's disease, and

modified the thought to something about learning disabilities.

He shrugged. "You have disabilities all right."

"Then that means I belong to a protected class and—"

I spouted off some crap about discrimination that I had learned on the web when I should have been working. He was nervous enough to usher me into a room of Russian abstract art that must have been too offensive for everyone else. One piece was a watercolor of a church that had breasts instead of domes. I couldn't help but compare the two domes and think of Lia and Luna, but I had to concentrate.

"I know you were with Lia when she visited Brandy Porter at the casino," I said.

"Opposition research is perfectly legal," he said.

He added that he had been doing the visit as a favor to Vladimir Stone, the man I called The Werewolf. He didn't know anything; it was all Stone.

"But you were going to pay her one hundred thousand dollars."

"If you'd read the election code, you'd know that was perfectly legal under the media exceptions. It's like hiring a local celebrity like Gene Hackman or Val Kilmer."

"Brandy is no celebrity. And the land deals?"

"Again, the deals were entirely legal," he said. "But they would be too complicated for you to understand."

"But you knew about Lia?"

He paused. "Everyone knew about Lia. She was the reason I hired you," he said. "I told her I was looking for someone. She said you were brilliant."

I had always thought the reason Joel had hired me was my mother. But it was Lia.

Joel picked up a Babushka doll and shook it like a rattle. Satisfied with its construction, he indicated to a distant clerk that he wanted to purchase it. He then looked at me, and stared.

"She was wrong," he said. "She's a bad judge of people."

He walked away. I accidentally brushed a shelf on another

wall. Ten Babushka dolls tottered on the ledge. Needless to say, if they broke, I would buy.

Most of them settled down, however one Babushka did fall, but I caught it in time. I gingerly placed it back on the shelf. Then I hurried out of the Brest-Litovsk before they threw me out

The cold air of Canyon Road threw its arms around me.

What the hell did Joel mean by that? That Lia was a poor judge of people. Did he mean me? Or someone else?

Off to See the Werewolf

JOEL HAD TOLD ME nothing. I went home empty handed and knew I would have to go see The Werewolf, personally.

"*Off to see the werewolf*," I sang to myself. Did that make Santa Fe, Oz? The Werewolf was the man behind the turquoise curtain. Albuquerque sure felt a lot like Kansas. It wasn't magical, but there was no place like home.

It took some convincing, but Eva set up with a meeting for me with The Werewolf. He was in Santa Fe as it was the heart of the legislative session.

"I don't know why I'm always helping you out," she said.

"Because I'm the *fiam*, the son, you never had."

"You pronounced it wrong, *Danika,* but I appreciate your effort. I'm playing fairy Grandmother here."

I noticed she was standing by a picture of her late son.

"You mean, fairy Godmother." I said.

"That too."

"Looks like we got us a convoy," I said, pretending to be a CB trucker as I headed up to Santa Fe the next morning. Twenty school buses, many with church logos from across the state, clogged the slow lane. The riders had signs in the windows: HONK IF YOU SUPPORT GOD, and HONK IF YOU SUPPORT VALUES.

I honked of course. Too much going on in my life not to believe in the need for some divine intervention. The people waved to me. They had nice warm smiles, as if they had just left church after an inspiring sermon and made the best blueberry pie at the entire bake sale. I waved back.

I passed the front of the convoy as they crawled up La Bajada. As I descended on the other side, I passed another convoy. This time it was a convoy of hybrid vans, many decorated with pink placards and rainbow banners.

They asked me to HONK IF YOU SUPPORT HUMAN RIGHTS! I honked for them too.

The traffic on St. Francis Drive dragged toward downtown. Several other convoys headed north, each holding placards for everything from increasing cocktail hours to returning cock-fighting.

I was from the D.C. area, but this felt more like Woodstock. In a state as small as New Mexico, people knew their legislators personally, or pretended they did. It was not always a good thing. Politics wasn't just local in New Mexico, it was personal.

New Mexico legislative sessions lasted either thirty days or sixty days. Most of the controversial issues took place in a sixty-day session like this one. Governor C de Baca had made many promises to many constituents, and they wanted him to pay up.

My car crawled on Paseo de Peralta past the New Mexico State Capitol, the Roundhouse. The Roundhouse resembled a Native American *kiva*, the ceremonial structure first utilized by the Anasazi. A *kiva* was a round building made of stone, or adobe bricks, and topped with stucco. The Roundhouse was a stucco building, but it didn't look like it would stand the test of time.

The building was adobe, of course, with long white columns. Unfortunately, it paled in comparison to the Native casinos I had passed on the way up. The people of New Mexico valued gambling over government, I supposed.

I felt excited as I searched for parking, like a school kid on a field trip. I had done Boy's State back in Maryland, and had played junior legislator for a day in Annapolis, the State Capital. I had even interned in the U.S. Congress for a Representative. Coming here made me feel young again. When I was in Congress, I was an unpaid cog in the wheel, now I felt more like a monkey wrench. I might as well have parked in Amarillo, I was so far to the east. When I finally hiked back to the Roundhouse, police in full riot gear served as an armed buffer between two diametrically opposed mobs. The phalanx of police left a narrow gauntlet to the entrance to the Roundhouse.

On one side were the churchgoers I had passed going up La Bajada Hill, on the other were the Human Rights activists I had passed going down on the other side. Both shouted angry slogans at each other.

Lia should be here right now, right here in the thick of it. God, I missed her.

In my gray suit, I looked like a legislator about to vote on the unfortunately named House Joint Resolution Sixty-Nine.

"No on Sixty-Nine!" came from the Right.

"Yes on Sixty-Nine!" came from the Left.

I stared straight and waved in both directions, like a celebrity going to a red-carpet premiere, not wishing to offend anybody. My limp worsened just as I hit the gauntlet. The red carpet lasted forever.

At the front door, I showed my ID to a very large state trooper. Thankfully I was on a list. I then attempted to navigate a metal detector. I beeped of course, and had to take off my shoes to show mismatched socks. The socks were both black, but one had a red stripe, the other a blue. I really had played both sides of the fence.

I repeated an old joke to myself. I was probably secretly "Bi," *Bi-partisan.*

Inside the building, I did a complete lap around the Roundhouse corridors, dodging junior staffers and high-priced lobbyists in the cramped hallways. It felt like an old episode of *The West Wing,* the lost New Mexico season. People walked and talked into their blue tooth accessories. Blue tooths (or is it blue teeth?) just looked wrong under a white cowboy hat. Maybe this would be the *Way Out West Wing.*

The criminal defense lobby was there trying to repeal a "Victim's Rights Bill." I waved to Mary, director of the Criminal Defense Lawyers' Association. She didn't wave back. She was pissed that I hadn't renewed my membership when I took the job with Joel.

I then smiled at a brunette intern who bore a passing resemblance to Monica Lewinski. She didn't smile back.

The biggest crowd gathered around the entrance to Governor C de Baca's office. People begged to pass, but a staffer was firm.

"No one else is getting in today!"

C de Baca had already vetoed every bill that Lia would have supported, including Article Seven's childcare amendments. Yet, the consensus was C de Baca was a leader. People didn't necessarily like what he did, but he got things done. *Newsweek* had already written a glowing profile of him as an "up and comer."

After another lap, I finally found the room number for Vladimir Stone, a.k.a. The Werewolf. His office had the long-winded title of Minority Tactical and Strategic Policy. His title was bigger than his office. He was a senior legislative advisor for one party, but he was probably the most powerful un-elected person in the building.

The Werewolf finished up a phone call as I waited.

"So you have a vid from someone saying she's a dyke?" he asked. He didn't realize how loud his voice was.

"Nah, not yet," he said after another moment. "We wait until he's about to veto Sixty-Nine."

He hung up when he saw me.

"All right, douche bag you have five minutes max," he said to me. "I'm only doing this as a favor to Eva."

I was alone with The Werewolf at last. I looked out the window. Still daylight, but I could see the full moon. The Werewolf looked like a male model from an Eastern European country. I remembered law-school discussions about how constitutional law used the word "narrowly tailored" to describe a strict interpretation of the State Constitution. He probably had a more expansive view of constitutional liberties, but his tight suits were narrowly tailored all right. He just didn't belong here; he was in an alpha wolf in a dingy stucco cage.

I flashed back to the Warren Zevon song, "Werewolves of London." He really could be drinking a piña colada at Trader Vic's. His hair was indeed perfect. As I had passed C de Baca's door, my personal pendulum had swung abruptly to the left as a reaction, but here in The Werewolf's office, the pendulum had swung right back.

In this kind of political environment, I felt I was in the middle of the old Iran-Iraq war and didn't know who to root for.

"What do you want to know, asshole?" he asked. "I don't have all fucking day."

He sipped an energy drink called "Zombie Juice." Back in the day, he had probably been a cokehead, his arms had that shake to them. I didn't know if Zombie Juice was an improvement.

"What was Ophelia Paz's official role on the campaign?" I asked.

"She put up signs. She did canvassing. She was a little nobody."

That didn't sound right.

"Why would the Governor's campaign manager pick up and drive this little nobody?"

He laughed. "We like to car pool and limit the impact of the environment, save gas and all. You got a problem with that?"

That was a lie. I smiled to indicate that I wasn't that stupid.

"She do any 'opposition research'?'"

He snarled. "The goddamn cheerleader thing. She gave us the names of some cheerleaders that C de Baca had supposedly molested."

"Brandy Porter?"

"Yeah. And the other Liquor Sisters. I already heard you visited that bitch, Brandy," he said. "But I heard she wasn't too goddamn helpful, right?"

"Brandy mentioned getting paid 'off the books.' Now just where would that money come from?'"

The Werewolf stared at a woman crossing the street below as if marinating her with his eyes.

"Did she give you an account number?" he asked.

"No, of course not."

"Brandy sign an affidavit?"

"No."

"Then why the fuck should I care?"

He had me there. Time to roll the dice.

"What about Agua-gate? A lot of campaign workers and contributors had links."

"What about it? C de Baca tried to take out my boy, but the Governor gave up a multi-million dollar deal to avoid the 'appearance of impropriety.' Again, so fucking what?"

I had to think of something. I had become too soft for Albuquerque, but now I worried I wasn't smart enough for Santa Fe.

He looked at his watch. "Three minute warning."

"Why did Portia Smith C de Baca go into Lia's house?" I asked. "Why did Portia Smith C de Baca happen to walk in that neighborhood? I know Albuquerque, and it's too big a city for Portia to just pick that house at random."

The Werewolf froze. I was taller than he was and I stood tall to let him know through my body language that I had beat off three tough teenagers from the *Burque*.

Perhaps he realized the door was closed and it was loud outside. I could take one small hairy dude or at least tear the fuck out of his expensive suit. He didn't know what I was capable of. I didn't either. *When you got nothing, you got nothing to lose.*

I had made a vow to Lia, and I wouldn't back down.

"Don't dis the burque, *ese.*" I muttered under my breath.

The Werewolf heard me. He yielded.

"Someone on our campaign staff made a phone call to the C de Baca campaign—told them a nice lady had the most C de Baca signs in New Mexico. They didn't tell them the signs were *anti*-C de Baca. We alerted the media too, a lot of networks and the bloggers. It was going to be a great photo op for the web. Portia Smith C de Baca posing with signs touting her husband as a child-molester. We had another few hours left at the polls, and I figured it was worth maybe a thousand votes or so."

So much for The Werewolf's car pool explanation. This was diabolic shit, but perfectly legal.

"Did Lia make that call?"

"Nah. We couldn't trust Lia Spaz with a call like that. The girl was a loose cannon. I don't know who made the call, someone lower down on the campaign. We never let Lia go out alone."

"The plan didn't work as planned, did it?"

"It was raining like a motherfucker in Albuquerque that day, remember? The news trucks didn't want to risk going out there and shorting out all their equipment. The bloggers were scared of the rain, getting shocked by the lightning or whatever. They didn't even want to leave their living room. The whole thing was for shit."

"For shit? Portia was killed."

I got closer to him, intimidated him.

"Well, that's something, I suppose," he said.

"So it wasn't Lia's idea to have the signs up? It was all a set up? Part of the campaign dirty tricks?"

He laughed. "Oh, trust me on this, it was Lia's idea. Those

were her signs. You can check the handwriting if you want. She would have had those signs up even if there wasn't an election. Just call us meeting her seren-fucking-dipity."

Us? Who was us? I tried to suck it up, looked him right in the eye.

"Who was in the house with Lia? Was it you?"

"I picked her up. That was all. I had campaign business in Albuquerque and she was on my way back here. If you need it, I got cell records proving I was always on the phone."

"Who was in the house with Lia?" I asked again. "I know you know."

I *don't* know," he said. "It wasn't me. I told you I picked her up. And I assume you don't have any fucking forensics or eye-witness accounts saying anything else. Maybe it was C de Baca."

"Governor C de Baca? You're saying he killed his own wife?"

"Why the fuck not?" he said. "I had access to the polling numbers. He was down in Albuquerque until the announcement that his wife had been killed. Then he won by a landslide. Do the math."

"The announcement came after the polls had closed," I said.

"You ever hear of something called the Internet?" he asked. "There were all kinds of rumors flying that day. Rumors on both sides. Rumors that our party had some dirt on her. Rumors that we were the ones playing dirty."

I would have been hard at work for Joel drafting interrogatories on the malpractice case, so I wouldn't have known. Before I could follow through, two agricultural lobbyists came in.

"The farmer and the cowhand should be friends," he said to the lobbyists.

I wouldn't let him shoo me out for the farmer or the cowhand.

"That's fucking bullshit and you know it," I said, surprised at my own rage.

The Werewolf looked at the lobbyists, and then at me.

"Give me thirty seconds," he said to them.

They waited outside. I realized I delayed the future of New Mexico agriculture.

The full moon was pretty bright for daytime and I certainly didn't want to risk another minute here. The Werewolf looked at me strangely; I must have been the first person to swear at him in a long time.

"You will interview Governor C de Baca, won't you?" he asked.

"I can try."

"I'll make a deal with you. Find a way to stick it to C de Baca and I'll help you out. You got spunk," he said.

I wasn't quite sure what spunk was. Was it something you wiped off a bathroom floor in an adult bookstore?

He laughed again. "You know, Governor Mendoza cost me a million dollars, so I wouldn't mind tearing him down a peg too. You'll interview him too, right?"

"I guess so," I said. "You want me to take down C de Baca *and* Mendoza?"

"Interview both of them. Tell me what you find out. Then I'll tell you what really happened that night."

I looked into his eyes. He was serious. The Werewolf could take me behind another turquoise curtain.

Friend of the Dust Devil

I WAS NINETY-NINE percent sure that The Werewolf had just lied to me. He had suggested that C de Baca killed his wife at Lia's house to improve his poll numbers. That would mean that C de Baca was there at the house with Lia, and that their decade-long feud was all a sham. I guess that would mean that Lia loved him all along. As I said, I was ninety-nine percent positive that The Werewolf was full of shit.

As a defense attorney I knew what that one percent chance was, *a reasonable doubt.*

I tried to call Lia, now that I knew she was back in Las Vegas at the hospital. The receptionist there was as rude as her Albuquerque counterpart. She would neither confirm nor deny that Lia was there. There was so much I wanted to ask Lia.

I tried to put the little information that I had together as I drove back to Albuquerque. The next step was talking to Governor C de Baca. I couldn't get to him through Eva, or my mother. In the middle of the badlands I figured a roundabout "in" to Governor C de Baca. I knew his brother Xavier, the "X-man." I had his cell phone number, from when he helped me with alternative sentencing for my more difficult clients. Thankfully the number was still good. He picked up on the first ring.

"Dan Shepard, I figured that someday you'd see the light."

A car honked at me. I'd better pull off the road if I wanted to talk. I wasn't quite sure where I was when I pulled over to the side of the road, in a valley somewhere between Cochiti and Algodones. This was an untouched part of the desert, it seemed almost out of biblical times. There was even a small cross by the road; someone had died in an auto accident here.

"I need to set up a meeting with your brother," I said. "I need to talk to him about . . . well, it's personal, but very important."

"He's a hard man to get to. He's got the weight of the world, the weight of the state on his mind."

"It's very important."

A tumbleweed hit the side of my car head on, and exploded. It was really dusty now. What did they call those mini-tornadoes, dust devils? A dust devil slowly emerged from the arroyo, half a mile away.

There was silence on the other end of the phone

"I'll do it," Xavier said. "You got to promise me something, though."

He was my only link to the Governor, so I didn't really have a choice.

"What?"

"One day, you're going to have to make a choice. Promise me you'll make the right decision."

"Sure, I'll '*Do the Right Thing.*'" He didn't realize that I was quoting the old Spike Lee movie.

The dust devil moved further down the highway, then jerked back, trying to make up its mind. Traffic on the interstate came to a halt in both directions due to the flying dust. It was now difficult to see.

"Seriously, Dan the man," X said. "You got to make sure you're on the right path."

"I'm not one of your convicts," I reminded him.

"Are you sure?"

The dust devil swirled a bit closer as the winds grew

stronger. Brush and other debris sailed through the air. A second tumbleweed came right for me like a heat-seeking missile. I honked. The tumbleweed ignored the honk, of course. Instead, it hit my car and shattered into a million little pieces.

No, the dust devil wasn't quite a tornado, but I didn't know whether to run or stay in my car. If I got out, a tumbleweed could easily do damage to me.

Another tumbleweed now raced across the freeway on a collision course.

"Okay, X-man," I said. "I'll do the right thing when the time comes."

"I have faith in you, Dan the man. I'll hook you up."

The dust devil disappeared. The tumbleweed fell to the earth. Traffic suddenly resumed.

I looked at the cross by the side of the road. X really did have power. But what the hell was the right thing to do?

Chimichanga Blues

XAVIER DIDN'T GET BACK to me right away, so I had to try to salvage something else. I hadn't talked to Luna since the New Year fiasco. I had avoided her office; I even avoided driving by it. But I knew something about getting to people so I went to Luna's sister Selena at the Grove. She said she'd put in a good word with Luna. It took Selena three days, and probably a lot more than three words, but Luna finally agreed to meet me for an early dinner.

She didn't seem happy when we met at *Garduno's*, the nicest New Mexican restaurant in town. She had her baby, Saca, with her, which made the situation more awkward. Babies made me nervous. Saca reminded me that this woman of my dreams had already dreamt of someone else. Luna's baby was fast asleep. I thought about the baby's namesake, Sacagawea, the Native woman who guided Lewis and Clark through the wilds, a baby at her side. Did I want Luna to be my own guide, baby and all?

Luna ordered the world's biggest taco salad, which had too much taco and not enough salad. It should not have been on the low fat menu. But hey, it was a salad.

I went with a *chimichanga*, which was technically Arizonan

rather than New Mexican cuisine, but then again, I wasn't a native New Mexican. This restaurant made it from blue corn, which made me nervous. I always wondered about blue food.

"So where are we?" I asked.

"I don't know," she said. "Where are you with Lia?"

I spilled a bit of salsa on my shirt. It looked like a blood stain.

"I'm her lawyer, that's all."

"But you care about her?"

"Lia's crazy, but people have taken advantage of that craziness and used it for their own purposes her entire life."

"So you don't still have feelings for her?"

"Someone has to look out for her. I'm her lawyer. Don't you wish someone had looked out for you when you were crazy?"

"How did you know I was crazy?"

I had been joking, but I apparently I had hit a nerve. She told me how she had once been "evaluated" for swimming naked in a pond in the middle of a murder case. Ironically, her evaluator was the same Dr. Romero who was now seeing Lia.

"You haven't killed anyone, have you?" I asked.

"Almost, but that was in Juarez, so it doesn't count." She thought for a second. "No, actually I was in El Paso, but I was still out of this jurisdiction."

"*I shot a man in Juarez just to see him die,*" I said, paraphrasing Johnny Cash.

"Don't joke about that," she said. "It's not funny."

There was silence. Luna pondered things over each bite of taco salad. She had refused several efforts by the servers to take it away. Luna softened by the time we had flan, a delicious custard dessert. Saca remained asleep.

"I need your help," I said. "Lia needs your help."

Luna thought for a moment. "My problem with Lia is not that we're so different, it's that we're so much alike. I'm probably just as crazy as she is."

I didn't know how to respond to that. Each woman had her

own strengths; each woman had her own unique brand of craziness.

There was an awkward pause. I munched on some more chips. Saca managed to stay asleep in a noisy restaurant, looking absolutely adorable. A baby wasn't the worst thing in the world, after all.

"Will you help me?" I asked. "I can't do Lia's case alone."

She thought for a long time. "I want you to understand one thing, I'm not doing shit for Lia."

"What?"

She put Saca back down, then took my hand.

"I'm doing it for you."

"What does that mean?"

"I don't know."

I got a call the next morning while I was still in bed. "This is X," the voice said.

"X-man!"

"He'll see you," Xavier said. "But you're not going to be alone. Diana Crater will be there too."

"No problemo," I said.

"Just remember your promise," he said.

What promise? I had already forgotten

Bishop's Dodge

THAT SATURDAY I DROVE to Santa Fe, took the northern part of the Paseo de Peralta Loop, then made a right on Bishop's Lodge Road, the old road that headed north from downtown to the village of Tesuque. The Governor's Mansion was still within Santa Fe's city limits a few miles down Bishop's Lodge Road, on the aptly named Mansion Road. The Governor's home wasn't the only mansion on it. I thought my parents lived in a swanky neighborhood, but this part of Santa Fe was filled with billionaires, a high-altitude Beverly Hills.

Star-struck by the homes, I missed the turn, and all of a sudden the pavement on Mansion Road turned to dirt. The mansions were even bigger on the dirt part of the road. Dirt, apparently, was a selling point in Santa Fe. Several homes stood even bigger than the Governor's residence. I was utterly incapable of doing the math to calculate their value.

Oprah had once had a house up here, along with other bold-faced names. Today, the neighborhood was deserted, as most of the residents came in town only for the opera season. The political season was an anathema to them. One big mansion had a tall mixed media art piece in the back yard that towered over the stucco walls.

After a few more wrong turns and a few more mansions, I

finally found the Governor's residence. It looked more like the adobe clubhouse of a country club than a political hang out. I don't know how I had missed the security fence when I had first driven past. It felt like Israel. Or Baghdad.

I had been nervous in the Roundhouse, now I felt as if I might as well be going to the White House. I did my best to fake it. I wore my nicest suit, a blue one, but I had already sweated through it. I decided to put on a red and yellow tie, New Mexico's colors.

Once I buzzed past the gate and parked, I walked with trepidation to the door. Xavier C de Baca opened it before I arrived. Up close, X was covered by religious tattoos. Each hand had a tattoo of a nail through the wrist. Over his left eye were small tattooed letters spelling out REPENT OR ELSE!

"Good to see you again, X-man," I said. We talked for a few moments about a few cases back in the day for his gospel ministry. He had specialized in lost causes like his brother. Maybe he could help me save myself some day.

X led me out to the mansion deck. He frowned despite the staggering beauty of the view.

"I'm worried about him," he said.

"The Governor?"

"My brother," X said. "This is a you and me conversation."

"Understood."

"I was in prison when he was in middle school. This was before I saw the light. Our father beat him very badly growing up." X paused. This was difficult for him. "Our father did something else to him, something far worse."

X didn't finish. C de Baca had been molested by his own father? I didn't know how to respond to that.

X continued. "So my brother, he had a lot of anger. He always had to prove that he was a man. A real man."

"What do mean?"

"I believed those girls."

"You did?"

"When my brother was drinking and doing drugs, he was a different person. I know about this because my first job was as a 'celebrity handler.'"

He mentioned the name of a famous teen "pop tart." He kept the girl away from alcohol as a "sober companion."

"That's basically what I do for my brother now."

"So is he drinking again?"

X thought for a moment. "I hope not. I can't watch him twenty-four seven. I'm someone who believes in repentance and redemption. For the rest of his life, my brother has proved himself."

X told me about his brother's accomplishments, his good works. It was rocky at first, but C de Baca had indeed done a lot for his community. Despite the nay-sayings of the Rhiannons of the world, New Mexico had not come to an end in the last few weeks. The economy was booming. New employers in high tech industries were pouring into Albuquerque. The UNM Lobos and New Mexico State Aggies men's *and* women's basketball teams were both winning on the road. Outside of Santa Fe and Albuquerque, C de Baca's approval rating was at ninety percent.

"I just hope he can hang on," X said. He quoted bible verses as he spread his arms over Santa Fe as if it was one big adobe Sodom. He talked about the various temptations his brother was facing. "I think losing Portia took him back to the street punk he once was."

"I'm sorry," I said.

I actually felt a bit of sympathy for C de Baca in spite of myself.

"I hope he'll be all right," X said. "I'm going away next week for a Bar Mitzvah, one of the department heads is having one on Long Island, where his daughter lives. I've got to be the Governor's rep."

I stared at his REPENT OR ELSE tattoo. I tried to picture him dancing the *hora* towering over a crowd of thirteen year olds from Long Island. My God, his iron cross alone would outweigh some pre-puberty Jews. "A Bar Mitzvah?"

He nodded. "Should I bring a present?"

The prospect of X buying a Bar Mitzvah present was as frightening as the thought of him dancing. My God, he might give a tattoo gun or worse, a real gun.

"A gift certificate would be fine."

"Wal-Mart?"

"Nah, Macy's or something."

"Good idea," he said. "Dan, you're all right."

"Thank you," I said. "So are you."

"Like I said, one day you're gonna have to make a choice. Make sure you make the right choice."

"Yeah, sure. You got it."

"*Vaya con dios.*" he said. "By the way, you need to find yourself a good wife."

"I'm working on it," I said.

Xavier made a call, then ushered me inside, past several doors and corridors, and soon I was in the Governor's private office. At first glance, this was a typical politician's office: pictures of the Governor with various bigwigs of his party, framed letters of congratulations and whatnot. He also kept portraits of his predecessors on the wall. Governor Mendoza's portrait hid off in a corner.

No one got up to greet me, so I stood there awkwardly, taking the whole room in. There was a Civil War era rifle mounted on the wall. A wooden label revealed that the rifle was from New Mexico's one Civil War battle in nearby Glorieta. The bayonet had dried blood on it. I wondered if the Governor had used it recently.

Religious art on another wall must have come straight from prison art class. Upon closer look, I realized it signed by C de Baca himself. Behind me, there was a wall dedicated to his late wife. I was too nervous to stare at it, so I looked out the giant window, at a view of all of Santa Fe, and then out to the Sandia Mountains of Albuquerque, sixty miles south. The ten thousand foot mountains looked so small, as if the Governor could stomp them down even further. The world was his. He wasn't Tony Montana, Al Pacino's character in *Scarface*, he was *Tony Nuevo Mexico*. I had been in jail cells before but I had never been so intimidated as in that room.

Governor C de Baca dressed casually in gray slacks and a black silk shirt opened at the top to reveal a silver cross. He looked more comfortable wearing a cross than a tie. He was the worst of both worlds. He was a Santa Fe power player who had learned to play rough in Albuquerque. There was no doubt that he could take me in a fight, both intellectually and physically.

The Governor stayed at his desk, and signed a few pieces of legislation. He scanned the final bill like Nero in the coliseum looking down at a Gladiator. It was the bill that the criminal defense attorneys had been lobbying for. He thought for a second, then put it in the box marked "veto."

Attorney General Diana Crater sat on the couch. She was in the Governor's shadow, literally and figuratively. She wore a gray pinstriped outfit that fit her badly. She had backed the wrong horse, just like me, and even her clothes looked uncomfortable.

C de Baca's personal lawyer, Stan Salazar, sat in a big easy chair. Salazar looked like a mob lawyer, and in fact had defended a big death-penalty case or two. The joke about him was he was better with his murder clients than he was with anything else.

Perhaps the Governor was a murder client.

For one brief moment, I wished I could be a big time lawyer like that, but then his phone rang.

"Tell Judge Lincoln in Metro that I can't be there right now," he said. "Tell her I'm with the Governor."

I could tell by Salazar's expression that Judge Lincoln apparently didn't care where he was. She would hold him in contempt, Governor or not. Judges were like that.

No, I didn't want to be Salazar after all. He hung up, but did not get up to shake my hand. Not a good sign.

Diana finally acknowledged me, shaking my hand in a firm grip.

"Mr. Shepard, Dan. I know your mother." She nodded at C de Baca. "Athena Shepard is his mom."

The Governor nodded as he vetoed another bill.

"I applied to be an assistant attorney general at your office," I said to Diana.

"I know. I remembered your application. It was unique."

"You didn't hire me," I said. "Five times."

"Well, you know how those things are," she said. "They can be political."

Diana then at least pretended to run the show, when she summoned in her personal court reporter, a petite woman dressed in off-white, so as to almost render her invisible.

Niceties over, Diana turned to C de Baca.

"Dan will ask you a limited number of questions on his investigation, but we will dove-tail your answers into our own joint task-force report."

What's a dove tail? There was an eternal struggle between the parties, like that of Good versus Evil with press releases. Lia was the tip of the iceberg. Agua-gate was just below the surface. Diana would go a bit deeper, and only God himself would judge what took place in the depths of this election.

C de Baca vetoed another bill and then smiled.

"As it says in Leviticus: Let's get ready to rumble."

I almost expected to hear a bell ring. The court reporter had already starting rumbling. I opened my notebook and gathered my thoughts. Might as well start from the beginning.

"How did you meet Ophelia Paz?"

"I was a teacher and coach at Albuquerque High her junior year. She was a student."

"Did you have a sexual relationship with her during Christmas break her junior year?"

There was an audible gasp from Diana. She had not expected me to ask that, especially not as my second question.

There was a pause. C de Baca looked at Salazar. Salazar then nodded.

"No, I did not." C de Baca said at last.

"Was there an investigation into whether you had a sexual relationship with her?"

"Yes, there was. No evidence was produced, due to the unreliability of the complaining witness, Ms. Paz."

He stared at me before I could think of taking an advantage.

"Do you have any evidence whatsoever regarding that?" C de Baca asked with a snarl. "If you repeat that question again, I will strongly consider a suit against you for defamation of character and I personally will—"

He stopped before he said the words "kick your," and "ass."

I looked at Diana. She wouldn't come to my rescue.

I then asked a question I didn't know the answer to. Big mistake.

"Then why did Ophelia Paz claim to have a relationship with you?"

He smiled. I had walked into a trap door.

"Because Lia's delusional. She tried to initiate a relationship with me. I rebuffed her. She tried again. I rebuffed again. She then complained to the principal on these trumped-up charges. You are aware that she was then institutionalized?"

"I am," I said. "Do you know what happened to her pregnancy?"

"Beyond the scope of his personal knowledge," Salazar said. "Also assumes facts not in evidence. Also—"

This guy was good. He kept going with five more objections. I had neglected to bring my rulebook with me. I had better move on.

"Did you ever have a relationship with Brandy Porter?" I asked. "She was in a group called the 'Liquor Sisters.'"

"No, I did not. I don't drink . . . liquor."

"What was your next contact with Ophelia Paz after high school?"

"Lia came to my wedding."

There was silence for a moment. Diana and I looked at each other.

"You invited her to your wedding?"

He spit into a wastebasket. "Of course not."

"Please explain."

"She showed up and stood outside holding a sign that said COACH C DE BACA MOLESTED ME! This was in front of a church, mind you. My father in law's church! Two thousand people."

Again, I felt sorry for him. I sensed anger and sadness in him and I remembered what X told me about their father.

"This was your wedding to the late Portia Smith C de Baca?"

"I've only been married once. I believe in the sanctity of marriage." He looked at Diana again before continuing. "That was eight years ago."

"Did she have any dealings with Portia that day?"

"No. Portia was safely inside the church. I didn't let her out off the building."

"What happened?"

"I don't know. Let's just say Ms. Paz disappeared before the ceremony began."

"Did you remove her?"

"My relatives took care of it."

"When was your next contact with her?"

"Would you count the time she called my employer?"

I hadn't heard this one. "I guess so. Please explain."

"I worked for the Mayor's Youth Campaign as a community organizer. She called the mayor himself and told him I was a child-molester."

"Do you have proof of that?"

He took out a white piece of paper that looked like a copy of a hand-written note. That couldn't be good.

"MAYOR NEEDS TO SEE YOU REGARDING SOMEONE NAMED LIA PAZ," it read.

"I can get you the original if you want."

"What happened with Lia's complaint?"

"The mayor put me on suspension, without pay."

"When was the next time you saw her?"

"A couple of years passed. I thought she had forgotten about me. I ran for mayor of the village of Los Rio Ranchitos. There were several incidents involving Ms. Paz and political signs in Los Rio Ranchitos as well. I still won."

"Continue."

C de Baca said nothing. He just stared at me.

"*Please* continue."

He smiled. "I have videotapes of her testifying at the Los Rio Ranchitos City Council meetings. These were televised on community access."

He pressed a button, and I heard Lia's voice behind me. I turned to see a giant plasma-screen TV. A younger Lia, dressed in pink with a pink flower in her hair, spoke rapidly about C de Baca's proposed bill to cut funding for a woman's clinic on the south side.

C de Baca pressed "pause."

"How many of these do you want to see?" he asked.

"How many are there?"

"Seventeen."

"Let's see one more."

The next tape was identical to the first, except Lia wore a different shade of pink, and her flower was a magnolia. She spoke in favor of sex ed in schools and how C de Baca was a hypocrite for opposing it, in light of his own sexual proclivities.

"His idea of sex ed is sleeping with his students," she said as her close.

"I don't see what the problem is," I said, stifling a chuckle. "Freedom of expression."

"The first amendment does not apply to everything under the

sun. Especially not defamation of character."

"I've seen enough." I took a deep breath. "So are you saying she's obsessed with you?"

"You're the lawyer. What would you say?"

I didn't know how to answer that, better keep going. "Do you think she's mentally ill?"

"I'm not a psychiatrist," he said. "Don't really believe in it. But no, I think she knows what she's doing. So no, I do not think she's incompetent to stand trial if that's what you're getting at."

I had to keep going. I didn't want to hear any more of Lia's past if I didn't have to. It made me uneasy. Where were we? Oh yeah. "Did you have any contact with her during your campaign for governor?"

"Not direct contact. But I heard rumors. Rumors of dirty tricks of Internet stories and blogs. A lot of e-mails were sent nationally to potential donors out of state."

He turned his computer on. There was an e-mail from a "Lia629" and I remembered that June 29 was Lia's birthday. The text in the subject line read REGARDING C DE BACA'S CAMPAIGN. There was an attachment to the email. He opened the attachment. It showed Lia getting roughed up at C de Baca's wedding.

In the clip, Lia minded her own business on her way to the church. Suddenly several burly security guards grabbed her and dragged her away. One had a button that said C DE BACA FOR LOS RIO RANCHITOS COUNCIL.

I had seen the video before, but never realized it was Lia.

"This went out to over a hundred thousand of my supporters. I filed a complaint with the election board, but now that I've won . . . ."

I tried to stick up for Lia. "Lia wouldn't have the expertise to send out that kind of video, or edit it. She wouldn't have access to your campaign list."

"Are you asking me a question? She worked on the Governor's campaign. Someone there would have had access to my campaign list. You're looking into that too, right Diana?"

"We're looking at a lot of things," Diana said as she looked out the window and sized up the view.

C de Baca then produced something else, a scrap of paper dated October first and addressed to Governor Mendoza.

It read, LET'S USE CRAZY GIRL.

There was something odd about the message. "Crazy Girl" wasn't used as an adjective; it was a proper noun. Lia's code name, no doubt.

"How did you get that?" I asked.

Salazar piped in. "That is beyond the scope of this investigation."

Time to keep moving. "Who was the note from?"

I expected an objection but Salazar indicated that I could ask away.

"We don't know," C de Baca said. "In case you're wondering, we did have it checked by a handwriting expert. It was *not* done by Governor Mendoza. My gut instinct tells me it was Stone or maybe someone else high up in the campaign. Another suspect is Rhiannon Goldstein Manygoats, a major contributor who worked on the campaign as a high-end fund raiser. No match yet. The note was written on an uneven surface, and handwriting analysis is an inexact science."

I thought of The Werewolf. And also Rhiannon. Perhaps the only person who would know would be the former governor himself. Perhaps The Werewolf wanted to set up Rhiannon as well?

"It isn't admissible as evidence," I said. "Well, I don't think it is."

"I know," C de Baca said. "But we've already given a copy to Ms. Crater and her team. And we've sent a copy of it to the administration."

"Administration? I thought you were the administration."

"The President's administration," C de Baca said. "They're offering Mendoza the Secretary of Interior job. The spirit of bipartisanship and all."

I tried to stick up for Mendoza. "He'll be the good guy for the bad guys."

C de Baca snorted. "He'll probably figure out a way to get the federal government to condemn that Agua-gate land for five times what the State would and pocket the difference."

Things were definitely out of my pay grade. Both parties were dirty.

"Where were you the night of the murder?" Time to play The Werewolf's hunch, even if I didn't believe it.

C de Baca had anticipated my question and nodded to Salazar who produced twenty time stamped photos showing C de Baca posing in pictures with supporters for the entire two-hour window time of death. So much for reasonable doubt. The Werewolf had been full of shit. I looked at the portrait of Governor Mendoza. The portrait made him look big and mean. I felt my internal pendulum begin to swing toward C de Baca.

C de Baca signaled to the court reporter that this was off the record.

"If you want the more likely culprit, it would have been my predecessor," C de Baca said. "He might have even been in the room with Lia when Portia was killed."

There was absolute silence. The court reporter hadn't taken any of that down. This was way, way above my pay grade. I thought again about The Werewolf. Perhaps he was gunning for the former governor himself.

I knew one thing: the chance of C de Baca being in the room with Lia was near zero. The chance of Governor Mendoza being there? Governor Gary Mendoza, whom she adored and who had a reputation of sleeping with half the gallery owners on Canyon Road, well that probability was much higher.

"Do you want to hear the tape of Portia dying?" C de Baca said.

"Do you have one?" I asked.

Diana was equally amazed. "Why didn't anyone tell me about this?"

"Nobody asked me," he said. "It's protected by executive privilege by the way. I will disclose it only after a court order. I'm still having my own people analyze it."

"The court order will take months," Diana said.

"I know," he replied.

C de Baca hit a button on his computer and brought up a digital file.

"She left a message on my machine. As I said, I'm exerting my executive privilege. I'm not releasing it without a subpoena and will not allow reproduction of any of it. Do you mind if I leave? It's very painful to me."

I nodded. C de Baca wiped his eye, then left. I looked at the pictures of Portia on the dedication wall—a place the Governor could see conveniently from his desk.

There was a picture of her in her missionary days. She had converted an entire city in China on her own. She had a perfect smile and big green eyes that made you know there was indeed a God.

Once C de Baca was safely out the door, Salazar pressed "play."

"Message sent November second at four-forty P.M.," a recorded voice said.

"It's me," Portia said. "I can't believe it, but this chick has all these signs up. Someone called and told me there was a woman with lots of pro-C de Baca signs in this neighborhood."

I looked at pictures of Portia in China, Africa and in New Mexico. I couldn't help but fall in love with her, too. I hated The Werewolf for trying to blackmail this nice woman.

"It's that woman who's always stalking you," Portia said from beyond the grave. She had an Eastern New Mexico accent, which was basically West Texas. "She's out front putting up another one . . . . Hold on . . . ."

The rain came down in torrents, muffling the sound. Portia yelled something. Lia yelled something back.

Did Portia leave her phone on for a reason? She had to have

known that it kept recording. Maybe she knew these were her final moments on earth.

A door opened. The rain stopped. Apparently she had made it inside Lia's house.

Portia then said, "It's you."

She couldn't have been talking to Lia, as Lia had already invited her in. She must have recognized someone else. I didn't know if she knew Rhiannon. Maybe it was The Werewolf. Maybe it was the former governor himself.

I heard a car honk. I heard doors open and close. Someone left. Could it have been Lia? Yes, but doubtful. Could someone else have come in? There was more confusion. It sounded like Portia left the phone in her purse, then went into another room. I could not hear any talking, just more muffled tones, far away. Doors opened and shut. Someone might have entered or left.

More words were exchanged. I couldn't make them out. Then there was a long silence. Then a gasp, almost like a strangulation. Then a thump. I grimaced when I heard the thumping sound. I remembered Luna pantomiming the many ways Portia could die. The sound could have been anything—Portia slamming into the table, or someone slamming her.

Another door opened, a screen door. There was the sound of more rain and then the sound of rushing water overpowered my ears. Portia must now be in the concrete arroyo.

Then there was absolute silence.

Chills ran down my spine.

Then the voice of the electronic message machine: "To delete, press one."

I stared at a picture of Portia shaking hands with a Native American child in full regalia on one of the reservations. The light changed just then, so it seemed that Portia's image had been deleted, right in front of me.

Salazar stopped the tape and buzzed C de Baca to return.

"That still gets to me," he said when he returned, a tear in his eye. "Still gets to me."

C de Baca definitely missed Portia. I noticed him glance at the Civil War rifle and the bayonet. I didn't know about the rifle, but the bayonet looked as if it was in working order.

I looked back at the picture of Portia and the little Navajo dancer. The dancer looked at her with the biggest smile. Portia had done a lot of good in her life. I should hate Governor C de Baca. I really should, but I felt a compulsion to say something to him.

"Mr. Governor," I said trying to be as delicate as possible. "I think Stone wants to bring out some damaging information about your wife before House Bill Sixty-Nine comes to your desk. Apparently they have *alleged* confirmation regarding some rumors."

Governor C de Baca frowned. He didn't bother to ask. He stared at Portia's picture.

I did feel sorry for the man. At least I did until he stared at the bayonet. He had blood lust in his eyes. What in the hell was he thinking?

He sat in silence for another moment. "This interview is finished," he said at last, his voice slightly slurred. "If you want more answers, you know where to go."

He pointed toward the portrait of his predecessor, Governor Gary Mendoza.

I went up to Governor C de Baca to shake his hand. Up close, I noticed a strong odor of alcohol and his blood shot watery eyes. I wanted Officer Nunez to give him a nystagmus test to look for "lack of smooth pursuit."

As I was walking out, Salazar stayed behind to ask, "Mr. Governor, could you issue a pardon on my contempt charge in Metro court before Judge Lincoln?"

Diana walked me out to the parking lot. "I hear you and Luna Cruz are friends now. We grew up together in Crater County."

"Is there really a crater in Crater County?"

"It was named after my family who pioneered the area. Luna and I always joked that the crater in the county was just a state of mind. We were best friends growing up."

Best friends?

"Luna's an amazing woman." Time to pretend to be Mr. Santa Fe insider. "Ms. Crater, you know Luna. You know my mom *and* you didn't hire me when you probably should have."

"Yes?" She was wary, as if trapped in her own private crater.

"Would you be able to set up a meeting with me and former Governor Mendoza? I'll give you any information I get. I can do it informally, so it doesn't look like you're out to get a member of your own party."

I liked being a power player.

Diana smiled. "I bet the real reason you want to meet Mendoza is to see if he slept with Lia. To see if he crossed the Mendoza line."

That was the first time I'd heard someone use that expression in that way. I didn't respond. I wanted to know if the governor had been in the room with Lia and Portia. I wanted to know how far up this conspiracy went. But yeah, I did want to know if Lia had crossed the Mendoza line.

Green Chile Goulash

LIA COULDN'T CALL, BUT she could write letters. And after carefully reviewing them, the hospital staff let her send a bunch of them to me at one time.

I sat in The Grove restaurant in Albuquerque and drank an endless cups of coffee (poured by Selena) and skimmed through the letters. Most were of the typical "I love you, you're so brilliant" Lia routine. Not all the pages were there. Did the staff censor her letters?

I missed her.

As Selena brought me another cup of *Flora Azul,* one image flashed through my mind. I doubted that Lia would have had intercourse with the former governor. One image got to me however. Had the former governor gone "oral office" with his star-struck little staffer?

I thought of Lia and Mendoza, and forced myself past a tinge of jealousy. Regardless of whether he had slept with her or not, Mendoza was a material witness. He knew of the plan to set up Portia. Or at least he should have known. C de Baca actually believed the former governor was in the room with Lia, and maybe killed Portia himself.

What did Mendoza know? And when did he know it?

* * * * *

On Monday, I called Dr. Romero. It would be another week, she said. Maybe more. The whole suicide thing had set the testing back way back, as had the mistaken diagnosis. Dr. Romero still didn't want me talking to Lia, pending the final report.

"Why not?" I asked.

"You're a lawyer. You might contaminate her answers."

I hated it on CSI shows when they talked about "contaminating the crime scene." Here, Lia's brain might be the crime scene.

"I'm her attorney, I *can* write to her."

"That might not be a good idea either," Dr. Romero said. "Your representing her might be a problem as well."

"A problem?"

"The evaluation is not going well," Dr. Romero replied. "Not well at all."

She hung up before I could press further. I knew I shouldn't pester Dr. Romero as it could possibly make the evaluation come out even worse.

Diana called later that morning.

"Mendoza can meet with you tomorrow in Washington. He's still up for Secretary of Interior. He goes before the Judicial Committee on Wednesday, but he can give you half an hour tops in the Secretary's office. They're helping him prep for the Congressional hearings."

"The Secretary?"

"The Secretary of the Interior. They control all the natural resources in America. He's working over there now."

"Will you guys pay for the trip?"

"No. This is unofficial. Off the books—like a lot of things in New Mexico these days. And besides, C de Baca has cut our budget to the bone."

* * * * *

At lunch, I visited Eva. She was at a potluck in the District Court's Fourth Floor Atrium. Most of the other staff had prepared "Frito pies," red chile stew littered with Fritos. Eva grabbed my hand before I could get near someone else's crockpot. She insisted I sample her goulash that she had spiced up with green chile, in addition to the traditional paprika.

"A concession to moving to New Mexico," she said.

The goulash nearly burned my tongue from both heat and spices, and gave my mom's cooking a run for its money.

"Grow some balls, Danika," she said with a smile. "Women like men with balls."

I blushed, then Eva and I talked for a few moments about Governor Mendoza.

"Do you think he—" I started.

"You'll have to ask him yourself," she said, reading my mind. "His last year in office we grew apart."

There was a wistful look in her eyes. Eva's professional relationship with the former Governor had been a long one. Who knew if she had ever crossed the Mendoza line herself? The relationship, professional and personal, had not had a happy ending.

Oral Office

DÉJÀ VU MUGGED ME at the Albuquerque airport. It was a magnificent *faux* adobe structure from some alternative universe where the tribes had conquered the Spanish. I had made this flight all the time when I worked as a public defender in the small town of Aguilar, New Mexico and my parents still lived in the Washington area. This was the first time I had gone back since they had left D.C. and moved to Santa Fe.

As I walked down the long hallway leading to the B gates, I felt like the prodigal son, except that Washington wasn't my home, had not been in a long time. I no longer had any relatives or friends east of the Mississippi.

When I boarded the plane, the flight was full, due to yet another march on Washington. My claustrophobia hit hard the minute the passenger in front of me leaned their seat back. I squeezed against the window and imagined breathing in fresh air from the outside. I had a full-fledged panic attack and had to close my eyes.

"Are you all right?" my seatmate asked.

"Could I sit by the aisle?" I asked. "I don't like being closed in."

*****

During the flight, the pilot went out of his way to announce every location.

Halfway there I opened another letter from Lia. She missed me; she loved me. She was innocent. I smiled as I put down the letter. Then I looked at my surroundings. I was indeed trapped. I finally shut my eyes just after the pilot announced we were flying over St Louis's gateway arch. In my dream, a woman gave me a back rub. I just saw dark hair covering her face. I tried to push the hair away from the face, but I couldn't.

Who was the woman in my dream—Lia, Luna, or someone else?

When I woke up, we had already landed at Reagan National Airport. Inside, the terminal was more crowded than Albuquerque's Sunport. The corridors seemed half the size, the ceilings much lower. This airport probably had twice as many passengers wandering around half the space. Outside, the wet cold seeped through my bones. I hadn't been there ten minutes and I already felt soggy.

I spent the night at a crappy place close to the airport in nearby Arlington, Virginia. This joint was actually called the "El Cheapo." A sign said PLEASE, NO PROSTITUTION! A couple arriving just behind me saw the sign, cursed and left.

The motel owner, a recent immigrant, did not believe that New Mexico was within the United States borders. We argued about it as he checked my credit card. Thankfully, it went through, once he dialed an international number.

"I told you New Mexico was foreign country," he said.

The best sex ever was in room six of the El Cheapo motel. The moans of pleasure were louder than any I ever heard. I did not know people really could go all night. I knew this because I was in room seven. As I tossed and turned in a lumpy bed smelling of curry, I became homesick. I had a craving for green chile and posole. Washington definitely wasn't home any more.

Déjà vu mugged me again when I saw the Washington Monument gracefully cut into the cloudy sky. The mall was far more cramped than I remembered. How many more monuments could they build here? If I hadn't screwed up working for my mom and taken the public defender job in Aguilar, I'd have an office with a view of at least one monument.

Was I really from here?

I dressed in a blue suit, a blue-and-white striped shirt, and a red and blue striped tie. When I lived here, I had dressed this way every day. I took the Orange Line, the Metro light rail system linking the Virginia suburbs to downtown Washington. Other than the college students at George Washington University, everyone my age wore some variation of red white and blue. I kept looking out the Metro windows as if I expected to see a mountain range or the mesa instead of blank walls that encircled us like a concrete coffin. In this part of town, the Metro ran underground.

I walked to the massive Department of Interior building, which was just off the mall. One could fit thirty roundhouses into the Interior's gothic architecture. It looked like a huge military academy. More people worked here than lived in some New Mexico counties.

Luckily, an official badge waited for me at the security gate. Diana had come through for me. I wanted to joke to the guard about "Not needing no stinkin' badges," but his face was blank so I thought I'd better not. I deliberately left my belt with its metal buckle at home whenever I flew. I now constantly had to pull my pants up, but at least I had clean underwear.

Security was extremely tight. Other than the White House itself, Federal buildings were the top of the totem pole. When it came to security guards, they were lean and sharp. Regardless of race, they all reminded me of members of Jack Bauer's Counter Terrorism Unit on "*24*," and not adverse to torture.

The hallways of the Interior building reminded me slightly of the floor of the Checkerboard Mile back at the Metropolitan detention center, but they were straight, too straight. A Jack Bauer clone came over to check my credentials. He ran it through a portable electronic scanner to make sure it was legit. He then personally escorted me to the Secretary's outer office. Jack waited at the door just in case I turned out to be a terrorist.

Inside the Secretary's outer office, I saw mementoes from home on the wall: pictures of the Roundhouse, Taos Pueblo, and a couple of Georgia O'Keeffes with her obscene flowers.

The receptionist, Wendy, was a clone of my old girlfriend Veronica, the receptionist at the jail in Aguilar. Why had the jail had had someone so pretty? Every inmate had tried to hit on Veronica during booking. Every lobbyist no doubt tried to hit on Wendy.

Behind Wendy, an African American woman typed furiously. It must be something important, perhaps an agreement to turn the Grand Canyon into a water park. I didn't know human beings could type that fast. It actually scared me. People moved so much faster here.

I glanced at a flowchart of the Department of Interior. I knew the Secretary had power over surface mining and national parks. I didn't know that the Secretary also had power over all the fish and wildlife in America. Kinda like God, I suppose. I was way out of my league here. I really was just a hick from New Mexico; worse, I was a hick from Albuquerque.

Finally, Wendy took me through several crowded rooms to the Secretary's inner office. Inside, the Secretary 'Pro Tem' of Interior, the acting Secretary, excused himself. Wendy patted me down one last time, then left me alone with Secretary-Designate Mendoza. I thought again about power, and about Lia. I could not help but imagine Lia spread out on his desk, or worse, underneath it.

Stop it! I told myself.

"Dan Shepard, right?" he said. "Athena's son?"

"Mr. Governor. Or should I say, Mr. Secretary?"

"Not yet," he said. "Not yet."

"Thanks for seeing me on such short notice."

"Well, Diana said you had some important questions to ask. Off the record."

"It's about the murder."

"Which murder?"

His only worries had been about a land deal that could ruin his nomination. He had actually forgotten about the murder.

"The murder of Portia Smith C de Baca."

He nodded. "What do you want to know? That was the night of the election party. I was in Santa Fe with you. You can be my alibi if you want."

"That's not what this is about."

I showed him a copy of the note that read, LET'S USE CRAZY GIRL, over an attempt to write the word "bitch."

"Who wrote this note?" I asked.

Mendoza stood up. He towered over me. As Secretary of Interior he could have me buried in any of the national parks and a few of the Trust Territories.

"How did you get that?" he asked.

"I'd rather not say."

"This is off the record," he reminded me again.

"Of course."

He thought for a moment. He wanted to say something, then thought better of it. Finally, he nodded as if he had gotten his own story straight in his mind.

"I got my mail from Stone." Mendoza said. "He gave me the note. He must have written it. Or Rhiannon."

I couldn't follow all the moves of the political chess game going on between all of these players. I just kept going. "What did you do when you got the note?"

"Nothing. I certainly didn't act on it." Mendoza said.

"C de Baca thinks you might have been in the room when Portia was killed."

"C de Baca thinks a lot of things."

"Were you?"

"No. Of course not. As I stated, I have an alibi. There's a record of everywhere I go. You know that. Anything else?"

He glanced down at his briefing folder. I couldn't imagine what it would be like to go before a Senate Committee. I was just a gnat to him.

"Do you think that Lia did it?"

"That's for a judge to decide."

I saw a picture of White Sands National Monument. I didn't know whether the picture belonged to him, or the Acting Secretary. The Acting Secretary was from New Mexico as well. The state had a long tradition of sending men to Washington for public service. For some reason I felt emboldened with the power of all of New Mexico behind me.

"So was the murder part of a conspiracy involving your campaign?" I asked.

Shit. Did I really ask that? Eva had told me to be myself. I guess I finally had grown some balls.

Mendoza didn't hesitate. "I certainly wasn't a part of that conspiracy."

It took me a moment to realize that he hadn't answered my question.

He smiled. "I hope you realize that Stone was the man who had the most to gain from Agua-gate. As I disclosed in my financial packet to the Senate Committee, I sold my shares before I became governor."

Aqua-gate was about the cronies, and not about the man himself. And something told me that the former governor wouldn't hesitate to turn on his friends if it got him into this office.

Mendoza changed the subject. "Lia was a lot smarter than anyone gave her credit for. She actually came up with some of our policy points, especially on children's and women's issues."

"So she did work closely with you then."

He smiled a shy smile.

"Anything else?" he said.

His eyes were on a dossier on his desk. Perhaps he was about to sell all the off shore drilling rights to the Saudis.

There was something I did have to ask, the real reason I had maxed out my credit cards and risked claustrophobia to come here. I took a deep breath.

"So you *did* know Lia. You had worked with her before, yet when I met you at the party you pretended you were barely aware of her existence."

"So?"

"Why?"

He laughed. "I didn't want to hurt your feelings. Lia had me swear that I would never say how well I knew her to you. She was afraid you would get jealous."

"Jealous?"

"We knew each other well."

"You knew each other well. I mean, totally off the record, did you sleep with her?"

Why the hell did I ask that? Did I care more about Lia than I had been letting on?

He said nothing for a long while. He looked out at the Washington Monument as if it was a representation of his personal power. I felt dwarfed next to him, and scrunched into my chair.

But then he smiled. "You got me," he said.

I froze. This was not a man who liked to be "gotten."

There was a long pause. "And yes, I did . . . proposition her, so to speak. As we were drafting a policy paper on children's health care."

"Article Seven?"

"Article Seven," he said. "But she said no. Do you know why?"

"No, I don't."

"Because she said she was in love with someone else."

I started to smile.

But he kept going before I could say anything.

"She said she was in love with the current Governor, Mr. C de Baca."

I nearly fainted. He laughed. He actually slapped his knees as if to announce that he had just given a "knee-slapper."

"I'm kidding," he said. "She said she was in love with you."

Anasazi's Revenge

A FEW HOURS LATER I took the night flight out of Washington, the last guy off the stand-by list. God himself didn't want me to stay in Washington and breathe that cold wet air another minute.

I had to talk to The Werewolf one more time. I would tell him that C de Baca had a note linking him to using Lia on the campaign. His old boss, the former governor, was not going to protect him either. I wasn't going to tell him I had spilled the beans about his plan to blackmail C de Baca regarding Portia.

Still, I hoped The Werewolf would keep his word. He had said he would tell me what really happened that night if I brought him back some useful information. The final vote on House Bill Sixty-Nine would be tomorrow.

The shit would hit the fan.

Early the next morning, I called the party office in the Roundhouse, and asked for Stone. The staffer was apprehensive. "Can you give me the gist of what you're going to tell him?"

"I talked to C de Baca and I talked with Mendoza," I said. "Both of them said things Mr. Stone needs to hear. Time is of the essence and I feel I should talk to him in person. He said he had information for me in return."

She called me back a few minutes later. "He's expecting you

around nine tonight," she said. "He's at the Inn of the Anasazi. Room 300."

"Did you say the Anasazi Room? Do you mean the one in the Eldorado?"

"No, the *Inn* of the Anasazi. It's on Washington Street, north of the plaza."

That sounded promising. The Anasazi certainly deserved their own inn. I hoped that the Anasazi would work their magic.

The Inn of the Anasazi was one of the nicest hotels in the state. I had been in Washington, and now I was on Santa Fe's Washington Street. The two could not be more different. Washington Street held a few nice stores and galleries, as well as the Santa Fe public library. There was power here, but it was subtle, ancient, intimate. Washington itself reeked of power, but the white marble buildings made the visitor feel small.

I paid for parking in the city lot a few blocks to the south, then ran across the plaza because it was so cold in the high desert air. The plaza was utterly empty; every store was closed, and the traditional Native American vendors lining the plaza were long gone as well. The roar of sirens and ambulances echoed through the narrow roads. They sounded as if they were headed toward Washington Street so I started running toward the Inn. When did I start chasing ambulances?

Emergency vehicles were parked at the Inn by the time I arrived. A young reporter stood in front of the main entrance. He spoke in soft measured tones, as paramedics wheeled two covered bodies out of the building.

"What happened?" I asked a cop doing crowd control.

"C de Baca and Stone got in a fight, and it turned deadly."

A deadly fight? I knew politics was dirty, but this was worse than I had ever imagined.

My statement to C de Baca about The Werewolf's plans might have had led to a series of unfortunate events. Telling The Werewolf that I had talked to C de Baca didn't help either. Was this my fault?

Every local law enforcement agency possible arrived in the
next few minutes. The Governor was dead. This was huge. An
FBI agent led a pack of men all dressed in the same black suit
and red tie. Uniformed state troopers worked crowd control and
told every one to stand clear of the door.

I felt another tinge of guilt. I certainly hadn't wanted anyone
to die. I suddenly felt colder. The FBI agents looked big and
scary. I would fold under questioning so quickly that I would
confess to Lincoln's assassination if they pressed hard enough. I
walked back across the plaza to my car.

On the way home, details on the radio were vague.
Announcers kept talking about a great tragedy for all of New
Mexico.

I finally learned the particulars on the early newscast the
next morning. The Werewolf had called C de Baca and the two
had had words over the phone. C de Baca then went over to the
room to settle the score. He went alone; Xavier was out of town
and couldn't stop him. I then heard the dreaded words you hear
with nearly every deadly accident in New Mexico: "Police suspect that alcohol was a factor."

Both men were armed. There weren't metal detectors at the
hotel. I had a vision of the Aaron Burr-Alexander Hamilton duel,
but this fight was far less formal than that. The words heated to
the point where both drew weapons and fired simultaneously.
Mutually assured destruction.

I had another pang of guilt. Had my questioning of C de
Baca pushed him over the edge? No, X had said the Governor
had been sneaking drinks. Still, I know my questioning about
Portia didn't help. X had said when his brother drank, he became
a different person.

X was right. Without Portia, C de Baca was a common street
thug and The Werewolf was no better. The Werewolf didn't
seem like a drinker. Perhaps his drug of choice was cocaine. As

a criminal lawyer I'd seen a lot of men in tailored suits do crazy things on cocaine.

Maybe they argued over disclosures regarding Portia. Maybe Lia's name came up as well. No one would know. Without staff members to hold them back, pure emotion had heated to a fever pitch.

I sipped a Mountain Dew to get my mind working that early in the morning. Shit, with The Werewolf gone, he could never tell me what really happened that night. I had lost a valuable source of information.

Then I realized who really wanted both Stone and C de Baca dead: The Anasazi, the ancient tribe whose name was memorialized in a room at the Eldorado and at the fated hotel. Both men had disgraced this beautiful state. Both men had disgraced the Anasazi's legacy. Even though my best contact was gone, I knew I would somehow find another source of information. Besides, I doubted I could trust either The Werewolf or C de Baca.

"Yay, Anasazi!" I said out loud.

Leaving Las Vegas

THE ENTIRE STATE SHUT down for several days, during which time few additional details emerged. Diana Crater released a terse statement that "everything was under investigation." Apparently Portia's death was just the tip of the iceberg. Attorney General Crater would investigate both political parties for months to come.

I kept waiting for the FBI to call me to ask me something, anything. But as more details emerged I got over my fear that I had caused the two men to kill each other. This feud between the political *Montagues* and *Capulets* had gone on for generations. The FBI had a long list of people they needed to talk to before they made it to me, if ever.

I couldn't help but quote Shakespeare. "A plague on both your houses," I said out loud. Mercutio's dying words in *Romeo and Juliet*.

A plague on both their houses indeed.

The hospital was on lock-down like the rest of the state but Lia somehow got through on a phone line toward the end of the week.

"The testing is done," she said. "Now they just have to write it up."

"So I can't contaminate you any more?"

"Something like that," she said. "I need to speak to you in person. There's something I have to tell you."

I couldn't read her tone. "What?"

"I have to tell you in person."

When I arrived at the hospital the guards directed me to a reception area with a wall of amazing pieces of resident art that could hold its own in a Canyon Road gallery. Some of the inmate art was actually for sale at a remarkable discount.

"Our prices are *insane!*" I couldn't help but say out loud. "We *cut* out the middleman."

A section of the wall had a big sign: WATERCOLORS BY LIA. The angel was there of course, along with a giant white bird flying out of the hospital. The bird was too big to be a dove and it had a big orange mouth that was carrying something. Was it a pelican carrying a fish? I was too far away to tell.

I wandered over to the receptionist to ask about buying some of the art. Unfortunately, they didn't take credit cards.

After what seemed like nine months, Lia finally arrived from inside. We sat there in the gallery right underneath her painting. I tried to pretend that we really were in a Santa Fe gallery on Canyon Road.

Lia wore a white sweater I had never seen before. She had progressed up the ranks enough that they let her wear a flower in her hair, a white daisy.

White meant innocent, right? Lia had a glow about her, and she'd gained even more weight. She had the apprehensive look of someone about to graduate from high school who was unsure of life after graduation.

"I'm leaving this week," she said. "Dr. Romero pulled some strings, and I'll be in a hospital in Albuquerque for the duration rather than at MDC."

"That's great."

"So what do you think will happen?"

"Depends on the report."

"I'm not incompetent or insane," she said. "You know me. Do you really think I'm fucking crazy?"

I bit my lip. C de Baca's stories had raised some doubts. I was also surprised by her profanity. Lia almost never swore.

"I can get letters from all the other residents here saying I'm not crazy," she said.

I remembered those residents from the party. There was a crazy lawyer. Maybe he had some weight.

"I don't think that would help." I tried to stare her down, but she wouldn't meet my eyes. "Who else was there with you that day? Your mom?"

"I made a promise. I can't tell you."

"Who did you make that promise to?"

"I can't tell you that either."

"I don't get it. Why is competency and sanity such a big deal to you? You've been here before in the hospital, for an entire year. You've survived."

That hit a nerve. "I would rather be guilty than crazy. Just don't ever say that I'm crazy! I'll kill myself if you say that I'm crazy!"

"But if you're convicted you go to prison."

She didn't bat an eye. "I checked online about the rules at the female correctional facility out west. It's run by a private company and they allow daily visitation. Daily contact visitation with immediate family if you're on honors. Especially for new mothers."

Who would have thought a woman's prison would be better than a mental hospital? Then what she said sunk in. "New mothers?"

"That's why I don't want to be here in an institution." She looked me in the eye. "If you're found incompetent, you can't be a mother."

"What?"

"It happened before. I was here when I was seventeen and they took my baby away. It's called 'TPR.' Termination of Parental rights."

"TPR?"

Through her tears, Lia told me when she was committed here when she was seventeen, the State took her child away. It was a closed adoption. She had never seen her daughter; a military family had taken her. In the last thirteen years, there had been no contact. She didn't even know if her daughter was alive.

I then looked at Lia's painting on the wall. It wasn't a pelican. It wasn't a dove. It was a *stork!*

Suddenly it dawned on me, the whole new mother thing. It was happening all over again.

"Are you pregnant?" I asked.

"I'm late," she said. "It happens sometimes. The doctors said I'm under too much stress. I usually hide it, but I'm freaking out and it's affecting my body. That could be why I've missed my period."

"You're in a hospital. Have you seen a doctor to get a test? Don't they have to test before they give you meds?"

I tried to do the math; she'd be around two months along. She wasn't showing, yet. Still, she had gained some weight. And she did have that glow.

She shook her head. "No. I told you I wouldn't take their meds. So they can't test me for anything. That's Article Forty-Two of the Mental Health Code. I know my rights."

"Your rights?"

"I don't want them to take my baby again. I'll be out of here before I give birth this time. I made up my mind, I'm keeping my baby."

"Papa don't preach, I made up my mind, I'm keeping my baby." I sang.

"Is everything a joke to you?"

"No, it's not a joke," I said. "But you might be keeping your baby in prison."

Then I realized who would have to care for the baby if that happened. I was not cut out to be a father, not at all. I could barely change my own underwear. Hell, I was in still in puberty and I was pushing forty.

After we talked a few more minutes, a guard came to take Lia away.

"Do you guys have any extra rooms?" I asked. "I think I might have to check in here."

Act III
Mama

Mostly Harmless

NEW MEXICO CONTINUED ITS lock-down during the next few days. The entire state was falling apart. The lock down finally ended, but the State's phones remained out. I couldn't ask Lia anything, even if I wanted to.

Later that week a uniformed courier hand-delivered Dr. Romero's report as if it was a matter of national security. I needed a place to read it, to digest the report. I almost went with Starbucks, but even in Albuquerque, Starbucks was crowded with failed screenwriters nursing a single cappuccino for hours. I had been a failed screenwriter once, and they were a surly lot. One of them might look over my shoulder and try to steal Lia's psych evaluation and turn it into a screenplay.

I finally decided on the Frontier, across from UNM. The Frontier was a collection of several bland storefronts topped by a bright yellow roof that was supposed to evoke a barn. Combined it was one of Albuquerque's coolest hang-out. It had been there for over a hundred years, when this stretch of Central Avenue actually was the final frontier.

The "barn" was packed with the usual transients and prostitutes, some of them boldly going where no man had gone before. I knew many of the transients by nickname now: Naked Guy, Calculator Man, and Flasher Woman. The sidewalk smelled of fresh urine from the throbbing mass of transients sleeping on the sidewalks.

The interior décor featured western memorabilia with UNM logos and paintings of cowboys. I don't think any of the major Santa Fe galleries had paintings of cowboys anymore. Diners included yuppies, students, and the few relatively lucky transients with borrowed change. I waited in line, ordered the "number one," *chorizo* instead of bacon, and replaced the tortilla with an extra pancake. Just to prove I was a real New Mexican, I put the delicious red-chile salsa on my eggs, over easy.

Lia's forensic evaluation report was five pages long. Lia had been there for weeks, and she was only worth five pages. The report didn't include any medical information, so the question of pregnancy was *not* answered, one way or another. I wondered if Dr. Romero had to rush the report and didn't have access to all the data because of the lock-down. I could barely write a report in college if my neighbors were loud. Imagine writing something in the midst of an asylum.

Dr. Romero was a big fan of the passive voice, unfortunately. She often used long words when shorter words would do. She repeated the same phrases over and over again. "Ophelia Paz, the Forensic Evaluation of" was not destined to be a bestseller or a literary masterpiece.

The report began with Lia's life history. Dr. Romero was unable to obtain a birth certificate prior to completion of the report. She did note that Lia had a normal childhood in Deming for the first few years and then Albuquerque until her dad died when she was thirteen.

I tried to play amateur shrink. Lia was always looking for a father figure. I sure hoped she wasn't looking for a father figure in me.

As to family life: "Subject's family history could not be

independently verified." Dr. Romero was unsure whether Lia's mother was alive, or exactly how her father died. Dr. Romero related that Lia offered conflicting information regarding her mother. Dr. Romero speculated that Lia was reluctant to convey information regarding her mother, since her mother "might possibly be an illegal alien subject to deportation." Overall, Lia's "narrative lacked internal consistency."

Dr. Romero next described the first "incident" with C de Baca at Albuquerque High. Lia stated that she had innocently flirted with C de Baca, who then forced himself upon her at a Christmas party. Dr. Romero stated she was unsure of Lia's "veracity." Why couldn't she just say she didn't know whether Lia was telling the truth?

I already knew Dr. Romero's next paragraph. Lia's assessment of rape against C de Baca "could not be independently verified." Dr. Romero did state that Lia displayed "obsessive behavior that could be a product of post-traumatic stress disorder." However she hesitated to make that diagnosis. Again, those magic words: Lia's narrative "lacked internal consistency."

Dr. Romero was aware of Lia's prior stay at the facility. That had been more than ten years ago, and she didn't have access to those records. Lia was also a minor at the time, which created another mass of red tape. Many of those records were "located in an unavailable area of the facility."

I had this vision of insurgent inmates taking over the archives and denying access unless a few hits of Valium were exchanged.

Dr. Romero did confirm that Lia had been the subject of a TPR action while in State custody. At least Lia had internal consistency on that point.

As for the account of the murder allegations involving Portia C de Baca, Dr. Romero also could not come to a conclusion. Lia's account again lacked "internal consistency." Dr. Romero did find Lia's assertion that Portia Smith C de Baca was alive when Lia left the home to be "highly improbable."

Dr. Romero then wrote, "Subject became agitated after interviewer continued with questions and kept repeating the phrase: "She told me not to tell." Dr. Romero stated that questioning stopped due to "patient's extreme agitation."

Dr. Romero did not learn the identity of the person who made Lia make that promise. The doctor speculated that it was Lia's mother, but could not confirm.

As to Lia's tendency toward violence, Dr. Romero used the unfortunate phrase "mostly harmless." Where had I heard that phrase before? And what did she mean by "mostly?"

In the next paragraph, Dr. Romero wrote that Lia had tremendous respect for her lawyer, and admired the great work he had done. Lia often described him as "brilliant." The report became part of the permanent record at the State Hospital, but at least generations of med students would have a good opinion of me, assuming they didn't store the report in an "unavailable area of the facility."

Dr. Romero next discussed Lia's stay at the hospital. It was "otherwise unremarkable, with the exception of the suicide attempt and some suicidal ideation."

Lia's suicide attempt was "not probative of anything, other than an example of a 'narcissistic personality.'" Perhaps the doctor gave the suicide attempt such scant attention because the hospital might have some liability if such an attempt succeeded.

Dr. Romero also repeated Lia's statement that she would rather be found guilty of murder than be found insane or incompetent as indicative of obsessive compulsive behavior.

That was another factor in her finding that Lia's reporting of her past history might lack veracity.

I glanced through the rest of the report. I reminded myself that competency and sanity were two different issues. Lia could have been insane at the time of the murder, but still be competent to stand trial, or vice versa.

To make it even more complicated, Lia needed the "ability to form specific intent" to be a legally sane and competent murderer. The fact that she was either bi-polar or obsessive compulsive didn't matter in a court of law. Even post traumatic stress disorder wasn't necessarily a symptom of insanity. I quickly turned to the conclusion page.

Dr. Romero stated: "Subject is either a traumatized young woman with mild paranoia and poor impulse control, or a complete sociopath. She does understand the charges against her. She is highly intelligent. She can assist her attorney at trial. That is all that is necessary for this reviewer to offer the opinion that Ophelia Paz is competent to stand trial according to the dictates of the New Mexico statutes."

Dr. Romero then turned to the issue of insanity. "Defendant is obsessive, but is certainly sane now, due to her treatment here. However, as previously stated, due to a lack of subject's internal consistency, this evaluator cannot make an expert opinion regarding sanity at the time of the incident."

Cannot make an assessment? I read the next paragraph. "Given the subject's utter lack of cooperation with this particular interviewer on certain essential topics, this was not an appropriate referral for a diagnostic."

Not an appropriate referral? Shit. Now what the hell do I do? I would have to go through a competency hearing next week with "not an appropriate referral?"

On my way out, a short woman in a skanky dress came over to me. It took me a moment to recognize Bebe Tran.

"How'd did you know where I was?" I asked.

I know everything," she said. "I'm a cop. Got some good news."

"I don't know if I like good news coming from you," I said. "Let's go back inside."

The restaurant was still crowded. No one looked like an undercover cop. Maybe I was getting too paranoid, but I still didn't trust Bebe.

"I thought you were in Vietnam for *Tet.*"

"My family in Vietnam made it quite clear that they didn't want to see me until I get a real job. They don't quite grasp the concept of a decoy. They confuse me and my mom. Speaking of mothers. . . . "

She shook her head, then handed me a photograph. I looked around. I didn't see a SWAT team anywhere.

I took the photo. "You find her mother?" I asked. "Her mother confessed? Is that your good news?"

"Well I guess it's good news for me."

I looked at the photo. The woman was identical to the woman in Lia's picture. Bebe then showed me a border patrol report indicating that woman was dead, shot near a border checkpoint.

"This her mother?" Bebe asked.

"Looks like the woman I saw in the photo."

"Well, I confirmed with Border Patrol that this woman did indeed die about ten years ago at the border crossing in the desert near Deming, New Mexico."

"I don't know if that's good news for me or not," I looked at Bebe. "Why is it so important for you for Lia to be found incompetent?"

Bebe stopped. I had asked her a question she didn't know the answer to.

Finally she said, "I headed the raid that picked up Lia. Her arrest was done by our mental health unit with the help of the SWAT team. I put my reputation on the line that in my expert opinion Lia Spaz was mentally ill, and not just your run of the mill misfit. I'm on thin ice over at APD as it is. Once you say someone is crazy, they better *stay* crazy or internal affairs comes down on you hard."

Bebe eyes were apprehensive. She wasn't playing this time.

"I'm counting on you to help a girl out here," she said.

I thought back to our last encounter. I didn't respond.

* * * * *

I sat in my car and didn't start it. I tried to think of another explanation, but my mind locked up. So Lia would have been an appropriate referral to the mental health system after all. The whole thing about her mother calling, that had to be a sign of it. If I could just get that information into the report.

But what did it all mean? Perhaps Lia had lied to me all along about her mother? Or perhaps Lia was mentally ill. Totally harmless, not just mostly harmless. I thought of the wig.

Had I knocked up this woman? Hopefully my craziness and Lia's craziness would act as a zero sum. If not, you might as well lock the kid up in Vegas *before* birth.

I tried calling the hospital, but no one answered and I didn't have a cell number for Dr. Romero. Instead, I called Eva.

"I want to delay the hearing. The report is incomplete and I've got new information."

I could barely hear her; Eva had a very quiet phone voice.

"The judge won't be *boldog,* happy, about that, *Danika.*" Eva said.

"Can't we continue the hearing for a later date?"

"Not without the prosecutor stipulating," Eva said. "I'll call the prosecutor for you, then get back to you."

I sat in my car in the parking lot for an hour. I didn't know what to do. I didn't know where to go. Bad things would happen to Lia. I wouldn't be able to save her. I was no white knight after all.

Lia was right. This wasn't a joke.

Eva didn't call me until after five. By that time I was trying to work off the stress on the Stairmaster at the gym. I had to get off the stairs to hear her.

Perhaps she'd learned to be so quiet on the phone growing up under a dictator and was used to whispering.

"So sorry, *Danika*. The State wouldn't agree. However, you can bring up your points up at the next hearing and maybe the judge will delay for you.

"So this will be the hearing about the hearing?"

"I have no idea what it will be," she said.

The End of the Roller Coaster

THAT NIGHT, I TRIED to find Lia again. They had moved her from Las Vegas to an undisclosed facility in Albuquerque. I called all the possible hospitals, but none would confirm or deny her admittance. Maybe they were hiding her for security reasons.

The next day, I hurried to Luna's office in Barrio Wells Park, the BWP. The city had put up NO PARKING WITHOUT PERMIT signs all over the place. I had to park a few blocks north, deep into gang territory. I thought of an old rap song that announced "wear the wrong color, your life could end." I wore a red tie. Hopefully the local gangs here wouldn't hold that against me.

On the walk south, I passed a few law offices that resembled fortified outposts. They had serious iron grating over their windows, and many had electronic cameras on their roofs. The cold war between gentrification and decay had escalated to the point of sectarian violence.

Gentrification might be winning, but decay wouldn't surrender without a fight. One resident had countered the lawyer onslaught by turning his lot into a menagerie of cats, dogs and auto parts. I heard barking and honking from several species as I walked past his house. A block later I saw a few lawyers in gray pinstripe walking down 5th Street to Metro court, side by side with their tattooed criminal clients. Law and disorder walking hand in hand.

* * * * *

Inside Luna's adobe sanctuary, Jen asked, "Are you paying rent here yet?"

"I'm working on it," I said.

I noticed that Jen had an opened a criminal procedure textbook. I had forgotten that she was in law school.

"You've got papers coming up?" I asked.

"Criminal Procedure today. Bankruptcy tomorrow."

"Sounds like my life," I said.

She laughed. Maybe she was finally warming up.

"I've already survived criminal procedure in real life," she said. "But that's another story."

She didn't elaborate, and changed the subject.

"I'll call Luna. I don't know how happy she'll be to see you."

"Why you don't like me much?"

"Because it's all about you. You've like totally got a crush on Luna, and also on that other girl, what's her name, again?"

"Lia."

I didn't want to bring up my latest predicament with Lia.

Jen continued. "But it isn't about them, their feelings, and their needs. It's all about you. Like totally all about you. Each of them has got something you need so you can fill some emotional void."

I didn't know how to respond to that. Jen had diagnosed me with Dan Shepard's Disease. She was much smarter than she looked.

I knew the disease, but what was the cure? They would need a whole wing up in Vegas dedicated to treating me—the Dan Shepard Disease wing. They'd probably have to fly specialists in from Zurich.

Luna's office door opened. She was dressed casually, about to go for a run at three in the afternoon.

"Jen, did you forget to file the restraining order against Mr. Shepard?"

"I'll take it over to the court right now," Jen said.

"Luna, I really need your help," I said.

We went into her office and I handed her the report. Luna looked at it as if I had just handed her an envelope full of anthrax, then opened the report and skimmed over it.

"At least it says she's a sociopath as opposed to a psychopath," Luna said. "And she's harmless, well mostly harmless."

"Where have I heard that before?"

"*Mostly Harmless* was the title of a book by Douglas Adams. It was a sequel to *Hitchhiker's Guide to the Galaxy.* It was how Ford Prefect described the earth before it was destroyed."

A woman who could throw out obscure citations just like me. She was good.

"You can concede the competency and go right to trial," she said. "They don't have an eyewitness to the actual murder. You can try to win on reasonable doubt, if you're man enough. You can blame it all on her mother."

"I don't think I can do that with a straight face," I said. I showed her the picture of Lia's late mother.

Luna frowned. "And Lia claims her mother is still alive?"

"She even takes phone calls from her," I said. "I guess they would be imaginary phone calls."

"Imaginary phone calls are not good," Luna said. "Well, it *is* a good thing if you want to prove insanity. You just have to get that information to Dr. Romero so she can put it in the report."

"Too late, " I said. "The report has been filed, and the hospital is apparently locked down for the duration. As I said, I need your help. I have no idea what to do."

Luna thought for a long time.

"Dan," she said finally, "we've been on an emotional roller coaster in the very short time we've known each other."

I expected her to say that it was too emotional, that perhaps it would be best if I just got on my way. I heard sirens wailing off in the distance.

"On my first murder case in Crater County, I didn't become a real lawyer until I got too emotional," she said.

"What do you mean?"

"I was a prosecutor back then. One of the victims had a silver cross. I found it at her house after she died. I started wearing it as a way of getting empathy for my client. I became a much better advocate on her behalf."

"Is that the same cross?"

"No, I lost it a few weeks after the trial." She shrugged. "This is a cheap knock off Jen bought me at a Korean church."

"So what should I do?"

"I think that's a question you need to answer for yourself. But why is it such a big deal for you to have my seal of approval?"

"Because with Lia in the insane asylum, and my mother on yet another world tour, you're the only sane woman I know."

Luna frowned and stared at some old movie posters. "Sometimes I think my clients want me to be that character in that Mel Gibson movie, the one where the guy got tortured and saved everyone at the end."

"*Braveheart?*"

"No the one with the Romans."

"*Gladiator?*"

"Wrong Australian, that was Russell Crowe. No, it was the one he directed."

I had never heard of the movies on her posters. What was she talking about? "*Apocalypto?*"

"I'm talking about the character in the movie who was tortured by the Romans, who then comes back and saves the world at the end."

"Jesus in '*Passion of the Christ?*'"

She looked me directly in the eye. "That's who your clients expect you to be."

The Hearing About the Hearing

EVA HAD VERACITY WHEN it came to setting hearings. She put the "hearing about the hearing" on Friday morning's pre-trial docket. Unlike his regular docket, Judge Kurtz held his pre-trial hearings in the jury room next to the courtroom. His bailiff, Rachel Santini, made all the lawyers wait in the courtroom as she stood at the doorway, shouting out case numbers. Rachel wore a hip black cocktail dress that made her look like the hostess of a restaurant specializing in Pan Asian Fusion cuisine.

God forbid if you weren't ready when Rachel called your number, or you went to the back of the line. The line was especially long today, as the rest of the judges were at a judicial conclave in Reno, of all places. Why would judges have a conclave in the only place with legal prostitution? That meant Judge Kurtz was now the law west *and* east of the Pecos; he had to tackle every emergency hearing in the building.

"You got a break last time, so he's putting you dead last," Rachel said to me. "Eva can't save you this time."

The docket was pages and pages thick. Dead last would take a long time.

"Could we leave and come back?" I asked.

"No. Once you're in, you're in for the day. He once held a lawyer in contempt who had to leave to do a sentencing in a death penalty case."

I gulped. I didn't bother to ask whether the defendant had been executed.

I had made it a point to dress well thinking it's better to look good than to feel good. Well, in my gray pinstriped Ralph Lauren suit and purple abstract Jerry Garcia tie, I sure looked good, even if I felt like day-old dog shit.

Despite my claim of becoming an Albuquerque lawyer, I was still an outsider here, so no lawyers greeted me in the court-room. I overheard low mumbling from two lawyers in the gallery, " . . . slept with his client."

I grabbed some coffee from the back room. Rachel had made it extra strong, and I could feel my veins turn dark brown as the caffeine flowed right to my heart.

I scanned the gallery. Most defendants dressed casually except the sex offenders out on bond. They wore suits and ties, some dressing better than their lawyers. The clothing store by the Frontier must have had a sex offender suit sale, 50 percent off, because they all wore the same polyester brown jacket and slacks. Sex offenders also liked yellow ties for some reason.

It was crowded in front, so Rachel indicated that I would have sit in the gallery with the defendants.

"Nice suit," one defendant asked me as I sat down. "What are you in for?"

"Attempted murder," I said. "One I'm about to attempt any minute now."

He backed off.

A few minutes later, Lia arrived accompanied by hospital security. She wore loose white clothing that hid any possible baby bump and a black plastic flower in her hair. Perhaps the hospital didn't trust her with a live flower on the outside.

The hospital security guard turned Lia over to a sheriff's deputy in a tan uniform. The deputy looked like a basketball power forward from Argentina when he stood close to the much shorter Lia. He made Lia sit down next to me. He then stood right in front of us, eclipsing the rest of the room.

"So do you know if you're pregnant yet?" I asked.

"Not yet," she said. "It still could be stress."

"And you still won't take a test?"

"Not until this whole competency issue is settled. I don't want them to know."

"Let's just get through this hearing first," I said. I wanted to bring up the issue of her mother, but I was too nervous.

We sat in silence for an hour. Even though the judge whipped right through the eight-thirty cases, the room grew more crowded from the nine o'clocks.

"Do you want this one too?" Power Forward asked.

He pointed to an inmate who wore a blue Department of Corrections (DOC) jumpsuit, meaning he'd already been sentenced. He was the real deal, a DOC lifer. He shook his shackles like Marley's ghost.

"Baby lawyer," he said. "You all growed up now."

It took me a second to recognize him, Jesús Villalobos, Anna Maria's husband, my first client when I was a public defender in Aguilar. His head was shaved now, and he had even more tattoos and bigger muscles than when I had represented him.

"Fresh white meat," he called out to me as if I was as green as the rookie prosecutor. "Don't you remember me, *ese?*"

I couldn't disavow my first client. "Of course," I said. "Officer, put him next to me. Just for a moment."

"Hey, *ese,* what's happening?" I asked, pretending to be cool.

Power Forward came closer, destroying any illusion of attorney client privilege. Jesús now had several more teardrops tattooed on his face. I had read once that the most popular name in joint was Jesús.

He looked at Lia, who was sitting on the other side of me.

"Who's your girlfriend?"

"She's not my girlfriend, she's my client. Her name is Ophelia Paz. She's innocent."

"Nice to meet you, Ophelia. Dan was my lawyer once. Long

time ago when he was a baby lawyer. He thought I was innocent too."

I didn't have time to explain that Jesús was not currently incarcerated on the murder charge I had represented him on, but Lia interrupted.

"Can we move?" she whispered to me, so Jesús couldn't hear. "I don't want to sit here with criminals like that."

As we moved to another row, I nearly tripped over Jesús's lawyer, Pete Baca, my old boss down in Aguilar.

"Guess you're not a big Hollywood lawyer yet, are you?" he said. "You're still in the trenches with the rest of us."

I was in the trenches all right. My God, could this day get any worse?

Rachel came over and reminded me to be quiet or I might never be called at all.

"You stay cool. I can still get my zapper. If you act up I can zap your ass."

"We're cool," I lied.

The morning dragged on. I called it the "physics of justice." Time always moved slowest when waiting in a crowded courtroom. The ten o'clocks were probation violators and they took more time in the back room because the judge had to set hearings for their old charge and for their violation.

Lia and I sat in silence. I was afraid to go to the bathroom because the judge would make me do the hearing with my pants down. The noon hour loomed closer and closer. Lia grew more agitated as Rachel called number after number.

"We got to get back or we'll miss lunch," Lia said.

Her body had been programmed in Vegas. They ate at noon, exactly, an institutional obsessive-compulsiveness. Missing lunch would not only mess with her stomach, it would mess with her mind.

The room was now filled way past capacity. If this wasn't an exempt courtroom, we'd have a fire hazard. My claustrophobia worsened as an obese sex offender in a brown suit and pink tie now squished Lia and me against the far wall. I privately called him Mr. Pink, due to his tie. It had the Japanese anime character "Hello Kitty" on the tie, which made it worse. His face was as ugly as the actor Steve Buscemi. Meanwhile, Power Forward's ass was now right in my face, another wall closing in on me.

Luna had a case today and Rachel had placed her on the pre-trial list ahead of me. It was the first time I had seen Luna and Lia in the same room since the election party. The difference was staggering. Silver and gold indeed. I watched Luna charm the prosecutor from a sentence of one year "community custody" down to a "conditional discharge" in less than thirty seconds. She might hate practicing, but Luna was the lawyer I had always wanted to be.

Lia noticed that I was staring at Luna.

"She doesn't love you," Lia said. "I love you!"

"Are you talking to me?" Mr. Pink, the obese sex offender, asked.

An hour later Lia and I repeated the same dialogue we had before. She insisted she was competent and refused to give up her mother. She still didn't know if she was pregnant, and didn't want to take a test yet.

Then she said it again and again.

I was now far more agitated than Lia. Hunger, claustrophobia and jealousy mixed like heroin and anti-matter in my gut. My stomach growled so loudly that Rachel came over.

"Be quiet," she said. "Both of you."

I put my hands up, didn't say a word. Voices roared inside my head. Fathering a child with a mentally ill murderer. Technically the conception had taken place before I was her lawyer. Still, that didn't make me feel any better. I felt like I was the one about to give birth.

Rachel might have told us to be quiet, but she let the other lawyers slide. She saw them on a daily basis. The lawyers in polo shirts talked at a steady hum, occasionally breaking into laughter at some private joke. Were they joking about me?

Luna came out when her pre-trial was over and walked right by us. She sat on the other side, flirting with one of the burly correctional officers.

Rachel excused herself find a file from downstairs. Once she left the room, the din grew louder.

"So what bills have they passed this session?" I asked Lia, hoping to get her mind off the proceedings.

Lia began talking about the House bills that had recently passed. A state senator had introduced a bill about bringing back cockfighting, which had been banned a few years ago. Another senator wanted a special exemption for smoking at cockfights.

Lia's prattling agitated me even more.

More people came in from outside and sat in the jury box with us. Mr. Pink moved closer. There was no air back here. None at all. Mr. Pink developed a case of hiccups.

Lia didn't want to talk politics any more.

"So what's going to happen with my case?"

Hiccup. Mr. Pink gave an embarrassed smile, and pointed to Hello Kitty on his tie, as if the kitty was the one doing the hiccupping.

"Do we have a chance?" Lia asked.

"I don't know."

"What's going to happen today?"

"It would help if your mother magically appeared."

Hiccup.

"I'm not giving up my mother."

"Then, I've got to prove you're insane. Whether you like it or not, it's our only hope."

"But that would be lying," she said. "I'm not insane, and you know it."

It was now well past noon. I passed my breaking point hours ago.

Hiccup.

I couldn't resist any more. "I don't think you have a mother," I said. "I think she's dead."

"I have a mother."

Hiccup.

"Where is she then?"

"She's here."

I looked around the courtroom.

"No mother, here."

I was about to pick up the photo and ruin her world.

"What is she, invisible?"

"She's here. In the building. I promised her."

Hiccup.

That did it. That damn hiccup. Something in me snapped.

"I'm sick of your fucking promise. I don't give a fuck if you go to a mental hospital until the end of fucking time. I'm trying to save your fucking life here!"

"I'm not crazy!" she said. "My mother is alive. And I want to be a mother! You can't stop me! You can't say I'm crazy!"

"You're fucking crazy if I say you're fucking crazy!" I yelled at the top of my lungs. "And if you want to live, and you won't give up your dead mother, you have to be fucking crazy!"

Lia was too shocked to respond.

I looked around to absolute silence. There was even silence in the jury room. Then I heard some muffled whispering from the judge.

Out of nowhere, Rachel came over to us.

"Mr. Shepard, will you come in to see the judge for a second?"

We would get in before Mr. Brown and Mr. Pink. Good.

I motioned for the transport officer to take Lia in, but Rachel shook her head.

"Just you. This *isn't* the pre-trial hearing. Your client won't be necessary. The judge wants to talk to you. Alone."

Hiccup.

The Lady Justice is a Tramp

I WENT INTO THE jury room where the judge and Eva sat with the court reporter. They didn't even bother to move Jesús out of the room. His face held a smirk.

This jury room was even more cramped than the other room. It was built for a jury of midgets apparently. There was an abstract portrait of a bare-breasted Lady Justice on the back wall. I forced myself not to look.

"Mr. Shepard," the judge said. "I'm giving you a minute to tell me why I should not hold you in contempt for your outburst just now. You've disturbed the decorum of my courtroom. You've destroyed any semblance of attorney-client privilege. I suspect this whole competency thing is a ruse because you have no real defense. I read the report where Dr. Romero said this was *not* an appropriate referral."

"But—"

"You have wasted the court's time, you have wasted thousands of dollars, perhaps hundreds of thousands of the taxpayers' money evaluating Ms. Paz. I am tempted to make you reimburse the state for the expense for her stay at the state hospital."

I didn't have the math skills to calculate that cost. It was more than I made in a year during my best year of private practice. It was even more than Joel would have paid me.

Lady Justice smirked at me.

"Your honor, I'm sorry. I'm trying to zealously represent my client and it got a little heated."

"Is that the best you can do?"

I thought for a minute. My mind had gone blank.

"Your honor, I'm going through a rough time right now. Could I have some extra time to prepare an explanation?"

"No, you may not. We'll have a contempt hearing at the end of the afternoon docket. Since the rule is anyone who represents himself has a fool for a client. I will allow you to retain private counsel. Someone who knows how to conduct themselves in my courtroom."

I thought for a moment. I only knew one lawyer on a first name basis.

"I'll hire Luna Cruz."

"You're excused, Counsel," the judge said. "But don't leave the courthouse."

Red or Green?

I HAD AN AWKWARD lunch with Luna in Court Cafe, the café in the courthouse. The deputy took Lia for lunch at an undisclosed location within the building before I could say a word to her.

The café served everyone who had to come to court. Nervous jurors, burly cops, powerful lawyers and even a few criminals out on bond. It was burrito day, and a white plastic board had a "fun fact for the day." New Mexico's official state question was: Red or green? Lawyers usually liked green chile; criminals usually went with the red. Red was hotter today. I didn't want to subject my stomach to the red hot chile stew, so I had a burger. Dozens of lawyers talked trial strategy with their felony clients, so no one looked at us closely. We were just two more lost souls. Luna was not in the best of moods, but she had made a promise to me, so she was stuck.

Luna had a good bedside manner. She calmed me down as best she could. She called Bebe, who managed to come over from her gig on Central still in her work clothes. Bebe was reluctant. She was missing a shift and they were docking her pay.

"Do you want to get into Stanford or not?" Luna asked. "I know how much you need them to find Lia incompetent. This is your chance."

Bebe agreed to testify that Lia was insane all along, and was probably delusional about her dead mother.

"I suppose I owe you one," she said to me.

"That you do," I said. "Do you mind changing clothes first?" She left without another word.

When Luna and I finished our consultation, she said, "You know, now that I'm your lawyer, I can't sleep with you." Then she laughed her amazing laugh. "You can fire me if you want."

I was about to say something, when she interrupted. "I was trying to get you to relax. You are so tense, Dan. Don't you know when I'm kidding?"

"Not yet."

The last of the afternoon's criminals had now left. The air was only marginally better. The sex offenders had left; their stench had not.

I sat in a sandwich between Luna on my left and Lia on my right. Luna had taken off her jacket to reveal a tight black sweater. Lia still wore white. I stared directly ahead. To make it even more combustible, Officer Bebe Tran, now dressed in a blue APD uniform, sat behind us.

Judge Kurtz came in and called the court to order. Rachel stood next to the judge, ready to zap out disorder in the courtroom. They didn't have a prosecutor there. Apparently Kurtz would play prosecutor—along with the role of judge, jury and executioner.

Luna stood, then gave a brief opening. I thought she was a little stiff. Luna pointed out that I had not raised competency in the first place, it had been raised by Bebe Tran at the arraignment. She talked about Bebe's files from the mental health unit. Luna might have been stiff, but she was solid.

Luna then had Bebe Tran testify.

"What was your first contact with Ophelia Paz?" Luna asked.

"The first was when she reported a rape to me, but I refused to file so she filed an internal affairs complaint against me."

The judge frowned. He took the rare step of taking over the interrogation.

"Did you take that complaint personally?"

"Yes, I did."

Luna took the questioning back from the judge.

"What other interaction did you have with Ophelia Paz that indicated she might be mentally ill?'

"I arrested her at C de Baca's wedding, and she filed another internal affairs complaint against me."

The judge stopped Luna.

"How many complaints has she filed against you?" he asked Bebe.

"Seven."

The judge let Bebe continue, but whatever she was saying, the judge wasn't buying. He didn't look as if he wanted to take a leap of faith, good or otherwise. Bebe began to talk about the dead mother issue, but the judge stopped her cold.

"Dr. Romero stated the defendant's narrative lacked internal consistency on that issue. Do you have actual proof that the mother of Ophelia Paz is dead? Do you have a death certificate?"

"No your honor."

"My mother isn't dead," Lia whispered in my ear.

I didn't want to risk saying a word to her.

The judge pounded his gavel.

"Your witness is not helping your case, Counsel."

"Nothing further with this witness, your honor."

Luna frowned. She didn't like losing. I watched her suck it up like a runner getting up after a fall and walking it off. There was dead silence in the room. Luna went back to the table and stared at a book with a page opened to contempt charges. She was making this up as she went along. Then suddenly I could see that she had a Eureka moment. I had a good feeling about this. Luna would be my white knight and save the day.

"Ms. Cruz." the judge glared, "do you have any other witnesses?"

Luna sucked it up. She was a competitor after all. Without looking at me, Luna said, "I call Daniel Shepard to the stand."

Daniel Shepard? Who's that? Oh wait, that's me. Why hadn't she told me she was going to call me?

Luna whispered as I got up. "Just say you thought she was crazy from the get-go, and this whole thing goes away."

I nearly puked as I walked to the witness stand, and then had a vertigo attack as I sat down. I had been in court a million times, but it sure felt different sitting up here. The lights were a lot hotter. I had also failed to get into the CIA and the FBI because I had failed the-lie detector test. The CIA polygrapher said the machine even jumped when I correctly told them my birthday.

I looked at the two women, Luna in black at the podium and Lia in white back at the table. I had lost them both.

The judge swore me in.

"So help me God," I said.

Luna asked me a few preliminaries, then quickly got to the money questions.

"Why did you tell your client, 'You're fucking crazy if I say you're fucking crazy!'"

I looked at the judge. "I'm sorry, Your Honor," I said. "My language was inappropriate and I was way too loud."

"Mr. Shepard," the judge said. "You definitely will be spending the night in jail on the swearing alone. As I said, I'm just deciding whether to have you disbarred."

"Disbarred?" I gulped.

The judge continued. "However, I don't like submitting stuff to the disciplinary board. Generally they give everyone probation."

I sighed. Cool.

"That's why I would rather utilize direct contempt. I can keep you in jail indefinitely, up to six months."

"Six months?"

"Now, answer the questions," the judge said. "Did you genuinely believe that your client was incompetent to stand trial?

Do you believe that your client was or is insane and could not form the requisite criminal intent?"

This was my official New Mexico State question.

To Bebe the answer was obvious. She lifted up her I-phone and played with it. Was that solicitation video of me stored in there?

"Just say she's crazy," Bebe said, a little too loud. "How hard can it be?"

The next six months of my life came down to this. Who was I kidding? If I went to jail for an extended period of time, I was basically dead or insane. I thought back to the casino and the Mayan Princess game. I had made it to the Sacrifice Bonus Round of my own life.

Time stopped. . . .

I looked at Luna in black.

She whispered to me. "You knew she was crazy."

It was painful to look at her. Luna was indeed the woman of my dreams. Just watching how she got back up after the judge knocked her down had clinched it. Luna didn't have to be here. But she was. For me.

I had said I wasn't sure I loved her. I lied.

She had said she didn't love me. And yet here she was, putting her ass on the line for me. Perhaps she had lied about not loving me as well . . . .

Then I looked at Lia in white.

"I'm not crazy," she said over and over again. Occasionally spicing it up with "I've never been crazy."

Was she crazy? I was about to bring up the mother thing, but Lia was so sure, so positive. Something had to be up. It didn't make sense.

Xavier had told me there would be a moment in my life where I would make a choice. It all would come down to faith.

Lia was a human being; she deserved a chance at life. And

we still didn't know if she was pregnant. Pregnant with my child, or so she said. Again, I had to take that on faith. I had an obligation to her in any event. To her child, to my child, if she was indeed pregnant. Her competence, her sanity, meant so much to her. If I said I had always thought she was crazy, or merely incompetent, she might snap again. And if they terminated her parental rights, that would definitely put her over the edge. She might succeed at suicide this time.

She wanted to be a mother more than anything in the world. I couldn't deny her that, could I? But how could I possibly believe her when none of it made sense?

It all came down to faith. . . .

"Dan, we're waiting," Luna said. "Just say it."

"Please don't say I'm crazy," Lia said.

Rachel stood directly behind Lia, ready to drag the poor girl off to jail.

I took a deep breath. Xavier had been right. I would now act on faith. Blind faith. I looked at Bebe. Fuck her. Let her blackmail me if she wanted.

"Your Honor," I said after another pause. "I *don't* believe that Ms. Ophelia Paz was ever incompetent to stand trial. She was competent all along. She was sane. She *is* sane."

I took a deep breath. It was now time to take one for the team, the Dan and Lia team.

"I don't know why I asked for the report. It was the tactic of a desperate lawyer. I guess I really was wasting everyone's time and resources."

"Are you sure?" Luna asked.

Bebe nearly fainted. "There goes Stanford," she said.

The judge stared at me. He gave me a chance to wiggle out of my statement. "Are you sticking by that, Counsel?"

I looked at Lia. She was beaming. There was no room to wiggle.

"Yes, I am sure. Even if it means that I have to go to jail on contempt. I knew, or should have known, that Ophelia Paz was never incompetent. She was never insane. And I knew, or should have known that when we addressed the court at arraignment."

"Be seated," the judge said.

I sat back down in between Luna and Lia. Neither said a word to me.

"I will skip closings," the judge said. He thought for a minute, played with his gavel, then jotted on a piece of paper.

"Mr. Shepard, please rise!"

I rose.

"Mr. Shepard, you did swear in my courtroom and I cannot allow that. The only 'fucking' that is done is done by me. The only person who will be 'fucked' is you. The fact that it was a pre-trial is not relevant; it was in a duly designated district courtroom. My district courtroom. We were handling a very serious matter, and you disturbed it. I will sentence you to twenty-four hours at the Metropolitan Detention Center. And—"

The word "and" was not a good word when it came from him. He wasn't done.

"*And,* for your actions in asking the court to spend hundreds of thousands of dollars in judicial resources to put the defendant in the state hospital and perform lengthy tests upon her I will lock you up *indefinitely* on direct contempt."

I forced myself to cowboy up. I had sacrificed myself for Lia. I had made my bed; I would have to sleep in it. I nodded at Lia. You can at least tell yourself that one person in the world believed you.

The judge smiled. "*But . . . .*"

I had a glimmer of hope when I heard the word "but." Perhaps he would suspend everything, and I would walk out of here without handcuffs.

"*But,* I'll allow you to post a cash-only bond of ten thousand dollars to get out tomorrow as an alternative to incarceration."

My joy was short-lived. Where the hell were my parents

these days? A spa in Tucson or on safari in Timbuktu? Actually, I think it was Hawaii. Since I had posted bond for Lia and then lost my job, I no longer had that kind of money.

"Your honor, I don't have ten thousand dollars."

"Then you will enjoy the next six months in jail."

Lia cried, "I love you. I love you. I love you. Thank you. Thank you. Thank you."

Luna was still a zealous advocate.

"Your Honor, he is a defense attorney and will be at grave risk inside the facility. You can't put him inside the jail. Perhaps house arrest might be more appropriate."

"Then he will be placed in the segregated unit under maximum protection."

I had mixed feelings. I wouldn't be knifed in jail, but the claustrophobia would be brutal. Paris Hilton had nearly gone insane after only a few days. I almost wanted to ask for the mental institution instead.

"All he has to do is one night in jail." The judge tried to be merciful. "Surely someone would be willing to bond him out tomorrow."

Someone? Any one? No one in the room said anything. What would my mother think of me now?

"One week from today, we will have another pre-trial hearing to determine whether the defendant's case will go to trial, and whether Mr. Shepard will remain as counsel," said the judge. "The defendant has already posted a bond and apparently *is* competent, so she is released from custody. We'll transport Mr. Shepard from jail, assuming he's still alive. I mean if he's still incarcerated."

Rachel whispered something about MDC's new policy of needing something called a "commitment order" on contempt cases.

The judge yelled into his intercom, "Eva! I need the new commitment order form!"

The sheriff's deputies didn't wait for the order. They pulled my hands behind my back. I felt my shoulders nearly jerk out of their sockets. Damn, that hurt.

I had to keep cowboying up. It was the Albuquerque way. I remembered the defendant who had cried during his sentencing. "No crying in prison," the judge had reminded him.

No crying in jail, either. I could do six months standing on my head, right?

I forced my body to stop shaking as Eva hurried to the judge with the form.

"I kept my promise to you," Lia said.

Promise? She had never made a promise to me. I then realized she was looking at Eva.

I had not seen them together since the night of the election party. I looked at them closer and tried to imagine Eva at thirty, with dark hair. I thought again about the obese Mayan woman in the photograph, and my own mother's comment that Lia didn't look Mayan. Lia looked a lot more like Eva than the dead woman I had seen in the picture.

Eva handed the form to the judge and nodded at Lia. She whispered, "Thank you," then turned and hurried from the room.

Lia had said her mother was alive and in this building. Had she made her promise to Eva? What the hell was going on here? The guards dragged me to the door as it started to sink in. Before I could say anything the door slammed behind me.

"I have something I have to tell the judge," I said to Power Forward.

"It's too late," he said.

"Do I get a phone call?"

"It's too late," he said again. He was happy to have a lawyer in his custody. "You're going to Seg. Ain't no phone calls in Seg."

He dragged me to an elevator. I had spent less than a minute in custody and I was already on the edge of a nervous breakdown.

Thankfully, he uncuffed me so I could go to the bathroom.

I hoped that someone, anyone, would bail me out. But who did I know with ten thousand dollars?

Full Circle

I BLINKED A FEW times to let my eyes adjust to the sunlight on the other side of the window. I was still inside, in the lobby, but someone had opened the door to the parking lot outside. Fresh New Mexico desert air blew toward me. It was the sweetest air I had ever breathed. It was surprisingly warm for January.

Then I saw her.

"Oh my God, it's you!" I said.

Why the hell did it have to be her?

"I bailed you out," she said. I couldn't read her emotions.

I turned to Heavyweight. "Could you please take me back?"

"No," he said. "Once you're out, you're out."

My night in jail over, the embarrassment was even stronger than the claustrophobia. I didn't want to face her at a time like this. Why couldn't it be someone else? There in the lobby of the Metropolitan Detention Center, I was surprised to see my mother. Of all the women in my life it had to be my mother who saw me at the worst possible moment. I cringed in embarrassment.

"We heard, and we flew back from Hawaii immediately. I came directly from the airport."

"Why you?" I asked. I was weak from shame. No mother, especially not mine, should ever have to bond her son out of jail. I knew she now knew everything. "Of all the women in my life, why did it have to be you?"

"Dan, remember one thing. I'm your mother. Of course I'm going to bond you out. No matter how badly you screw up you'll always be family. I'll always be your mother."

Something nagged at me as I got into my mother's hybrid Subaru. As we began the descent down Nine Mile Hill it hit me: my life hadn't been resolved. I was still torn between two women. If Luna had bonded me out, I would have known that she really loved me. If Lia had bonded me out, it meant she had put her money where her mouth was. Any one can say "I love you." It takes real love to bond someone out.

"I know about everything," she said. "Let's *not* talk about it. Lia, Luna and all that. Someone told me what happened."

"Someone?"

"I talked to Judge Kurtz. I cannot express how disappointed I am at this moment."

I couldn't think of anything to say to that.

"What should I do?" I asked her.

"Just think about everything that happened," she said. "It's not over yet."

I wanted to ask my mother to solve my problems. I wanted her to tell me that she was proud of me, but I was too numb to talk.

She dropped me off at my apartment. "I don't want to go inside there, do I?"

I shook my head.

The Lowest Point in New Mexico

MY ROOM SMELLED WORSE than my jail cell. My socks had staged a coup while I was gone and somehow had taken over my refrigerator. So much for freedom.

I threw my suit into the trash and changed into gym clothes. Then I opened all the windows and propped open the door to let fresh air flow inside. Once the room was almost bearable, I turned on my computer and began searching. The earliest record of Eva Jonas in New Mexico was when she took the oath of citizenship in Luna County, New Mexico twenty-nine years ago.

Luna County. Where had I heard about Luna County? No one was from Luna County. Not even Luna Cruz was from Luna County. Except Lia. She was born there.

Thirty years ago was one year before Eva became a citizen. That meant Eva would have been an illegal alien. Maybe Eva was the "illegal alien" on Lia's birth certificate. From the picture on the mantle, Lia's Mexican mother looked obese and Mayan. Lia herself once said she was not full blooded; she did look a lot more like Eva than she did her mother from Mexico.

I then tried to cross-reference adoption data bases, but I couldn't get through the security firewalls. I thought back to my conversation with Lia in the jail. She had mentioned something about her mother, but in the confusion during the fight with Knockout Noriega, I didn't catch it.

So Lia had told me the secret all along. Eva had never wanted to be in the same room as Lia. Eva had been nervous about
me putting two and two together. Eva always helped me out
when she could. She was my fairy grandmother.

Shit, she would soon be a fairy grandmother!

I had thought Lia was protecting her mother from Mexico.
Or worse, that Lia didn't have a mother at all. But Eva had been
her mother all along. Lia had made her promise to Eva. Lia had
not lied to me after all. Lia might indeed be sane.

I then had an unsettling realization. Eva could have been
there that night with Portia. Was Eva the killer? Eva had always
been so nice to me, the mother I never had. Had the whole thing
been a sham?

But that's not the thing that bothered me most of all.

I had Eva's phone number stored in my phone, so I called.
She was at the courthouse, working on a Saturday, catching up
on paperwork.

"If you hurry, you can still catch me," she said.

I don't think she realized I only lived a few minutes away,
or how fast I was willing to drive. When I arrived, she had
already left the district courthouse and was headed across
Lomas Boulevard to the Peter Domenici Federal Courthouse, as
if hoping to make a break for it. She had no intention of talking
to me whatsoever.

The Peter Domenici Federal Courthouse was a massive
brick building that almost looked colonial. Protesters dressed in
black lined up along the front sidewalk, facing traffic on Lomas
Boulevard. It was a new cause every week, yet the same people
protested. The Domenici Courthouse had been built after the
Oklahoma City attack, so to deter car bombs or protesters, the
parking lot was not under the building. Instead, the lot was
under a small park in front of the courthouse. If a bomb went off
in a car, it would only take out a few pigeons.

Eva had already gone inside. They knew her, or thought they
did. Security probably waved her right through.

The last remnants of my sprained ankle were gone, so I could run like the Dan Shepard of old. Well, the Nordic Trek was no substitute for running hard. I was out of breath when I entered the security checkpoint. Then I had to sign my name and fill out a form.

I paused when I saw the space marked "reason for coming." I didn't know why I was there. I froze for a moment, until I noticed the guard was looking away, toward the sunset. It was the end of the day. This particular guard didn't care about another apocalypse, unless it happened on his overtime. I scribbled a few semi-legible words in the blank.

It took three attempts, but I finally made it past the vicious metal detector. I took the stairs down to the parking garage, went along a long dark corridor, then down a few more stairs to an even lower level.

The lot was dark and empty for the weekend. At least the jail was well lit. I was in the lowest point in Albuquerque. Right on cue, the claustrophobia kicked in. I heard footsteps ahead. Eva had started her BMW.

I sprinted to her car, pounded on her window.

She let out a shriek and opened her window . . . a crack.

"I've got to ask you something," I said, cutting quickly to the chase.

"Make it quick. I'm heading to Washington. Mendoza just got confirmed as Secretary, and I'm going to be his executive secretary. Secretary to the Secretary. Sounds great, yes?"

"Congratulations," I said reflexively. I didn't have much time, so I got to it. "Lia's your daughter. I can get DNA. You were there with her! You were—"

Her face fell. She looked twenty years older.

"I'm not saying anything to you without an *ugyved*," she said. "And I'm going to get the best lawyer, I can find."

She put the window up, but I managed to get my finger inside. I wailed when it squeezed tight, then cowboyed up.

She took mercy and let the window down all the way.

"What are you doing? I'll call security!"

"Why did you let Lia take the rap for you?"

That hit a nerve with her. "Did she tell you?"

"No. She kept her promise."

Eva frowned. She lit a cigarette.

"Well, she can break her promise now. It's a long story. Let her tell you."

"So what are you going to do?" I asked.

"There used to be a game show on American television when I first moved here, *Danika*. I watched that show to learn English."

"A game show?"

"The show was called *Let's Make a Deal*."

There was one more thing that bothered me.

"One question," I said. "It's not about the case. If Lia's your daughter, why the hell did you want to set me up with Luna instead? What's the matter, I'm not good enough for your daughter?"

"I love you, *Danika, my fiam*. Let's face it, you and Luna are made for each other, with all your whining. You're right, you're not good enough for my Ophelia. You've got too many damn issues!"

I wanted to call Lia. It took me a few moments to remember that the judge had released her on her existing bond. I hurried to Lia's house.

"Eva was there with you," I said when she opened the door.

Lia finally looked like she would reveal what had gone on that night. Finally ready to tell me the truth, the whole truth and nothing but the truth.

"Come in," she said.

I walked past the spot where Portia had died. I walked gingerly, afraid I would step on her ghost. "I talked to your mother," I said. "Your real mother."

"I know," Lia said. "She called me. She released me from my promise. I'll tell you what happened that night. I thought you knew about it when I told you in jail."

"I heard you say 'illegal,' I thought you were talking about how your mother was illegal. The mother in Chichen Itza."

"I said I was worried that dragging a body away was illegal." She stared at me. "Don't you ever listen to me? I've been telling you the truth all along."

Return of the Rattlesnake

EVA HAD ALREADY REPORTED herself into Federal custody while the going was good. She now played the bonus round of "Let's Make a Deal." She had a lot of deals to make.

Luna had worked the case while I was in jail. Her old boyfriend, an FBI agent with the improbable name of Jorje Washington, located Eva in the Federal system. Eva was now a material witness staying at an undisclosed location. I wondered if it was the mental hospital where they'd stuck Lia while she was waiting for court.

New Mexico Attorney General Diana Crater wanted Eva for conspiracy to commit election fraud. The Feds wanted her for Agua-gate, which now had ballooned to other land deals across America. Even the Albuquerque "Safe City Strike Force," the city's zoning enforcers, wanted her for littering with left-over signs and billboards from the campaign.

"I set up a deposition of Eva the day before the hearing with Judge Kurtz," Luna said. "Hopefully Eva will give us the information we need."

"Give me the information I need," I said. "This is something I have to do. You may be my lawyer, but Lia is my client."

"I didn't think you were up for it after everything," Luna said.

"I'll have to be up for it."

* * * * *

In the four days before the deposition, I concentrated on becoming a lawyer again—an Albuquerque lawyer. I also utilized the research and writing skills I learned during my brief stay in Santa Fe to unlock the conspiracy. I guess that made me a hybrid, a La Bajada lawyer.

I would be the last person to get a bite at Eva, who had given statements to everyone in the legal solar system. I would not have access to those statements, unfortunately. I may have been last, but I didn't want to be least. I had cowboyed up, so I figured I should round me up a posse: get Luna and Jen to have my back.

I dug up my old rattlesnake cowboy boots that I had bought ten years ago when I'd been in the self-proclaimed "Fighting Fourteenth Judicial District." They hurt a bit, but they still fit. I thought about the sign I had first seen when I had entered the Fourteenth: WATCH FOR RATTLESNAKES.

Time to become the Rattlesnake Lawyer, one more time.

The deposition took place on the top floor of the highest building in Albuquerque, the rocket building, the one that reminded me of the Washington Monument with a weight problem. The U.S. Attorneys were down below on the eighth floor, but occasionally they used the big conference room of the major law firm here in the nose cone.

I suppose this was the most Albuquerque part of Albuquerque. I could see the entire city from the summit, and onto the Sangre de Christos up in Santa Fe. They looked very small from this high up.

"Don't dis the Burque, *ese*," I said.

At counsel table Luna wore white, and Lia wore black. Lia also wore a red rose.

"For passion," she said.

Jen wore a pink t-shirt that said GEISHAS FOREVER, that was totally inappropriate for the hearing, but Jen would be Jen.

Eva sat there with a female U.S. Marshall. The Marshall was taller than I was, even with my boots on. Eva and Lia were about to talk, but the Marshall stopped them.

"They can't talk, they're co-defendants. I have specific orders."

Lia and Eva stared at each other. There was so much the two had to say. We didn't start on time, of course. Eva had us wait for her lawyer, who was coming from Santa Fe.

"I've got the best *ugyved* in New Mexico," she said.

"*Bring it on,*" I said. I realized too late that I had quoted a teenage cheerleader movie as opposed to a cowboy flick.

I planned ahead. I brought energy bars so I wouldn't get hunger pains. Unlike the hearing in Judge Kurtz's courtroom, I felt stronger with every minute.

It was noon when the lawyer, arrived. High noon. I should have expected what came next. There was only one best lawyer in New Mexico. I heard some swearing outside when the elevator closed too quickly. The lawyer finally made an entrance.

"Dan, good to see you," the lawyer said.

"Mother?" I said. "God, you were serious when you said you knew everything."

She handed me a waiver of conflict form, which I signed immediately. What else could I do? She was my mother.

Eva conferred with my mother in another room. When she emerged alone, my mother was quite specific about the terms of the immunity deal. We could ask limited questions. She gave me another form to sign saying we understood.

"Dan, you don't have to do this now," my mother said. "You've been through a lot."

Lia touched my shoulder. "I want Dan to do it. He's my lawyer, you're not."

I took deep breath. "This is my case. Well, it's my case until tomorrow, and I'm not afraid of my mother."

My mother nodded at me. "Ready when you are, Dan."

Athena looked at me expectantly. For the next few minutes, she was Athena the goddess of wisdom, rather than merely my mother. She would give me no mercy, but I hoped she wanted me to win. She had fired me way back when, maybe she hoped I would prove her wrong.

Eva came in from the rest room and sat down. The court reporter gave a thumbs up. We went through the preliminaries, then I got to the good stuff.

"Eva, how are you related to my client, Ophelia Paz?"

"She's *lanyom*, my daughter. I was working in the hospital in Deming, nurse's aide work under the table. There was a shortage of help. I figured it would be my path into citizenship. Her father, Octavio Paz, was in charge of maintenance at the hospital. It was a typical hospital romance."

Both Jen and Luna snorted.

"I had severe post-partum depression, and Octavio left me for another woman. They moved to Albuquerque, taking my daughter with them. I stayed behind in Deming."

"How did an illegal nurse's aide from Deming get to be assistant to Governor Mendoza? And then assistant to the Chief Judge?"

"That's not relevant," Athena said.

"It is to me," I said. "I'm laying a foundation."

Eva nodded as if she wanted to tell her story.

"Once I recovered from my depression, I worked for a another year. I got my citizenship. The hospital sponsored me. I moved to Santa Fe and grew active in health issues. My paths crossed with the *Kormanyzo* the Governor—"

I hoped I'd hear about an affair, but Athena interrupted.

"We don't need to hear her whole life story," Athena said.

"You're right, let's move onto how you met Lia again after all those years."

"A few years ago I was doing opposition research for the party. I had heard rumors about Lia and I recruited her to work on *valasztas*, the election. She was reluctant at first, but once I told her who I was, she was eager to help."

Eva verified what C de Baca said about the campaign using Lia over the years.

"You used your own daughter?"

Athena grew testy. "Dan! Please move on."

"Nothing personal," Eva said. "It was just politics."

"But I thought you were a state employee and couldn't do anything political," I asked before my mom could object.

Eva shrugged. "This is New Mexico. Everything is political."

Time to go with a hunch. "Did you write the note Let's Use Crazy Girl?"

Eva looked at Lia. "I hope you understand. We want the same things. I want to change the world just as much as you do. I thought this was the only way we could take down C de Baca and all that he stood for. I never thought you were crazy."

Athena gestured for me to move on.

"Did you call Lia on the phone?" I asked.

"Yes," she said.

"Why could I never hear you?"

"I'm used to whispering," she said. "I grew up in troubled times. Besides, I never wanted to be overheard by the Governor. There was a phrase he used. I don't remember it in English."

"Plausible deniability," I said, repeating a Watergate word. "Did you ever use other women on campaigns?"

"Information regarding the so-called Liquor Sisters is not germane to your line of questioning," Athena said.

Not just Brandy Porter, but all three of the Liquor Sisters. I got the feeling that the campaign was not just dirtier than I imagined, it was dirtier than I could possibly imagine.

"Okay, let's move on to what happened that night in November."

"Can I take a cigarette break?" Eva asked.

Eva and Athena left. Jen went down to smoke as well.

"I thought you quit," Luna said.

"Once a year," Jen said. "After sex."

"Sex?" I asked. "You call this sex?"

"Look around you," she said. "They got U.S. Attorneys and immunity agreements. Don't you get the feeling we're about to get screwed?"

Higher Noon

LUNA, LIA AND I sat there in silence. I didn't think the moment could get more awkward. I was wrong.

"I still don't know if I'm pregnant," Lia said.

"You slept with me, knowing she was pregnant with your child?" Luna asked.

"I didn't know she was pregnant," I said.

"You slept with her?" Lia asked.

"I thought you already knew that," I said.

"I thought you were just *with* her," Lia said. "I didn't think you were stupid."

"Let's get back to the questions," Athena said, returning to the table.

"Great idea!" I turned to Eva once the court reporter was ready.

"Why were you there that night in November. The night of the election?"

"Lia trusted me," she said. "I was her *anya*, her mother. I came through the back, on the trail that ran right above the arroyo ditch. She let me in. No one saw. I was going to take some video to post on a site. The election could go either way."

My mother looked at Eva, who nodded. "You have immunity, dear."

Eva then told how Portia came in out of the rain. They talked for a while. And then Eva then asked Lia to leave.

"Why did you ask Lia to leave?"

"Because there was something I had to say to Portia alone."

"What was that?"

I wasn't surprised when my mother stopped me.

"That's under the immunity deal. You can't ask about that."

I expected that. I had overheard Stone talking about a lesbian affair. I looked at Lia, she was all that mattered now. "So what happened next?"

"I told Portia the information we had on her, then she collapsed."

"She collapsed?" I asked. "You didn't hit her?"

"No."

"Was the information you had on her that bad?"

"No," Eva said. "I don't think the information was what caused her to collapse."

My mother now piped in. "We've had an independent medical examiner complete a report that says Portia Smith C de Baca died of an aneurism brought about by exhaustion and dehydration. She had already hiked several miles that day. She apparently fainted and hit her head on the stone on the table. She was dead on the floor."

That was one of the scenarios that Luna had come up with. Luna looked at me and nodded.

I looked at a report that had magically appeared on the table below me. Sure enough, the independent medical officer offered confirmation. Political infighting had stalled the inquest for months, but my mom had the power to have an examination right way. I didn't want to know how.

"Why didn't you say anything to the authorities?"

Eva frowned. "Would you say anything, *Danika?* The wife of *Kormanyzo*'s worst enemy dies in front of me right before the election. I had violated the election laws by campaigning while a state employee and deliberately used an *orult* woman to torment a candidate and his wife. I had just given her some terrible information, then she faints and hits her head, then dies. Oh and by the way, I had a million dollars or so riding on the outcome."

"Don't call me *orult*," Lia said. "I thought you were my mother, or my *anya*, or whatever."

"That's the first time you ever talked back to me," Eva said.

"I guess I'm growing up," Lia said.

I didn't want to open that Pandora's box.

"How did the body get to the arroyo?" I asked.

"I have immunity for that, yes?" Eva asked.

"Yes," Athena said.

"I dragged the body out. Lia's computer too, because it had a lot of the web marketing we did."

I shuddered to think how they had used poor Lia. That computer was long gone, broken into a million pieces, some of which might have made it to the Gulf of Mexico by now.

Eva continued. "I went down the bike path, the one by the arroyo, in the rain. Because I parked further down the street no one saw me come or go."

"What about the deaths of C de Baca and Stone?"

"That's beyond the scope of your questioning," Athena said. "Please move on."

"Why didn't you come forward earlier?" I asked. "I saw you every day."

"She was up for a job in Washington which she's now jeopardizing," Athena said. "She didn't want to say anything until she was guaranteed immunity, Dan. You should know that. "

Eva laughed. "And you're the biggest blabbermouth in the world. You told me everything about everyone. I couldn't trust you with any sensitive information about me, or my daughter."

I ignored that. Time for the big finish.

"So it is your testimony today that Ophelia Paz did not have anything to do with the death of Portia Smith C de Baca. And she did not tamper with evidence by helping you dispose of the body?"

"Yes. That is my testimony."

"Was she actively involved in the conspiracy?"

"Please rephrase," Athena said. "Which conspiracy?"

Athena was right. Lia was neck deep in campaign dirty tricks, but the state wanted her for murder, not illegal election-eering, a misdemeanor. I nodded.

"Eva, was there a conspiracy between you and Ophelia Paz involving the death of Portia C de Baca?"

"No," Eva said.

"I have one more question. Why?"

"Why what?"

"Why everything?"

"She doesn't have to answer that," Athena said.

"I know," I said. "I just think we all have a right to know."

My mother gestured to the recorder to stop recording.

"I lost my family in Hungary," Eva said. I noticed that Eva's accent seemed to vanish, as if she was trying to put her past behind her. "I lost everything. I came here on a student visa, overstayed and then had to work my way up in Deming, New Mexico, the middle of nowhere. I try to get pregnant as a way to get citizenship, and then that man rejects me. I was depressed. I was institutionalized. I lost my daughter to adoption, whom I loved very much."

I tried to picture Eva, the epitome of power and grace, in an institution. I saw Lia in her eyes. They were far more similar than they looked.

Eva continued. "But once I was released, and became an American citizen, I wanted the American dream. I proved that I could make it, despite all the odds. I wanted it all. I wanted the dream more than anything. And I wanted justice for people like me, people on the edges of society. I once had nothing. And once I was with Governor Mendoza, it looked as if I would finally make it. And until now, I thought I would make it. Achieve that dream."

Eva turned to face Lia. "I am so sorry for what I did to you, my Ophelia. I never wanted any of this. I figured once your lawyer got you to the asylum, you'd be fine. The dust would settle and we would get you out."

"Thank you," I said. "No further questions."

My mother nodded toward the Marshall. Lia and Eva talked for a moment then Eva looked at me and shrugged.

"You could do worse," she finally said.

The Marshalls took Eva away.

Athena was my mother again and gave me a hug.

"Well, you really are a lawyer now," she said.

"Thank you."

"So are you going to stay here in Albuquerque? You can always work for me in Santa Fe."

"I don't know."

Jen gave me a hug.

"You're not that bad," she said.

I had a feeling that Jen would somehow become an important player in my life.

Luna hugged me when we got out to the lobby, but it was a weak "let's move on" hug.

"Getting Lia pregnant is a deal breaker to me," she said. "Sorry. If you are a father, you should *be* a father to your child."

A father? My anxiety increased and I felt a deep pang in my gut.

"Luna, did we ever have a chance?"

"You'll never know," she said.

Luna and Jen took their own elevator down.

Lia and I were alone. She hugged me harder than I had ever been hugged in my life. I worried that she would crack a rib.

"Lia, I can't breathe." I said. "I have claustrophobia you know."

She released at last. "So what happens now?" she asked.

"We send this transcript to the D.A.'s office and hopefully they'll drop the charges."

As we waited for my mother, I took one last look at the three hundred sixty degree view of Albuquerque. I looked at the

Sandias and felt a major triumph. I couldn't see La Bajada, but I knew it was there.

In almost every way, Santa Fe was superior to Albuquerque. Santa Fe was prettier, the air was cleaner, the people were more interesting. Santa Fe had thrown me out on my ass, however, and Albuquerque had embraced me. Except for the time I got beat up in the Albuquerque High parking lot. Well, that and the spending the night in jail part.

In every way Luna was superior to Lia. Luna was smarter, prettier and less crazy, but she didn't love me and Lia did. Lia loved me as much as Anna Maria loved Jesús.

My mother emerged from the bathroom and went down with us on the elevator.

"Welcome to our family," my mother said to Lia. "I promise I'll never use you in a campaign."

"Can I call you Mom?" Lia asked.

"Why not, she calls everyone else her mother," I added.

Lia smiled, rubbed her belly. "Well Mom, there's something I have to tell you. . . ."

Mother and Child Reunion

IT TOOK SOME MAJOR legal wrangling, but the state dropped the murder charge against Ophelia Paz. They eventually granted Lia immunity on the tampering charge, once she agreed to testify against Mendoza and his campaign.

My mother also managed to get Eva a deferred sentence for her various infractions. Eva now had become the biggest winner ever on "Let's Make a Deal."

Judge Kurtz lifted my contempt charge without a hearing. My mother pulled strings on my behalf.

I had some nightmares about my brief stint in Seg, but they faded after time. I renewed my old "conflict contract" with the public defender. I had one contract in Albuquerque, and one out in a small rural county. I decided to get my own office downtown.

Lia had her period the day after the deposition. It was just stress after all.

After an interim election, Diana Crater became Governor. Diana was hardly the smartest person in the room, but Luna told me that at least she was honest and her heart was in the right place.

I applied for a position in the executive branch as a "crime advisor," but Diana promptly rejected me. She appointed my old boss Joel, of all people, even though he had never tried a criminal case in his life. As Diana and Eva had said, it was political. In New Mexico everything was political.

Oh, and Bebe decided not to blackmail me after all. "I'm glad Lia isn't crazy," she said when we crossed paths. "She actually wrote a letter to Stanford on my behalf."

I kept working out at Midway, often at the same time Luna did serious free-weights with Rutger the EMT. It was clear from Rutger's stares that any chances I had with Luna were long gone. I watched her stare at him and those tattooed arms. I had rescued one person. He rescued people every day. He could easily bench more than my IQ. Every other Wednesday afternoon I talked to Luna for five minutes before she went into her aerobics class. Rutger had his afternoon shift on those days. Those five minutes were the highlight of my week.

I always asked myself "What if?"

Jen began working out at the same gym, as did Bebe Tran. I suddenly remembered the long dormant Asian fetish I had. I worked out a lot too, and soon found myself in the best physical shape of my life. Even Luna gave me a second look every other Wednesday, before she went in for aerobics.

Lia kept me on as a lawyer for one more task. Now that I had become something of an Internet information wizard, I located the military family who had adopted Lia's daughter. Custody now lay with an Anita Armijo. Armijo was the mother of the original adoptive mother, a female soldier who had been all over the world and recently died in Iraq. Anita took custody of her adopted grandchild.

Thankfully, Anita was now just one state over, in Tucson at the Air Force base there. Over a few days of e-mails, I became surprised how eager Anita was to bring the child, Ariel, to meet her birth mother.

"She's a handful," Anita e-mailed. She even hinted she'd be willing to give Lia custody. Full custody.

"You mean visitation?" I e-mailed back.

"No, custody," Anita replied immediately. "Ariel's a handful!"

When I related that information to Lia, she nearly burst with tears of excitement. She asked me to start the adoption papers. It was a long complicated process. Since there was an issue of paternity, Lia asked if I could get C de Baca's body exhumed for a DNA test to prove everything once and for all. I called X. He made it clear that wasn't going to happen. He even refused to give his own DNA sample.

"You're just going to have to take it on faith," he said over the phone. We took some time to catch up. He had actually testified on Eva's behalf.

"Eva's seen the light," he said.

The mother and child reunion was set for a Friday night in March. Lia made a party of it. Eva even showed up, now that she had her life together thanks to X's help. Eva didn't get to be Secretary to the Secretary after all. Through Jen Song's mother, Nurse Song, Eva returned to nursing with a staff position at the local hospital.

Lia and Eva had normalized their relationship as much as possible, and had made up for lost time. As a grandmother, Eva was as excited to meet Ariel as Lia was. She really would be that fairy grandmother she had always wanted to be.

Rain wanted to break out all day and March rains were far worse than the November rains. It was snowing in Santa Fe, but I didn't care. I was firmly settled here now, on the lower side of La Bajada.

When I arrived at the house, I looked at the black clouds mixed with sunlight. As the sun set, I saw the biggest rainbow I had ever seen over the Sandias. I also noticed that Lia had replaced her political signs with flowers. It was a big improvement.

"Let a thousand flowers bloom," Chairman Mao had said. He was right.

Damn, I loved New Mexico on days like this. Damn, I even loved Albuquerque.

I walked up Lia's drive way. I remembered thinking this place reminded me of the Bates Motel. I heard thunder off in the distance. The rainbow vanished. Storm clouds now lay directly overhead. The rain then began in earnest, so I ran the last steps to Lia's door. When she opened it, Lia looked as if she'd undergone a major renovation. Eva had done a full make-over on her daughter, and now Lia could pass for Hungarian royalty as well. Lia was a work in progress no more. Except for one thing: she still had a big flower in her hair. Eva now wore one too.

I wasn't sure what I wanted any more. Time would have to pass before we could get back to where we were. Was I willing to take that time? I didn't have to remind myself that Portia Smith C de Baca had died on a night like this. Lia gave me a kiss on the cheek and invited me inside. We savored Eva's world famous green chile goulash.

I noticed the flowers.

"What are they?" I asked.

"I think they're called *colitas*," she said. "That's what the clerk said, but I couldn't find a *"colita* flower" in any encyclopedia."

I laughed, then sang. *"On a dark desert highway, cool wind in my hair, warm smell of colitas rising up through the air."*

I kept singing "Hotel California" for Lia's amusement, but stopped when I got to the line about checking out and never leaving.

"You can never leave?" I sang to myself.

I suddenly had a feeling of dread.

The lyrics *"Can't kill the beast"* echoed in my head.

The beast? Portia had died in this very room.

* * * * *

The Armijos' flight had been delayed because of the rain. Around eight o'clock, during the worst of the rain, a small rental car pulled to the driveway. Anita Armijo, a tough grandmother, emerged from the rental. She opened an umbrella with military precision, then looked at the house as if checking for insurgents.

There was panic in the living room. Anita appeared to be alone. Was Ariel coming?

Before Anita made it to Lia's door, a twelve-year-old girl hurried out of the car without an umbrella. Ariel was the name of the Little Mermaid of course, and this little mermaid practically swam through the water to get to the door, despite Anita's yells for her to wait.

Lia didn't wait either and hurried through the rain to greet her.

"Mama, mama, mama," Ariel yelled. She, too, had a flower in her hair just like mother and grandma. She was twelve, but she was as excited as a five-year-old. She hugged Lia immediately.

"Grandma," she yelled as she hugged Eva.

Ariel was a handful indeed. The girl talked faster than humanly possible.

I just nodded and stayed inside the living room. I didn't want to get wet.

Once they were all safely inside, it was obvious that Ariel was indeed Lia's daughter. Ariel quickly wowed everyone with trivia about the places she had lived all over the world.

Did the young girl, Ariel, look like C de Baca? I would never know for sure.

There in the living room, the women caught up amidst tears and laughter. I didn't say anything, preferring to watch from a corner of a couch.

Lia came over to me and whispered in my ear. "You're fired as my lawyer," she said.

"Fired? But the job isn't done yet," I said. "It will take weeks to finalize the adoption."

"I want you to amend the papers and put your name on there, too. It's what you want, right? To be part of a family?"

"Are you proposing to me?"

"I'm proposing to propose," she said.

I didn't have time to respond before Ariel tugged on Lia's shirt asking her another trivia question about the tallest mountain in North Korea.

I smiled for a moment. This could be the rest of my life. I headed to the screen door and view of the mountains. I was in a relatively large living room, yet I had the worst claustrophobic attack in my life. Suddenly the rain ended. Another rainbow appeared.

All the women then got together for the big group hug.

"We can be one big happy family!" Lia said to all of them.

One big happy family? That's what I always wanted, right?

While they were in the midst of the group hug, I stared out at the window.

"Open Cell 42."

One Scene Too Many?

"*DEJA FREAKING VU*," I said to myself as I looked around the room. Another year had passed, or had it? I was forty now, officially an adult.

We were back at the Eldorado, the Anasazi room, just like before. The people here were the same as the last election party. Rhiannon Goldstein Manygoats even hit me up as a potential buyer until I politely shooed her away.

Joel was there. He had already been fired by Diana. The papers said he just didn't get criminal law. He came over to me and tried to offer me a litigation position.

"I'll get back to you *forthwith*," I lied.

Tonight was a fundraiser for all of the party's candidates all over the state. The guest of honor: the President of the United States.

Other than a speech at the Washington Mall, where I had an obstructed view, I had never even seen a President before in the flesh.

Diana had sponsored the party, and Luna was on the guest list. She was now up for judge and I was helping Luna with her campaign. I was the poorest person in the room of course, but damn it, I was in the room.

My mother came over and told me how happy she was now that I finally wanted to settle down.

As I stared at my companions, I realized I had transcended Albuquerque versus Santa Fe. I was finally a powerful New Mexican. Hell, I could influence national politics without leaving the state.

When "Hail to the Chief" began playing I nearly fainted with excitement. I never thought I'd make it this far. Who knew how far I would go now that I had straightened my life out?

The President gave a good speech that was thankfully short.

My fiancé joined me on the receiving line, just in time to shake the President's hand.

"I'm Dan Shepard," I said.

I was surprised he didn't mention my mother, who had been a big contributor. His attention wasn't on me of course. He stared at my companion as if he had X-ray vision.

I smiled. It had taken awhile, but I finally was in love.

"This is my fiancé," I said to the President. "Jen Song."

He smiled. "I know," he said. "We've met."

THE END

Author's Note

I am *not* Dan Shepard. He is a fictional character who is far more neurotic than I am. He crosses lines with clients that I most certainly have never crossed. My parents live in Albuquerque, not in Santa Fe, and my mother is *not* the basis for the character of Athena Shepard. While I am a criminal defense lawyer in New Mexico, I have not been to jail on contempt charges . . . yet.

No New Mexico governor's wife has ever been murdered. I would like to think that politics in New Mexico are not as nasty as I have described in this novel.

The state hospital is indeed in Las Vegas, New Mexico, but every event and resident mentioned is fictional. The hospital would never allow some of the events to occur, although I do hear that they throw a great Christmas party.

Jen Song only had a minor part in this book, (she's still recovering from *Volcano Verdict*), but she and her cousin, a golfer, will have their own stories told in an upcoming book.

Ophelia Paz is completely fictional. As of this writing, I have never dated a woman who has been held incompetent by a court. Have I ever dated a criminal? Three words: attorney, client and privileged.

Everything good about Luna Cruz is based on many of the outstanding female attorneys that I have met in New Mexico. Everything bad about her comes from me, of course.

Albuquerque is a real place and is much as I've described. The city of Santa Fe is completely fictional.

—Jonathan Miller
March 2008